Extremely Hot

JENNIFER APODACA

KENSINGTON PUBLISHING CORP.
http://www.kensingtonbooks.com

BRAVA BOOKS are published by

Kensington Publishing Corp.
850 Third Avenue
New York, NY 10022

All Kensington titles, imprints and distributed lines are available at special quantity discounts for bulk purchases for sales promotion, premiums, fund-raising, educational or institutional use.

Special book excerpts or customized printings can also be created to fit specific needs. For details, write or phone the office of the Kensington Special Sales Manager: Kensington Publishing Corp., 850 Third Avenue, New York, NY 10022. Attn. Special Sales Department. Phone: 1-800-221-2647.

Brava and the B logo Reg. U.S. Pat. & TM Off.

ISBN-13: 978-0-7582-1451-5
ISBN-10: 0-7582-1451-0

First Kensington Trade Paperback Printing: November 2007
10 9 8 7 6 5 4 3 2 1

Printed in the United States of America

Acknowledgments

Thank you to Calista Cates Stanturf for being so generous with her knowledge of radio stations. Calista provided me with terms and jargon, pictures, and answered my endless questions. In the end, only a fraction of the information made it into the book, but it was all invaluable to me when writing the book. Any mistakes are mine.

Thank you to Marianne Donley for helping me when I had my regularly scheduled meltdown at the three-quarters point in the story. Marianne saved this book. I'd have shredded it if she hadn't stepped in, read the pages, and assured me the book could be saved.

I'd like very much to thank my editor, Kate Duffy, for always being just a phone call away when I need to talk out a character or plot.

Prologue

Excerpt from Interview with Professor Regina Parker

"*Is it true you know the Urban Legend? Is he as hot as everyone says?*"

"I thought we were going to talk about the Jade Goddesses of Fertility and Virility. The statues are at least five centuries old and have a fascinating legend of sex, love, and murder. Once you see them, you'll feel their power."

"*Sex, love, and murder, wow. That sounds like something that would attract the Urban Legend's attention. Has he seen the statues?*"

(Audible sigh) "No, he's been too busy treasure hunting and honing his reputation as a sex legend. Now can we talk about the statues? I will be taking the statues on tour . . ."

"*How do you know he's honing his reputation as a sex legend? Have you had, uh, personal experience?*"

(Bigger sigh) "No, back to the statues, they were carved by a powerful sorcerer to set up meetings with the woman he loved but could never have. They used the statues to pass messages of where and when to meet to conduct a passionate affair."

"*Oh my, how romantic.*"

"Indeed. As best we can tell, the Jade Goddesses of Fertility and Virility came from the Aztecs. They had a highly structured society based on religion, magic, and science. A society that prevented two star-crossed lovers from being together. The powerful sorcerer would not be denied, however, and he carved the statues out of two pieces of jade, including the traditional oblong space for a jade heart. But when he crafted the hearts to fill the oblong space, he made them hollow. The two lovers communicated by leaving messages inside the hearts to set up clandestine meetings."

"They wrote notes to each other?"

"They didn't have the same written language we have today. We believe they left markers of some kind inside the hearts that indicated a place and time—perhaps gems, locks of hair, who knows? It's quite romantic to consider, until, of course, the tragedy struck."

"Tragedy? What happened? Were the lovers caught?"

"Infinitely worse. Someone stole the hearts of the goddesses, and the legend goes that the two lovers died instantly."

"That's horrible. But how could such a thing happen?"

"Because the man who carved the statues was a sorcerer, and the two hearts were crafted with the blood of their love. It's said the statues have been looking for their deepest desire ever since then. Even today, the power of the statues lives on. They bring out people's deepest desire, deepest lust."

"What does that mean exactly? If someone like the Urban Legend came in contact with these statues, he'd get even more sex? That wouldn't really be anything extraordinary, would it?"

(Pause) "It would depend on what the Urban Legend's deepest desire is. What he really lusts for."

"Hmm, you might want to guard those statues carefully, Professor. A lot of women may want to steal them to seduce the Urban Legend." (Shuffling, clearing of throat) *"Or maybe some woman out there thinks she can use the statues to catch the Urban Legend permanently. Now that would be extraordinary."*

(Academic sniff) "The statues aren't a matchmaking service, they are an exceptional and exquisite piece of history with a fascinating and provocative legend."

Chapter 1

The door to the office kitchen was closed.

Ivy York stared at the dingy beige door, a knot of anxiety ballooning in her stomach. She'd never seen the door closed before. She'd been working at KCEX radio station in Claremont, California, for over two years now. Not once had she seen the door closed.

Nor had she ever heard those particular sounds coming from inside the office kitchen.

She put her hand out and touched the cold doorknob. *Open it,* her brain insisted. *You don't want to know,* the little girl in her replied. But she was a grown-up woman with responsibilities, not a child. She turned the knob and shoved open the door.

She swept her gaze around the room, barely taking in the left side of the kitchen with the beige Formica countertop, stainless steel sink, coffeemaker, and microwave shoved up against the old brown refrigerator that hummed like a DC-10. The brown table and chairs in the middle of the room didn't catch her attention either.

But the sight that met her gaze on the right side of the room damn near seared her eyeballs. She got an eyeful of her mom kneeling on the cracked, brown linoleum, the backs of her Pilates-toned thighs cradling a man's white pumping ass.

His pants were puddled around his hairy thighs; his hands were digging into her mom's bare hips.

He grunted and pumped.

Her mom seemed to have her head halfway in an opened cupboard, but she managed to praise the man with, "You're so big!"

Ivy was *so* nauseous. "Mom! For God's sake!"

They both froze, cutting off the sound of slapping wet flesh. "What the hell!" The man pulled out of her mom, then shoved her mom out of the way to close the cupboard door.

She couldn't look away, it was like an X-rated traffic accident. Her brain asked her why the man was more interested in closing a cupboard door than covering up his rapidly deflating penis. But the daughter in her didn't care about the man one way or the other.

"Ivy." Her mom got to her knees and yanked her skirt down.

Another stray thought pushed into her head: *Was today Underwear Optional Day?*

Her mom said, "The door was closed." Smoothing her long dark hair, Mallory York stood up, looked at the man, and said, "Pull your pants up."

The full impact of what Ivy walked in on finally pierced her horrified shock. "Mom, you swore! You swore that if I got you this job, you'd concentrate on the job, not men!"

Mallory straightened her tight sweater over her short skirt. "I am working. I've hired him to build new storage cabinets to replace this mess of old filing cabinets and cupboards. We were measuring and got distracted." She shrugged.

"Distracted?" Ivy turned to the guy. Oh yeah, he was her mom's typical *distraction*, the kind of man who came with hot packages and no money or ethics. They flocked to her mom's short skirts and tiny shirts with alarming regularity. Not only was her mom a sucker for rippling abs and sexy grins, she took pride in snagging the bad boys. In *having fun*. Then when it all fell apart, when the bad boys managed to screw her in the nonorgasmic way, Ivy was left to pick up the pieces.

The man—she so didn't want to bother learning his name—got his jeans buttoned and his T-shirt pulled down. He ignored Ivy and said to Mallory, "Later." Then he headed to the door and left.

"He's leaving? I thought he was measuring for new storage units. Where's his tape measure?" The right side of the kitchen was a makeshift storage area.

Her mom sighed. "I don't think he's right for the job."

For the love of . . . "Do you want to get us both fired? You can't have sex in the radio station!"

Her mom was an interior decorator, and Ivy had hired her to renovate the KCEX offices. Her mom had begged Ivy for the job, claiming her company, York Interior Designs, was on the verge of bankruptcy. Again. Ivy did most of the hiring these days for her boss while Leah went out and did what she did best—sell the radio station to advertisers.

Her mom pursed her lips in disagreement. "Leah Allen isn't going to fire you."

True. Ivy's radio show, the *Economic Sex Hex,* had grown into a cultural phenomenon, catching all of them by surprise, most of all Ivy. It had been a combination of anger and desperation that drove Ivy to pitch her show idea to Leah Allen three years ago. Now it was KCEX's biggest show. Ironic, considering Ivy had been as disgraced as humanly possibly and no one would hire her in her chosen field of accounting. But now she'd put her reputation on the line to hire her mom for the decorating job, along with her promise that she'd make sure her mom stayed on task. Not on the first available male hot bod. Crap.

"Mom—"

Mallory cut her off. "I'm your mother, not a loser calling into your show. And I'm not impressed with your semi-fame."

No kidding, like when had her mom ever been impressed with her? Exactly one time, when she had dated Dirk Campbell. There was a memory she didn't want to think about. Ivy stalked over to the fridge and pulled out a bottle of iced tea. She screwed off the lid and took a drink before replying, "You swore you'd concentrate on the job, Mom. You know how you are when you get involved with a man."

Slapping her hands on her hips, her mom said, "Just because you want to live like a monk doesn't mean the rest of us do."

She clutched the cold bottle tightly in her hand. "I date sometimes." Damn it, she walked right into her mom's trap.

Her mom adjusted her handmade crystal necklace that matched her lavender top over the black skirt. "You date men scared of their own shadows. I doubt they even try to kiss you, let alone make love to you. And your show is making you sound like a frigid, bitter, number-cruncher, not a woman."

No matter how hard Ivy tried, they ended up back to this same old argument. It'd been this way all her life; Ivy was the adult and her mom was the hormone-ridden teen. Why couldn't she have just ignored the closed door to the office kitchen? Because she had spent much of her life pulling her mom out of trouble—the kind of trouble that came with rippling abs and a randy penis. Sighing, she simply said, "I'm not bitter. I'm realistic."

Her mom shook her head. "You're alone. Maybe you're making money, but does that keep you warm at night?"

"Actually, yes. Because I pay the gas bill, which keeps the heat on. I'm toasty all night long."

Her mom shook her head. "You're too safe, Ivy."

She liked safe, damn it. Ivy had fallen for a mysterious, handsome man once and darn near ended up in prison for it. Never again. She controlled her own fate, and she stayed out of trouble, and out of pain. "Mom, just stay focused on the job." She lifted her tea bottle in a silent salute and walked out. She ignored the dingy beige walls and weird gold carpet to make her way to her little office. There was nothing wrong with safe. Besides, she was helping other women, and she liked her life.

Mostly.

Inside her office, she ignored the plain white walls that her mom called a symbol of her vanilla life. Ivy had painted them white for a clean, professional look. Her home was full of warmth and color. At work, professional was the color chart she worked from. Her office furniture was directly from Office Max, thrifty yet functional. She had the whole set—computer desk, filing cabinet, and shelving unit.

She sank into her chair and picked up the e-mail from Leah.

> Ivy, I know how hard you've been working since I'm out of the office so much. To help you out, I've hired an assistant and call screener for you. I only promised him a two-week trial, but I think you'll be very happy with his work. His name is Luke Sterling. He came highly recommended by several excellent sources and I checked him out myself. He should arrive for work Tuesday afternoon. Call my cell if you have questions. Leah.

Ivy wasn't really surprised. Although she did most of the hiring these days, she'd bet her last dollar that Leah had hired this Luke Sterling for a two-week trial to seal some deal. Her boss was clever and aggressive at sales. It's what made a small A.M. station in a college town do so well.

And hadn't Leah spotted the potential in the show Ivy pitched to her?

She'd give the man a fair shot. As it was, too much burden was falling on the sound board engineer Ivy had just hired. Having a call screener would help out Marla Rimmer. Putting aside the e-mail, she turned to her computer to do a last check of tomorrow's show.

A sharp knock interrupted her before she put her fingers to the keyboard. Turning back, she saw a man in her doorway. He was wearing tan work pants and a lightweight jacket. His hair was black and wavy around his blue eyes, and he had a shy dimple when he smiled. "Hi."

He was hot and she had zero reaction. Maybe her mom was right and there was something wrong with her? Hell, she was letting her mom get to her. No more of that. She stood up. "You must be Luke"—she glanced down at the e-mail from Leah—"Sterling?" She walked around her desk and held out her hand. "I'm Ivy York." She was a few feet away when she saw the small smile had turned hard and mean.

He stepped into her office, shut the door, and turned around holding a knife. "Just the bitch I'm looking for!"

Odd thoughts passed through her mind. The feel of her skirt slithering around her calves. The scent of the man, grease and aftershave, and the size of the knife, bigger than the man's hand. It was one of those switchblade types, a silver color that gleamed wickedly in the overhead office light.

The same light that her mom told her made her skin look sallow.

She didn't want to know how her blood would look.

Reminding herself that she was known for being calm, cool, and controlled, Ivy kept her voice soft and low. "What are you doing?"

"I'm not Luke."

Well good, because she wasn't going to hire a man who had a knife, no matter what her boss promised some client. "Who are you?" *Wait, shouldn't I scream? No, get to the phone, dial 911.* The buzzing in her ears was probably shock or fear.

His voice was smug. "Ed Bailey. Ring a bell?"

Oh God. Yes. Ivy had helped his wife find the money Ed Bailey had tried to hide during their divorce. "Mr. Bailey, what can I do for you?" Her voice shook, betraying her fear.

His eyes narrowed. "Payback. You cost me a hell of a lot of money, bitch, and I'm gonna get my payback. Where are they?"

The door behind him slipped open.

Ivy's heart swelled up into her throat. Please, please, let it be the police. Let someone have called the police! Don't let it be anyone she worked with, or her mom. She didn't want them to get hurt. She shifted her gaze to the doorway.

It was a man, wearing wire-rimmed glasses, a black turtle neck, and a wrinkled tan coat. He stuck his head in and said, "Excuse me, I'm looking for Miss York? I'm Luke—"

"Get out!" Ivy hissed, hoping he'd run, warn everyone else in the building, and call 911 from someplace safe.

Ed lunged for her, grabbing her around her waist and shoving the business end of the blade against her throat. He positioned Ivy in front of him and said, "Don't move or I'll make this ice bitch bleed."

The nightmare just kept getting worse. His hand holding the knife smelled like a cheeseburger, greasy meat and old cheese. She could feel him breathing fast. Her own heart pounded. Her palms were slick with sweat and the office seemed eerily quiet.

Luke put his hands out in front of him, his gray eyes widening. "I'll just sit down in that chair." He waved his right hand to the chair facing Ivy's desk. It was directly between them. "See, I'm walking slowly to the chair." He took a step.

"Stop, Goddamnit!" Ed yanked his arm around Ivy's waist, cutting off her breath. "I'm not leaving here without getting what I want."

The blade dug into the skin of her neck. She was afraid to swallow, afraid to breathe, afraid to do anything. She stared at Luke, silently begging him to run and get help.

But Luke frowned. "I'm against violence. I'm a peace activist and I'm a big fan of Ms. York's radio show."

God help her, just when she needed an alpha hero type she got Mr. Rogers. She was going to have to get herself out of this disaster, but how?

Knife-wielding Ed said, "Shut up and sit down!"

Luke nodded and took a step while saying, "Sure, yeah." He took another step. "We'll talk and—" He snagged his foot on the shag carpet, pitching forward face-first.

Oh God! The knife hitched against her throat as the man behind her jerked.

Luke reached out to stop his fall and latched on to Ed's knife arm.

It was so fast that Ivy wasn't sure what happened. The blade lifted from her throat, the man screamed, and suddenly she was free. When she looked, Luke had fallen on top of the man and was flailing around trying to get up.

Ed curled up in a ball. "My arm! He broke my arm! Get him off me! My arm!"

Ivy hurried to the phone and dialed 911. While she reported the attack, Luke bent down and talked to the attacker in a low voice.

All the while she answered the questions of the 911 operator, she stared at the back of the man who had saved her with his earnest clumsiness. He had his brown hair pulled back in a stubby ponytail. An aging hippie type? Maybe. His shoulders looked so big and wide she wondered if he padded that coat.

The attacker screamed again.

Luke's voice rose enough to make out the words. "Don't try to get up. It's too painful."

He was comforting the bad guy? But she didn't have time to think about it as people poured into her office and the sounds of sirens screamed up the street.

"Ivy!" Marla Rimmer broke through the knot of people. "I called the police. What happened?" She turned her dark eyes to the man writhing on the floor. "What did he want?"

"Payback," Ivy muttered.

"Who is that?" Marla gestured to Luke.

Luke stood and turned. "Luke Sterling, I'm Ms. York's personal assistant and call screener."

Marla's chunky blond hair brushed her shoulders as she swiveled her head back and forth. "What? Call screener? But I screen your calls."

"Leah hired him, but I haven't agreed yet. Don't worry, Marla. You're the best sound engineer we've had. Leah was just trying to take some of the workload off of you." She was seriously annoyed that Marla had to find out this way. Leah should have talked to them before dropping her surprise on her and Marla.

"Sure, okay, I just . . . Are you okay?"

Her mom's voice cut through as she skidded into the room. "Ivy! Oh God, you're bleeding!"

Startled, she said, "I am?" But now that she thought about it, her neck did burn.

Luke slid up next to her. He grabbed several tissues from the box on her desk. "Sit down." His hand closed around her shoulder and pushed her into the chair.

The touch of his hand jolted through her. He slid his errant glasses back up his nose; then he touched her chin, moving her head up, and gently pressed the tissues to her neck. "It's just a small cut." He looked down into her eyes.

She stared back into the icy gray depths and felt a twang. Something about his eyes . . . or maybe she was in shock. "Thanks. Your clumsiness saved me." She winced at her choice of words. She'd meant to thank him, not insult him.

He laughed, a small, warm chuckle. "I knew my two left feet would eventually get me the girl." He quirked up an eyebrow. "Or at least the two-week trial for a job?"

Ivy kept Luke's sincere gaze and answered, "Can't very well say no to a hero, now can I?" She reached up to put her hand on the tissue Luke was holding and was surprised to see that her hand shook.

Luke wrapped his hand around her trembling fingers and pressed them gently against the tissue at her throat.

She hissed in a breath, aware her office was filling up with curious people and the police. But the feel of his warm hand, surprisingly strong, made her suddenly breathless.

Shock. Or maybe it had just been a long time since a man touched her. How long? God, she couldn't even remember.

Luke leaned closer to her face, close enough that she could see an emerging five o'clock shadow on the hard planes of his jaw. For a man who appeared to be a clumsy hippie peace activist, he had an overpowering aura. "Then say yes."

Damn. "Yes."

Luke had been looking forward to meeting the woman who had pulled off the heist. Ivy York had to be the brains behind the job, not her ditzy mother or the dupe they had conned into doing the actual theft.

But as he followed the light blue Toyota RAV4 through the streets of Claremont, California, he was having trouble reconciling the woman with a knife at her throat with a master thief.

The protective feeling surprised the hell out of him. Taking a knife to a woman was a disgusting, barbaric thing to do. He'd seen firsthand the damage a knife could do. The thought of what might have happened if he hadn't gotten there when he did . . . he shook it off. Ivy York was an opponent, not a victim. It was entirely possible that Ed-with-the-knife was some kind of buyer with a grudge. Luke intended to ask her about Ed, and then he'd run a check on Bailey tonight.

He couldn't let himself be distracted by Ivy's blond, blue-eyed, all-American-girl package. Hell, she'd masterminded the heist of the Jade Goddesses of Fertility and Virility from a private collector. The statues were valued at over five million dollars, not just for their exquisite beauty, but also for their legendary claim of power. A power that's often misunderstood. The statues were not exactly an aphrodisiac, but many thought they were. Over the last couple of centuries people had killed to get their hands on the Jade Goddesses.

But Ivy York had done it without lifting a finger or spilling any blood.

The insurance company that held the policy on the statues hired Luke to find them. And he would. His blood simmered with the challenge. He never felt more alive, more vigorous, than when he was on the trail of a thief.

Or making love to a woman.

But sex was recreation, while tracking down thieves was his job, his life. He turned the corner, following Ivy onto a street filled with long shadows as the sun set behind the old trees. She pulled her RAV4 into a driveway that led up to a . . . Christ, the woman lived in a life-sized gingerbread house. Victorian, he guessed she would call it.

Luke parked his rented car at the curb, reached for the bag of food, and walked silently up the stone driveway just as Ivy slid out of the car.

She whirled around, her blue eyes wide, her face pulled into a tight mask of fear. "Good God, Sterling, you scared the hell out of me."

Luke stopped short about four feet from her. "Not my intention, Ms. York." He held up the bag of food. "You've had a rough day, and I thought—"

She slammed the car door, clutching her purse and keys. "Thought you'd scare me some more?"

He took a breath, doing his best to look harmless and contrite. "Look, both of us went through a trauma, okay? It's dinnertime. I picked up some food, came by to make sure you were okay and see if you were hungry too. That's it." He was counting on the bonding experience that often happened to victims. He was no victim, but she didn't know that. Just like she had no idea he'd intentionally taken down the prick with the knife and purposely broken his arm. Years in the Special Ops had turned him into a skilled killer when the situation called for it.

She studied him. "How did you know where I live?"

Smart, but he'd already known that about her. Hadn't she gotten away with stealing three million dollars from her previous employer? That took smarts and balls. "You gave the police your address, remember? I was standing right there." The lies just rolled right off his tongue. They always had. He was an excellent liar, having learned at a very young age how to tell people what they wanted to hear. He'd had to just to survive in the series of foster homes he'd been dumped in.

"Right. Look, Luke, I'm sorry we didn't get to discuss the job and your two-week trial. We'll do that tomorrow or . . ."

No way was he getting brushed off. Getting into Ivy's house was a bonus he hadn't expected this soon. "Ms. York—"

"Ivy."

He heard the tiredness in her voice and he used it. "You have to eat, right? We don't have to talk business. Let's just have some dinner, and I'll leave." He narrowed his eyes on her neck. "After I take a look at your cut." Women usually fell for a protective, nurturing man. It was hardwired into their hormones.

"The paramedics . . ."

"Wanted to take you to the hospital, but you refused. I know they bandaged you up, but I want to make sure you're okay. I feel responsible; if I hadn't tripped, that knife—"

"No, no, it's not your fault."

He had her. "Just the same, I'd feel better if you let me feed you dinner, and take a look at the cut on your neck. Then I'll get out of your way."

Her gaze went to the bag he held. "It does smell good." She lifted her gaze to his eyes. "Dinner it is."

He followed her over the stone pavings and up the stairs to a circular gazebo-like front porch and noticed something interesting about Ivy York. She had a killer ass beneath that long, flowery skirt. He watched the graceful sway of her hips as she climbed the stairs and felt his body tighten with white-hot lust. He imagined the soft material of the skirt in his hand as he lifted it up to reveal her secrets. Hot skin and her wet . . .

Jesus, he needed to get a grip. Walking into her house with a full-sized boner would blow his cover as a sensitive guy. He usually had iron control over his body. He had to snap out of it. He shifted his gaze to the back of her blond head. That was safe.

Unless he pictured her head bent over his cock.

Note to self: get laid. Later. Right now, he had to keep his mind on business.

"Come on in. The house is a work in progress."

Her voice wrapped around his guts and slithered down to fill out his cock and balls. Holding the bag of food in front of his pants, he forced himself to concentrate. He looked around as he stepped inside the cool house. It smelled old, like aged wood, fresh sawdust, lemon oil, and old books. Not unpleasant, actually, but rich and soothing. They entered on the upper level of the house into the high-ceilinged living room that opened into a dining room and a kitchen. To the left of the dining room was a staircase leading down to another floor. Farther left was a hallway that he presumed led to a bedroom or two. He refused to think about bedrooms or any room with a bed.

The living room had a heavy couch covered in deep brown suede, a coffee table, and a TV. The walls looked like they were stripped of old wallpaper, ready to be painted or something. Long, thin strips of wood rested on the wood floor against one wall.

"Chair rail," Ivy said. "I'm going to paint the walls beige, paper the top half, and put a chair rail up."

Luke turned to see a slight flush on her creamy white face. "You're doing it yourself?"

She shrugged. "Mostly. It's a hobby. My aunt left me the house last year. Uh, we'd better eat. Do I need to warm up the food?"

He followed her into a dining room that had a built-in hutch and sideboard. It was all sanded down to the naked wood. The kitchen appeared to be the only finished room. It was painted a soft cream with a wallpaper border of big flowers. Brand-new appliances gleamed. Luke sat the bag of food down. "It's probably warm enough. Roasted orange chicken, rice, salad, and brownies."

She reached up to a glass-fronted cabinet, her short-sleeved sweater lifted to reveal a strip of white skin across her back, and took down two plates. "Sounds good. Do you want some wine? I don't have any beer, but I have soda if you'd rather. Or iced tea."

"Wine." He started dragging the packages from the bag. He had to keep his mind on business—finding the statues.

He had believed the statues were hidden at the radio station, but now that he'd seen Ivy's house, he wasn't so sure. She and her mom could have hidden the statues in the house, especially with the renovation Ivy was doing.

Still, the trail had led him to the radio station. It was a complicated trail, starting with the mom's boyfriend. Mallory York dated Trip Vaugn, a small-time scammer. From interviewing Regina Parker, the owner of the Jade Goddesses, Luke was certain Trip stole the statues. He'd worked for Regina as a bartender for several of her parties.

Trip then passed the statues off to his girlfriend, Mallory, and Trip went into a hole; no one has seen him.

Mallory suddenly got a job redecorating the very radio station her daughter worked for. The same daughter, Ivy, who had been under suspicion a couple years ago when three million dollars was stolen from the investment firm she worked for. Ivy had been fired from her job but not charged. The employer and police had believed her pathetic, poor-me-I've-been-scammed-by-my-bad-boy-boyfriend story.

Luke wasn't buying it. Not for a second. Hell, look around this house—it had to be worth millions. Inherited from an aunt? Her mom didn't have any siblings, and her father hadn't been in the picture since Ivy was a baby. No child support trails . . . nothing. He was pretty sure Ivy sat on that money, probably grew it with her big fat money brain and then invested in this property.

Then she needed more money for all these improvements. So she set up another big heist. Using another stupid man, leading him by his dick, no doubt.

He watched as Ivy filled two glasses with wine and thought, *Not this time, sweetheart.*

God, he loved his job.

Chapter 2

Ivy watched Luke's long, straight fingers as he ate the last piece of the toasted garlic bread. She didn't want to admit it, but she was actually glad he had shown up. For the first time in years, she had been a little scared to go into her own house. She knew the police had arrested Ed, but still . . .

It's not every day a woman gets to feel the sharp end of a knife at her throat. She felt better after eating the chicken and drinking a glass of wine.

Luke picked up the wine bottle and refilled their glasses. "I've been wondering, why did that man attack you?"

She sipped her wine, set the glass down, and debated what she should tell him. But if he was going to work for her, he should know. "I helped his ex-wife find the money he hid during their divorce proceedings. Courts take a very dim view of that kind of behavior. As do I." How would Luke react to that?

He raised both his dark, arched brows over his steel-gray eyes. "Was this a favor for a friend?"

Ivy leaned back in her chair and studied Luke. Was that skepticism she heard in his voice? She was getting a mixed reading on the man. He seemed like a gentle-giant type, clocking in at over six feet tall and wearing at least 190 pounds. His clothes were all wrong, like he wasn't comfortable in his own skin. And yet, when she looked into his eyes, she saw the organic male confidence of a well-seasoned man. When he leaned close to her, she could practically smell his testosterone thumping in his veins.

What was he? The bad boy woman-user type or the thinking, mature man type?

He intrigued her. But if he was working for her, he was off-limits sexually. She didn't date coworkers. In fact, she rarely dated; but when she did, they were mild, undemanding men who scratched her itch. Well, truthfully, she didn't have much of an itch to begin with. And there was a place she didn't want to go. So what if sex wasn't fireworks and blazing orgasms? She'd been burned once, and no way was she getting burned again.

To answer him, she said, "I do investigative accounting for women screwed over by the men in their lives." She waited for his reaction.

His eyes never moved from her face. "Get a lot of clients?"

"Enough."

He nodded. "What about men? They've been known to get screwed by women. And not in a good way."

Something shifted low in her stomach. She hoped to God it was the wine, but it felt suspiciously like desire. Why now? "I've had a few male clients, but it's usually women. It's the Economic Sex Hex that tells women they should cook, have sex, and let the men worry about money. Even *their* money. Trust me on this, women are conditioned to hand over access to their money to men. It's the whole Cinderella fable—the hot guy with rippling abs and clever fingers will come take care of you. All you have to worry about is making sure you look sexy. Then the next thing you know, both your money and the guy are gone. The hot guy turned out to be a scamming bad boy of Urban Legend proportions." She took a breath and realized Luke was dead quiet. She'd gone off on a rant, fueled by a long day, tiredness, and the second glass of wine. Resolutely, she put down her wineglass.

Mildly, he said, "Urban Legend. You talk about him a lot in your shows."

"He created a whole Web site of Urban Legendites to feed his bad-boy ego. He made himself into a myth, calling himself the Urban Legend." She shoved her empty plate away in disgust. "Then the media got wind of it, and when he refused to give any interviews, they started interviewing the women. They refused to talk about the supposed work they are doing for him, but they were happy enough to brag about his sexual prowess."

He asked blandly, "You think he built the Web site for sex?"

"Undoubtedly. He may have told those stupid women that they are part of some kind of network to recover stolen artifacts, or whatever that treasure hunter really does, but it's just a ploy. And it's working; women flock to the sight and beg to be allowed to join. He probably has horny women all over the country hoping to meet him in person and find out if he's really as good as the rumor says he is."

Luke grinned. "Good at sex? Is it so wrong that women might want sex?"

She glared at him. "One orgasm is like another. They are being used, that's what irritates me. Women have got to start thinking with their brains not their emotions, or their—" She clamped her mouth shut.

His eyes widened. "I really want you to finish that sentence."

Ivy couldn't help it, she laughed. "I bet you do. Sorry for going off, I just don't like the Urban Legend. No one really even knows his name. He won't let his picture be taken. Who knows what he's taking these women for?" Damn, she was still ranting. Standing up, she started picking up plates and took control. "I'll make some coffee to go with the brownies; then we'll call it a night."

Luke followed her into the kitchen and took the plates from her. "I'll do the dishes while you make coffee."

Suspicion coiled tight in her chest. "What do you want,

Luke Sterling? Why did you really show up at my house with food?"

He rinsed the plates and leaned over to put them in the dishwasher. "I told you why."

Her gaze went to his ass. That unfortunate jacket lifted, and the material of his jeans pulled tight, revealing a real hand-squeezer. God, she'd had too much wine. Ivy grabbed the coffeepot and filled the carafe with water. "Are you worried about the job?"

"No, I'm getting a head start on the job. Being a personal assistant means knowing my boss and what she needs." He turned off the water and shifted to rest his butt against the counter. "And I was concerned about you."

So not falling for that. She poured the water in, added coffee, and turned on the machine; then she got down a couple plates for the brownies. She went to the fridge and pulled out some vanilla ice cream. After setting that on the counter to soften, she fixed her gaze on Luke and decided to draw the boundary lines. "My needs are professional."

He shoved off the counter and closed the distance between them. "Looks a little bit physical at the moment." Lifting his hands, he reached toward her neck.

Ivy recoiled, jumping back so fast she slammed her hip into the counter. Pain shot through her hipbone.

Luke closed his hand around her upper arm. "Easy, I meant the cut on your neck. I just want to take a look at it."

He had a rich, clean, and distinctly male scent. His eyes settled on her face like a touch, confident and soothing. "Sorry, I'm just jumpy from today." She felt a little silly.

His smile rolled out over his face, lifting the corners of his mouth and crinkling his sexy eyes. "You're safe with me unless I trip and fall on you. Or make a sudden move and cause you to slam your hip into the counter." He loosened his hand holding her arm and rubbed the bare skin down to her elbow and back up to her sleeve hem.

"You're big." She could have bitten her tongue off for that

dumb-ass comment. But next to her, he was big. Overpowering. Not at all like the biddable, mild man he had seemed to be in her office.

"Always have been. A bull in a china shop, always bumping into stuff or tripping over my own feet." He let go of her arm and reached up to her neck. "I'm going to lift the bandage and take a look. Do you have a first-aid kit?"

She felt the edges of the bandage pull away from her skin. He leaned in close, his hair tickling her cheek. The stubby brown ponytail didn't look so ridiculous now. His hair smelled like forest and cedar. She had the insane urge to pull out the rubber band and bury her fingers in it.

He lifted his head, bringing his mouth just inches from her. "We need to change this bandage. The bleeding has stopped, but you need a clean bandage."

What is wrong with me? A small voice in her head answered that question: *Horny and lonely, a dangerous combination.* But she wasn't ruled by her hormones. "I'll do it." She took hold of his hand and stepped back at the same time. Unfortunately, he didn't let go of the bandage fast enough and it ripped off her neck.

"Damn," he said softly.

"It's fine." She waved a hand at him and went to the cupboard to get out her first-aid kit. Setting the white box on the counter, she was acutely aware of Luke in her kitchen.

And the sound of the coffee dripping in the otherwise silent room.

"You know, as your personal assistant, this is probably one of my duties." He moved up next to her, reached into the white box, and pulled out a square bandage and a small tube of ointment. He set the items down on the counter, then turned and looked at her. "Don't panic."

"I don't . . . What are you doing?" He put his hands on her waist and lifted her to the counter.

"You already mentioned how big I am. This way I can see your neck without slamming you into counters." He put a dab of the ointment on his hand and smoothed it over the cut. Then he covered it with the bandage. "There you go, all fixed up."

He stood at her knees, which were demurely covered by her skirt, and yet she felt . . . vulnerable. "Move so I can get down."

He reached for her waist and lifted her to the ground before she could protest.

This time he didn't move his hands. They stayed warm and firm on the curve of her waist. Her entire body started to hum. This was so not good. "Look, Luke, I'm not sure the personal assistant job is a good idea."

He quirked an eyebrow. "Why not?"

She moved his hands off of her. "Because of this. You keep touching me." She went to the coffeemaker and filled two cups. Time to send him home. Maybe she should make his coffee and brownie to go.

"Don't trust yourself, Ivy?"

Startled, she turned while holding the coffeepot. "Don't be ridiculous."

He folded his arms, pulling that ugly jacket tight across his shoulders. Muscles seemed to bulge against the material. "So we're sexually attracted to one another, we're both adults."

"Well, yes, but—"

A raw challenge heated up his gaze. "Or is it that you think I can't possibly control myself? I'll admit, you're attractive, but I think I can hold myself back."

Was he laughing at her? To buy time, she shoved the coffeepot back on the warmer and dumped the brownies on two plates. Then she rummaged for the ice-cream scoop, finally remembering which drawer she had put it in.

"Or we could have sex now and get it out of the way."

She dropped the ice-cream scoop. It clattered onto the wood floor. She picked it up, then slammed it down on the counter. Then she turned and faced him. "I'm not having sex with you."

He shrugged. "Then my working for you won't be a problem, will it?"

"Nothing wrong with your verbal skills," she muttered as she picked up the ice-cream scoop and ran it under hot water.

Luke took the scoop from her hand and served the ice cream. "And there's nothing wrong with admitting I'm attracted to you. It's just sex. Besides, that remark you made earlier bugged me."

She frowned as he put the ice-cream scoop in the sink. "What remark?"

He turned to hand her a plate and cup of coffee. "One orgasm is like another." Shaking his head, he said, "I can prove to you that's a fallacy."

Her mouth went dry. "This is exactly why I can't have you working for me. That's a totally inappropriate comment." And it made her hot as hell. Restless. Wondering what she'd been missing. How the heck did this Clark Kent rip-off make her hot?

Picking up the remaining plate and cup, Luke grinned at her. "Just honest communication, Ivy, like you talk about on your *Economic Sex Hex* show. You know, men should be honest about what they want? That stuff? If it bothers you, I can probably muster up a Neanderthal grunt." He headed into the dining room.

Ivy followed him, watching his tight butt. "You'll be lucky to last the full two weeks, Sterling."

It was Wednesday morning and Luke was surprised how many calls came through for the *Economic Sex Hex* show. Being a natural-born cynic, he had suspected most of the calls as being fakes, setups. But tons of women and a few men jammed up the phone lines trying to talk to Ivy York. He sat on the outside of a U-shaped desk and answered a multilined phone. Marla Rimmer engineered the program at the control board, where she patched all callers through to the sound booth through a phone interface by Gentner. She also controlled the system's CD player and recorded all calls and programming through a digital recorder. Marla was really good at what she did; Luke could see why Ivy hired her. She was attractive enough with her blond-streaked hair, gleaming brown eyes, and smoky voice.

But his gaze kept going back to Ivy. He watched her in the booth as she dealt with the latest caller, Amanda.

Amanda said, "I'm not going to stop, you know, sleeping with hot men. But I want to protect myself financially."

Ivy adjusted her headphones to keep her hair off her face and answered, "Okay, fair enough. My first suggestion is not to have them to your house at all. But if you do, make sure they don't get access to your records, like your banking records, your credit card numbers, your social security number, not even your date of birth." She took a breath and said, "A lot of that information is available in your purse. All it takes is for you to go in the bathroom and your sexy bad boy can go through your purse and clean you out the next week. Do you write down your PIN number for your ATM card and other accounts?"

"Umm, yeah. It's that easy?" Amanda's voice sounded thin with new worry.

Ivy's answer was stern. "That easy. I understand that you want the fun of good sex." She lifted her gaze back to Luke.

Luke felt like his breath had been sucked out. The impact of her blue eyes, along with the phrase "good sex" punched the air right out of his lungs.

Ivy went on, "But you might be putting your financial future at risk if you don't safeguard yourself, and your financial information."

Amanda said, "But I get lonely; I'm a woman too. What do you do for sex?"

Luke stared at Ivy. He wanted to know the answer to that question. Bad.

She kept her gaze on him as she assured the caller. "I get real. Sex with bad boys isn't all it's cracked up to be. The truth is that deep down we want to tame those bad boys and bring them to heel. We use sex to try and do it. It's really not about the orgasm, but about the challenge. Buy a vibrator; you'll be a lot less frustrated and a lot more solvent." Ivy ended the call and pulled her gaze from Luke to study the computer screen for her next call. "Hello, Julie, what can I do for you today?"

"I slept with the Urban Legend."

Luke straightened up in his chair. The hell she had! She hadn't said anything about sleeping with the Urban Legend when he screened her call! *Shit, shit, shit.*

The caller went on, "I know who he is, and he's—"

Luke shot to his feet and stared at Marla. "I put the wrong call through!" Sweat popped out on his face and under his arms.

Julie finished her sentence, "—been in secret military—"

"Fuck. Cut the call!" The panic in his voice was entirely real, just not for the reason Marla probably thought.

Marla swiftly cut the call.

"Julie? Are you there?" Ivy's voice asked the dead air.

Marla keyed the mike. "I'm sorry, Ivy, we've had an unavoidable technical problem and lost Julie." Her gaze moved to her computer screen. "But we have another call from Mary, who has been fired from her job."

Ivy didn't miss a beat, her voice was silky and concerned as she said, "Mary, welcome to the *Economic Sex Hex*. Let's talk . . ."

Luke sank into his chair. That had been close.

Marla looked over at him. "Breathe, dude."

"I put the wrong call through." Thinking fast, he added, "I knew she was a nutcase when I talked to her. Damn, I screwed up my first day." He didn't give a rat's ass about screwing up, he had been worried the woman would tip off Ivy to the Urban Legend's real identity—him. The Urban Legendites started as a private Web group when Luke had been tracking a legendary diamond that had been stolen. He loved legends that told the story of gems or art that had survived generations while the people that owned them died off. Art survived when people didn't. Luke had pooled his resources into a single Web site. It worked like a charm. Over the years, he'd added more resources—pawn shop owners, private art dealers, jewelers, cops, anyone who has their ear to the ground on high-dollar thefts. If any tips led to Luke recovering the item, the tipster got a reward. It had worked beautifully.

Until his cousin got wind of the Urban Legendites and went to the media, trying to ruin Luke. But the media glommed on to the sexy side, getting the impression that the Urban Legend, Luke, was some kind of modern-day Romeo/treasure hunter, like Michael Douglas in *Romancing the Stone*. He just ignored all the rumors going around about the Urban Legend and his sexual prowess. Women, often women he'd never met let alone slept with, got themselves face time on TV or in tabloids by claiming to have slept with him.

Marla's voice cut through his thoughts. "Don't sweat it, Sterling. This shit happens in live radio, and Ivy knows it."

He smiled his thanks, then turned back to the phone lines that were lit up like a Christmas tree in Rockefeller Center. Luke got back to work screening the calls. By the end of the hour-long show, he was surprisingly tired.

Ivy signed off the show and stood up while Marla went to commercial. She walked out and looked at Luke and Marla. "What happened with the Urban Legend caller?"

Marla said, "I patched through the wrong call."

Luke added, "Because I lined it up for her. It was my screw-up."

Ivy nodded, her slender shoulders rising in a sympathetic shrug beneath the thin pink sweater she wore over the slim black skirt. "It takes a little practice. Keep following the question sheet in the procedure book. You're doing fine."

"Uh, thanks." He'd expected her to lay into him. The more

he talked to and observed her, the more Ivy puzzled him. Intrigued him. She wasn't what he expected. He'd thought she'd be beautiful, cold, calculating, and manipulative. But while beautiful, she came across as warm and genuine. There was an excellent chance it was part of her good-girl-used-by-bad-boy act. But there was always the possibility he'd been wrong.

He intended to find out. Needed to find out. Anticipation streamed through him. Peeling back the layers to find the real Ivy York was a challenge he embraced.

Luke closed the notebook he'd been working from and stood up to follow her into her office. "It doesn't bother you?" he asked her back, his gaze dropping to her ass in that black skirt.

She stopped at the door and looked back. "What?"

"Talking about getting fired from your last job?" She'd commiserated with Mary about getting fired and used her experience as an example of moving on.

"Of course it bothers me. But it happened and I had to make the best of it. So does the caller. I can't help them if I'm not honest myself. The caller needs to accept the reality that her job is gone and find a new one." She walked into the office, went around her desk, leaned down, and pulled her purse out of her drawer.

Luke watched her from the doorway. "You blame your ex-boyfriend for getting you fired."

She jerked upright, her blue eyes going dark and stormy. "I blame myself for blindly trusting him, and that trust allowed him to get access to my clients' money to steal more than three million dollars. I accepted responsibility and I paid the price. When I was fired, I couldn't get a job doing bookkeeping for a donut shop. I had to figure out a way to make a career for myself, just as the caller does."

Defensive, interesting. Ivy was so damn smooth, so convincing in her good-girl role, that Luke almost found himself wanting to believe it. He pushed her a little further. "I guess people would just use the information to attack you if you didn't talk about it."

She picked up her briefcase. "They'll do that anyway. I have a meeting. I'll be back in an hour or two. I've signed some head shots and written replies to fans." She tilted her head to the pile on her desk. "I need you to mail them out."

Startled, he asked, "Where are you going?"

Her blue eyes frosted. "Meeting. I'll have my cell on if you need me." Then she walked by him and was gone.

Luke inhaled the scent of berries clinging to her hair before he shook it off and moved around her desk, sat in her chair, and started going through the fan letters to look busy. He'd checked out Ed Bailey last night. The man clearly had the IQ of a bark beetle judging by his small-time arrests. He might have been after the statues, but he doubted Ivy had set up a deal with him as the buyer. The man didn't have enough assets to buy the statues, and he didn't have enough brains to get the money.

Since he couldn't follow Ivy without arousing her suspicion, he put his time to good use by searching her desk.

Nothing.

He went to her filing cabinet, picked the lock, and looked there. No statues.

Nothing on the shelf unit. Unless she had a hidden safe behind the diplomas on the walls, the two Jade Goddesses were not in her office.

He doubted they were in the reception area; it was too public. There were a lot of possible hiding places in the radio station. He couldn't check the on-air studio until the station went off the air at sunset as mandated by the daytime permit. He sank back into the chair and started addressing envelopes for the fan mail replies while thinking it out.

Ivy's office was too obvious.

Her mom, Mallory, originally had the statues after having gotten them from her boy toy, Trip.

Ivy was the mastermind, but that didn't mean she actually touched the statues.

Mallory was redecorating the radio station. What would she have access to? Most everything, except maybe the on-air studio. But she'd have access to the other offices, including the station owner Leah's office, the conference room, bathroom, storage area, and kitchen.

It was a start. Luke could hit the conference room and kitchen. He picked up the stack of work and went down the hallway. The conference room was across from the on-air studio, so Luke lifted a hand to wave at Marla, then turned into the room.

It was twice the size of Ivy's office and had a nice mahogany table running down the center. Matching credenzas ran along one wall. There was an LCD TV on a stand in one corner, along with a video and DVD player. The room had several wall-mounted speakers, with a switch to turn on KCEX's program. He put the stack of work down on the conference table and spread it out.

A pile of signed photos. Fan letters with Ivy's reply attached. Envelopes. Some promo crap Ivy wanted included. He pulled off the ill-fitting sports coat and draped it over the chair to make it look like he was working. Then he went to the credenzas and started opening drawers and doors. He found two overhead projectors, computer equipment, pads of paper, pens and pencils, a couple white boards, a box of KCEX coffee mugs . . .

"Something I can help you with?"

Her voice was like a purr. Luke recognized the voice as belonging to Ivy's mom. He pulled his head out of the cupboard and stood up. "I'm running out of envelopes. Do you know where they are?"

Mallory had an interesting walk, one that made her short skirt ride up higher on her thighs. She stopped right beneath his chin. "Envelopes, huh? Anything else interest you?"

She was shorter than Ivy, and she shamelessly advertised

her goods. He was a man, he looked. But damn, he found himself thinking of Ivy, how she smelled, how her ass looked in her soft skirts, the feel of the skin on her neck when he touched her . . . Shifting as if uncomfortable, he said, "I need to get this work done before Ivy gets back."

She leaned back with just enough arch to display her expensive breasts. "Trying to impress my daughter, huh?" She ran her gaze down his body.

Luke fought a grin at the blatant sexual appraisal.

"You might be just what Ivy needs." She lifted her gaze back to his eyes. "She could use a little fun, and beneath those unfortunate hippie clothes you could have just the right equipment for her to play with."

She had his attention. Either this was a test, or Mallory York was a very interesting woman. Staying in character, Luke said mildly, "I have two weeks to prove myself and make my job permanent."

She sighed, the overt sexiness melting a bit. "Shame, still think you're hiding a hot package." She turned and walked out.

Ivy got her coffee from the 12-year-old-looking Starbucks barista and returned to the table. They had purposely met outside of Claremont, choosing the city of Diamond Bar to protect her client's privacy. Returning to the table nestled into a dark corner, she missed the individual charm of her little Claremont Village coffee shop. This shop had the usual small round tables and a cluster of chairs. About a half dozen people were in the coffee shop.

"So you'll be able to find it?" Beth Lawrence asked as she twisted a wad of tissue in her hand.

"Yes, I think so." Ivy took a sip of the hot coffee and added, "I have your husband's name, birth date, and social security number, along with all the places you know of that he's had bank accounts. I'm certain I can find where he hid the money he uses to gamble." She added the caution, "If there's any money left."

Beth's mouth turned white with worry. "I can't believe he's done this. That money was supposed to go toward a down payment on a house. I was so tired and sad when my mom died, I just put the inheritance in our savings account, then never checked. Never did anything . . . until I listened to your show."

Same story, different face—women not paying attention to the money in their marriage, always blindly trusting the man. "Hang in there, Beth."

Beth's eyes welled up with more tears. "I hate this! He's lied to me, to everyone. Just lied and lied, and I kept making excuses, believing he'd change." She dropped her eyes to the table and swept up the pieces of her shredded tissue into a soggy pile. "It's my fault for being so stupid, so gullible."

"Beth, all of us make mistakes. What makes us strong is fixing the mistakes."

The woman looked up, resolve lifting her shoulders and firming up her face. "I know. I'm angry that I let it go this far. I have nothing to lose since I don't have to pay you unless you find money, right?"

She opened her mouth to agree when a voice said, "Hey! You're that radio talk show chick. The sex hex one. I'm Cindy Mason and I'm a huge fan."

Ivy forced a smile and looked up. The woman wore a dark pantsuit and carried a large bag in place of her purse. She had a wide grin on her face. The man she came in with was standing by the counter waiting for their orders and talking on a cell phone. He hung up the phone, looked around, and stalked over. "Damn clients are bitching that we're late. How long does it take to make the drinks?"

"Joel, this is Ivy York! That sex hex woman." She turned back to Ivy. "We listen to your show when we're in the car."

Ivy guessed they were salespeople out making calls and said, "Hope you enjoy it."

Joel snorted. "She listens to that rubbish. I don't take financial advice from people who get fired."

She heard Beth's sharp intake of breath but ignored it. "Your choice. Nice to meet you." She hoped they would go away.

"Take a pill, Joel," Cindy said, then looked at Ivy. "I took your advice on credit cards. I cut all but one up and am paying them down. I plan to buy a house—"

Joel cut her off to glare at Ivy. "What's your problem with men anyway?"

"Actually, Joel, I don't have a problem with men. Grown-up men are great. It's bad little boys masquerading as men I have a problem with. Boys who are rude and impatient because their coffee isn't ready by the time they get off their cell phones."

Joel's blue eyes narrowed. "Enjoy your vibrator, honey. No man's going to want to touch an ice bitch like you." He stormed over to the counter, grabbed the two coffees, and stormed out the door.

The woman sighed and shook her head. "I'm really sorry. I just wanted to tell you how much I enjoy your show."

"Thank you," Ivy said. "It was really nice to meet you."

As Cindy left, Beth said, "Wow, Ivy, does that happen a lot? I mean people being so rude?"

Ivy turned back to Beth and shrugged. "It comes with the territory."

"It must be hard."

She had no idea. Ivy always had to be "on" and it got tiring. The only place she was able to let down and be herself was when she was working on her house. "It's part of the job. But lately, it makes doing this"—she picked up the information that Beth had given her on her husband—"harder. I have to skulk around to meet with clients."

Beth tilted her head, studying her with intense green eyes. "Then why do you keep doing this? With all the excitement and glamour of a radio show, maybe you don't need to do this. After you are done with my case," she added with a smile.

Ivy stood up, not wanting to tell Beth that being an accountant was her love. Accounting made sense—there was always a number trail. Growing up, her life had been an emotional and financial roller coaster. Men came and went in her mother's life, always in a dramatic fashion. Ivy longed for stability—a home and financial security. After she'd been fired and humiliated by the theft from the investment firm she worked for, the radio show became a way to achieve the security she needed. But Beth was just being nice. "I like doing investigative accounting. I'll be in touch as soon as I have any information for you."

Ivy got in her car and started back toward Claremont when her cell rang. She checked to see who the call was from and answered, "Luke? What's up?"

"I got a call from an electrician verifying a job at your house at three. Something to do with ceiling fans. Ring any bells, because I don't have it on the schedule for you?"

"Damn it! My mom set it up for me with one of her contractors. She told me, but I completely forgot. I'm having ceiling fans installed and he's checking all the electricity. I need to show him everything today and sign off on the plans." She jumped on the freeway and mentally ticked off everything she needed to do. "You can go home, Luke. I'll go by the office tonight and work on my program for tomorrow."

"Actually, I have a few more things to go over with you. Why don't I come by tonight after I finish up here? I'll bring your file for tomorrow's show."

Ivy thought it over. "Okay. See you then."

Chapter 3

Mallory hung up the phone. She had nearly all the contractors lined up that she'd need to renovate the radio station. They'd do the bulk of the work at night when the radio station was off the air. It was a little more expensive to get people to work nights, but the job would be done faster, so the costs should balance.

Ivy would like that. She did like her numbers.

Mallory winced at the thought of her daughter walking in on her the day before in the kitchen at KCEX. But Trip had wanted her so much. How could she explain to her smart, beautiful, accomplished daughter that being wanted by a hot guy made her feel . . . sexy and valuable. That it made her feel alive.

It was late, time to head home. Where Trip waited, hiding out until his soon-to-be-ex-wife stopped trying to take the heirlooms that belong to Trip's family. He'd want more sex. Mallory sort of wanted to watch TV, maybe have a glass of wine and relax.

God, she was 47 years old, not dead! She was still hot, still liked to party. It was Ivy and her nagging that was making her—

The door to her office opened. A tall, slim man dressed in dark slacks and a designer shirt walked in. He had sky blue eyes set in a strong face. "You must be Mallory York."

She felt a ping, a rush of interest. Standing up to let him get the full impact of her tight shirt and short skirt, she said, "Yes, can I help you?"

"Actually, I'm here to help you." He pulled out a small leather case and extracted a business card. "I'm Arnold Sterling, with Sterling Investigations."

Her skin pebbled and her interest went cold. "I see." She reached out and took the card. "Are you planning to redecorate your office?" *Trip*. This had to be about the feud between Trip and his estranged wife. For a few seconds, dogged tiredness weighed her down. Why was she letting herself be dragged into another mess?

"You know, that's not a bad idea. I do have a suite in a building in Irvine. But today I'm here to warn you about another investigator, Luke Sterling."

"Warn me . . ." *Luke Sterling*, that name rang a bell. "Luke . . . oh!" Her daughter's new personal assistant. She glanced down at the card in her hand, then back up to Arnold as she made the obvious connection. "You both have the same last name."

A distasteful look tightened his mouth and brought out the lines around his eyes. "We're cousins. Normally we stay away from each other. But when I heard Luke hooked up with your daughter, the radio talk show host—"

Mallory leaned forward, her blood going hot. "Luke is working for my daughter."

"Is that his game?" Arnold asked in a regretful tone.

Mallory narrowed her eyes, concern for her daughter firing her temper. "Arnold, exactly what is your point?"

He met her gaze. "My cousin got the job under false pretenses. Luke is a private investigator. He's known as the Urban Legend . . ."

The rest of his words were lost in a furious buzzing in her head. *The Urban Legend!* What was he after? Could Trip's soon-to-be-ex-wife have hired him to find the statues? But why would he go to work for Ivy? She brought her attention back to what Arnold was saying.

"I'm afraid Luke is going to use your daughter for some kind of publicity stunt. She's known to dislike him on her radio show. If he seduces her, it would give him an edge—either to blackmail her or he'd reveal it to the media and destroy Ivy York's reputation."

The buzzing turned to a roar of rage. And suspicion. "Why are you telling me this? Why not tell my daughter?"

He sighed. "Luke charms the women; he has a way of being whatever they want him to be. They never see what he really is until too late. I doubt she'd listen to me."

Ivy thought of Luke in his unfortunate clothes, hippie ponytail, and glasses. His sincere eagerness to please Ivy with his work. Oh yeah, that was exactly what would work on her daughter. The bastard. No way in hell would she let him trick and disgrace Ivy. "Do you have proof?"

"Actually, I do. Can you get online?"

She sat down in her chair and turned to her computer.

Arnold came around the desk, stood behind her shoulder, and directed her to a celebrity watchers Web site. He leaned close, his mouth near her ear. "This one, where the caption reads, 'Urban Legend caught'? That's Luke."

She noticed his scent of balmy aftershave, but it did nothing for her. Her full attention was on the picture. She studied the image. Take off the glasses, update the wardrobe, cut and style the hair, and it's Luke Sterling. The rat-bastard.

Mallory was sure he was after Trip's family heirloom figurines and using Ivy to get them. Ivy didn't know a thing about them. "I'll take care of this."

Arnold turned his gaze to her face. "Your daughter is lucky to have a mom like you."

Yeah, sure. A mom known as the town slut. Mal shoved the thought away. Damn it, she was getting morose lately. She could see the vivid interest in Arnold's eyes, his appreciation for her full breasts straining her sweater. She just didn't care. "Thanks."

"How about I take you to dinner tonight? Some place nice enough for a beautiful woman like you."

She tilted her head back and remembered she had a man hiding out in her house. And a daughter to warn. "I'm sorry, I have—"

The door opened.

Arnold straightened up and Mal swung around to see Isaac Kane. Uh-oh. She had redecorated his Victorian home for him; then she'd casually dated Isaac a couple times, but he wasn't her type. He was . . . old. Frumpy. A lawyer! Nearly bald. She knew the type: They liked to cage women and control them. Maybe to the world they seemed nice, conservative, and gentle. But her dad, a man the community loved and respected, had taught her how very different those men could be at home.

They were the type to call their daughter a slut and hit her.

She shrank the screen before Isaac could see the picture of the Urban Legend and accuse her of trying to seduce him or something like that. "Isaac, did we have an appointment?"

He shifted his intelligent puppy-dog sweet brown eyes to Arnold. "No, just came by to see if you wanted to pick up some dinner and watch a movie tonight."

She lifted her chin. "I can't, I'm working tonight."

Isaac walked up until the edge of her desk touched his perfectly pressed slacks. "You've lost some weight, Mal. Are you eating?"

She gritted her teeth. She hated the way he pushed through her words to see her. To worry about her. "Of course I'm eating. A girl's got to watch her figure." She laughed and looked up at Arnold with a flirtatious smile.

He grinned. "A very nice figure it is."

Isaac shifted from puppy-dog sweet to shark instantly. With a single glare, he had Arnold fidgeting. Then Arnold said, "I'll talk to you later, Mallory. You have my card; call me if you need anything else." He hurried out the door.

Mallory rolled her eyes. "What was that for?" she demanded of Isaac. "He was perfectly nice!"

He didn't look a bit remorseful. "He was sniffing around you like a dog in heat." Leaning his hands on the desk, he fixed his gaze on her. "You're a lovely, talented woman, not a sex toy. You deserve better than him."

She hated it when he did this, when he made her feel soft inside, and cared for. It was a trick, a defense lawyer's trick. The man wore a sweater vest as casual attire! He was not her kind of man. She liked her men young, hot, and eager. Not old, slow, and seductive with confident smiles and a gentle touch. Because it was a lie. She'd rather have the truth—sex for fun and nothing else. Rubbing her forehead, she said, "Go away, Isaac."

"What's wrong, Mal? Do you have a headache?"

She dropped her hand and met his gaze. "No, I have work to do. Go away, Isaac."

He glanced at her computer screen. "What are you hiding?"

"Nothing! You're not my father! Get out." Her voice sounded shrill and tired even to herself.

"Mal . . ."

The warning tone sent her over the edge. It made her too damned aware that she didn't have anything deep and lasting, except her daughter. That was all she'd ever have. Seriously, what would an accomplished, successful man like Isaac want with the town slut? If he wanted her at all, it was just to try to change her, reform her, mold her into something fake that would kill her spirit. "Get out. I mean it, Isaac."

He glared at her. "When are you going to stop running?"

"Never."

She was covered in paint by the time the doorbell rang. Wearing torn jeans and a barely there tank top, she looked down at herself and grimaced. "Perfect for a Wednesday night work meeting." She'd lost track of time. Setting the paintbrush down, she walked over the plastic sheets she'd put down to protect the wood floor and opened the door.

"She's driving me out of my mind."

It wasn't Luke, but Isaac Kane. A friend, criminal defense lawyer, and man-in-waiting. Waiting for her mom. But Isaac was middle-aged and looked it, with dark-framed glasses over brown eyes, a small potbelly, only remnants of his brown hair on his shiny head, and a killer smile. The kind of smile that made children trust him and men want to have a beer with him. But women? Women thought the smile was too open, too honest.

Too boring.

At least her mom did. Ivy personally wished Isaac was twenty years younger and she'd marry him. He was safe. He'd come home every night, be a good dad and a loyal husband. He was everything she dreamed of, except he said he was too old for kids.

And he had it bad for her mom.

Isaac stormed in wearing his hopelessly out-of-date loafers and a—swear to God—sweater vest over his shirt and tie. "She's up to something. I know it. She had some man in her office and hid what they were doing on her computer from me. Threw me out of her office!"

Ivy left the door open and followed Isaac into the living room. "Why do you do this to yourself? There must be dozens of women who would love to date you."

Isaac turned around and stared at her. "I want Mallory. I love your mom."

Ivy snorted. "For a smart man, you are blind when it comes to my mom. Or stupid. Take your pick."

"I'm serious, Ivy! I'm running out of patience!" He scraped a long-fingered hand over the skin on his head and into his remaining hair.

She stopped on the plastic-covered floor and stared at him. He did look more harassed than usual. "Seriously, Isaac, forget my mom. She's into flash, not substance. I'm sorry, but I'm not going to sugarcoat this for you." He was the male version of the women who called in to her show, sure they could change the men they were in love with. Except that Isaac was never stupid with his money. Nor would her mom ever swipe his account numbers and access codes to steal his money. But the emotional aspect was the same. It hurt her to see a good man, a solid man, throwing away years waiting for her mom to grow up.

"She's just scared."

Ivy blinked. He did know her mom, maybe he understood her mom better than Ivy realized. But her mom wouldn't change. "She's stubborn and determined to be twenty-nine years old until she dies." The bubble of her frustration popped, spewing out to the one man she knew would understand. "She doesn't want to be an adult! She never wanted to be an adult. She chases after any man with hot abs and a sleek car. I'm so damned tired of rescuing her."

Isaac moved faster than Ivy had ever seen, grabbing hold of her upper arms and looking into her face. "Then don't. Stop rescuing her. Let her fail, Ivy. Damn it, I'll take care of her."

She wasn't afraid, she wasn't even annoyed. She knew Isaac right down to his argyle socks. He was a tough man packaged in an easy-going, soft frame. He'd kill anyone who hurt her mom, but he'd never hurt a woman. He was, in a weird way, almost a father figure to Ivy. And she'd seen him take care of her mom when Mallory had a nasty flu bug. Ivy had been there with her mom and was exhausted. Isaac came in and ordered Ivy to bed. Ivy told him no, and he'd gotten into her face and told her she'd help no one if she got sick. Then he'd told her to go to bed or he'd put her there himself. He wasn't above doing it either. The easy-going charm worked in the courtroom, but he had layers and layers of steel beneath that charm. Ivy respected that. "Don't be an ass. You don't want her just because she has nowhere else to go."

"I'd almost settle for that."

She didn't miss a beat. "Then you're not the man I thought you were." She meant that right down to her toes.

He fought with himself for a second. She could see it in the hard lines of his face, the anger in his jaw. Then he started to pull her toward him to hug her. . . .

"Move away from her, now."

The fierce, threatening voice froze Ivy for a second.

Isaac jerked his gaze from her to the door and tried to shove her behind him.

She sidestepped his maneuver and turned to see Luke. He wore a loose button-down plaid shirt over a "Peace Activists Get More SEX" T-shirt and baggy jeans, his hair was pulled back in that ridiculous stubby tail, and he held two plastic bags from the grocery store. It was Luke, but not the Luke she knew. His eyes were an icy, threatening gray behind the glasses. There was nothing soft and cuddly about the man standing in the foyer of her house. He rolled to the balls of his feet, his knees going loose and his gaze taking in everything.

"Do you know him?" Isaac asked as he attempted to step in front of her again.

Trying to recover her wits, Ivy answered, "Yes, he works for me." Turning to Luke, she said, "What's wrong with you?" It wasn't just his posture. He gave off the vibe that he was ready to attack, and if he attacked, the victim was going to get seriously hurt. It made her stomach tighten in fear, and something else that she didn't want to think about too much.

He settled back from the balls of his feet and shrugged. "I thought you were being threatened. This guy had his hands on you."

He'd been protecting her? There it was again, that warm, safe feeling. Damn, she must be inhaling too many paint fumes.

Isaac said, "Excuse us." Then he took hold of Ivy's arm and tugged her toward the kitchen.

"Ivy, do you want to go with him?" Luke asked; this time his voice was slightly less threatening.

She looked back at him. "He's a friend, Luke." She went into the kitchen. "Isaac, what's gotten into you?" She knew the answer—her mom. Her mom was driving him to insanity.

His brown eyes, magnified by his glasses, bore into her. "Who is that? You hired him?"

"Luke Sterling. Leah hired him for a two-week trial as my personal assistant. Why?"

"Hmm."

"Hmm, what? What does that mean?" She put her hands on her hips and gave him her best stare.

Isaac pulled his mouth tight. "Honey, I don't know who you think you hired, but that man is dangerous. He would have gone after me if he thought I was a threat to you." Then his mouth relaxed. "On the other hand, that's not such a bad thing. I could see his point. I did have my hands on your arms; it could have looked threatening."

She shook her head trying to keep up with his male reasoning. "He's just bringing me work." She remembered the bags in his hands. "And probably dinner since he seems to like to eat." He was big, she imagined he had to eat a lot.

"Okay, then. As long as you feel safe with him, I'm off." He leaned down and kissed her cheek.

"Wait, I didn't say I felt safe with him."

Isaac did that easy smile. "I know you, Ivy. If you'd felt threatened, you'd have hurled a can of paint at him and called 911 before he regained his senses." He walked out of the kitchen.

"Where are you going?" She yelled at his back. He'd been really upset about her mom.

"To make a plan. I'm tired of waiting for your mom."

She went back to the living room and stopped by the couch. Isaac said something to Luke she didn't catch, they shook hands, and then Isaac was gone. What plan? What was he going to do?

Luke shut the door and walked with a loose-hipped stride

into the dining room where he tossed files onto the table. Then he disappeared into the kitchen. He didn't look at her, didn't say a word.

She pulled herself together and followed him into the kitchen. From the plastic bags, he pulled out a bottle of wine, salad fixings, and a container of lasagna. "Luke, uh, thanks. But that didn't quite seem like you out there. What gives?"

He turned around, the full impact of his molten gaze landing on her. Then he shrugged, rearranging his body into a nonthreatening slouch. "Just trying to do my job. You looked like you might have been in a tight situation. You've got some harsh critics out there."

"Oh." What was making her uneasy? He hadn't done anything violent; he'd just told Isaac to let go of her. Maybe she'd been so startled by the tone of his voice that she'd imagined that whole I-can-kill-you-as-easily-as-look-at-you thing. She decided to change the subject. "What's the food for?"

"Again, just doing my job. If you wanted to work tonight, I thought we might get hungry. I didn't notice a lot of food in your house last night." His gaze strolled down her, from her hair pulled back into a rubber band down to her bare, paint-spattered feet. "But it looks like you have other plans. I put the files on your table. Call me if you need anything else."

Before he could leave, she said, "I lost track of time. I meant to be cleaned up by now. I'll put the stuff away and we'll get to work." She turned and walked into the living room, suddenly conscious of how disheveled she looked. She was a mess.

"Do you have another paintbrush?"

She stopped at the couch. "Sure, but why?"

He looked around. "Get me a brush. We'll finish the living room."

Suspicion tightened her gut. "You're going to help me paint?"

Facing her, he said, "At the end of two weeks, you aren't going to be able to live without me as your personal assistant." Then he stripped off his flannel shirt and tossed it on the couch.

Her mouth fell open. Holy God. His arms were solid with ripped muscles. Right up to where the damned T-shirt covered his biceps and shoulders. She had the odd feeling that, layer by layer, the soft teddy bear was being stripped away to reveal something else. Someone else. Someone hot. And dangerous. Sex hex dangerous.

"Paintbrush?"

She forced her gaze away from his arms, taking in the ridiculous lime green shirt hanging from his shoulders like a tent. As if he had no definition beneath it. As if he were soft and formless. "Right. Paintbrush." She grabbed a roller and handed it to him. At the touch of his warm, dry fingers she yanked her hand away and got busy painting.

She reminded herself that she was in control since Luke had two weeks to prove himself or she could fire him.

Two hours later, the living room was finished. They'd opened all the doors and windows, plus brought in lights. Ivy was beat and starving. After cleaning the brushes, she put her hands on her back and arched.

Luke moved up next to her in the kitchen. "The lasagna will be ready in fifteen more minutes. You have time to grab a shower."

He was too close. She could smell his warm skin, feel his heat. "Fine." She laid out the brushes to dry and hurried out of the kitchen. Halfway down the hallway to her room, she had an attack of conscience. Luke had worked nonstop for two hours painting her living room. He hadn't talked about anything but work, planning shows and schedules. The least she could do was offer him the use of her second shower before they ate dinner. She went back into the kitchen, stopped cold, and sucked in a breath.

Luke had pulled the shirt off, yanked out the rubber band, and stuck his head under the faucet. The muscles surged and rippled in his back and shoulders as he cupped water over his head and neck. Hearing her, he pulled his head out of the stream of water and turned.

Rivulets of water sluiced over his jaw, down his neck, winding over the curve of his shoulders and . . . God, he was hot. Fireman hot. With his pants hanging low on his hips, she just stared.

"Forget something?"

How to talk? "I was just going to tell you there's another shower . . ." she trailed off to watch a line of water slide between his pectorals and down his flat waist. He had a light dusting of crisp hair that made her fingers itch. Finally, she looked up. Without his glasses, he appeared less studious and more edgy. Sexy.

He walked toward her, slowly, as if stalking prey. "Do you need me to wash your back, boss?"

Oh God. She had to pull herself together. "That's an inappropriate question."

He smiled, an all-male smile. "So is the way you are looking at me."

She had to get out of this. Lifting her chin, she said, "I'm just surprised. You didn't seem like the gym-rat type. I thought you had better things to do with your time than grunt and sweat to make your muscles bigger."

Stepping closer, he slapped a hand on the doorjamb over her head. "I think you like what you see. I think you might even want sex, but for all your tough talk when you're hiding behind that microphone, you really are afraid to go after what you want."

He smelled of paint and pure man. With his arm over her head, his skin close enough to lick, she felt cornered. Small. Almost protected. Those feelings were the kind of emotion that made women careless and stupid with men. Forcing her coldest smile, she said, "I always go after what I want, Sterling. I just don't want you."

The air crackled between them.

She could hear the frantic beat of her heart; it sounded something like, *Li-ar, li-ar, li-ar.*

Then Luke dragged in a long gulp of air. "Do you always get it, Princess? What you want?"

Princess? What the hell? She answered him with a sharp "Yes." When she was thinking *no.* Because right now, she wanted him. She wanted the feel of a man's arms around her. She wanted to feel a connection to someone who wasn't looking for advice or answers from her. She just wanted to be a woman with needs and desires. But she couldn't do that, she couldn't let her guard down. She had done that once and darn near ended up in prison. Nor did she want to end up like her mother—always trying to tame the bad boy who uses her time and again.

Luke's gaze was locked on to her. Slowly, he drew his hand down from the doorjamb and curled his fingers over her cheek. "Let me know if you decide you want sex from me; otherwise, I'll continue to do my job." He dropped his hand and walked across the kitchen to check on the lasagna.

She had to get the upper hand back. "I'll let you know tomorrow if you still have a job."

The next afternoon, Ivy's mom burst into her office. "Ivy! I have to talk to you."

Ivy looked up from the computer where she was preparing for Friday's show. The day was tense. She had done her best to keep Luke busy and out of her office. It was embarrassing to be so attracted to her personal assistant. Today he wore pressed jeans and a polo shirt that dropped beneath the hem of his tan sports coat. He had his hair pulled back in that almost ponytail and kept his glasses firmly in place.

Clark Kent was back and she had the hots for him. Her stomach clenched in frustration. This wasn't like her.

"Are you listening?" her mom demanded as she shut the office door.

She yanked her brain out of her panties and shook off the raging hormones. Narrowing her gaze on her mom, she said, "Where have you been all day? It's nearly five." Worry gnawed at her gut. "Mom, Leah has big plans for the radio station, and the redecoration is part of them." Although Leah hadn't shared just what those big plans were yet, Ivy knew her boss really wanted the station to look professional. "I don't want to let Leah down. You swore you'd lay off men and work on this job. No men," she added. Unless her mom had a sudden personality change and realized that Isaac was perfect for her. He wouldn't interfere in her mom's work. In fact, he'd be a steadying influence on Mallory's creative brilliance.

"You're going to thank me for going after *this man*." Her mom strode to her desk and tossed down a computer-printed picture. "Take a look."

Ivy picked up the sheet of paper and studied the picture. It was a man in a club. The lights cast shadows over his face and body. It looked like a cell phone picture, not the best quality. He had short wavy hair, a face cut hard, almost brutal except for the full mouth. There was something naggingly familiar about him.

"Imagine the hair longer and pulled back into a ponytail, and put a pair of glasses on him."

It slammed into her. "Luke." She looked up. "This is Luke? Why are you showing me this?"

Her mom sat on Ivy's desk, her skirt hiking up to her panty line. "I got suspicious when I caught him snooping in the conference room."

Frowning, she said, "Snooping?" She leaned back in her chair and studied her mom. Her mom had dropped a couple pounds, a sure sign she was trying to catch a man. "What's this really about?"

Mallory met her gaze. "The Urban Legend."

She jerked forward in her chair, snatching up the picture and staring at it. "What are you saying?"

"You never think I'm smart about men, but this time you're

the one who screwed up. You hired the Urban Legend as your personal assistant and call screener."

Bile burned up Ivy's esophagus and left a bad taste in her throat. "Luke? You're sure?"

"After catching him in the conference room, I got to thinking. Remember your show when that woman said she'd slept with the Urban Legend?"

"The call that got cut off?" Her thoughts were a tangled mess. Then it dawned on her. "Luke cut the call, or he had Marla cut the call. He said it was a mistake, but if he is the Urban Legend—"

Her mom's smile was triumphant. "He didn't want to take the chance of the caller revealing his identity to you. So I went online last night and found this picture of the Urban Legend." She reached across the desk and tapped the paper in Ivy's fingers. "This is the only one. But it's him."

She dropped her gaze to the picture. She'd seen Luke without his glasses last night. It was him.

Why? What was he doing pretending to want a job with her? Maybe he was working with another radio station to set her up? A tabloid? She frowned. "He's some kind of treasure hunter or . . . It doesn't make sense."

"Fire him, Ivy. He's lying to you and he's bad news."

She looked up at her mom. And finally, the anger and betrayal kicked in. She'd been a total idiot. Her instincts had been warning her since the first night at her house. The Urban Legend was the ultimate bad boy. He'd built a Web site to lure stupid women into believing they were helping him recover stolen artifacts when he just wanted sex. And he probably used them to find the stolen art, too, and cash in. No one knew his name, not even all the people on his Web site. TV and print journalists seemed more interested in his sexcapades than in exposing him. They ran clips of interviews with women claiming to have slept with him.

You could have had him last night, a little horny voice whispered in her ear. Found out for yourself if sex with the

Urban Legend was mythical or orgasmic. She jerked her thoughts back into line.

She met her mom's dark eyes, fury boiling hard in her veins. "For once, we agree on something. I'm going to fire him. But right now, I have to think."

"Think about what? You need to get him out of here."

"About my show. Maybe it's time to expose the identity of the Urban Legend."

"Just as long as you get him out of here, like now." Her mom got up to leave.

Ivy looked up. "Where are you going?"

"Uh, back to my office. I'm lining up all the contractors and ordering supplies to get started on the renovations."

"Mom, don't blow this job."

With her hand on the doorknob, her mom looked back. "You just deal with Luke Sterling. I'll worry about the job."

Ivy watched her go. It was late, past five. She needed to catch Luke before he left for the day. But what did he want? What was his purpose in the little charade? Dressing like a teddy bear nerd? Then half-seducing her? Was his plan to have sex with her, then tell the world she was a hypocrite? Or did he have something else in mind?

She didn't have time to work it out. Instead, she got to her feet and went to look for her personal assistant. As she walked down the hallway, another thought occurred to Ivy.

Her mom had a homing radar for bad boys, so she totally believed Luke was who her mom claimed he was. That made sense. What was a little odd was her mom's insistence that Ivy fire Luke. Why wasn't her mom all over Luke? Mallory York had spent her life trying to tame bad boys. The Urban Legend would be the ultimate challenge.

Was her mom losing her taste for the game? Getting too old? Maybe Isaac was making progress?

Her thoughts ground to a halt when she spotted Luke leaning one arm on the reception desk and talking to Carrie, one of the college interns they used as a receptionist. Her anger shot up to unreasonable. It was a struggle to say in a calm voice, "Luke, I need to see you in my office. Now."

His gaze swung to hers. "Sure." He pushed off the desk.

Ivy turned and strode to her office, her heart pounding and her palms sweating. She turned to confront him. "Shut the door."

He closed the door and faced her. "Problem?"

"You're fired."

He took a step, his shoulders going back and his face hardening. "Any particular reason why?"

Even his voice dropped to an edgier, dangerous tone. Like last night when he'd seemed to think that Isaac was a threat to her. She forced herself to stay still and meet his unflinching stare. "You can drop the hippie, peace activist act. The press loves you as the Urban Legend—"

"You're not serious. Me? Come on, Ivy, what's really going on here? You can't believe that I'm—"

"Cut the act, Sterling. You are the Urban Legend. But even if you won't cop to the truth, the fact is, you're fired. I gave you two weeks, but it only took me a couple days to make my decision. Get out." God, she was mad. Now, NOW, she could spot his smooth game behind his Clark Kent look. She couldn't resist adding, "You disgust me." She was as disgusted with herself as with him. She fell for it, damn it.

He took off the glasses and hooked them over the front of his shirt. "Disgusted with *me*?" He laughed like the snap of a whip. "You're good, sweet cakes, but you aren't that good. I know exactly what you are. But I'm willing to cut you a deal. Give me what I want and I won't turn you in." He took a long step to bring him toe-to-toe with her. "Although, I really do think your pretty ass belongs in prison."

What? Prison? She stared up into his gray eyes. "Leave."

"Not without my statues."

Huh? "Sterling, I don't know what you're talking about, but I am one second away from calling the police to escort you out of the building."

"Go ahead. I know the statues are here. I'll find them by the time the police arrive. Then it'll be you and your mom wearing silver bracelets and riding in the backseat of a cruiser."

Alarm bells blared in her head at the mention of her mom. Sweat prickled under her breasts. Holding her line, refusing to move an inch lest he smell her sudden anxiety, she said, "What are you talking about?"

He lifted the corners of his full mouth in a smirk. "You can't hustle a hustler, baby girl. I've been in this game a hell of a lot longer than you."

Oh man, she was getting a seriously bad feeling. "What the hell are you talking about?"

"The Jade Goddesses of Fertility and Virility. They are valued at over five million dollars, and people have killed to get their hands on them. But your mom—"

She stretched every muscle, tendon, and bone she had to stand taller. "My mother is not a thief!" *She wasn't!* She made bad choices in men, but she didn't steal!

He arched an eyebrow and tilted his head. "Leah wasn't so sure of that. She hired me as your assistant, and she knows who I am."

Leah did that? The old shame, embarrassment, and humiliation fired in her stomach. The sense of powerlessness. "Get out!" She knew she was screaming, but she didn't give a shit. She'd worked for years to live down that whole ordeal of the stolen money. Ivy hadn't stolen it, her too-good-looking, smooth-talking sack of horse shit ex-boyfriend Dirk Campbell had. And by the time the money had been discovered missing, Dirk was out of the country. Ivy was fired and spent months fighting to prove she didn't steal the money.

But she had been careless enough to let Dirk get a hold of the account numbers and passwords. She was lucky she hadn't been prosecuted.

A smug male smile curved his mouth. "You can't fire me, Princess. Your boss hired me to do a job, and I intend to do it."

Her fingers curled with the urge to smack that smirk off his face. She pulled out her biggest weapon. "Wrong. I'm the star at KCEX. If it comes down to a choice, Leah will back me, her moneymaker, over you." Or Ivy would walk out.

His smile iced. "Last chance, Ivy. Either you help me or I'm going to take you down. And your mother. The two of you are a menace to all horny men."

Tears threatened, but no way in blazing hell would she cry in front of Luke Sterling—the Urban Legend in his own sick mind. Last night, she'd wanted to believe he was different. He wasn't. "Rot in hell, Sterling. You have two minutes to get out of the station before I call the police."

His shoulders and chest swelled. "You're making a mistake."

The hell she was. "One minute and fifty-three seconds left."

Chapter 4

Luke went back to the small studio apartment he was staying in. The unit had been added on to an existing house as a rental unit for students. Because Claremont had seven independent colleges, there was never a shortage of students looking for housing. The unit was set back from the house and was basically a living room that doubled as a bedroom, small bathroom and small kitchen.

Perfect for him. Hell, at his home base in Riverside, California, he pretty much lived in his office when he wasn't on the road. He hadn't had a real home in twenty-six years. His life was all about the chase, not home and roots.

Going into the apartment, he was grimly determined. The key to staying in the game was to be flexible and adaptable. No way in hell was Ivy York going to beat him. He'd given her a chance to work with him, and she'd thrown him out on his ass.

The thing that puzzled him was how confounded and frightened she had seemed under all that anger. Her fiery anger had bloomed her skin to a warm rose and made her eyes sparkle. But once he'd started threatening her mom, the color bleached out and her eyes went flat. But she'd never looked away from him.

Damn, she was either the absolute best hustler he'd ever come across . . . or she was real. His need to know which was

starting to overshadow his drive to find the statues. No problem, he assured himself, he would do both: find out who the
real Ivy York was and find the statues.

Now it was personal, and a little more interesting. He
grinned as he pulled on his black jeans and black T. He went
into the bathroom and used clippers to shave his dark hair
down to military short. He tossed the glasses in the trash can.
Then he packed what he'd need—his gun, knife, laptop, cell
phone, and a few toys.

He figured either Ivy or her mom would try to remove the
Jade Goddesses now that they knew he was on to them. Luke
had seen Mallory York leave the radio station right before
Ivy fired him. She hadn't carried anything more than her tiny
purse so he was confident that she didn't have the statues
with her.

His money was on Ivy. Luke stored what he needed inside
the hybrid Camry that he'd rented in an effort to prove to Ivy
he was harmless.

Note to self: get a kick-ass car. Not that the hybrid drove
too badly. But still, he was going into his dark and dangerous
personality; a hybrid just wouldn't cut it. He went to the trunk
and got out two magnetized signs that read "Ace Private
Security" and slapped them on the driver's and passenger doors.
Then he got in, started the car, and headed toward Ivy's
house.

He wondered if she had a buyer lined up for the statues?
No way could she sell the statues on eBay. The Jade Goddesses
were too identifiable. Christ, he wondered if she was being
careful. People had killed for those statues in the past, not for
their monetary value, but their rumored power that the statues were supposed to have.

Pulling onto Ivy's tree-lined street, he noticed it was dark
and quiet, and the houses glowed with yellow lights. First he
cruised the street for a little reconnaissance. He noticed that
her living room window blazed with light and her RAV4 was
parked in the driveway.

Circling the block, he parked two houses back where he could see her front door, but she wouldn't be able to see him out her front window.

Did she have the statues in the house with her now? Or was she going back to the radio station in the dead of the night to retrieve them? Or could she be innocent and caught up in a web? He was going to find out. He settled in for a long night.

An hour later, a sleek black Lexus pulled up in front of Ivy's house; then a man wearing a suit got out and walked up to Ivy's door.

Luke went on high alert. He grabbed his long-range listening device, got out of the car, and sidled up to the side of the house. Pressed against the siding, he slid the earpiece into his ear and pointed the device to the upstairs front door.

"Miss York? My name is Bob Harris. I got your name from a friend. I should have called, but I'm kind of desperate. I need to find out some information about my wife, and you come highly recommended."

Luke wondered what Ivy would do. It didn't sound like the man was there for the statues, but rather for her side business.

Ivy's honey voice slid over him. "Mr. Harris, what exactly do you want to know about your wife? I'm not a private investigator."

Luke nodded to himself. Good, she was being cautious.

The man sighed. "I need to get an accurate picture of how much money my wife owes in credit cards. I just found out that she's been getting cards, charging them up, and hiding them from me."

Luke winced. *Ouch.*

He went on, "I love my wife, but she's going to financially ruin us." There was a pause. Then he added, "If she's lying to me about money, what else is she lying to me about? I'm at work all day . . ." His voice trailed off, then came back strong. "I need to get a clear view of how much money she has charged up. If she's hiding money somewhere or has some kind of problem, I need to understand what would make her do this. I trusted her to take care of the money. I don't lie to her. If she's going to up and leave me, I want to be prepared."

"All right. Tell you what, you think about it overnight. If this is still the avenue you'd like to pursue, call me tomorrow."

There was a silence, but he heard Ivy moving around. Then she was back. "Here's my business card."

"Thank you, Miss York. I'll call you tomorrow."

"Good night."

Luke heard the door close softly. He stayed against the side of the house and watched the man get back into his Lexus and leave.

Turning over what he'd heard, he tried to figure out Ivy's game. If she was so interested in fast money, why didn't she get a down payment from this guy tonight? Strike while the guy was vulnerable, angry, and confused? That's what a cold-blooded hustler would do. It would be an easy enough job— the guy would have his wife's social security number and birth date. Ivy could easily pull her credit history. Instead, she'd given him the night to think it over.

After the car pulled away, Luke slipped back to his car. The house stayed quiet. He moved positions a couple times, and eventually he parked a few streets over and did surveillance on foot. The neighborhood was quiet, people seemed attentive, and he'd noticed, protective of her.

Around eleven P.M. he was resting against the side of her house in the shadows when he heard a car roll down the street. From the rough sounds of it, he figured it was an older car. It stopped a few houses down; then he heard the soft slam of a car door.

Luke rose silently to his feet and moved to the front of the house. A man wearing a long-sleeved black jersey, black sweatpants, and a dark baseball cap walked toward the house. He turned left and headed between the houses and directly toward him.

Luke stepped back deeper into a lush vine dotted with purple flowers. All his senses were on high alert. He could hear his own heartbeat in his ears. His night vision felt magnified by adrenaline. Whoever it was walked with a purpose, and a bit of clumsy stealth.

A buyer? Oddly, Luke felt the sting of disappointment at that thought. Did he want Ivy to be innocent?

He shut it all down and willed himself to become a part of the shadows. The man walked right by Luke, reached up and opened the gate to Ivy's backyard, then shut it slowly, as if trying to be quiet. Luke grinned—an amateur for sure. No way could Ivy not have heard the gate creak open and clang closed.

Unless that was the signal to meet? Maybe the buyer didn't want to be caught at Ivy's front door? Or maybe it wasn't a buyer at all?

Luke intended to find out. He silently scaled the fence and dropped into her backyard. Walking in the shadow line of the house, it didn't take him long to find the man trying the exterior door that led into the garage.

The door popped open, startling the man into stumbling backward and falling on his butt. Ivy stormed out to stand over the man. "Just what the hell do you think you're doing?"

Luke melted back out of view, but his gaze was locked on Ivy. Good God, his blood heated and poured into his dick at the sight of her. Christ, all Ivy wore was a black tank top and a pair of shorts so skimpy he could almost see the delicious curve of her ass. Her long blond hair gleamed a rich gold in the moonlight and streamed down to the middle of her back. She looked so damned gorgeous it was like seeing a real live princess. Untouchable, except that she was made for touching. And he ached to touch her, every delectable morsel of her five feet seven inches, right down to her bare toes.

"Ivy!" The man crab-scuttled backward on his hands and feet. "Don't spray me!"

Spray him? Luke forced his brain into gear. In her left

hand she held a canister with her finger on the trigger. Pepper spray. *Good girl,* he thought approvingly. In the other hand was a cordless phone and a wad of something else that he couldn't make out.

Ivy glared at the man. "You're trying to break into my house! Why shouldn't I spray you?"

The man rolled over to his knees and climbed to his feet. "Come on, Ivy, I was just stopping by for a visit. Why do you have to be like that? Besides, we both know this should be my house."

Okay, this was some weird shit. Who the hell was this guy?

"Leave or I'm calling the cops," Ivy said.

"You call them, and I'll tell the media that you called the cops on your own father."

Luke drew in a breath of cold surprise. *Her father?* Far as he knew, Ivy's father hadn't ever been in her life. He was unknown on her birth certificate.

"Who's there!"

Her voice filled with real fear. Shit, he'd given himself away. He could slip away before she caught him, but Luke couldn't make himself leave her. Not with the man she clearly didn't want in her backyard. The guy may or may not be her dad, but he hadn't been skulking around her backyard trying to sneak into her garage to wish her a happy birthday. "It's me. Luke." He stepped out of the shadows and walked into the light of the moon.

Her eyes widened and her finger twitched on the trigger of the pepper spray. "What are you doing here!"

Her fear ate at him. "Easy, Ivy. I followed this guy into your backyard. My intention was to make sure he didn't hurt you."

"Oh, right, like I should believe you." Her eyebrows drew together. "I should call the cops on both of you."

"Give me some money and I'll leave," the man claiming to be her dad said.

Luke watched Ivy, saw the tightening of her mouth and

that hunch of her shoulders at the man's words. Pain. He knew pain when he saw it. Finally, she walked over to the man, and dropped the handful of paper she'd been holding on the grass at his feet.

He fell to the ground, scooping up the bills.

"Are you kidding me?" Luke demanded, outraged. "What the hell are you giving him money for?" He took a step toward the guy.

"Don't," Ivy's voice snapped out.

The man stood up clutching the money. "Listen to her. Ivy doesn't want any bad press. She owes me and she knows it."

Luke took another step until he could clearly smell the sour scent of beer on the guy's breath. "She wants you gone." He grabbed the man's arm and tugged him toward the gate.

"Don't hurt him." Ivy followed after them, her bare feet barely making any sound.

He pushed the guy through the gate and shut it. Then he turned around. "He's really your dad?"

"Greg Beaman. My proud father."

Her deep blue eyes caught the light of the moon, so clear he felt like he could see into her soul. A little girl wishing she had a real dad, not a drunk who obviously never claimed her. It took a conscious effort to ignore the pang of sympathy. His job was to get the statues, which meant he had to figure out just who Ivy York was.

"You look different." She backed up a step. "What happened to your hair?"

He watched her. She was taking it in, seeing the man he'd hidden beneath the personal assistant persona he'd created for her benefit. "Cut it."

"You're different, more scary."

She had no idea. "Scary as they come, sweet cakes."

She backed up another step. "Who are you?"

"Luke Sterling, private insurance investigator and ex-military. Right now I'm determined to find those statues and best you at your own game. But I don't hurt women to win."

He didn't care if she thought him a bastard, he was. She didn't care if she thought him a killer, he'd killed. He didn't care what she thought of him, as long as she didn't think he'd brutalize her to get what he wanted. He'd outsmart her, use sex if it got the job done, but he wouldn't physically hurt her. Even he had some standards.

She took it in, processed it, and spit out at him, "God, that's what you're doing here! You think I have your statues." She laughed. "You're on the wrong trail, tough guy. You have some serious holes in your theory. I don't even know anything about the jade things."

She intrigued the hell out of him with her quick mind. "Sure you do, baby girl. Your mom seduced that dumb shit loser, Trip, into stealing them; then he passed them off to your mom. Your mom stashed them at the radio station, and now all you need is a buyer."

Her body twanged like a bow, all the long lines snapping at the mention of her mom and Trip. "My mom is not a thief!"

Luke could see that she was shaking. Her face was flushed, her nipples hard and poking against the thin material of the tank. She flexed her jaw and swallowed hard, struggling for control. It made him feel helpless, and like a total bastard. Why he cared, he had no clue. He took her arm and led her back to the garage.

She stopped at the garage door. "What do you think you're doing?"

Hell if he knew. "Getting you inside and checking your locks." Yeah, that sounded like a good, solid plan. Very reasonable.

"I'm not letting you in my house!"

He arched an eyebrow at her. "Don't trust yourself? I've been in your house a few times, Princess. I haven't accosted you yet, so I know you're not worried about me. Must be your self-control you're worried about."

"That's the biggest line of bullcrap I've ever heard."

He tugged her through the door into the garage. He'd

done two things with his little speech—reminded her that she'd trusted him for a couple days at least, and gotten her back up enough that she now had something to prove to him. He really was a ruthless SOB. He took in the two-car garage that had assorted power tools, paint cans, and saw horses that went with renovations. He led Ivy in the door to the house.

She'd turned on a light, so he saw they were in the downstairs hallway. On his right was a bedroom, and on his left was a bathroom. The hallway led to a staircase. Beyond the staircase was a big room, like a bonus room or media room, and on the other side of that he saw a second short hallway with doors. Probably another bedroom. "Any other outside doors down here?"

She shook her head, her long hair swaying. In the process, she pulled her arm from his hold and started up the stairs.

He was pretty sure her dad was gone for the night anyway. Luke put a hand on the polished oak of one of the two newel posts that flanked the bottom of the stairs, and looked up. Ivy's ass in those shorts made his mouth go dry. God, she was hot. She sure as hell wasn't an ice princess, but he already knew that. He'd seen desire in her eyes when she'd caught him with his shirt off.

But Ivy didn't do things impulsively. He'd worked with her for a couple days, seen her up close and personal. She had weighed and calculated having sex with him, and decided it wouldn't work. She did everything with forethought and a set of personal standards that he was beginning to believe was real.

He wasn't sure what to believe. Where the hell were the statues? What was Ivy's role? The puzzle, the need to find the real Ivy was as compelling as her luscious ass. Starting up the stairs, he was determined to find the statues and uncover the mystery of Ivy.

As he reached the top, he saw she'd marched right to the front door, then turned and faced him. "You're leaving."

Like hell he was. Curious, he moved toward her and asked, "Why did you give your dad the money?"

She looked away. "None of your business, Sterling. Leave."

Her misery and vulnerability was like a pulsing, living thing. He decided to use it. Reaching out, he touched her shoulder and damn near lost his train of thought at the warm feel of her smooth skin. "I'm worried about you. First you're attacked by a guy with a knife, and now your father is trying to sneak into your house late at night. I don't want anything to happen to you. Let me help you."

She lifted her gaze. "Don't touch me. And don't try to charm me. All you want from me is the statues you think I have."

Desire ripped through him, and something else, something he couldn't quite define. Lifting his hand, he used his finger to draw a soft circle on her exposed shoulder. "See that's where you're wrong, baby cakes. I want more than the statues from you."

She made a female sound of disgust deep in her throat. "You really are the ultimate bad boy. Cocky enough to think I'd fall for your lines. Wanting sex is like breathing to you. Big deal."

Yeah? He didn't miss her nipples puckered in that thin little tank. She was attracted to him; he could read the signs. He moved in a bit closer. "I'm not a bad boy, Ivy. I'm not a boy at all. I haven't been for a long time." Not since he was six years old.

She rolled her eyes. "You lied to me and used me to get what you wanted."

"Not denying it. I was undercover and I lied. I'd do it again if it worked. But it didn't. So now we're going a different route."

"How's that?"

"Honesty." He slid his hand under her hair and rubbed the tense muscles of her neck. A deep need came to life in him. "I'm after those statues; but if you don't have them, then you have nothing to fear from me."

She stated flatly, "You'll use sex to manipulate me, whether I have the statues or not."

"I would have, yes." He lowered his head toward her. "But now, I'm being honest—I want you. It's two separate issues. Sex is for pleasure. But it doesn't change the fact that I'm going to find the statues."

"Then go. Now. Go find them and leave me alone." She stared at him, but she didn't move to shove him away or open the door.

There it was again—vulnerability. It tugged hard at his buried feelings. Ivy was hurt, hurt by his betrayal. It made him feel decidedly odd, almost like he cared. He was horny, that had to be it. Too long without the release of sex. And Ivy, she was hot, sexy, and standing right in front of him. With his hand on her warm neck, he leaned down toward her face, looked at her full lips, and said softly, "You don't want me to go, Princess."

She leaned her head back, forcing his gaze up to her eyes. "You really believe that one kiss would get you in my bed, don't you? You think you can live up to your own legend?"

"One way to find out." He put his mouth to hers.

She stood immobile, her arms hanging down at her sides, her hands clenched in determination. As if she wanted to prove to them both that she wasn't susceptible to the combustible chemistry sizzling between them.

Luke took the challenge. He slid his hand off her neck and into her thick, soft hair. Then he spread his other hand over her lower back and pulled her into his body.

She resisted for a long second, then she softened with a frustrated sigh. Her mouth slid open as she exhaled; her rigid spine eased against his hand and she put her arms around him.

Surrendering? God, he hoped so. Then her tongue touched his and lust swamped him. His blood pumped fast and hard while his dick throbbed. He sank his tongue deep inside her, tasting Ivy, a flavor so real and intoxicating that he forgot about statues, jobs, fathers . . . His entire world narrowed to the woman in his arms.

"No!" Ivy jerked her whole body away from him. She ran her hand over her mouth, her gaze losing the haze of desire and icing to frustration, maybe anger. Then she grabbed the doorknob, pulled open the door, and said, "Time for you to go."

What the hell just happened? He reached out to touch her, to reconnect.

Ivy smacked his hand away and glared at him. "Leave."

Damn, he'd been doing a good job of seducing her. "Ivy, you liked the kiss as much as I did. Don't lie."

She shoved her hair back out of her face. "So what? I don't think with my hormones, Sterling. You're just another dime-a-dozen bad boy."

Ah, that was it. She was tough, he'd give her that. Which just made her all the more interesting. Intriguing. Sexy. "You don't mind using bad boys to get what you want." She'd used his Urban Legend persona often enough on her radio show to prove her points. To tell the world what a bastard he was without ever having met him.

Her mouth thinned and her eyes narrowed. "Are you suggesting I sleep with you to get you to back off?"

He shook his head. "I'm not backing off whether you have sex with me or not."

She made that female noise in her throat again. "God, you're annoying. I can't believe all those ditzy Urban Legend fans actually fall for your bull. I liked you much better in your Clark Kent character."

He couldn't help it, he laughed. She'd been the one person who had gotten him to break character, and she'd been intrigued by him in spite of herself. Drawn to him. "Yeah, well, this is me, sweet cheeks." He leaned toward her. "I'm not a bad boy."

She put her arm against the edge of the door as if she were amused by his ignorance. "No? Then what are you?"

"A badass."

A light flared like a crystal star in her gaze. "The difference?"

Ivy York was such a pretender. That flare in her eyes told him how very much she liked dangerous men. He suspected it was because, deep down, Ivy possessed the same drive to survive and to succeed, a need to prove to the world that it couldn't destroy her. To answer her question, he said, "A bad boy throws tantrums and punches for no reason other than he's a spoiled brat with a man-sized cock."

Her lips twitched. "With you so far, *Urban Legend*."

She managed to make Urban Legend sound like something right out of a garbage can. He leaned his body closer. "A badass takes care of business and gets the job done." He slid through the opened door, thinking she could chew on that for a night.

"Hey, Sterling."

He turned at the top of the stairs and caught his breath. She stood silhouetted by the porch light in her black tank and tiny shorts. Her breasts jutted out with perky nipples, while her shorts cupped her hips where he longed to bury his dick. Her blond hair flowed down around her shoulders and damn it, she was hot. "What?"

Her smile was slow and sensual. "You really are a legend . . . in your own mind." She shut the door.

Chapter 5

Friday morning, Luke woke up tangled in the covers, sweat covering his body and nausea burning his belly. He snapped on the light beside the sleeper sofa, desperate to chase away any remaining shadows of his nightmares.

He didn't remember the scene in his waking hours. He had no real memory of gathering up the bloody pieces of his two closest friends and flying them home. But his nightmares remembered, and they tried to replay it for him every damned night. To torment him and remind him of his guilt, of his failure. Ray and Sanders. The two men he hadn't been in time to save. The two guys who had been the closest thing to a family Luke had since his grandmother.

He'd failed them when they needed him.

He sat on the edge of the bed, braced his elbows on his clenched thighs, and rubbed his eyes. His neck and jaw ached from the silent screams in his nightmares. "Christ." He rubbed his forehead one last time, then got up and headed to the bathroom to shower. He turned the water as hot as he could bear it. Then hotter.

"Survivor's guilt," the head-shrinkers had said, nodding and looking very pleased with their diagnoses.

No shit. What a group of useless assholes. Like he didn't grasp that he shouldn't be alive and they shouldn't be dead?

How many years of school did it take for them to figure that one out?

But did they know how to fix him? How to stop him from feeling dead inside? Nope, they told him that was up to him. He had to forgive himself, understand that he deserved to live or some psychobabble bullshit like that.

Assholes. Two things made life worth living at all—chasing a puzzle and screwing a woman.

Getting out of the shower, he focused on his latest puzzle—finding the Jade Goddesses. Today, the gloves were off. He'd failed playing the mild-mannered assistant. But he was going back to the station as the Urban Legend, and he was going to convince Ivy and Leah that it was in their best interest to let him freely search the radio station. Since Leah knew her bread was buttered by Ivy's incredibly successful radio show, he knew he'd have to seduce Ivy into agreeing.

And so he would.

Ivy stopped off at her favorite village coffee shop on her way to work. The smell of the coffee beans inside the shop was almost enough to clear her so-tired-she-felt-hungover fog.

After her dad and Luke's late night visit, she hadn't fallen back asleep until three A.M. and it showed in the bags under her eyes. She smiled and said hello to the old men playing chess. But today, she didn't stop to debate the state of the economy or give them a chance to fix her up with their sons or grandsons. She was too . . . edgy. Some sexual frustration, and some real unease.

What drew the Urban Legend to KCEX? Luke was famous for finding stolen artifacts. Could her mom have hooked up with the wrong guy?

Again?

Her head throbbed badly enough to make her teeth ache. Ivy got into her car, set the hot coffee in the cup holder, and pulled into traffic. She had to believe her mom would not get involved with a thief.

Okay, sure, she'd gotten involved before with guys who were trouble. There was the one who seemed to have too much money and no job. Ivy and her mom discovered the source of his money when the cops arrested him right in front of their house. Ivy had been seven years old. She vividly remembered standing at the front door in her Cinderella nightgown and bare feet, and being terrified the police would take her mom away too.

Then there were the boyfriends who slept at the house, ate their food, bummed Ivy's lunch money. . . . They were always handsome, always had a story, and never had any money.

Never mind her dad. He'd been married to another woman when he'd knocked up her mom. Her mom seemed to miss that little detail, and over the years, she'd believed he'd dump the wife and come live with them. Mallory had talked about him, but Ivy had only seen him twice—until the *Economic Sex Hex* made her semifamous. Then her dad showed up, looking for a handout and threatening blackmail.

How many times had Ivy pulled her mom out of trouble? She'd given her money, paid her taxes before they were late, smoothed things over with clients her mom sometimes ignored, helped her at the last minute to finish a job she'd neglected because of a man. . . .

She sighed. It was possible her mom had tangled up with the wrong guy. Just admitting it made her stomach knot. She pulled into the radio station and parked. What to do? Luke had mentioned some man named Trip. She'd have to confront her mom and go from there. Getting out of her car, she was surprised to see her mom pull into the parking lot. It was only five-thirty, a half hour before KCEX signed on air.

Maybe she was wrong, maybe her mom was one hundred percent committed to redecorating the radio station and was taking a break from men. And if she believed that, then she might as well believe her mom would wake up and see that Isaac Kane really loved her and could make her happy if she'd just let him. If only her mom would just believe that she deserved someone like Isaac.

Her mom parked her car, opened the door, and slid out.

Ivy noted that skirt was short enough for a Dallas Cowboy cheerleader. Deep down, her mom believed she was good enough for sex, but not real love. Ivy bit back a comment and forced a smile. "Mom, you're here early." It was possible her mom had a sleepless night. Ivy had woken up many nights while growing up to find her mom had insomnia and was working on a decorating project in the house. Her best memories were of those nights when her mom let her help. They would work and talk for hours.

Mallory fell into step beside her and yanked her out of the memory by saying, "What's up with the tired and frumpy look?"

"Don't start, Mom." She took a long drink of her coffee to keep from snarling that it was better than looking like a warmed-over hooker. She liked her feminine skirts paired with shells and a nice jacket. She'd worked hard to be a professional, and she enjoyed dressing the part. Her skirt today was black with pink flowers.

"Did you fire Luke?"

They were at the front door of the radio station. Just thinking of Luke made her feel odd. A little betrayed, a little angry, and a whole lot confused. The man could kiss. The change in him was purely stunning. Last night, he'd looked like, she didn't know, half tough cop and half renegade. And he'd kissed like . . . heaven. Forcing herself to focus, she said, "Yes, but I wanted to talk to you about that. Luke claims that he's on the trail of some stolen jade statues." She unlocked the door and held it open for her mom.

Mallory walked in and turned. "He's probably fishing."

Ivy shut the door. Since they weren't on air yet, the radio station was quiet. She relocked the door, and said, "That doesn't make sense mom. KCEX is a small radio station. Why would he think the statues are here?"

Her mom put her hands on her hips and glared at her. "Ivy Rose York, just what are you accusing me of?"

She desperately needed a handful of Advil. Striving for patience, she kept her voice low and even. "Mom, you were screwing a man in the radio station kitchen just a couple days ago! What's his name? Was it Trip?" That was the name Luke had mentioned to her.

"I came here to work, not listen to accusations from you." She turned and stalked away on her insanely tall high heels.

Ivy followed her mom, dragging her feet and trying to figure out how to have a civil conversation and get the answers she needed. She was just passing the on-air studio when her mom's shriek sliced through the silence.

"Mom!" Fear dumped buckets of adrenaline into her blood. Ivy dropped her coffee and ran down the hall, hanging a skidding right into the kitchen, and stopped. Her eyes saw it, but her brain couldn't make sense of it.

A man lay on the floor in a puddle of brownish blood. "Oh. Oh God. Mom!" She hurried to where her mom stood still and pale, staring down at the man. "Mom." Ivy grabbed her mom's arm; her skin felt cool. "Are you okay?"

Her mom slowly turned her head and looked at Ivy. "It's Trip. Trip Vaugn. I think he's dead."

Oh my God. *Trip.* It had to be the man Luke had been talking about. And her mom knew him. She turned back to look at the dead man. He was leaking blood all over the radio station kitchen from what she guessed was a gunshot wound. Her mind had slowed to that sluggish underwater sensation. Her skin prickled with cold chills, yet she was sweaty. Her stomach rolled.

He was the same man she'd seen her mom having sex with.

What did she do? "I have to call 911." She let go of her mom's arm to pull her cell phone out of her purse and dialed.

While Ivy tried to stammer out the situation to the operator, her mom walked over to the storage units. Ivy watched her drop to her knees and rummage in one of the cupboards. In her ear, the operator told her that Ivy should get out of the building now in case someone was still inside.

Oh! She hung up. "Mom! We have to get out of here. Come on!"

Her mom said in a flat voice, "I can't find them."

"Mom!" Ivy rushed over to her and grabbed her arm to try and pull her to her feet. "Whoever shot Trip could still be in here!"

Her mom looked up. "No, he's gone. And he took them with him."

Shit! It finally struck her what her mom was looking for. "You had them, didn't you? The statues. Oh God, mom! Why?" Her ears buzzed, her sweat-slicked hand slid off her mom's arm. "What have you done?"

Standing up, her mom frowned. "I was helping him! He and his wife were getting a divorce. The jade statues were family heirlooms and she was trying to get them in the divorce. They belonged to Trip's family! His wife probably killed him to get the statues!" Her voice quivered and broke. "He's really dead."

Staring at her mom, Ivy heard the clang of her lifelong fear closing in on her. Her mom in prison. Because of a man. She always knew that someday Mallory would get in too deep. "Mom, he stole those statues! What have you done!"

Covering her mouth with a shaking hand, her mom shook her head. "No. No, Ivy, it was a divorce fight. That's all. His wife killed him. She found out and killed him. That's. What. Happened."

Tears burned behind her eyes and clogged her throat. Her mom had always done this—told the story she wanted to believe and refused to listen to reason. Sick panic rolled over her in huge, wrenching waves. How was she going to save her mom this time?

* * *

Ivy watched as her mom was being escorted toward a patrol car. Next to her in the parking lot of the radio station, Leah was trying to calm down Marla.

"Marla, just breathe. You don't have to go into the kitchen, I just need you to stay in the sound room, watch the control board while the tapes play. Cue the station IDs, the commercials, we'll have to get the news on live . . ."

Marla's pupils were dilated, and the faint freckles stood out against her pale, sweat-slicked skin. "I can't! I'm sorry, I just . . . I have to go. I'm not going back in there where a man was murdered! They haven't even moved the body. He's—" She slapped her hand over her mouth and ran to her car.

Leah sighed. "I'll call in an intern; until then I'll do it myself."

Ivy heard her, but she was focused on her mom. One of the two cops opened the door to the backseat of the car.

"This looks bad, both for Mallory and for KCEX," Leah said, and started to pace the small sidewalk that led to the front of the radio station. Her cell rang and Leah took the call.

Ivy had called her boss the first chance she had to let her know the situation, and that she was going to run tapes in place of the live shows while the police did their work.

The radio station was a crime scene.

Since Ivy and her mom found the body, they had been separated and questioned. It didn't take long for them to zero in on her mom. They were taking her to the police station for more questioning. She wasn't under arrest . . . yet.

Seeing her mom's shocked, tired, tear-stained face in the back of the patrol car tore Ivy to pieces.

Leah hung up her phone. "That was the radio station lawyer. He wants us to run any statement by his office before issuing it. The media is already working up into a frenzy."

Her head throbbed. "I have to go to the police station. I already talked to our lawyer, he'll meet us there." Isaac wasn't exactly their lawyer, but Ivy was grateful to him. He made her tell him as much as she knew, then didn't even pause, just said he'd meet her mom at the station and do what he could.

Leah put her hand on Ivy's arm. "I know."

She turned to look at the woman who had hired her when no one else would. Leah had given Ivy her self-respect back and a chance at a career. She wanted to help her boss, but she was terrified for her mom. "My mom didn't know the statues were stolen. And she didn't kill Trip Vaugn."

Leah's hazel gaze was sympathetic. "If you want to help her, Ivy, go talk to Luke."

Anger tightened her muscles. "Luke? He blames my mom! He won't help her. If you had just told me why Luke was here, I could have talked to my mom and resolved this before a murder happened!" God, she was so frustrated.

Regret thinned Leah's mouth. "I didn't like doing it that way. But Luke insisted, and he was right. When it comes to your mom, you'd never believe she might have been involved with stealing the statues. Everyone in Claremont knows how protective you are of her."

Ivy fought the denial that rose to her lips. She *was* protective of her mom. People always gossiped about her mom, but few of them knew the heart of Mallory York. The way she loved Ivy, stood up for Ivy. The way she'd fought to keep Ivy when her own father wanted to take Ivy from her. The way Mallory had been forced to learn to protect herself from pain. Her mom was a free, creative spirit, but her spirit was easily crushed. And Ivy couldn't bear her mom getting hurt. Taking a deep breath, she said, "I don't like being tricked, Leah. A man like Luke is dangerous, and you gave me no warning."

Leah's gaze sharpened. "Dangerous? He's just doing his job."

"He thinks my mom and I are some kind of mother–daughter team of master thieves!" And she had kissed him! Even knowing that. What did that make Ivy?

"He never said that to me . . ." Leah trailed off, looking

around at the media pulling up. She turned back to Ivy. "Look, regardless of his beliefs, Luke was obviously on the trail of the statues. He tracked them to the radio station and he was right. If you want to find out the truth to help your mom, go find him and get him to help you."

A stew of emotions simmered inside of her. Leah did have a point. If they find the statues, they will most likely find the killer and her mom will be cleared. "He's probably long gone." A deep loneliness added to the mix of emotions. Even though they were often at odds, Ivy's mom was the only real family she had. She would do anything to save her.

Leah tightened her fingers on Ivy's arm. "Go talk to him, Ivy. Cut a bargain with him. Get his help and give him your help. Frankly, you're already behind the curve on this and your mom is in serious trouble."

Leah was a good friend and she truly cared about Ivy, but she was also a businesswoman. "Finding the killer will help the radio station."

"That too," she nodded her head without apology. "We have a problem. The question is what are we going to do: whine or kick ass?"

Ivy didn't have it in her to smile, but she squeezed Leah's hand. There was a reason Leah was her friend. "Kick ass."

Luke stormed into his apartment ready to rip the head off of anyone stupid enough to get in his way.

He'd fucked up. He'd been so distracted by Ivy "too damned sexy" York, and he'd lost the statues. Trip Vaugn was murdered right in the Goddamned radio station while he was staking out, and trying to make out with, Ivy. How had he let this happen? Now it seemed dumber than shit to stake out Ivy instead of the radio station.

He'd been thinking with his dick. He couldn't remember the last time that had happened.

"Shit." He went to the couch, sat down, and stared at the floor between his feet. He'd just spent an hour and a half at the police station explaining who he was and what he was doing in Claremont. The cops were not in a good mood.

He was in a worse mood.

A knock sounded on his door. He snapped his head up and glared at the white gloss-painted door. Another cop? He shoved himself off the bed and yanked open the door.

"I talked the insurance company into hiring you because you're supposed to be the best. How did you screw this up?" Regina Parker walked into the studio and dropped onto the couch.

He shut the door, leaned back against it, and glared at his current landlady, Urban Legendite, and friend. "Followed the wrong lead."

She settled her worried brown gaze on him. "Which was?"

"Ivy York." He bit the words out, then added, "I'll find the statues." He had no idea how. Ivy had been at home, she hadn't killed Trip. Her mom? Was Trip double-crossing them? And why didn't he believe that Ivy was capable of murder? He'd sure as hell believed she had masterminded the theft of the statues when he began this case.

Regina's desperate voice dragged him from his thoughts when she said, "I need those statues, Luke. I can't believe that little weasel stole them from me." She leaned her head back and sighed. "I leave in a month for the Jade Goddesses Tour. Without the Jade Goddesses . . ."

He knew. She'd spent years revitalizing the interest in the Jade Goddesses through lectures, a Web site, newsletters, and including some clips on selected TV shows. Regina believed in the "power" of the statues. She was passionate about it and wanted to share their beauty and power with those who appreciated it. She'd succeeded in building enough interest to schedule a six-month tour for the statues and herself. The tour would take her around the world to true art and legend lovers.

She took a deep breath and stared at him with her light brown eyes. "I'm worried, Luke. Those statues tend to stir people's deepest desires. Virility and fertility symbolize the primitive essence of men and women, not just to procreate, but to exist. And that tends to tap into some serious emotion—desires, jealousies, fears—and bring them to the surface. You may not believe, but it's true. It's what has driven people to kill for those statues in the past."

Regina's face, a face suitable for a forty-something art history professor, took on the glow of her love and awe of the Jade Goddesses. He'd seen too much to be an unbeliever, but all he said was, "Well, something sure as hell is happening." Like the fact that he'd watched Ivy instead of the radio station.

She sat forward, her eyes bright with excitement. "You've felt something? Like what?"

And he thought shrinks were bad. "Indigestion at the statues getting snatched from right under my nose."

She waved away his comment. "Stop being stubborn. If the statues have affected you, maybe it'll help in tracking them."

Oh yeah, he had to hear this. "Help how?"

"I don't know until you tell me."

Luke crossed his arms over his chest. Still leaning against the closed front door, he debated what to tell her. He went with some questions instead. "Are these, uh, emotions the statues release real? Does the person have to touch the statues?"

She shook her head. "No, just be in the vicinity. And yes, the emotions are real; that's what makes them so dangerous."

He spoke before he thought. "I broke his arm."

Regina's voice rose. "What?"

"The first day I met Ivy I heard a man threatening her in her office through the door. I didn't want to break my cover as a nonviolent man, so I planned on accidentally getting between Ivy and the knife. But when I saw him cut her . . ." He uncrossed his arms to run a hand over his short hair. "It pissed me off and I broke his arm. Compound fracture."

She tilted her head. "Purposely?"

"Yes."

"What would you have done if you saw a man do that to a woman on the street?"

Luke considered the question. "Depends on the circumstances, but I'd hurt him. The thing is, I was supposed to be in character as a man who doesn't purposely hurt someone. I don't ever slip character. I'm good at being whatever I need to be to get the job done." He'd done it most of his life.

"What else?"

He pushed off the door and decided to end this conversation. "I'm horny as hell. Think that's the statues?"

Regina stood up. "Yes, I think the statues are forcing up your deepest desires, the ones you've repressed."

A knock on the door interrupted her.

Relieved, Luke turned around, opened the door, and almost forgot how to breathe.

"Luke, I need to talk to you," Ivy said, looking pale, tired, and more beautiful than he remembered in a black skirt with pink flowers and a pink shirt.

He almost reached out to touch her, as if touching her would calm the storm inside of him and assure him she was okay. It was all the talk of deep desires and odd powers messing with his mind. Angry at his reaction, at his colossal screwup, he slapped his hand on the edge of the door and said, "Did you come here to confess?" Being a bastard came naturally, and it helped him steel himself against the attraction of Ivy.

"Please, Luke. It's a mistake! My mom didn't know the statues were stolen. Now the police think she did it, that she killed that man!"

A bitter laugh tore up his throat. "Not my problem." He started to close the door.

She stepped in so that the door bounced off her shoulder.

Her wince was fleeting; then she lifted her chin. "You have to listen to me!"

Swear to God, he thought he saw a glimmer of tears in her eyes. Gritting his teeth against the persistent urge to touch her, he snarled, "Don't stand in doorways if you don't like getting hurt."

"I'm not hurt, I'm desperate. I have to find who killed Trip, and I need your help to do it."

Luke's guts twisted viciously. He had no doubt he was seeing the real Ivy, stripped down to her naked vulnerability. Her prim skirt and top, her blond hair brushed back into a low ponytail, her vivid blue eyes wide and beseeching were all window dressing around the truth—she was shaking with real fear for her mom. She had the brains to be a master thief, but not the heart. And she sure as hell wasn't a killer. He'd seen too much of her in the past few days to believe that. The truth was that he'd been lying to himself so he'd have an excuse to be close to her.

She kept talking. "I'll help you. I have some skills. I am very good at forensic accounting. Get me access to everything you can about Trip, and I'll see if I can find the trail to the statues."

That caught his attention. Right now he had very few clues, maybe Ivy could shake something loose.

She kept at him. "I don't care what you think of me, Sterling. But you need me. Those statues are gone—taken right out from under your nose. If we work together, I think we can find them and Trip's murderer. Please. I have to prove my mom didn't do it. I have to. If she goes to prison, I'll be alone."

Shut the door, he told himself. There was a chance her mom was guilty. Luke didn't need distractions like Ivy, he needed to find the statues. But he couldn't make himself shut the door. He couldn't make himself abandon her. Because Ivy had touched on the one thing Luke couldn't turn his back on—family loyalty. She was a woman who stuck by her family when they needed her.

Talk about deep, repressed desires.

He opened the door, and said, "Get in here."

Ivy walked in and stopped when she realized that someone else was in the apartment. She looked at Regina, then him.

Luke closed the door. "This is Professor Regina Parker. She is the owner of the stolen statues."

"She hired you? I thought the insurance company hired you?"

Regina said, "I asked the insurance company to hire Luke. I've known him for a while through the Urban Legend site."

Ivy held out her hand. "I'm sorry about your statues. And now there's been a murder. It must be awful for you." She took a deep breath, and said, "My mom really didn't know the statues were stolen. Trip told her they were family heirlooms and that his wife was trying to take them in the divorce."

Luke snorted.

Regina looked over at him. "That sounds just like Trip, you know."

He paid attention. "What do you mean?"

"Trip was charming, friendly, and convincing. I believed his hard-luck story about his impending divorce, how his wife was trying to get all the assets of his business and needed me to pay him in cash." Regina shrugged in embarrassment. "I trusted him, so much so that he saw where I put the keys to the locked case where I kept the statues."

Okay, he knew that. Regina had been kicking herself hourly for her stupidity. Trip wasn't that smart, but maybe he'd had plain old dumb luck. It happened. Then maybe he'd tried to sell the statues and gotten himself killed? Luke had to admit, the puzzle was getting more intriguing.

Regina asked Ivy, "Do you really think you can track the statues through forensic accounting?"

"If there's a money trail attached, I might be able to. It depends. I have to start with Trip and work from there. I think that if we can find the statues, we can find the killer."

Regina started to look better, more hopeful. "Luke, you should work with her. She might be able to help. It's imperative to find those statues right away. They are dangerous in the wrong hands."

"Dangerous?" Ivy asked, then amended, "Well, obviously someone killed for them."

Regina nodded. "Exactly. The Jade Goddesses possess powers to draw out people's deepest lusts and desires. They were made back in the Aztec times by a powerful sorcerer to be used as a way to communicate with his forbidden lover. They used the removable hollow hearts to leave messages for each other. But one day the hearts were stolen. The sorcerer and his lover died instantly—but the statues live on, continually seeking their deepest desires and bringing out the desires of any who possess them. Their legend really is a tale of sex, love, and murder."

Ivy looked nonplussed. "You believe they have powers? That they could really control someone's actions?"

Luke knew how Ivy felt about that. She'd told him last night that she didn't think with her hormones. Every decision she made was carefully thought out. She wouldn't like the idea of some statues taking her control away.

Regina answered, "I absolutely believe it. It's why I'm taking the statues on tour—housed in an appropriate container to keep their powers enclosed—to show the world. Just seeing them in person will make you a believer." Regina looked over at Luke. "Find them, Luke. Before something else bad happens." She left.

Ivy asked him, "Do you believe in the power of the statues?"

"I believe that artifacts live on when people die off and that is something of value to the world." In fact, he loved valuable artifacts and legends. They endured and lived on when people disappeared and died. He loved recovering stolen art and returning it to the people who made sure the pieces and their stories endured. He wasn't exactly a believer in superstition and legends, but objects that lived generation after generation had to have some power to keep existing.

She seemed surprised. "I always thought you did it for the money and women."

He shrugged, telling himself that he didn't care what she thought.

She asked him, "So we'll work together?"

He pushed off the door and took a step toward her. "We have a problem, Princess. I think your mom might be guilty. And if she is, she's going to jail." What the hell was wrong with him? He should have just let her think whatever the hell she wanted to, gotten all the information her accounting skills could access, then done his job.

Not warn her first. Christ, this was not his standard operating procedure. He did whatever it took to get the job done, and he didn't explain himself. Ever.

A fleeting wince danced across Ivy's expression, then melted beneath a resolved look as she lifted her chin and said, "My mom's not guilty, so there isn't a problem."

He didn't buy that for a second. Ivy loved her mom, she'd choose her mom over him every time. But if she wanted to play with the bad boys, then he'd oblige her as long as she was useful to him. "There is the other thing."

Distrust etched faint lines between her eyebrows. "What other thing?"

He laid it out for her. "I'm the boss. And I don't have any no-sex rules. In fact, I have very few rules at all. Can you deal with that?"

Chapter 6

What choice did she have? It was bad enough to ask for help from him, but on top of that, some desperately scared and lonely part of her ached for him to touch her. Just once, she wanted someone to tell her to have faith and things will work out. Just give her some crumb of reassurance. How freaking pathetic was that?

Besides, Luke was looking for sex, not intimacy. Not the kind of touching she wanted, the kind fueled by caring and kindness.

She took a breath and said, "Let's just focus on finding the statues and the killer."

"All right." Luke folded his arms over his chest. "How did your mom get involved with Trip and the statues?"

He was testing her, seeing if she'd tell the truth. The humiliation wound through her, reminding her of the interviews with the cops when the money had been stolen from her accounts at the investment firm. Everything she had said was suspect, every move she'd made studied and analyzed. But she had to do this; Luke was her best chance at clearing her mom. "She met Trip at a bar and started dating him. After a few dates, he talked her into holding the jade statues for him. Just like I told Regina, Trip told my mom that he and his wife were in a bitter divorce, and that the statues were his family heirlooms and his wife was trying to get them. He said they were all he had left of his parents. Together, my mom and Trip came up with the idea of stashing the statues at the radio station so his wife wouldn't find them."

"You believe your mom." It wasn't a question.

She went to the edge of his ugly green couch and sat down. The apartment had a sturdy Berber carpet in browns, minimal furnishings, and no personality or style. It looked like a dorm room. She assumed the couch was a sleeper sofa. She forced herself to tell the truth. "My mom has a history of getting involved with men who are trouble. She always believed their sob story that ended up wreaking havoc with her life."

"Ah, the bad boys you talk about on your sex hex show."

She didn't rise to the bait. "What else do you want to know?"

He stood in the middle of the room. Didn't sit, didn't fidget or rock, just stood still and watched her with his arms crossed. "What's your story for the more than three million that went missing from your clients' accounts?"

She'd braced for the question, but she still flushed with the shame. Folding her hands in her lap, she tried to explain, "Three years ago, I was going on a business trip, so I had brought my laptop home from work. My boyfriend, Dirk, came over, spent the night, and he cracked into my computer while I slept. He transferred money from several accounts. Obviously he'd been planning it for a while."

"How did he get your passwords?"

She brought her hand up to rub the ache between her eyes. "Over time, I got careless. He was around me when I worked at home and he picked up my passwords."

"You aren't that stupid."

She sighed. "I was. Dirk had been an investment broker in New York; then he moved to the West Coast to start his own business as a financial advisor. We had a lot in common, and it never even occurred to me that he'd do something like steal millions of dollars from my clients."

"You never checked him out?"

She dropped her hand from her forehead and met his gaze.

"Not until after. It turned out he'd been fired from the investment firm he had worked for in New York. His financial planning business never took off. He was charming people out of their money and funneling it into his own accounts. Then he went for the big money—thanks to me letting my hormones think for me—and he was gone." She tried not to care what Luke thought. She'd been stupid and trusting. Dirk hadn't loved her. The old embarrassment drove her to her feet. She walked around to stand behind the couch. "What else?"

His gaze followed her. "You saw Trip's body in the radio station, how was he killed?"

Ivy put her hands on the rough fabric covering the back of the couch. "He was in the kitchen. My mom had hidden the statues in there. He appeared to have a gunshot wound to the head." God, she'd didn't want to remember, didn't want to see Trip's dead body in her mind. She looked down at her hands to focus on her short nails and white knuckles.

"How many wounds did you see?"

She blinked and stared at her fingers. "I only saw one, but I guess there could have been more. I didn't want to look."

"You okay?"

"Fine." She just hadn't ever seen a murdered man lying in his own blood before. Cold chills broke out on her skin. It had been hours since they found the body. Why was she getting weak-kneed and queasy now? She tried to focus on the couch's ugly fabric. When she heard Luke move, she looked up.

He stood beside her. "Never seen a dead body before?"

"No, but I'm fine. I can start work if you have information on Trip. Full name, social security number, and birth date." *Focus,* she told herself. *Concentrate.* But her deepest fears kept streaming through her head—someone had killed Trip. Her mom had been involved with Trip and the statues, what if they had killed her mom? Then she'd have no one. She clasped her hands together to stop the tremors. "Just tell me what to do."

"Try breathing." He put his hand on her shoulder. "Damn it, you're shaking."

Ivy stiffened and took a step away. "I'm fine. I'll be fine. I just . . ." she stumbled over the words and stared hard at the ugly green couch. "I saw him, and when I realized my mom was involved, it could have been her. She could be dead."

"Fuck this," Luke said. Then he turned her and hauled her up against his chest.

Stunned, Ivy inhaled his rich scent, a combination of forest-smelling soap and male skin. Luke wrapped both his arms around her. She curled her fingers around the soft material of his T-shirt, struggling to get control of herself. "I—"

He tightened one arm around her, locking her to him. "Shut up," he snapped, while gently stroking her back.

For a couple minutes, she let him hold her, let the warm strength of Luke surround her and keep her from falling apart. She felt the sensation of his soft T-shirt covering a hot and hard chest against her face. She nearly groaned at the comfort of his large hand stroking between her shoulder blades and down her spine. And finally, she conquered her tears and weakness. Into his shirt, she said, "That's some bedside manner you have there, Sterling."

He laughed. "Honey, if you want my best bedside manner, you have to be naked."

She leaned back to see his face.

"You have color back in your cheeks. Maybe now you can stop playing around and get some real work done." He let go of her and headed to the desk that was shoved up against a wall where he picked up his keys and his wallet.

Ivy watched him slip his wallet in the back pocket of his jeans; then her gaze caught on the noticeable bulge in the front of his pants. Luke was . . . hard. Her mouth went dry. From just hugging her? A deep, primitive pleasure washed over her, a flush of power at arousing him.

God, what was wrong with her? She needed to save her mom, not get all starry-eyed over a man like Luke Sterling. He was the Urban Legend, the poster man for bad boys every-where.

Luke walked toward the door. "We're going to Kat Vaugn's house. She and Trip were in a nasty divorce. I think she'll co-operate if you dangle the ultimate carrot in front of her."

"Which is?" She almost ran into his back when he stopped to open the door.

With one hand on the doorknob, he turned around to look at her. "Using your skills to find any money Trip hid from her."

That helped her get on solid ground again because that was something she knew how to do. "Let's go."

He didn't move. "We're not done talking about sex."

She straightened her spine. "Can't you go five minutes without thinking about sex?"

"Not around you."

Pleasure warmed her and made her mad at the same time. "Stop trying to charm me, Sterling. I just want to find the killer and clear my mom."

"Good for you. I just want to find the statues and have sex with you. Lots of hot, sweaty, messy sex."

"No." There. Done. She could move on and not think about sex.

He grinned. "Baby cakes, I don't follow the rules, remember?" He laughed and opened the door. "After you, Princess."

Damn. She was thinking of sex.

Mallory paced her living room. "Just look what they've done!" Her little house, a tiny two-bedroom that Ivy had helped her buy, was a disaster from the police search. She and Ivy had worked hard to open up the small space while mak-ing it modern and elegant. The focal point wall had a fire-place in the middle, bracketed by two floor-to-ceiling windows. Mal had painted the fireplace a clean white, then used a white molding to frame the wall over the fireplace. There she'd painted three blue geometric designs. Then she'd painted the walls around the windows in a rich, creamy beige. The windows had white sheers with blue drapes that hung to the wood floor. She'd placed beige chairs on either side of the fireplace with blue and white pillows. A rug, couch, and some beautiful tables finished it off. Now the room was torn apart, cushions tossed to the floor, the rug shoved aside . . . It was awful.

Isaac's voice cut through her misery. "Are you sure you've told me everything? Every detail about your affair with Trip?"

She turned to him. He'd calmly replaced the cushions on a chair, and now he sat there with his legal pad balanced on one knee as he took notes. His expression was severe behind his glasses. He looked every single day of his fifty-five years. "Yes, I told you yes." Except the parts that would make him yell at her some more. She was exhausted from the police questions, then Isaac's relentless probing.

Looking up over his glasses, he said, "So he just showed up at the radio station with the statues? And he convinced you to stash them there?"

A flush crawled up her chest to flame her face. "I had agreed to hide them, but then I sort of balked when he showed up."

"I see." He wrote something down. "How did he convince you?"

She picked up a blue pillow off the floor. Studying the smooth fabric, she said softly, "Sex."

"What?"

Damn him. Throwing the pillow on the chair, she forced herself to look him in the eyes. "Sex. I said sex. Trip kissed me, nuzzled my ear, stroked my breasts, and begged me to let him ride me. I get that a lot. He also begged me to help him, told me that he needed me, needed my help and my body."

Isaac's stare pierced her. "In the radio station kitchen?"

Wait for it. Oh yeah, he'd say it now. "Yes." She cocked her hip out, and waited. Waiting for the words that she refused to let hurt her.

Isaac pulled off his glasses, threw them and the legal pad on the floor beside the chair, and stood, rising to his full height.

Mallory fought the rush of fear drumming blood through her ears. The metallic taste of regret washing up the back of her throat. The sheer self-disgust.

With measured steps, he walked toward her. "Did you come?"

She gasped, causing her to inhale his expensive scent. "What?"

He narrowed his brown gaze, a red flush staining the crest of his cheekbones. "You heard me. When this punk mounted you in the office kitchen, did you come?"

Oh God, did he know? How could he know? Had he figured it out because she'd been stupid enough to sleep with Isaac—twice? She backed up. "None of your business!" Why the hell didn't he react like she expected him to? Why did he look like it mattered to him?

He growled out, "Wrong. Everything is my business now. Answer the question. Did he care about your pleasure? Treat you as you deserve to be treated?"

Like she deserved to be treated? He had to be setting her up. "I . . . what?"

"Like I treat you? You come for me, do you know why, Mal?"

She knew better than to mess with Isaac. He was smart, too smart for her. She could handle sex-starved boys; but a man like Isaac, he'd destroy her. "I don't want you!" She had to make him stop.

"Yes, you do. Because you know I care about you. I would not treat you like that and you damn well know it. When I make love to you, it's in a bed, with privacy. You have my full attention. Where I can concentrate on every breath you take, every inch of your skin, and every orgasm you have."

She hated him. She did. He made her vulnerable and scared. "No, stop it. You're just trying to trick me, or trap me!" Like her dad had done.

You can tell me anything. You know I'll help you. Then

he'd smacked her so hard she'd had a black eye for two weeks. Called her a slut. Then he'd thrown her out of the house. She'd tried to tell him she hadn't known Greg was married. She hadn't! She had been only nineteen years old. She wasn't as stupid as everyone thought. She knew Isaac stirred in her a need for safety. Security. The kind her dad had never given her. He somehow made her wish that it was okay to be flighty and creative. But she knew better, she knew people like her didn't get real love. She had to make him stop.

Desperate, she said, "I'll get another lawyer!"

His famous control slipped and he roared, "The hell you will! You can't afford another lawyer, and I'm not about to let some wet-behind-the-ears mouthpiece screw up your life!"

She couldn't do this. She just couldn't. Tiredly, she said, "Go away. I have to clean this up. I have to—" She turned around, trying to figure out how her world had become chaos, just like her house. It always happened. And Ivy always came to her rescue. Shame just made her angry. She was tired of being ashamed of who she was.

He touched her shoulder. "Mal, you'll stay at my house."

She flinched. "No! This is my house, my home." She hadn't ever been able to afford a real home. She and Ivy had always lived in whatever rental she could scrounge up. She liked it here, or at Ivy's house. Her head was starting to throb when the phone rang. She hurried to answer it.

Isaac grabbed the phone from her hand. "Hello?"

She smacked his arm.

He ignored her. "No comment. Miss York will have no comment to any media questions." He hung up. "You can't stay here. The media will be all over you. Pack a bag, you're coming home with me."

That trapped, caged feeling made it hard for her to breathe. "I'll go to Ivy's." She had to make sure Ivy was safe. Whoever killed Trip was still out there. She'd never admit it to Isaac, but it was possible that Mallory might have accidentally endangered Ivy. She couldn't let anything happen to her daughter, to her baby girl. Ivy was the best thing in her life. She'd step in front of a speeding train for Ivy.

"Mal—" He moved toward her, his expression softening.

She backed up. She didn't want him to touch her. Didn't want him to know how desperate she felt, how scared. "No, I want to go to Ivy's house. I'm going to my daughter's house!"

In the passenger seat of the car, Ivy reminded herself that she was supposed to be the ice princess, or as some liked to call her, the ice bitch, and resistant to the charms of the devil and bad boys.

Not. What was wrong with her? For three years, she'd trained herself to choose her men carefully. Not to take risks. She knew she occasionally had a tiny weakness for strong and dangerous men, the kind of take-charge, I'm Tarzan-you-get-naked-now-and-don't-worry-about-a-thing guy. It was cliché, but some men were intimidated by her intellect, which made her long for the man who wasn't intimidated by anything. Who treated her like a desirable woman, not a walking brain. Recognizing that dangerous flaw, she ruthlessly controlled it. But now, it felt like she was losing control. Luke had walked into her life and shattered her control. She wanted to just be a woman. Go on dates, laugh and flirt, get a little bit drunk, and have great sex.

What would great sex be like anyway? Maybe great sex happens to women who don't worry constantly about the future. Maybe great sex just happens to other women.

She was so wrapped up in her thoughts that she was shocked when Luke slid the car to a stop and parked on the street in front of a small peach and tan house. She must be getting sick. Probably with the sex hex. She was thinking about Luke and sex when she'd seen a murdered man's body this morning, and now she was going to see the widow. Even if Kat and Trip had been divorcing, they'd still shared love once. She winced even more—her mom had been sleeping with this woman's husband.

"Ready?" Luke asked.

She pulled herself together. Her mom had poor judgment in men, but she wasn't a thief or murderer. Ivy had to help her. "Let's go." She got out of the car and started up the walkway. Luke fell into step beside her with a long-legged, confident stride. Shoving her Luke confusion aside, she knocked on the peach-painted front door.

The woman opened the door and instantly recognized her. "Ivy York? Why are you here?"

She was startled that the woman recognized her but recovered. "A couple reasons, but the most important is that I wanted to offer the condolences of KCEX. We are all so sorry." Kat Vaugn had blond-streaked hair pulled up into a clip. She wore a pair of low-cut sweatpants, a T-shirt, and a few extra pounds that softened her face into gentle prettiness. Her eyes had faint lines that Ivy assumed was strain, maybe grief. She was probably mid-thirties.

"Thank you. I can't believe this happened. Why was he at the radio station? I mean, I guess he stole those statues, but . . ." She sighed. "I always thought he was going to get shot by a husband, or maybe a pissed-off woman. But that doesn't seem to be the case."

Ivy's heart squeezed at Kat's grief.

Before she could think of what to say, Luke stepped up and said, "Kat, I'm Luke Sterling. We've talked, remember? I'm investigating the missing Jade Goddesses of Fertility and Virility and we talked?"

Kat turned to look at him. "Sure, I remember but—"

A man slid up to stand beside Kat. "Hello, Luke."

Ivy stared at the man, who obviously knew Luke. He looked a shade or two under six feet tall, and lean in his oatmeal-colored golf shirt and dark pants. His pale blue gaze watched them both. She felt Luke shift from relaxed to vigilant beside her. It was subtle but he rolled up slightly on his feet and dropped his hands loosely to his sides.

"Arnie," Luke said in a voice that passed for civil while sending chills down her spine.

The man ignored Luke and said to her, "I'm Arnold Sterling, Ivy. I'm a big fan of your show."

"Sterling?" Ivy looked at both men and saw a resemblance. Luke was taller and had more muscle, but their faces had a similar structure. The differences were that Arnie had thinner lips, his brown hair was longer, and his eyes had more blue, while Luke's had more gray. To Luke, she said, "The same last name as you. What's the deal?"

Luke turned his gaze on her. "Arnie is my cousin. We're both private investigators." Turning back to face the door, he added, "I was under the impression that I was the only PI working for the insurance company."

Arnold nodded. "You were . . . until the murder. I'm here now to do anything I can to help." He turned to Kat. "You have my card if you think of anything else. I want to help you, Kat."

"I don't know anything else." Frustration, confusion, and grief saturated her words, made them thick and heavy.

Ivy took her cue. Stepping into the opened screen door, she put her arm around the woman and said, "Let's go get you some water. Or maybe you'd like some tea? Coffee?" She started steering Kat into the house, then looked back at Luke, silently pleading with him to let her talk to Kat.

Luke's jaw bulged with anger, and his eyes were cold and flat as the London fog. She knew it had something to do with his cousin. To her, he nodded.

Ivy let the screen close behind her.

"Thanks," Kat said, leading the way to her kitchen. "I just feel like no one believes me. I mean, I know the police and investigators have to ask questions . . ."

"Believe me, I understand," Ivy said as she took in the small room with butterfly stenciling on the walls and lots of warm touches. It wasn't professionally decorated, but it was sweet and homey. Away from the weird strain between Luke and his cousin, she turned her full attention on Kat. "I went through something like that myself, although no one died."

Kat got down some mugs and filled them with coffee. Looking back over her shoulder, she said, "Yeah, I guess you have. I listen to your show, so I know you were fired when your boyfriend stole all that money."

"That's why I want to be really honest with you about why I'm here. No lies or games."

"Something to do with Trip." Kat set the coffeepot back on the warmer, turned, and studied Ivy. "Were you sleeping with him too?"

There was sad resignation behind the words. It made her more determined to get the truth out. "No, but my mom was. Trip told her the two of you were going through a divorce, and dragged her into this mess with the statues."

Kat set the coffee in front of her along with some cream and sugar; then she took a seat at the small table. "So you're here why?"

Ivy took a sip of her coffee, then said, "I need to clear my mom, but in doing that, I may be able to help you. If your husband was hiding funds from you and your lawyer, I can find the money for you."

Kat tilted her head and studied her. "Why?"

"Two reasons," Ivy said confidently. "First, I have a business of doing investigative accounting in divorce cases. It's something I really love. But it will also give me a chance to see if I can track the statues that the police believe your husband stole. Obviously, I'll waive my usual fee."

"I'd get any money you find?"

"I can't say for sure. Any money your husband got for the statues might be a police matter. But if he was hiding assets from your marriage, that you'd get."

Kat thought it over, then asked, "I've got nothing to lose?"

Ivy shook her head. "I don't see how. All I need is some information to get started. But you've been through a lot; I'll understand if you'd like to take some time to think about this. I can give you my card."

Kat shook her head. "I want the truth too. Trip is, uh was, younger than me. Handsome. A dreamer. But I thought he loved me. The last two years of my life have been miserable because I didn't want to face the truth. I'm facing it now."

Ivy put her hand on Kat's shoulder. "I'll help you do it. I just need some information from you; then I'll get started."

"Don't forget the business accounts," Luke said as he walked in and stood behind Ivy's chair.

Ivy stiffened. She and Kat had established a connection, the last thing she needed was the two men making Kat uneasy. Craning her head around, she gave him a "get lost" look and said, "Luke, we're talking. Wait outside with your cousin."

He didn't budge, just looked down at her with his light-colored eyes. "He's gone."

"It's okay, Ivy," Kat said. "I did a lot of the bookkeeping for Man for Hire until I got fed up with Trip's lies and cheating.

"Man for Hire?" Ivy turned back to Kat and did her best to ignore Luke. "What's that?"

Kat filled in the blanks. "That was Trip's business. Sort of an upscale handyman. He hired himself out, usually to busy, single women, to do whatever a husband or boyfriend might do. Take the car into the mechanic, do repairs around the house, walk the dog, play bartender at a party, or escort the woman to a party." She shrugged tiredly. "I convinced myself that he wasn't screwing them, but he was. Any chance he got."

Luke said, "That's how Trip met Regina. She hired him for some jobs, and that gave him access to the statues."

She tilted her head back to see Luke. "Gave him a key to her house?"

Luke nodded. "It was pretty obvious who stole the Jade

Goddesses. But no one could find Trip. We still don't know where he holed up."

Kat's mouth flattened. "Trip was convincing. It was the one thing he could do—charm anyone." She sighed heavily. "But he was stupid or arrogant enough to think he could get away with stealing statues that are obviously valuable if the insurance company is sending out private investigators to recover them. I wonder if he even knew what he had?"

Luke said, "Or what made him recognize their value? I'm thinking that someone nudged him in the right direction, or maybe hired him to steal the statues."

Kat's eyes widened. "Trip would do that. If somebody dangled enough money in front of him, he'd do it."

Ivy thought about that. "Can you give me all the information you have on Trip's clients? I'll see what I can track."

Chapter 7

Luke put the car in gear and pulled away from the curb. He kept a tight rein on his anger.

What was that sniveling prick doing snooping around his case? Trying to show Luke up? Find the statues and get the money for himself? Or something worse? He and Arnie had a long-standing agreement to hate each other. What the fuck was he doing?

Ivy asked, "What do we do now?"

Forcing his mind from Arnie, he said, "We start going through everything we have and try to figure out who hired Trip to steal the statues."

"You think he was double-crossed? Do you have any idea who it is?"

He looked over at her in the passenger seat. Blond strands of her hair escaped her ponytail. Her blue eyes were tired. And yet, she still looked pretty. What struck him was how wrong he'd been. He'd been sure the good-girl veneer was all a game. But Ivy might just be the real thing. And he might just get to be the lucky dick who destroyed her world. "Your mom springs to mind."

Her mouth turned down at the corners. "You just can't let that go, can you? How are you going to find the real killer if you don't quit beating a dead horse?"

Shrugging, he turned his attention back to the road and focused on the job. "Doesn't matter, I just follow the trail until I find all the pieces of the puzzle."

"We're sure Trip didn't just decide to steal the statues on his own?"

He took the ramp onto the freeway and merged into traffic. "Could have. But he'd still look for a buyer. He didn't try to sell them on eBay."

"You looked?"

Her surprised voice amused him. "Sure I looked. I'm damned good at my job. Which is why you begged me to help you." He looked over at her.

She rolled her eyes, then frowned. "What's the deal with you and your cousin? Does he always get involved in your cases?"

He figured she'd get around to that. Without looking, he knew she was twisting her fingers, worrying. "Take my advice, stay away from Arnie. My cousin has always been jealous of me." Talk about irony since Arnie had everything Luke had always wanted while growing up—a family.

"Why?"

The knot in his gut twisted. "Drop it. He can be dangerous, that's all you need to know." He knew damn well he couldn't outrun his ghosts, but that didn't mean he had to lay his damaged soul bare for little Miss Radio Shrink to analyze.

"Hell no." Her voice rose. "I'm not going to drop it. It's my mom's future at stake here."

He ignored her and drove.

She kept pressing. "How is he dangerous?"

Frustrated, he said, "The kind of dangerous you don't see coming until too late. Your choice, either you believe me or you don't. Trust me or you don't." He pulled to a stop in front of his apartment next to the house, shut off the car, and stormed inside.

Ivy grabbed her purse, slammed the door, and followed him into his apartment. "If we're going to work together, we have to talk. You can't just shut me out."

He turned around to find her standing by the door with her hands on her hips. Her blue eyes were huge, loose strands of her blond hair fell around her face, and her soft skirt swished around her legs. A beautiful woman, Ivy was. And determined. She had rebuilt her life from sheer fortitude. But she had a weakness. He'd seen it last night. Bluntly, he reminded her of who he was. "I work or screw women, but I don't chat."

She clearly wasn't buying it. "Cut the tough talk, Sterling. Your anger is just a cover for some kind of . . . I don't know . . . hurt."

"Hurt?" He laughed. "Honey, getting shot hurts, watching your buddies die hurts, growing up living out of a suitcase in one foster home after another hurts." He went stone still when he realized what he'd said.

Her blue eyes went all womanly and concerned. "Foster homes? What happened to your parents?"

Luke refused to accept her pity. Shutting down all his emotions, he said, "Which part of working or having sex do these questions fall under?"

She took a step toward him. "Don't change the subject. What happened to your parents?"

He tried another tactic to get her off the subject, the unvarnished truth. "My dad died in prison and my mom died with a needle in her arm. I lived with my grandmother until she died of cancer. Then I went into the system."

She frowned. "But if you have a cousin, then you had family. Arnie's parents would be your aunt and uncle, how come they didn't take you in?"

He breathed in and out, forcing his body to stay relaxed and not reveal how much he hated talking about his past. He took a step toward her and arched an eyebrow. "Are you trying to save me?"

She jerked back as if he'd slapped her. "I'm only interested in saving my mother."

His lips quirked in a half grin. "Liar. I'm you're biggest weakness, sweet cakes. A dangerous, broken man that you can't control. Damaged goods." He took another step. "I'm *that man,* the one you warn all your listeners about in your safe little booth while hiding behind your microphone. I scare you."

Color crawled into her cheeks and she straightened her spine. But she didn't look away from him. "You're a bastard." She lifted her chin, "And for your information, I'm in control of myself."

She believed that. Interesting. He was close enough now to smell the fresh berry scent that clung to her, probably from her shampoo. It was enough to send his thoughts into hot and heavy naked territory. "That so?"

"Yes." She nodded vigorously.

"So if I pull you into my arms—"

She froze, then stepped back. "Don't you dare!"

Her horrified reaction made him feel unworthy. Not good enough. Unwanted. He stepped closer to crowd her. "Don't what? Tempt you? Seduce you? Make you feel raw and aching lust? Make you burn for what only I can give you?"

She swallowed hard and squared her shoulders. "Trying to scare me off, Sterling? Keep me from poking at your wounds? Don't bother, you're not worth the effort." She turned and walked to the door, then she looked back. "We have a deal. You help me find the murderer and I'll help you find the statues. I'll start doing financial searches on Trip and see if I can—"

The sight of her walking away from him spurned him into motion. He reached her before she finished talking. Curling his hand around her shoulder, he bent down to her ear. "Damned right we have a deal."

She turned to stare at the door. "I'm going home now to start searching. That's my part of the deal."

He felt the tremor in the muscles of her shoulder. He didn't think it was fear. Stepping closer, he pressed his body into hers, felt her warm softness mold to his harder angles. Hot lust raced through him; his dick rose and reached for her. The sense that they fit together, the hot flash of need, made him want to force an admission from her. "The truth, Ivy. Can you admit it? That you're attracted to me, that you want to have sex with me." He figured she'd run. Put some space between them.

Instead, she turned around and said, "Do you know what the biggest sex organ on a woman is? Don't answer, because you'll be wrong. It's her brain. And my brain says no." She lifted her chin, her blue eyes shining with triumph.

He placed his hand on the doorjamb over her head and leaned in toward her. "That's a nice line of bullshit, sweet cakes. Your listeners eat it up. All that sex hex mumbo jumbo, your tidy little lectures about being in control of your hormones and finances sounds so smart, so evolved. But you forgot one thing."

"Maybe when you're done flexing and trying to crowd me with your big, manly muscles, you'll enlighten me as to what I've forgotten?"

He had to admit, he loved sparring with her. He was doing exactly as she accused him—crowding her, reminding her he was bigger and stronger. He hadn't missed the way she looked at him, she liked his body and his muscles. "If you'll stop lusting after my manly muscles, I will tell you."

"You wish."

He smiled. "The thing you forgot? Sex is a primitive, elemental drive in all of us. You can try to dress it up any way you want, but in the end, it's a magnetic pull that all of us have. Even you." He dropped his gaze slowly, taking in her full mouth, and slid his stare down to the base of her throat where her pulse jumped. He lifted his free hand, draped his fingers over her shoulder, and stroked the beating pulse with the pad of his thumb. "Your body is reacting *primitively* right now."

She swallowed hard, then said a little breathlessly, "But I'm still thinking. I'm still in control."

Her skin was warm beneath his hand, and the erratic

dance of her pulse beneath his thumb matched the beat of his own heart. He knew that if he made love to her, he'd feel that same beat—a wet, hot pulsing—surrounding his cock. Lust squeezed his balls. He hadn't wanted a woman the way he wanted Ivy in . . . a helluva long time. He admitted it, this was fun. He kept thumbing her pulse and lowered his face until he could feel her breath fan over him. "Then think about this. It's just sex. You're in control of your emotions, right? If that big brain of yours is in control, why not take what you want? It's not like you're going to fall for me. You know better."

She stared at him.

He left the thrum of her pulse to run his hand up her neck and cupped her warm skin beneath her ponytail. "Afraid? Worried you aren't in control? Or is it that you want me too much? The need to fix the broken man inside of me is just too much temptation?"

"No, you're just not my type."

He laughed. "I am exactly your type, and that's what has you fighting so hard." The silky length of her hair spilled over the back of his hand. He pulled his other hand from the wall to press it on the small of her back and draw her closer into his body.

Where he needed her.

He skimmed his lips over her mouth, just enough to make her shiver. "Prove it to me, Ivy. Prove you can screw me and walk away. Prove you're immune to the Urban Legend." He wrapped her ponytail around his hand and kissed her with the fierce need pounding inside of him. His blood went hot, the need hammered in his head and all the way down his spine until he forgot everything but the woman in his arms. His world narrowed to the feel of her mouth against his, her tongue mating with his.

Jesus! Luke pulled back before he lost control. He'd been horny many times, but Ivy aroused him to a whole new level. He struggled just to breathe and force his brain out of sex-neutral and into drive.

"We can't do this. My mom, I have to help her."

Ivy's eyes were unfocused and her breasts heaved against his chest. He reached up to touch the frown line between her eyes. "I'll help you, Ivy. I told you I would." Her loyalty to her mom was something he couldn't turn away from.

"And no sex?"

He grinned. "There's going to be sex. A lot of sex. Because there's no chance you'd fall for me, right?"

She pulled out of his hold. "Right. But that doesn't mean I'll sleep with you." She turned around and yanked open the door.

Luke said to her retreating back, "Liar." He shut the door and was alone. Again. He was used to being alone. Ivy was just a distraction. An entertaining distraction. But he'd been right about one thing, women like Ivy didn't fall for him.

Ivy pulled into the radio station parking lot. The police were gone.

Which meant the body was gone.

She shuddered. Trip might have been another bad-boy type, but he hadn't deserved murder. Her head throbbed and she was more tired than she ever remembered. But she knew Leah would be there, and Ivy had work to do.

She owed Leah everything. And she had to take care of her mom.

No sex with Luke. It was the stress making her vulnerable.

Getting out of her car, she walked into the reception area. The intern behind the reception desk jumped, then said, "Oh, Ivy, sorry. I just . . ." she trailed off and shrugged. "It's an awful day."

Forcing a smile, she said, "I know, Carrie. We're all on edge." Without warning, she thought of Luke pulling her into his arms and holding her when she'd freaked out a little bit at his apartment before they went to Kat's house.

Carrie nodded, then said, "A man has been calling for you

but he won't leave his name. And he didn't want me to put him through to your voice mail."

"Would it be too much to hope that it's just a shy fan?"

Carrie offered a half smile. "He had a sexy voice."

"Ivy." Leah walked out of the hallway, looking as tired and strained as the rest of them. "We need to talk."

She nodded. "My office okay? I want to get started on some things."

Leah nodded and headed down to her office. When they passed the on-air studio, Ivy said, "Marla didn't come back?"

Leah's shoulders bowed. "She was too upset. We're running tapes and the intern is doing fine."

Following her boss into her office, she circled her desk and dropped into her chair. "Leah, I'm sorry. This whole thing, the statues, the murder—"

Her boss's naturally curly mop of shiny brown hair trailed limply around her lightly freckled face and weary hazel eyes. She sat down in the chair and stated bluntly, "The media is crawling up my ass and the advertisers are making ugly noises. Tell me some good news."

Ivy leaned back in her chair and rubbed her eyes, wishing she had more to tell her. "Luke Sterling agreed to help me. We talked to Trip's estranged wife this morning, and I'm going to start some searches now. It has to be someone connected to Trip Vaugn." Ivy recapped the conversation with Kat and running into Arnold Sterling.

"Arnold Sterling? He's been calling and he stopped by once, asking for you."

She frowned and searched her drawers for some Advil. "Luke said he's dangerous. But I couldn't get him to be specific." Probably because he had his tongue in her mouth. Idiot.

Leah's gaze narrowed. "You're blushing."

She snapped her head up. "I am not. It's just been a long, awful day and—"

"Don't lie to me, Ivy York."

She dropped the pretense. "Luke kissed me. Twice."

"Interesting. Isn't he the dreaded Urban Legend?" Leah tensed and leaned forward in her chair, the energy returning to her gaze. "Did you sleep with him?"

"No!" *Not yet.* But how could she work with him and not sleep with him? Until she met Luke, Ivy would have sworn that she could control her libido. It was the foundation of her sex hex theory—that women could conquer their primitive side and make intelligent, informed choices, while protecting themselves and their finances.

But Luke was testing her self-control. He made her want to let down her guard. To lose control. To trust. Worse of all, she wanted to lean on a man.

Stupid. Stupid, stupid, stupid.

"But you are, right? Going to sleep with him?" Leah asked.

Frowning at her boss, she said, "Don't you have a disaster to spin or something?"

Leah flashed her infectious grin. "I can multitask. And damn, Ivy, when was the last time you had fun with a man?"

She bristled. "I've dated."

"They were boring whimps. When was the last time you dated a real man? A man who made your mouth go dry and your heart pound? A man who made you want to get hot, wet, and naked?"

Rolling her eyes, she said, "Last time I did that I almost went to prison. Which reminds me, I have work to do to keep my mom out of prison and keep the radio station in the black." She pulled all her notes out of her purse and booted up her computer.

Leah stood up.

Ivy said, "I'll find a way to make this mess work out, Leah. I know you're worried. It's my fault for hiring my mom. But my mom means well, she just gets—"

"Stop. Just stop."

Startled, Ivy looked up.

"You're doing all you can by working with Luke. And maybe it's time you had a little fun too." She turned and walked out.

Ivy worried that the stress was getting to Leah. She hunkered down and started working on the computer, accessing every account that Trip Vaugn had that his wife knew about. Kat had given Ivy everything, including the access codes, so she could reconstruct Trip's financial history. She was hoping to find a thread that led to the killer. Maybe a big deposit that wasn't tied to a job . . . anything.

She lost track of time as she worked.

When her phone rang, she reached out and answered it on automatic. "Ivy York."

Her mom said, "When are you coming home?"

"You're at my house?" Ivy looked at her watch to see it was after seven P.M.

"The police searched my house and made it a mess. The media kept calling and pounding on my front door. Then there's Isaac. Swear to God, just because he's my lawyer doesn't mean he runs my life. He's getting bossy."

Isaac's comment that her mom was scared went through her head. If Mallory hadn't been scared before the murder, she sure had to be now. Gently, she said, "Mom, he's trying to help you."

"I made dinner, when are you going to be home?"

Her mom changed the subject. Ivy let it go. At least her mom wasn't talking to the media. "I'm leaving now." She shut down her computer and began gathering her stuff. "Stay there, I'll be home soon." Ivy grabbed her purse, double-checked to make sure she locked the door to the radio station, and hurried to her car.

By the time she pulled into her driveway, exhaustion made her arms and legs feel like lead weights. She got out of the car and trudged up the stairs toward her front door. No matter how much trouble her mom was in due to her own bad decisions, if she had dinner made, Ivy would forgive her anything. It was all she could do to open the door and walk in.

Then she stopped. And stared. Her mom sat at the dining room table and was eating with a man.

Arnold Sterling.

They both stopped talking and looked at her.

"There you are, Ivy. Come eat. I've made Chicken Pasta Primavera." Her mom started filling a plate.

At least they'd set her a place, Ivy thought grimly. But she didn't like Arnold showing up at her house out of the blue, especially after Luke's terse warning that he could be dangerous. She noticed that her mom was casually dressed in tight jeans and a flirty sheer shirt meant for a teenager, not a forty-seven-year-old woman. Her eyes were tired but she had color in her cheeks.

Because she was *flirting*. Just freaking great. They had found her most recent boyfriend murdered this morning, her mom had spent a good part of the day at the police station under suspicion, and now she's flirting with a man they didn't know. Perfect. Her head throbbing, she dropped her purse on the couch and walked into the dining room. "Arnold, what are you doing here?"

He sat at her mom's right, with his back to the door. Flashing a smile complete with a dimple, he said, "I can't resist home cooking. I've been trying to get a hold of you. Finally, I came by your house and found your mom here."

Walking around to the empty place at her mom's left, she narrowed her gaze on Arnold's face. "Why?"

"Ivy, don't be rude. I know Arnold; he's the one who told me that Luke is the Urban Legend," her mom said, and filled Ivy's glass with wine.

He had? She should have realized her mom didn't just stumble on to Luke's picture. "When?"

"He came to my office Wednesday night."

Arnold cut in, "I didn't know what Luke was doing, just that he was skulking around you. I thought about trying to talk to you, but women . . ." He shrugged and gave her a small smile. "They are sucked in by Luke's charm. At first, anyway. So I decided to tell your mom. I figured she'd be able to warn you."

She wanted to smack herself, but instead turned her glare on her mom. "That's why you were so hot for me to fire him! You thought he was there looking for the statues."

Her mom looked down at her plate. "I thought Trip's wife had hired him. Trip warned me to be careful." Then she lifted her head, squared her shoulders, and said, "But it's okay. Arnold is investigating this whole mess with those statues. He's on our side."

When was her mom going to learn? She kept trusting the wrong men. What made her think Arnold was legitimate? They didn't know *why* he ratted on Luke to her mom. All Ivy knew was that there was some kind of bad blood between the cousins. "You have a lawyer to handle this stuff, Mom. Isaac will hire investigators, not you!" He was going to blow a gasket when he heard about this. What was Arnold doing here? Why?

Arnold said quietly, "I am on your side, Ivy, and I'd be happy to talk to your mom's lawyer. I came over to your house to make sure you are okay. You didn't return my phone calls, and well, frankly, I got a little worried." He glanced at her mom, then back to her. "Luke is . . . unpredictable."

A strong urge to defend Luke surprised her. Lifting her wineglass, she decided to get some answers, "What exactly do you mean?"

He met her gaze. "You should know this. Luke left the military because he caused the death of two men. He wasn't charged or anything," he added in a rush. "But it did something to him, made him even more . . . troubled."

Luke had told her he was ex-military. So he had made a

mistake? She decided Luke would be the one to ask. She tried a question that Arnold could answer. "Why are you butting in on Luke's case?"

Arnold tilted his head to study her. "Because the insurance company asked me to. With this murder, things have taken an ugly turn, and Luke lost the statues on top of that."

Staring over the top of her wineglass, she asked, "They fired him?"

"They've marginalized him and hired me to get the job done. The only reason the insurance company doesn't blatantly fire him is that Luke has developed quite a loyal following as the Urban Legend. Insurance companies like to keep things quiet and dignified."

Could be true, or not. The fact was that she didn't have enough information. She couldn't get Luke out of her head. Not the man who stirred her lust to dangerous, nearly painful levels, or the thought of the boy being shuffled from foster home to foster home. "What is the story with you and Luke? Why do you two hate each other?"

He took another bite of his pasta primavera and set his fork down. "It's not very pretty dinner conversation, Ivy. The best thing for you is to not trust Luke."

Mallory pushed her food around on her plate. "Maybe we should listen to him, Ivy."

Turning to her mom, she waved her arm toward Arnold. "Luke said the same thing about him. They are both free with the advice but mighty short on explanations." Her temper was bubbling to the surface. Who did she trust? How did she keep her mom out of prison? Why were men so damned much trouble!

His pale blue gaze rested on her. "Luke's the one with the secrets. I'm an open book."

"See, Ivy," her mom said, sipping her wine.

Ivy sat back in her chair, her hunger forgotten. "Then tell me why Luke grew up in foster homes."

His mouth went lax and his eyes widened. "Luke told you that?"

"I don't think he meant to. I'd like you to tell me why that happened. Why didn't your parents take him in?"

He nodded and drained the wine in his glass. "I warned you, it's not pretty. Luke's parents were dead and he lived with our grandmother. She wanted so much to believe Luke was perfect, but even when he was five or so, Luke was troubled. He shook his head at the memories, and asked, "Are you sure you want to hear this?"

Oh God, did she? "Yes."

"The day our grandma died, Luke attacked me with a kitchen knife. I had to have ten stitches in my side. My parents knew they couldn't risk keeping him, so they put him into a place where he could get the help he needed."

Mallory gasped. "Oh, Arnold, that's terrible. Of course your parents couldn't take him."

Ivy looked over at her mom. It was always this way—she fell for the story. For herself, she just didn't know. And damn it, it seemed to her that no one was ever on Luke's side. Luke had held her today when the fear for her mom, and the memory of the dead body, finally overwhelmed her. That had been real and genuine.

But later, when she poked at his wounds, he'd gone very Urban Legend. He'd turned it all to sex. Pure, primitive sex.

God, she was confused. She didn't really have the track record to trust her own judgment. That's why she had rules. And Leah—Leah trusted Luke. It wasn't just her.

Arnold turned to look at her mom. "Luke broke my mom's heart. She kept track of him, visited him, and when he got out of the service, he came to work for my mom's private investigating business. He broke rules, caused problems, and when my mom died—"

Ivy stopped listening when she saw the front door ease open; then Luke strode into the house. Like he belonged there.

He cut Arnold off by saying, "I was there with her when she died and you were out getting drunk and chasing skirts."

The room shrank and heated as Luke rounded the table to stand next to Ivy, and stare down his cousin. She looked up at his hard face. "Luke, I didn't know you were coming over."

He dropped his gaze and his lips curved. "Obviously. I just came from the radio station."

She couldn't keep up. "The radio . . . Were you looking for me?"

He shook his head. "Nope, Isaac and I were searching for the statues, making damned sure we didn't miss anything. Isaac is still there."

"And you came here, why?" Ivy wanted answers.

He gray eyes hardened. "Figured Arnie would come sniffing around."

Arnold rose from his place and put his hands out in a calming gesture. "Luke, don't take it out on her. I came over here to talk, to help. I told you that the insurance company . . ."

His mouth thinned. "I called the insurance company. Did you think I wouldn't?

"I should hope you called them. That's part of being a good private investigator. I'm sure they explained that I'm here to help you, and to look out for Ivy and Mallory." Arnold's voice was full of calm confidence.

"After you called them and offered your services." Luke pivoted and walked into the kitchen.

"Ivy," her mom whispered. "Should I call the police?"

Arnold frowned. "I'll handle this." He tossed his napkin on the table and started to move around the table.

Luke strode back in, carrying a plate, silverware, and a wineglass. He set the dishes next to Ivy and pulled out a chair. Sitting down, he handed her his plate, and said, "Smells good, serve me some, will ya?"

Still standing, Arnold said, "Luke, you can't just walk into someone's home and help yourself to dinner."

Luke took the filled plate from her. "Sure I can, Arnie. I went to strangers' homes all the time while growing up." He forked a large bite into his mouth, then reached for the wine bottle to fill his glass.

Her stomach knotted and her chest tightened. Foster homes, he was talking about the foster homes. She felt ill just thinking about how scared and lonely he must have been. Unable to help herself, she picked up the basket of garlic breadsticks and put two on his plate.

Arnold sat down and sighed. "Don't fall for it, Ivy. He's playing the pity card. You talk about emotional manipulation men like Luke use on women in your *Economic Sex Hex* show."

It was like a splash of freezing water. She blinked and turned to study Luke.

He grinned and winked at her, then broke off a chunk of the breadstick and ate it.

Damn. She *was* falling for it. God, she wanted to smack herself. "Enough, both of you. I didn't invite either of you to dinner. And you, Arnold, have been charming my mother."

He looked wounded. "But she's beautiful and in trouble. I'm just trying to help."

She'd made a deal with Luke. He had been right about Trip, the statues, and to some degree, her mom's involvement. She'd worked with him for a couple days, albeit he was pretending to be someone he wasn't, but she still knew him better than she knew his cousin. She didn't know anything about Arnold. She had to rely on Luke. "We already have help, Arnold. I've made a deal with Luke."

Her mom set down her wineglass with a thud. "And I've made a deal with Arnold."

She whipped her head around to glare at her mom.

Mallory continued, "Don't you give me that look. You damn near went to prison by trusting the wrong man. In spite of all your blathering on your radio show, in the end, you aren't any better judge of character than I am."

Chapter 8

Luke was furious, but he didn't let it show. Arnie interfering in his case annoyed him. He needed to find out what Arnie's purpose was, but he'd keep an eye on his cousin and deal with him. What infuriated him was that Mallory intentionally hurt her daughter, the daughter who was desperately trying to save her, and that was not acceptable.

He wouldn't forget the pain and fear in Ivy's eyes today in his apartment. She loved her mom, needed her mom, and Luke would make damn sure her mom didn't go to prison.

And he would find the statues. That was his number one priority. Not Ivy or her mom. Christ, he had to remember that. He washed down the pasta with a swallow of wine, and said, "We'll all work together then. Mallory, tell us how you met up with Trip, and what you know about him."

She glanced at Arnie, who nodded; then she pushed her plate away and picked up her wine. "I met him at a bar. We talked, danced, and he went home with me."

Luke saw Ivy wince. He was getting to know her enough to think it wasn't a morality issue as much as her mom's safety. He agreed but kept his mouth shut.

Mallory went on, "The next morning, we talked about work. I told him I was an interior designer and that I had a big job coming up soon with KCEX. He told me he did odd jobs and gave me his card in case I had some work for him."

She picked up the wine bottle and splashed more into her glass. "We dated a few more times, and he gradually told me that he and his wife were in a bitter divorce. He was doing some work for a woman and staying in one of her extra bedrooms."

Luke nodded. "Mrs. Santos. Emily Santos. She hired Trip to dog-sit while she went on a cruise with her friends. When she got back, she had to make Trip leave after he tried to charm her into letting him stay there."

Mallory said, "He probably liked her, just wanted to have some fun."

"Fun," Ivy said. "Fun doesn't pay the bills."

Her mom gave her a sharp look. "Fun is better than boring and judgmental. And being alone like you are."

Luke thought that maybe he hadn't missed out much on the whole family thing after all. He cut off the bickering by saying, "I know Trip stole the statues when Regina was at a work function; then I tracked him right to your house, Mallory."

She flushed. "He was sort of staying with me."

"Mom," Ivy shook her head and sighed.

Mallory ignored her. "Trip came home Monday night upset, shaking and mad. He said that his wife had threatened to destroy the statues. He begged me to hide them, and not at the house because she was probably having him followed. He was so upset; I wanted to help him." Her mom sat back in her chair. "Trip and I decided that the radio station was the best place to hide the statues." She looked at her daughter. "They are beautiful, Ivy. Exquisite. The green jade is so pure, the forms perfect except for these carved rectangular empty spaces in their chests. A space for their hearts, but I guess the little hearts were lost long ago. They are actually warm to the touch." Her brown eyes nearly glowed. "Once I saw them, I had to protect them, had to keep them from being destroyed."

Luke raised an eyebrow at that and made a mental note to tell Regina the effect the statues seemed to have on Mallory.

Arnie said, "Perhaps you were under the influence of the statues."

Mallory tilted her head. "What influence?"

Arnie explained, "The statues are the Goddesses of Virility and Fertility. They are said to bring out the most primitive and basic desires in people."

Luke didn't want to get into a theoretical discussion about powers. "Mallory, did you tell anyone where you'd hidden the statues, or that you were holding them for Trip?"

She shook her head. "No."

Ivy turned to look at him. "What do we do now?"

He wanted to touch her. Wanted to feel her skin beneath his fingers, and reassure her. "I have some feelers out."

Arnie snorted. "I bet. But I doubt your little group of bored and horny housewives will be able to help."

Luke turned a dry look across the table. "Then why don't you tell us what you have, Arnie?"

He squared his shoulders and looked down his nose. "I've just started. It's going to take time to unravel the mess you've made of this case. I think it'd be better for everyone involved if you bowed out gracefully."

He laughed. "Not gonna happen. Hell, it's never happened." He stared Arnie down. "I never let go once I get my teeth in a case. I will find those statues."

Arnie used the smile he'd perfected when they were kids—innocent and a little sad or baffled. Then he stood up. "Thank you for the dinner, Mallory. I'll call you tomorrow. You have my number if you need to reach me." He turned to look at Luke. "It's time for you to leave."

Luke stared back at him. "I'm staying."

"It's late, Luke, almost nine o'clock. You're imposing on the women."

He shrugged.

"Fine, then I'll stay."

Ivy stood up. "I've had enough. Both of you go home."

Luke looked up at her, seeing the protectiveness for her mom and the fatigue and uncertainty on her face. Fury and the need to protect her surprised the hell out of him. Grabbing her hand, he said, "I'm not leaving you and your mom unprotected. I'll sleep in my car." Letting go of her hand, he stood up and said, "Thanks for dinner."

Luke worked on his laptop. He'd pulled his car into the driveway and settled in. The Urban Legendites were putting out feelers all over to find out who was seriously interested in the Jade Goddesses. Interested enough to kill.

So far, one name had popped up. *Pierce Jordan.* Luke went to the man's Web site. He was an entertainment lawyer based in Sherman Oaks, California. Luke would check with Regina in the morning to see if the name meant anything to her. She'd been in contact with hundreds, probably thousands of people about the statues. But maybe this name stood out.

He leaned his head back, closed his eyes, and hoped like hell that they got lucky and this was the break they needed.

A sound jerked him upright. He looked toward the house. Ivy was walking down the stairs with a sweater wrapped around her shoulders. She marched to his car and opened the passenger side door. "You're really going to stay here all night?"

"I said I was, didn't I?" Why was she ragging him?

She slid into the car and shut the door. "I thought you believed me."

"About?"

"My mom. You saw her tonight, she's just gullible." She pulled her sweater tighter and shivered.

Noncommittally, he said, "Just covering my bases." She was right, though. He didn't think her mom killed Trip. Or masterminded the theft. Nope, her mom had been the patsy. But who was the brains? He didn't share that information with Ivy—she was already turning him inside out. When he'd walked in tonight and saw her sitting there at dinner with Arnold, listening to what that sniveling prick said about him . . .

Luke had cared.

Goddamnit, he'd cared what Ivy York thought of him.

She turned those blue eyes on him, and exhausted or not, outrage burned there. "All right, let's do this. Come on." She opened the door, slid out, and hurried toward the stairs.

Luke had to scramble to catch up. Carrying his laptop and keys, he caught her at the top of the stairs. Turning her to face him, he said, "What the hell?"

She said levelly, "You're going to search my house. You think my mom did it. She must have hidden the statues at my house because the police already searched hers, right? That's why you're sitting in the driveway. So go find them." She lifted her hand toward the closed door.

The muscles in her arms were taut with anger, but he could feel the effort it cost her. Beneath that anger was real fear. Ivy didn't like being afraid. And he didn't like her being afraid. Unable to stop himself, he said, "I believe you."

She dropped her hand. "Then why are you camping in my driveway?"

He wondered if she knew how beautiful she looked standing in the porch light, her hair falling around her shoulders, dressed in a pair of tiny sleeping shorts with a sweater wrapped around her shoulders. And bare feet. He stared down at her long, smooth legs to her naked feet and wondered why the hell she hadn't put shoes on? What if she'd stepped on glass or something? Finally, he lifted his gaze and told her the truth. "I figured Arnie would turn up here. He tried Regina; she wouldn't talk to him. He talked to Kat. I knew he'd look for your mom. It looks like he hit the jackpot by finding both you and your mom here and inviting himself for dinner. I showed up and ruined his game. Now I'm staying."

She drew her brows together. "Arnie was here when I got home. My mom invited him for . . ." Her brows cleared of confusion and rose in accusation. "What is this? The two of you are so intent on beating each other and my mom and I are just pawns?"

He shrugged, unwilling to go down this road in his life again. Few people believed him until it was too late. "Little competition adds excitement to the chase."

Ivy narrowed her eyes. "Spending the night in a cold car doesn't sound exciting. What's the real reason?"

It was damned annoying the way Ivy never bought his act. Well, she had at first when she hired him as her personal assistant, but even then he'd had a hard time staying "in character." Now she seemed to see through the layers to the real him. "In case you hadn't noticed, Princess, all roads keep leading back to you and your mom. If Arnie can follow that trail, anyone can. I'm here in case the killer stumbles onto the road."

She revealed the whites of her eyes as she grasped the danger. "Oh. If the killer comes here, you'd catch him? Solve the case? I guess that makes sense."

Damn right it did. It was cold logic, nothing more. The hot urge boiling in his belly was about solving the case, not protecting Ivy or screwing Ivy. He'd decided at dinner that he didn't like the way Arnie schmoozed her mom. Just like Trip had. Who would show up next? The killer trying to tie up loose ends? And Mallory would just open the door for him? Yep, staying in the car parked in her driveway was just cold logic. "There you go. Then there's the fact that you didn't call me and let me know Arnie was in your house. Having dinner. Even though I warned you—" he bit off his own words. She didn't trust him. Get over it. She'd made a deal with him in her desperation to save her mom—a mom she didn't even seem to like that much. But she didn't trust him.

"You didn't tell me why I should believe you over him!"

Oh, this was just perfect. "But Arnie did, huh? He explained it all to you? If you believe him, you'd better lock your doors since I'm not budging from your driveway." He turned to get the hell away from her. He got two steps down the stairs when her words hit him in the back.

"I didn't believe him."

Keep going. Do the job. Sleep in the car and keep watch. He told himself these things, but he turned back anyway. Her face was pale, and she'd curled her bare toes into the wood of the porch. He was out of his freaking mind, but he went back to her. "No?"

She didn't flinch from him. "No, I don't know the truth. But he was warning me that you're dangerous and I'm damned sick of all these warnings with no facts to back them up."

So Arnie had started giving her facts, *lies,* to make his case. His cousin had done that as far back as Luke could remember, and it had worked remarkably well for him. He nodded once. "Go in and lock the door. I'll be out here if you need me."

She reached out and touched his arm. "You can't sleep in the car. You'll be miserable. I have another bedroom besides the one my mom is using."

The feel of her hand on his arm was soft and warm. He didn't look at her, just stared out to where his car sat in the driveway. "I've slept in jungles and deserts, the car is fine." He only slept two or three hours at a time anyway.

"Don't be stubborn. I won't sleep worrying about you."

Stunned, he turned and looked at her.

She blushed and stammered, "Uh, you'll be cold and uncomfortable and I'll feel guilty. Just stay in the extra bedroom."

He closed the small space separating them. "If I'm in your house, I'm going to imagine you warm and sexy in your bed. I'm going to remember both kisses." He was going to imagine it in the cold car too. He was imagining it right now.

"I don't control your thoughts, Sterling. But I do control my actions." She slipped by him and went inside.

Luke followed her in. She kept going, turning left down the hall, and then hooked a right into a bedroom. She flipped on a light. "Bathroom's across the hall. I'm going to bed. Good night." She went to her room and gently shut the door.

In the soft glow from the bedside light, he saw a room done up in blue and yellow. The quilt over the bed had mounds of pillows, there was a reading chair in the corner with a separate light, bouncy curtains brightened up the dark window set against cozy yellow walls. It was warm and inviting and weird as hell for him. He stowed his laptop, stripped down to his boxers, and climbed into the bed.

He turned over a couple times, feeling . . . odd.

When he had been a kid, he'd longed for a room like this. The safe and warm feeling of a bed covered in good-smelling sheets. A woman who slept not far away who would come running if he had a nightmare. Eventually, Luke had accepted that those things would never happen for him. He lived his life hard and he liked it that way. He didn't have to feel betrayal or grief if he didn't love anyone.

Finally, he drifted to sleep.

He saw himself flying the helicopter, his hands and arms bloody from scrapes and scratches. He'd had engine trouble. It'd taken him two hours to fix the problem and get back into the air.

"Let them be there." It was his mantra the entire flight. His mission was to extract Sanders and Roy, his two buddies who were the closest thing he had to family. The back of his neck tightened in twisted ropes of agonized worry. Every instinct he had screamed at him to hurry. But he finally made it to the pickup spot.

At first, the two of them were just spots on the ground. The relief let him draw his first full breath in half a day. They were there. They'd made it.

The spots grew as he closed in.

And grew.

Into bloody body parts. No longer recognizable as Sanders and Roy. Dead. Not just dead . . . butchered.

* * *

Luke woke up in the pitch black, sweating with his heart hammering so fast he couldn't catch his breath. Bile burned his throat. He was alive.

And they were still dead. It'd been Luke's job to get them out when the mission went bad. He'd failed.

The covers tangled around his legs. He kicked them off and rolled to his feet. The room felt close and hot as a coffin, as if he were locked in hell with the dying screams of his buddies.

His gut rolled up.

"Fuck." He walked to the door, opened it, and was struck by the light and voices.

"Get this bubble."

It sounded like Mallory's voice. Frowning, Luke blinked against the light and walked out into the hallway. Then he stopped and leaned a shoulder against the wall.

Ivy and her mom were hanging wallpaper in the middle of the night. Mallory had on a pair of long purple PJ bottoms and a pink T-shirt. She was on the ladder, working the top section of the paper with her long, thin brush.

Ivy had on black girl-boxers and a tank top that outlined her body and left lots of bare skin. She bent to the spot her mom had pointed at with her foot and swept her brush across the spot. She said, "You were right about this print—it's perfect."

"The house is coming together. Oh! I found a lovely fabric for tie-back drapes. I left the material at home, though. But I think you'll love it."

"That's great, Mom. I've looked everywhere and couldn't find anything I liked. You have a knack."

Her mom shrugged and climbed down the ladder.

Luke's nightmare faded away as he watched them ready what looked like the last strip of paper to hang on that wall. The paper was going only halfway down. A chair rail would

separate the painted wall from the paper section. He didn't
know shit about decorating, but it looked okay to him.

Course, he'd slap a big-screen TV in a room and call it
home.

He watched as Mallory went back up the ladder and the
two of them aligned the paper. "I never meant to cause all
this trouble."

"I know, Mom." Ivy arched her back, grabbed the brush,
and attacked the paper. "It'll work out, I promise. I'm going
to track every financial thread I can. Luke's helping. We'll
find the killer."

"I just want you to have some fun."

Ivy stopped brushing. "What?"

Mallory never missed a stroke. "You're young, beautiful,
and smart. You shouldn't have to always pull me out of trouble. You need to have fun. Date, laugh, have great sex."

"Mom, guys are what get you into these messes."

Mallory tilted her head in a sort of wincing acknowledg-
ment. "I have an exciting life."

"You're lonely, Mom. It's not me you're talking about, it's
you. You've tired of boys, tired of the meat market. But it
doesn't have to be like that." Ivy's voice was soft, like warm
water. "You don't have to be lonely. Isaac really cares about
you."

Mallory shook her head while smoothing the paper. "No,
he doesn't; he just wants the chase and to save me. Once he
did that, he'd be bored. What would we talk about? He'd
want to talk about the law and the stock market. I'd die of
boredom in a week."

Ivy laughed. "You're exaggerating. He's a nice man, and
he's—"

"He's a shark in sheep's clothing. Don't let his easy-going
manner fool you. That man is headstrong and stubborn, and
he'd turn me into . . . into . . . Donna Reed."

Ivy stared up at her mom. "Donna Reed?" Giggles started

out in tiny bubbles that eventually rose to a full boiling laugh. "You? Donna Reed?"

Her mom's laughter mixed in. "See? You think it's as ridiculous as I do."

Ivy brushed the back of her hands over her eyes, then said, "He cares about you."

"He's bossy and driving me crazy. My dad was exactly like him. Everything had to be perfect, exactly right, and he knew what was best for everyone, including my mother."

Ivy stopped laughing. "And you."

"Yes, and me. He tried to force me to give you up. I'll never ever let a man do that to me again." Mallory turned back to the wall, ran her brush over a spot, then said, "I think we've done all we can for tonight."

Like a body slam, Luke got it. Staring at the two women, he got it now. What bonded them—decorating. Ivy was the caretaker while her mom had the artistic creative streak. There was a lot more to these two women than appeared on the surface. In their daily lives, their personalities clashed. But when they decorated, there wasn't any fighting or bickering. How many times had they worked in the middle of the night and talked? Probably countless times.

Ivy turned and spotted him. "Luke. Uh, sorry, did we wake you?"

He smiled. "Just woke up thirsty and stopped on my way to the kitchen for the view."

"I'll get you a bottle of water." Ivy scurried off to the kitchen.

But her mother headed right for him. In the harsh light of the bright lamps, with her face free of makeup, she looked her age. She was surprisingly attractive that way. Real. She stopped just below his chin. "I know you want to sleep with her—"

Entertained, he said, "You know that, do you?"

"Of course, I do. You think I can't see the way you look at her? She can use some fun." She boldly shifted her gaze down his chest and stomach, then back to his face. "And you're sexy enough for some hot fun, but don't you dare hurt her." She walked away, disappearing down the stairs to the lower level.

He stared after her until Ivy's voice said, "Here's your water."

Taking the cold bottle, Luke opened it and took a long drink. Then he said, "Can't sleep?"

"Sorry if we woke you. I'm used to living alone." She shrugged, leaned one exposed shoulder against the wall, and stacked one bare foot on the other. "Ever since I was little, I'd help my mom with projects in the night. I loved waking up to the sound of her working."

Twin sensations ran through him simultaneously. A strong twitch in his cock and a pull deep in his chest. She looked so female and vulnerable in her little tank and short set, and yet there was such love in her actions with her mom. Ivy knew what family was.

He didn't.

Shifting his gaze, he studied the newly papered wall. "Looks good."

"I found a large cash deposit in Trip's account. Eight thousand dollars."

Luke whipped his head back to Ivy. She chewed her lower lip. "Hadn't been sure about telling me, huh?"

She stopped chewing and glared at him. "No, I didn't have *enough* to tell you. It was cash, which makes it hard to trace. What I need now are suspects and access to their accounts. If I can find a matching withdrawal, then we might have our buyer and possibly the killer. But there are ethical and practical considerations."

"Humph. Ethical? Murderers don't get ethical consideration from me." He drank more of the water.

"They do from me. I can't just break into people's checking and savings accounts. Besides, I have to have access information to get in anyway."

Luke studied her curiously. "I might have a suspect. Pierce Jordan, an entertainment lawyer who lives in Sherman Oaks." He filled her in on getting the name from his Web group, the Urban Legendites.

"So your fan club really is a working group."

He ignored that. "We'll talk to Regina tomorrow. But for now, let's say we find reason to believe Jordan is the buyer of the statues. The person we think paid Trip to steal the statues and maybe killed him. And you have what you need to get into their accounts to see if they have an eight-thousand-dollar cash withdrawal. Would you do it?"

Shaking her head, she said, "No, not without permission."

This was revealing. "Even if it means your mom going to prison?"

Determination firmed her jawline. "I'd try to find another way, maybe trick them into giving me permission."

"Isn't that the same thing?" Her lines were interesting.

"No, because I'm following the letter of the law. There are rules for a reason."

"Mostly to be broken in my book."

She shifted, walking into the living room and turning off the lights. "I like rules. It's the only way I know to tell the good guys from the bad."

Luke watched her in the gloom as she walked back toward him. Light from her bedroom spilled down the hallway behind him. "That's why you need me. Maybe it takes a bad guy to catch one."

The weird thing was, Ivy made him want to be the good guy.

Chapter 9

Ivy watched Luke go into his room and close the door. She stood in the hallway, feeling achy and empty. Alone. Restless.

Luke had looked warm, rumpled, and sexy. Hot. In just a pair of blue boxers, he'd looked *extremely hot*. She'd had to run to the kitchen to keep from begging him to touch her.

To let her touch him.

The worst part was his eyes. Their gray-blue depths had been as open and unguarded as she'd ever seen them. Vulnerable. Real.

She cleaned up the wallpaper mess, then booted up her laptop and sat alone on the couch in the dark living room. She didn't want to go to bed, close her eyes and see Trip's dead body. Or worse, imagine her mom dead. Shoving those thoughts away, she searched for Pierce Jordan. She found the Web site for the lawyer, but what did that tell her?

Nothing.

She couldn't get into his financial records. "Think," she muttered. How to backtrack from Trip's cash deposit? But she knew there wasn't any way to do it.

She pulled up Trip's bank accounts, trying to look for any other threads.

It all blurred. She was too tired, too scared. Too alone. She'd been afraid of this day since her earliest memories. The day when a bad boy would take her mom from her. It was scarier than when Ivy had been the one in trouble.

Her mom was all she had.

Hot tears filled her eyes and her throat closed up. She hated herself for being weak when she needed to be sharp and strong. Clenching her jaw, she slapped away the tears and struggled to focus on the computer screen.

She heard Luke's door open followed by the sound of his footsteps. Felt him move around the couch and saw his legs come into her peripheral vision. Finally, she felt the weight of his stare, but she kept her gaze on the screen. "Go back to bed, Luke."

"Can't." He sank down on the couch next to her, took the laptop from her, closed it, and set it on the floor.

She wondered, "Why can't you sleep?"

He leaned his head back on the couch. "Nightmares. You?"

"Same. What are your nightmares about?"

He was silent.

The tears burned again. Her anger surfaced. "You always demand answers from me, but you won't tell me a blasted thing." She heaved herself forward, half rising when he caught her. Wrapping his hand around her arm, he tugged her down onto his lap. He pressed her face to his chest and circled her with his arms.

The warmth of it, the sheer comfort, locked her in place. She couldn't remember the last time she'd felt a man's skin against her, his arms around her.

"My nightmares are about two friends. My job was to extract men from tight situations. My last mission, Ray and Sanders were in trouble. They got to the pickup location, but I was too late. I landed my helicopter in a bloody bath of body parts."

"Oh God." She curled her fingers against the curve of his chest. "That's the two men Arnie said you were responsible for—" She realized what she was saying and shut up.

She felt his body tighten. "Arnie's a liar, but in this case, he was right. It was my fault. My helicopter had mechanical problems an hour into the flight. It took me two hours to fix it and get it back into the air."

That wasn't his fault, that was a horrible twist of fate. God, it outraged her, made her sick. And it made her realize that even though she was scared, her mom was still alive, not dead like Luke's two friends. "I'm sorry."

He rubbed her back, his body relaxing. A few minutes stretched out. A silent time filled with warm comfort and fueled a desire for more. "What are your nightmares, Ivy?"

"Not as bad as yours. Just that this is the first time I saw someone killed like that." She was afraid she would lose her mom, but compared to Luke, who had lost his friends and his family, she had nothing to complain about. Still, she shuddered at the memory of Trip dead.

Luke wrapped his arms tightly around her and slid his warm hand under her shirt to more intimately caress her back. "What you're feeling is what makes you human. Scared and vividly aware that you're still alive. Desperate to feel alive."

She didn't know if he was seducing her or comforting her. She didn't even know what she wanted. His hand skimmed over her back in warm, easy circles. And yet, her body wanted more. Keeping her face buried in his chest, she asked, "You use sex for that? To feel alive?"

His hand slid up to the back of her neck, working the knot there. "Yes, and you use hanging wallpaper in the middle of the night with your mom. We all do what works for us."

She could feel the entire length of his arm against her back under her shirt and his hand easing her muscles at her neck. This was a side of Luke she hadn't seen—easy, comforting, and self-confidently sensual. Sexy in a way that melted her bones. Lifting her head, she looked at his face. The light from her room at the end of the hallway was just a mist, but it showed her his gray eyes. "Ask me again."

He lifted an eyebrow. "Ask you what?"

It was a leap of trust. This man would walk away from her, but she could live with that. *Rules,* as long as she understood the rules, she could do this. Take comfort and, please God, a little pleasure in sex. As long as she didn't believe Luke cared. She swallowed against her suddenly dry mouth. "If I want to have sex with you."

Blue flared hot in his gray eyes. "I'd rather find out for myself." He moved his free hand to her knee and slowly drew his fingers upward.

Sensations shot through her; her nerves twitched and begged for more. Overwhelmed and feeling like he was already ahead of her, she said, "You're going to go out of order, aren't you?

His fingers froze on her leg. "Out of order?"

Heat bloomed in her face. Why didn't she just shut up? He knew what he was doing. She was the one who wasn't very good at sex. "Nothing."

"Oh no. I want to hear this. Start talking."

God, she didn't even know what to tell him. "I don't, I mean I thought maybe kissing . . . it just seems a little fast . . ." If he laughed, she was going to put on her high heels and kick him.

His face softened. "Fast. As in not giving you an orgasm?"

Embarrassed, she tried to sit up.

Using his hand on her neck, he locked her in place and lowered his face to hers. "No hiding. There's nothing wrong with wanting as much pleasure as your partner. Nothing wrong with asking me to slow down and telling me what you like. This?" He skimmed his finger up her thigh, under the boxers and under the elastic of her panties. "This is just for me." He gently brushed over her pubic hair, separating her folds.

While watching her.

Ivy couldn't look away from his face, his eyes.

He slid his finger along her folds and deeper. "It's like a little roadmap. Finding what I'm going to need to give you as much pleasure as I can. Like this." He rubbed her clitoris, circled it. Touched it. Petted it.

She shuddered and pressed herself closer to him.

His skin grew warmer against her face. "You're slick and hot. Not ready, but damned tempting. And here," he groaned as he penetrated her with his finger. He went deep, adding a second finger.

She curled her fingers into his chest. "Luke." She wanted to move, to ride his fingers. How did he make her feel this way so quickly?

Using his hand on her neck, he tugged her head back. His eyes were fierce. She could feel his arousal beneath her. In a low voice, he asked, "Feel good?"

Wasn't she supposed to be doing something? "Yes, but—"

"No buts. I'm just getting started discovering you." He took his hand out. Lifting her in his arms, he stood and walked into the guest room, kicked the door shut, and set her on her feet by the bed. Before she could catch her breath, he dragged her to him, kissing her. Luke put his hands into her hair and held her as he tongued her mouth, touching every place she had and making her shiver with thickening desire.

Breaking the kiss, he angled her head to see her face. "I'm good for sex, Ivy. Nothing more. Don't forget that."

She felt that low in her belly. Warning her not to get hurt. Not to get stupid. "I won't."

He dropped his hands to the hem of her tank and pulled it off.

The cool air mixed with the heat of his gaze, making her nipples pebble and her thighs ache. He dropped to his haunches and stripped down her shorts and panties, leaving her bare to him.

"God. You're so pretty, so sexy." He reached out, cupped her hips with his hands, and tugged her closer to him.

She looked down, seeing his head, his shoulders. His face at her thighs. It was too fast, too overwhelming. She wasn't going to get this right. Luke was experienced, he was going to figure out she needed a diagram or chart to get it right. She wasn't naturally creative and sensual. Putting her hands on his shoulders, she said, "You don't have to do that."

"You don't like it?"

Self-conscious, she shifted back a step and tried to tease her way out of it. "You're out of order again."

He narrowed his eyes, studying her. Then he rose to his full height. He stripped off his boxers.

She took him in. He was fireman hot and calendar cut. She loved the shape of his face, the long lines of it, the flat cheeks, the way his full mouth wore a curve as if he had a secret. Fascinated by the sprinkle of hair across his chest and marching down his abdomen, she visually followed the line to his long, thick erection. He was already hard. Rock hard. She guessed a man with his package had a right to wear a secret smile. But he was more than big and powerful, he was . . . Luke. Full of mysteries, and yet, she'd felt a kindness in him. Like tonight. She looked back to his eyes.

He opened his arms. "Come here."

She walked into his embrace. He closed his arms around her. His erection strained into her belly, and he lowered his mouth to her ear and said softly, "There's no order to sex. There's just what feels good. Going down on you will feel good for both of us."

She turned her face into his chest. "Not everyone likes it. You don't have to do it. I'm ready."

"You're not even close. I'm too damned close. So we're going to even things up a little." He walked her back to the bed and eased her down onto her back. Followed her. Covered her body with his and kissed her.

Ivy's nerves melted away and she sank into the kiss. He made her feel hot and sensual, hyperaware of the cool sheets on her back, and his hot body pressing against her. The rough shadow of a beard on his face, the crisp feel of his chest hair against her breasts, the wet feel of his tongue rubbing hers. His erection against her thigh.

He moved his mouth over her face, down to her ear, then her shoulder. Sliding down her body, he cupped her breast, brushing his thumb over the nipple.

She arched beneath him. The orderly way he was doing this made her feel more secure, more sure. She knew what to expect next. When he shifted and took the other nipple in his mouth, suckling and nipping, it was more than she expected. She gasped and lifted her head. "I want to touch you."

He let go of her nipple to smile. There were more secrets in his smile. "Do you?"

"Yes." She knew how to make him feel good. Knew what she was supposed to do. Dirk had needed a lot of stroking, licking, and sucking to get hard. Luke was already hard, but still, she had to do her part.

"You're going to have to earn it, Princess."

"Huh?" She didn't understand. "I thought that's what you wanted?"

"Oh, I do. But I want something else more."

She didn't believe him. "What?"

He slid off the mattress to his knees on the floor, took hold of her legs, and pulled her until her bottom was at the edge of the mattress. "I want to make you come with my mouth. Then we'll talk." He grabbed a pillow and put it beneath her hips. The angle arched and opened her to him.

Oh God, she'd didn't want him to do it, then not like it. "I don't think . . ."

"Perfect. Don't think." He dropped his gaze, pressed her legs open, and touched her with a fingertip. Gently. Stroked her. Then he leaned forward, his wide shoulders catching on her thighs. He lifted her legs, draping her over his shoulders, and slid his tongue over her clit.

She stopped thinking. She couldn't think. Fisting the sheets, she just . . . felt. The wet roughness of his tongue lapped at her. Her head filled with a buzzing, her body was hot and liquid, and *need* flashed bright and pulsing in her veins. There was no order, nothing to grab on to. If he stopped, she'd cry. "Please." She was begging.

He sucked her clit gently and penetrated her with a finger. Then another finger slid in to fill her up.

No order. The buzzing in her ears exploded; she arched up and came. Hard, pulsing spasms that left her panting and heavy with pleasure.

Luke watched her pleasure. Intense and beautiful. He'd never seen a more beautiful woman than Ivy when she let go of her careful world. He didn't know who hadn't liked using their mouth on her, but they were a fool. It made him proud, arrogant, and damned pleased to get her to trust him enough to make her come.

She was wild and trusting at her very core. She just didn't seem to trust herself enough to let that woman out. But for the night, she was his. He rose up, grabbed his pants, and fished out a condom.

"I want to touch you."

He looked over at her. She'd scooted off the pillow he'd put under her and back up to the proper place on the bed. But her hair was tousled, her color high, and the hair at her thighs was wet with her pleasure. He enjoyed messing up her order. God, he loved seeing her like that. Going to the bed, he looked down at her. "About that, I lied." He tore open the condom and put it on. "Feeling you come against my mouth made me too horny to wait."

Her eyes widened. More heat bloomed in her cheeks and over her breasts. God, she was fun. Chuckling, he debated scandalizing her some more. Or just taking her face-to-face where he could watch her as he thrust into her. Hold her hands so she wasn't thinking about what she was supposed to do with them. That deep need won out. Luke put his knee on the bed.

She reached out and curled one hand around his dick; the other hand cupped his balls. He sucked in a breath. Pleasure shot through him. She gently squeezed, and swear to God, he saw stars behind his tightly closed eyes. Through the condom, she stroked the sensitive tip and he shuddered. His balls drew up. Chills and heat chased down his spine. He grabbed her wrist. "Scoot down the bed a bit." His voice was rough and hoarse, he couldn't help that, but he kept his hold gentle on her wrist.

She edged down.

He let go of her wrist and covered her body with his. "Put your arms up over your head."

"Why?" She slid her arms up.

"You're going to hold on to my hands while I'm inside of you. You're not going to think about anything but how I'm making you feel." He took hold of her hands, laced his fingers with hers, then looked down into her face.

Then he thrust into her. All the way. Deep into her.

"Oh." Her breath rushed out and her fingers twined tightly with his.

Luke saw her eyes fill with heat, the same heat that closed and pulsed around his dick. He didn't need a roadmap to her body—it was made for him. He'd hit her core first try. Amazed, he held her hands and levered up enough on his elbows to swing his hips, first out then back into her sweet spot.

And his. Jesus. Sweat popped out all over him. His cock loved the feel of her, the glide of her. And the next thing he knew, instinct took over. Need. He was driving into her, going higher, pushing her higher.

She made desperate sounds in her throat, sounds that inflamed him to a primitive, aching need. The whole world narrowed to the woman beneath him, to their pleasure. He looked down into her heated blue eyes and felt the last of his control rupture. He drove her until she shattered, her body arching in bliss. His own release raced down his spine and exploded.

When he finally could breathe, he held on to her hands for a second longer to look down into her flushed face. He couldn't help the splash of pride he felt. "You have a fun side, Ivy York. A wild streak that we're going to have to explore."

She unlinked her hands from his and tried to shift him off of her. "You're imagining things, Sterling. I'm a mild-mannered accountant."

He rolled to the side, then caught her when she tried to scoot away. He pulled her back to his chest. He wasn't ready to be alone, wasn't ready to let her go. "A mild-mannered accountant would not have turned a career disaster into a radio career," he said, liking the feel of her in his arms. The scent of her hair in his nose. The feel of her ass against his dick.

She looked back over her shoulder at him. "I guess sex with an accountant would look pretty boring on the Urban Legend's résumé."

He felt his teasing grin slide away. "I don't talk about the women I sleep with." He hadn't been the one to spill the beans about his private Web-based group. Luke liked sex, hell he loved sex. But he liked an honest partner, not another woman looking for bragging rights and a chance to get on a tabloid.

She turned her face and tucked into his hold. "Lighten up. It's not like I'm going to tell anyone. I'd be a laughingstock."

His gut kicked over at that. He should be relieved, glad that she wasn't using him to get more fame. But it wasn't much fun to be an embarrassment either. "Your secret is safe with me."

Saturday morning, Ivy stared at the specially made bullet-proof glass case in Regina's living room. The case was empty and Ivy had the oddest sense of loss looking at it.

Like when she woke up alone this morning? She shook off that thought. It had just been sex. Comfort sex that got a little hot. Luke had woken up before her, went home and showered. Changed his clothes. Got his point across that it was just sex. Then he had called and asked her if she'd like to talk to Regina with him. Point number two—back to work.

Regina stood next to her. "I should never have kept the statues here at the house. But I couldn't let them go either. They are so compelling. That's the thing about those statues, they release our deepest passions and judgment gets trampled."

A quiet grief coated each word. Ivy looked down at one of the pictures of the statues in her hand to give the woman a little space. They were exquisite in detail; although she didn't have the eye her mom did, she could recognize the beauty.

And she was beginning to believe the myth of deepest passion. How else did she explain her actions with Luke? Curiosity made her ask, "Do they do that to everyone? How long does it last?"

"Ah. No, the statues don't have the same effect on everyone. Some people aren't susceptible. There are theories that they have no deep passion. Or that they already know what their passion is and are pursuing it."

Ivy understood numbers. They were concrete and made sense every time. But this, this was not something she could grasp. "So they are like an aphrodisiac?"

Regina smiled. "No, but many people have thought so. The power of the statues is all about the thing you want most. For me, it's the statues themselves. I am passionate about them and showing them to the world. For you, maybe sex is a part of it. But no, your passion lies deeper."

Ivy blushed. "I wasn't asking about me. I never even saw them."

Regina looked over to Luke, who was thumbing through the police report and the lists of people who had contacted Regina about the statues. He looked up, his gaze colliding with Ivy's.

She forced herself to break eye contact. *Rules.* Rules were what she lived by, what kept her safe. She was breaking a lot of her rules with Luke, so she created new ones to cope.

Regina said, "Most people don't really know what their deepest desires are." She turned her gaze on Ivy. "And you were close enough to the statues to be affected. You and Luke both."

What? Was she wearing a sign that said "I got sex last night"? Uncomfortable, she handed the pictures back to Regina. "My mom touched the statues, held them. She's the same."

The woman's light brown eyes crinkled when she smiled. "Perhaps her passion just isn't what you think it is."

Ivy rolled her eyes. "I know my mom's passion. That's why she's in trouble. Men. Bad boys. It's always been her passion to be the woman who finally tamed the bad boy. Now she might end up in prison."

Regina asked kindly, "It's always been your passion to rescue your mom?"

She blinked. "No, it's just . . . what I do. I mean, we're family." Her gaze caught on Luke. He stared back at her, his eyes were like gray mirrors, bottomless and intense. What was he thinking? *Stop*, she told herself. Luke had told her what he was thinking—sex, not relationship. *Work*. She needed to focus on finding the statues. "How did Trip steal the statues from the case?"

"He got the keys out of my spare bedroom office and un-locked it." She shook her head. "Trip did bartending for me when I had parties. He was here after the parties cleaning up. During parties, I keep the keys with me to open the case and show off the statues. He could have easily seen where I put the keys when the party was over."

Luke walked up holding a guest list. "Pierce Jordan has come to a couple of your parties. He's very interested in the statues."

"Yes, Pierce has tried numerous times to get me to sell him the statues. He's offered me a lot of money. I'm not interested in selling. He knows that."

"What's he like?" Luke asked.

"Smooth, charming, sophisticated, and not a killer or a thief. He wants the statues, wants them more every time he sees them. But he's not a killer."

Luke narrowed his eyes. "Got a thing for Jordan?"

Regina shrugged. "He's not interested in me. Has a girl-friend, I think."

"Who?"

"I don't know. Once I heard girlfriend, I backed off." She set the pictures Ivy had returned to her on the coffee table and added, "It's not Pierce."

"I'm going to check him out."

"You're wasting your time." The skin around her mouth and eyes tightened. "And I don't have time to waste. This whole mess is all over the news. I'm getting calls left and right; all my backers are talking of pulling out, and the places we've booked want to cancel."

Ivy could feel Regina's tension just standing next to her. "Regina, why don't you call Pierce and ask if he'll talk to Luke and me? We have to check out every possibility."

"I'll go call him." She walked out of the room.

Luke's face was coldly blank. "Good idea. We'll go talk to Jordan." His gaze drifted toward the hallway where Regina had gone.

"You care about her." A pang of envy sliced through her. Luke wanted Ivy for sex, but he didn't care. He seemed to genuinely care about Regina.

He looked back. "Those statues mean more to her than any amount of money. They are her life's work. Damn right I care, and I'm going to get them back."

How much did he care? Oh God, she had to stop that! "All right."

Luke wasn't finished. "The fact that they were stolen out of the radio station means we have to check out everyone who works there. Can you get into their bank accounts?"

She shook her head. "It's not that easy. In some cases I might be able to, but—"

Luke sighed. "You said you were going to help, do your part.."

His icy voice reminded her that she and Luke weren't friends. They were two people thrown together by circumstances. The sex was a side benefit. Probably chemistry she'd heard so much about. "I'll do what I can."

"Okay." Regina walked back into the room. "Pierce will see you in his office. But just so you know, he's spent last week at a conference on the East Coast. He just flew in last night. He's catching up on stuff at the office."

Luke went to Regina and put his hands on her shoulders so they were face-to-face. "Hang in there. I'm going to find those statues. You'll have your tour."

"I believe you. Those statues belong with me. I think they just had some work to do before they come back."

Okay, Ivy thought, that was a little too weird for her.

Chapter 10

Pierce Jordan looked a little bit like Barry Bostwick in his late forties or early fifties. Distinguished and smooth. He met them in the marble foyer of his office, striding toward them with his hands out. "Ivy York! This is a real pleasure. I listen to your show every chance I get."

Luke knew six ways to kill the bastard if he didn't let go of Ivy's hands. Hell, he could drop him face-first onto the marble floor without breaking a sweat.

Ivy squeezed his hands. "Thank you, Mr. Jordan. What a lovely compliment."

His smile warmed. "Well deserved. Please call me Pierce, and be forewarned, I am an entertainment lawyer and you are in entertainment. It's a perfect match."

Taking her hands back, Ivy laughed and said, "I'm not on your level, Pierce. I am strictly small town."

"Not true. You have some serious potential, and people have noticed. I could help you make some connections that—"

Luke had enough. "We're here to talk about the stolen statues not Ivy's career."

Pierce turned to him and held out his hand. "Of course. Regina told me that you are Luke Sterling. Sorry for being rude, but a beautiful woman like Ivy distracts a man."

Luke nodded and shook his hand, but he glanced at Ivy. She seemed pleased. Hadn't he told her she was beautiful? Or had he? Had he complimented her at all? Or had he just taken advantage of her when she'd been tired, desperate, and needed a little human connection? He'd known that sex would help him sleep without nightmares, so he'd basically used her.

Pierce turned and took Ivy's elbow. "Come into my office. I'm sure Regina told you that I was in New York over the last week. I can assure you I had nothing to do with the theft or the murder. I'll be glad to help you however I can. If I can't have the statues for myself, then I want Regina to have them."

Luke followed behind and struggled to concentrate. Damn hard to do when Ivy was wearing a pair of cream slacks and a black button-down shirt that ended at her hips. Her trim back, narrow waist, and rounded butt kept snagging his attention.

Pierce's office was bigger than the entire studio apartment he was staying in. Plush carpet muffled their footsteps. Pierce ignored his massive desk to guide Ivy to the couch and two chairs. "What can I get you? We have coffee, tea, or I have some cold champagne?"

Luke stayed on his feet to keep the advantage and remind himself to stay focused. Around Ivy, his concentration was shot to hell. Or maybe it wasn't Ivy at all, maybe it was the statues. The sooner he found them, returned them to Regina and went back to his life, the better it would be for everyone.

Ivy moved past Pierce to sit in a chair. "We're fine, Pierce. We don't want to take up too much of your time."

Luke took his cue. "How long have you been interested in the statues?"

Pierce put his hand on the back of the chair Ivy sat in. "I've been interested in them for years. They have a fascinating history and I'm an amateur collector of jade. After seeing a clip on a TV show about the statues, I contacted Regina through her Web site, and eventually I was invited to one of her parties. The statues are alluring. There's a quality to their beauty that's hard to resist."

Ivy tilted her head. "Do you believe the statues have some power?"

He studied Ivy. "I'm a romantic at heart, Ivy. I want to believe in magic."

Luke wanted to puke.

Ivy said, "That's a nice sentiment for a lawyer."

Pierce blinked, then broke into rich laughter. "Touché."

Luke cracked his knuckles. "Do you know Trip Vaugn?"

Pierce sobered and shook his head. "I know he was the bartender at Regina's parties, that's about it. The most I talked to him was to give him my drink order. Rest assured, if I wanted to steal those statues, it'd have been done right. I'd never hire an evident amateur."

That was a comment Luke understood and respected. The lawyer meant it.

"Besides, stealing the statues would be pointless because then I'd have to hide them. I'm not interested in that."

That rang true, Luke thought. "Did anyone else at the party seem overly interested in Trip?"

Pierce broke out his expensive smile. "The man charmed the women. I noticed that."

Ivy sighed. "Is there anything you can tell us that would help?"

He looked down at her. "Only that I will let you know if someone contacts me in an attempt to sell me the statues. My interest in them isn't a secret. I want Regina to have them back; then I will do my best to convince her to sell them to me."

"She won't," Ivy said.

He nodded, stuffing his hands in his pockets. "I'm aware of that, but I rather enjoy trying. She's quite an interesting woman and she knows a great deal about art." He walked to his desk and opened a drawer, then came back with a business card. Handing it to Ivy, he said, "Call me if you have any more questions. Or if you are interested in expanding your career. You have an extremely bright future in front of you. I'd like very much to talk about it with you when you have the time."

Ivy stood up and shook hands with him. "Thank you for your time, Pierce."

He folded both his hands around hers. "My pleasure."

Luke clenched his jaw at the picture they made. Ivy with her polish and cheerleader looks, Pierce with his older man sophistication and easy charm. The truth was that Pierce probably could make a famous woman out of Ivy. Give her the security and safety she craved; it was a custom-made match for Ivy.

All Luke could give her was a few mind-blowing orgasms. *Damn it.* "One more thing before we leave," Luke said sharply.

Dropping Ivy's hand, Pierce said, "What's that?"

"I thought Regina told me you have a girlfriend. What's her name?"

Pierce narrowed his gaze. "I did. Now I don't."

Ivy headed toward the door. "Luke, we've taken up enough of Pierce's time."

Ignoring her, he pressed harder, "Did your girlfriend go to any of the parties at Regina's house? What's her name?"

He stared back at Luke. "Simone Waters, and no, she never went to Regina's parties. Simone is a singer, not an art collector."

"Do you represent her professionally?"

Pierce said smoothly, "I don't think my client list is relevant. Have a good day."

"Luke," Ivy said in that very female way and grabbed his arm.

He planted his feet and said, "It was a simple question, Jordan. Do you have something to hide?" Of course he did, he was screwing his client. Luke wanted Ivy to see exactly what kind of man Jordan was before she signed with him to make her a star.

Pierce raised both eyebrows and laughed. "I keep the secrets of many of my clients, Sterling. But the fact that I represented Simone is not a secret. The curious thing is how you see that as having anything to do with the missing statues."

He didn't, but he was smug with having proved that Jordan screws his clients. "Just covering all my bases."

Pierce just nodded, then said, "It was interesting to meet you. Please don't let me keep you from your next appointment. I'll show you out." He strode past them both into the marble foyer.

Once they were in the car, Ivy snapped her seat belt into place and demanded, "What is wrong with you?"

Luke looked over at her angry face. "Doing my job, Princess. That requires dropping the niceties and asking real questions. And by the way, that guy wants to screw you, not make you a star." *Fuck.* Luke slammed the car into gear and drove.

"Good to know. I'll make an appointment for a bikini wax."

"You don't need a bikini wax." What the hell was wrong with her? Now she was going to torture herself for that lawyer?

"Maybe I should get another opinion. You seem a little bit easy to please. I'm pretty sure Pierce is more . . . discriminating."

He choked and coughed so hard his eyes watered. Finally catching his breath, he looked over at her. "You're messing with me, aren't you?"

She shrugged. "How naive do you think I am, Sterling?" She held up a hand. "I know I'm not that good at sex, but I'm a very good businesswoman. I can read men. Pierce is after a piece of my career if I were to break into bigger markets. Sex would be a bonus, but it's not the goal."

Luke heard every word, but his brain hung up on *not that good at sex.* "What do you mean you're not that good at sex?"

She rolled her eyes. "It's not a priority for me. And I'm pretty much a sex-by-the-numbers girl."

He had no fucking clue what she was talking about. "Where did you come up with that?"

She crossed her arms protectively over her middle and stared out the front window at the freeway. "I overheard Dirk describe me to his friends that way. They were laughing so hard they didn't see me standing there for quite a while."

Oh hell. Anger arced up his spine and slammed into his head. Ivy had been sweet and fun in bed. And sexy as hell. Luke had realized she hadn't been with a lot of men. So what? She responded with such passion, he'd enjoyed finding ways to make her come. He'd been thinking about her since he woke up this morning. It'd been all he could do to quietly slip out of bed and let her sleep, instead of waking her up with his mouth on her lovely tits. Christ. He opened his mouth to say something when the radio caught his attention.

"This is Zeke Levy of *Ethics Today,* and we're talking about media hypocrites. The Urban Legend is hot on the trail of the Jade Goddesses, and rumor has it, the tail of Ivy York, talk show host of the hottest show on daytime radio, the *Economic Sex Hex*. Has Ivy York been scamming the public? Preaching no bad boys on air while secretly lusting after them? Or is she falling under the legendary power of the statues? Or the Urban Legend himself? What's your ethical take on this? Call in now!"

Hell. He was used to this publicity, but Ivy . . . He turned to look at her.

She looked out the front windshield, her eyes glassy with anger or embarrassment. He could see her teeth were rigidly set, making his own jaw ache in sympathy. She squeezed her hands together in her lap until her knuckles were white.

"Ivy, it'll blow over. People will forget, move on to the

next sexy story." He tried to make her feel better. "Your ratings will probably go up from the exposure."

Flatly, she answered, "Yeah, ratings. That'll make Leah happy."

She still looked frigid and miserable. What the hell was he supposed to do? He was who he was. She'd just have to get over her embarrassment of being linked to the Urban Legend. He muttered, "Thought you were tougher than this."

"I don't care what you think. What I want to know is who leaked to the media that you are on the case, and that I'm working with you or sleeping with you? Who knows that, Luke?"

His first thought was, "Your mom?"

"She's not talking to the media on the advice of her lawyer."

It hit him then. "You think I did it?"

Her shoulders dropped with a sigh. "I don't know, Luke. I suppose it doesn't matter. It was going to get out. Zeke's show is new and he's fighting for ratings. Guess I'm good for ratings."

A roil of feelings irritated the shit out of him. Like the fact that Ivy didn't trust him. She trusted him fine in bed, so what the hell? That her reputation was being shredded, thanks to him, didn't exactly sit well either. He didn't like her being used. But she did have a point; who knew they were sexually involved?

No one, but maybe her mom.

Who might have guessed? And who wasn't above using it? His smarmy weasel cousin, that's who. "Arnie," he said.

"What?"

Luke turned to meet her gaze. "Arnie is the one who went to the media with the story of my Web site. He told them I created a Web site to lure women, then seduce them. The media contacted me, through the Web site, and I refused to talk. So they started calling me the Urban Legend and interviewing women who supposedly were on the site and had slept with me."

"He thought it would ruin your business?"

Luke split his attention between the road and her. "My business name is Legendary Treasure Investigations. But Arnie's little sabotage effort turned me into the Urban Legend and easily doubled my business."

Ivy thought about that. "What would he gain from telling the media about you and me?"

He kept it simple, knowing he'd never be able to explain the hate dynamics between the two of them. "He'd irritate me, which was probably just a happy bonus for him. The real reason is that it would get you mad at me, and then you'd shut me out and turn to him."

"So it is a competition between you two."

He shrugged, then changed the subject. "We're going to take a detour and go to Arnold's office. I want to see a couple things. Like what made him sniff out this case. He doesn't do this kind of PI work usually. So maybe he's having financial problems or he got a tip."

Her voice was incredulous. "That you'll steal?"

"I like to call it investigating. I also want to see if he's been contacting the media." Luke changed direction and headed toward Irvine.

Ivy's cell phone rang. Fishing it out of her purse, she looked at the display, then answered, "Marla?"

Luke turned to see Ivy listening.

"Marla, I think it's safe now. The statues are gone. There's no reason for anyone to break into the radio station now. You don't have anything to worry about."

Luke wondered why Marla was calling Ivy.

"We don't know who did it. But they are long gone by now. They got what they wanted." She listened, then said, "The police haven't told us anything. I'll let you know if I find out anything, I promise. Take the weekend off and by

Monday you'll feel better." She put her cell phone away. "I've never heard Marla like that. She's a rock under pressure."

"This isn't pressure, it's murder. Everyone handles it differently. Why was she calling you?"

She tilted her head. "We're becoming friends, and she's scared."

He left it alone and drove. Nearly an hour later, he got off the fifty-five freeway down by the John Wayne Airport and pulled into an industrial park.

Ivy asked, "Do you think he'll be in the office? I mean, it's Saturday."

Luke parked and turned to face her. "No."

"Then why—oh God, you're going to break in!"

He got out and shut the door. Ivy caught up to him as they headed to the unimaginative mirrored block of a building. "Luke!"

He glanced over at her. Worry knit her eyebrows in a way that made him ache to smooth the lines away with his thumb. Maybe with his mouth. "Ivy."

"Are you really going to break in?"

"I'm going in, yes." He went into the lobby and strode to the elevator and raised his eyebrows when she stopped outside the doors.

She hurried in and the doors slid shut.

They rode in silence up to the sixth floor. Luke was being a prick, but it irritated him that she didn't trust him. She'd thought he ratted out their sex-fun to the media? The elevator stopped. He strode off and headed to Arnie's office. He waited until he got to the dark door with the shiny plate that read STERLING INVESTIGATIONS. For a second, he could smell his aunt's rose-scented perfume and hear her voice. Through all the foster homes, she'd kept track of Luke. Visited him, remembered his birthday. And when he'd gotten out of the service, she'd stayed up with him one memorable night, both of them getting drunk as any sailor, and she listened as Luke told her what happened on his last mission. She hadn't played with his head like the idiot head-shrinkers, hadn't asked him how he Goddamned felt walking through the bloody body parts of his friends. How it felt not to be able to remember what they looked like alive, but he got to see them in bloody pieces every night. She'd just listened.

Christ, he missed her. She'd been human, made mistakes and later tried to fix them.

He took a breath and let it go. She was gone. He reached into his pocket and pulled out his keys. Selecting the correct key, he slid it into the lock.

"You have a key?"

Her breathless, shrill voice made him smile. "Yep, my aunt left me a share of the business."

"You work together? You said your business is Legendary Treasures Investigations."

He went in and held the door for her. Shutting the door, he said, "No, I have an office in Riverside and I run my own business. But it's fun to know that I can demand my share of this business if Arnie the asshole pushes me too far. He walks around knowing that any second of any day I can demand my share. I can bring in an army of accountants to look at the books. In general, I can annoy him at will."

She turned away from him, walking around the office. She went past the rich mahogany desk in the middle of the room to the shelves covered in pieces of art. His aunt had loved art, particularly statues and figurines. There were only a few pieces on display. Ivy touched the ivory music box. "So letting me think you were going to break into the office was payback for me thinking you leaked sex with me to the media?"

Moving to the desk, he sat in the chair, booted up the computer, and pulled up the Internet program. He started looking to see what e-mails Arnie had sent and received. "You're the one who jumped to the conclusion that I'd break into the office."

"You told me you break the rules."

He looked over his shoulder to see her carefully cradling the silver and ivory music box in her palm. She ran her finger over the intricate ivory design on the lid. Luke had sent that to his aunt when he first went into the service at eighteen. The sight of Ivy holding it made his chest ache oddly. His feelings had been dormant for so long, it surprised him. What were they talking about? Oh, rules. "It's the badass versus bad boy thing again. I only break the rules that get the job done. Bad boys break rules for attention." And to destroy the cousin they hate. He turned back to the e-mails. He didn't see anything interesting. Arnie had a pretty extensive grapevine, so it'd be easy enough for him to find out Luke had gone undercover at the radio station. Then go to Mallory to rat him out.

"Want me to look at his financials?"

He lifted his gaze to her intense blue eyes. He'd known she wouldn't be able to resist digging into Arnie's financials. It was in her blood. "Yes, see if he's suddenly desperate for money. Try to find a clue why he has a sudden interest in the statues." He got up and moved.

She wasted no time, quickly sorting through the files on Arnie's computer to find his bookkeeping system. She was instantly absorbed. Leaving her to it, Luke nosed around the desk, trying to find some clue as to what Arnie's motive was in horning in on his case. Or evidence that he'd been chatting with the media.

Nothing.

"Do you think Arnie stole the statues and killed Trip?"

Her accuracy at guessing his thoughts surprised him. "It's crossed my mind." Dropping his gaze to her mouth that was only inches from his, he said, "It's possible. Even if it's just to make sure I don't recover them, or to force me to sell my share of Sterling Investigations to him." Her lips were shiny with a soft-colored gloss. He really wanted to taste her mouth with that stuff on her lips. Heat washed through his groin and woke up his dick.

She kept his gaze. "What about murder? Would Arnold commit murder?"

Arnie had come after him with a knife once, but he'd been drunk. Truthfully, he said, "Anyone can kill, but I doubt it."

She kept his gaze for a few seconds, then turned back to the computer and said, "There's no obvious expense of eight thousand dollars in the bookkeeping program."

Her brain was fast at tracking financial clues. "So he probably didn't hire Trip to steal the statues." It was a long shot, but he needed to rule out all the possibilities.

Ivy said, "Are you on the business bank accounts?"

"Yes, I make sure Arnie doesn't run the business into the ground. He's been staying in the black, bringing in enough to cover expenses. I don't draw a salary."

Her fingers stalled over the keyboard. She glanced at him and asked, "Why not? You're due the money if you are part owner."

Every time she moved her head, he caught the berry scent of her shampoo. It was making him hungry, and not for food. "Don't want it."

She seemed to look straight inside him.

The door opened. Luke snapped up straight and stared at his cousin. Arnie's blue eyes narrowed; his face hardened and colored with rage. He shut the door and stalked across the room. "Now you're desperate enough to search my office? My computer? I told you I'd help you."

"Don't need your brand of help. You've already caused Ivy enough embarrassment."

"Me? I'm not the one who tricked her into thinking I'm a harmless personal assistant. And now the media has picked up on it. How many lives do you have to destroy?"

Stepping back, Luke moved away from Ivy and around the desk. "Don't try your spin, asshole. I know your methods when it comes to the Urban Legend." He expanded his chest and added, "Newsflash, I'm not selling out my portion of the business to you."

Arnie visibly controlled himself. He brought his shoulders down a notch and smoothed out his voice. "You don't understand, you never can grasp when someone is trying to help you. You're in over your head. I want to help you."

It was like pushing a button and all the buried anger burst free. "Bullshit. You want to beat me and you never will. So you have to horn in on my cases, and . . ." he dropped his voice to icy disdain, "living vicariously through my sex life. Calling the media and telling them Ivy and I are having sex gives you a perverted thrill. Do you stay awake at night imagining it?"

Ivy's gasp made him regret the words immediately.

Arnold rocked forward and clenched his fists. "So like you to be rude and crude. You're embarrassing Ivy, and she doesn't deserve that. She's not like your sex groupies." He took a breath. "I don't have to explain myself to you. I'm trying to save the Sterling name because you screwed up the case. The statues are gone and a man has been murdered. How proud do you think *my* mom would be, huh, Luke?"

It was a solid hit. Luke repressed the urge to kick his teeth down his throat. "Probably as proud as she was when she figured out what a pathetic liar you are."

In a flash, Arnie's smooth exterior shattered and he took a swing at Luke.

Luke shifted to the side, grabbed his arm and shoved.

Arnie stumbled but caught himself on the desk. "Get out. Get out of my office." He shuddered with pent-up anger and looked at Ivy. "I'll take you home, Ivy. I don't want you near that bastard."

The hell he would. If Arnie touched her, Luke would kill him. Crush the breath from his body.

Ivy's face was pale, her blue eyes flitted between them. Then she said, "I'm fine with Luke." She walked past them both and out the door.

Luke caught up with her inside the elevator.

She jabbed at the ground floor button and demanded, "What's the story with you two?"

"We're not kissing cousins." The fury hangover roiled inside of him.

She turned her gaze on him as the doors slid shut. "Do you hate him so much because he had a family and you didn't?"

Her words were honey soft and they had the effect of yanking back a scab from his old wounds. He didn't want to think about the day his grandma died and his aunt and uncle refused to take him in. He didn't want to think about being alone and scared. A scared that never went away, only grew bigger as his longing for a real family grew dimmer. He couldn't stand it, couldn't deal with her knowing. He hit the Stop button on the elevator, then spun around to trap her by putting his hands against the wall on either side of her head. "There you go again, Princess."

She blinked in surprise. "What?"

He could feel her pity. It twisted in his gut and reminded him that he was good enough to fuck, but not good enough for anyone to find out about it. That was bad enough, but on top of it, she felt sorry for him. "Thinking I'm damaged and that you can fix me. It's in your voice and stamped all over your pretty face."

She opened her mouth.

He dropped his gaze to those full lips shiny with gloss and knew he had to cut off her reply. "You know what fixes me? The only thing that fixes me? Sex. Lots of sex. Hard sex. Sweaty, hot sex that lets me finally sleep more than three fucking hours a night." Goddamn it, he hadn't meant to tell her that last part. She just ripped out more of him than he was willing to give. More than he could afford to give. He tore himself away, slapped the ground floor button, and said, "Unless you're ready to get naked, leave me alone."

Ivy was tense enough to scream by the time they got back to Luke's studio apartment. After that scene in the elevator, they only talked about the case. She hadn't been afraid of Luke, she was afraid of herself.

Luke slammed the car door and said, "I'm going to check out Trip's clients from that list we got from Kat. Try a face-to-face and see if I can pick up any leads on who knew Trip had those statues."

Ivy nodded. "I have to go check on my mom, but I can meet you—"

"No." He fell into step beside her and walked to her RAV4. "You stay home and work the financial angle."

"Okay." She wasn't going to fight him. Ivy had begged Luke to help and he was. He didn't need her down his throat every second. He didn't need her at all. He'd been up and gone before she'd woken up this morning. He might use sex to sleep, but sex with her didn't get the job done.

Story of her life. That's why she stuck to numbers. They never let her down. They didn't pull her into a myriad of confusing feelings like Luke did. He was right, embarrassingly right. She wanted, needed, to help him. To show him he was worth more than just sex. She was just as pathetic as all the other women out there falling for bad boys.

She pulled open the door to her car and climbed in.

He caught the door. "Don't waste your kindness and compassion on me, Ivy. Just don't. If you want sex, call me and I will make you come all night long. Anything else isn't going to happen." He shut the door.

She drove home, trying to get her thoughts into order. She kept reminding herself that she was in control of her actions. That part of her hadn't wanted to drag Luke into his apartment and give him exactly what he claimed he needed—sex.

Once she arrived at her house, she recognized the car in her driveway. She parked and went up her front stairs to find Isaac sitting on the top step. His argyle socks showed where his pant legs hiked up. He had his elbows resting on his knees and a forlorn expression that gave him an almost hound dog face. "Did Mom lock you out?"

"She's not here. She's at her house, cleaning up with her crew."

"Crew?" Ivy dropped down next to him. "Like a group of young men with no shirts?"

His mouth twitched. "No, Marla Rimmer was helping her clean; then Arnold showed up. She let him in but told me that if I want to see her, I had to make an appointment since I'm only her lawyer."

She rolled her eyes, then studied the steps in front of her. "What makes us do this?" She wasn't surprised at Marla. She was fairly new in town and still making friends. She and Mallory had gone out for a drink once or twice.

She felt the weight of his gaze as he asked, "Luke?"

"You'd think I'd have learned from Dirk. Stay away from the bad boys."

Isaac snorted. "Luke's not a bad boy. He's a man, Ivy. A hard man, but not a bad one."

Surprised, she looked up into his face. "And you know this how?"

He put his arm around her. "Honey, you're important to me."

"You checked him out!" She smiled in spite of her confusion. It was nice to have someone care enough to do that.

Gently, he added, "I heard some of the nonsense going around the media today."

Ivy blurted out, "I slept with him."

He pulled her closer. "He treated you right?"

This had to be the most surreal conversation she'd ever had. "Yes."

"Trust yourself, Ivy."

"He told me he was good for sex and nothing else."

He was quiet, just letting her rest against him. Then he said, "Luke and your mom, I think they really believe that. It's up to us to show them what they are really worth."

"You love her that much?"

He looked down into her face. "We both do. We both know how special your mom is. She's the one who doesn't know it."

True. Ivy stood up. "I'll go over there."

Isaac stood. "I knew you would. I'm going to look into Arnold. I don't like him just showing up."

Because he was jealous. But she just nodded, leaned in, and kissed his cheek. Then she hurried over to her mom's house. Once there, she spotted Marla's light green Jetta, and she assumed the black Suburban belonged to Arnold. Why had he rushed to her mom's house after the confrontation with Luke? What was Arnold really after?

Ivy walked into the house, smelling a combination of Windex and orange Pledge. She walked to the small hallway and saw Marla vacuuming the bedrooms. The beds were stripped bare, but everything looked tidy. She turned and looked in the bathroom to see Arnold was mopping the floor. He looked at her and grinned. "I got bathroom duty." Backing out of the bathroom, he finished up, then fixed his gaze on her. "Ivy, you okay? I can't believe I let things get so out of hand in my office."

"You and Luke have issues."

He nodded, then leaned over to pick up the basket of cleaning supplies, complete with rubber gloves. "I can't reach Luke, no matter how hard I try. I let him push my buttons and suddenly we're both hotheaded kids instead of adults." He sighed and added, "The last thing my mom asked me to do was keep an eye on Luke. I've let her down." He walked down the hallway.

She walked with him, thinking that there seemed to be one set of facts with two interpretations. Who was telling the truth and who was lying? They passed through the living room and into the surprisingly roomy kitchen for a small house. Her mom was putting sandwiches on a tray while wearing jeans, bare feet with brightly polished toes, and a siren red T-shirt. She had her hair pulled back in a red ribbon. "Ivy, good, put some chips in a bowl and let's take all this to the table. Arnold, go get Marla, that woman has worked like a demon helping me clean."

Arnold shut off the water where he'd been washing his hands and went off to find Marla.

While Ivy helped her mom set all the food on her table topped with beautiful mosaic tile, she said, "You need to be careful. We really don't know that much about Arnold."

Mallory set the sandwiches on the table and said, "He's just being helpful. He cleaned both my bathrooms. How many men do you know who do that?"

She had a point. Ivy hesitated, unsure what to do. She hadn't seen anything the least bit incriminating in Arnold's office. He hadn't done anything to seem physically threatening to anyone but Luke. But it had looked like he'd have beaten the crap out of Luke if he could have.

What was interesting was that Luke held back. He'd been mad, but he hadn't gone after Arnie. She didn't know, maybe she should call Luke? But he'd told her to call only if she wanted sex, not if Arnold showed up.

Arnold and Marla walked in together, and they all sat down to eat. Marla smiled tiredly at Ivy. "I needed to keep busy. You were right, you know. I was overreacting. Freaked out, I guess. Then I felt bad; after all you and your mom found Trip, not me. So I came over to see if I could help."

Ivy picked up a sandwich. "We always feel better if we can do something."

"She did a lot," Mallory added. "Thanks, Marla. And, Arnold, I appreciate it."

Ivy looked at Arnold across the table from her. She wanted to learn more about him, try to figure out what his real motive was. "How did you become a private investigator?"

"My parents were private investigators. My dad died in a car accident and my mom kept the business going. It's in my blood, I guess."

"You specialize in recovering art?"

Arnold put down his sandwich and settled into talking. "My mother did, I've branched out some. Before going into private investigating, I worked for an armored car service, and now I investigate the employees as a PI. Many times, robberies are inside jobs. Having worked in the business, I can conduct undercover operations and catch these employees before they can get away with the theft."

Ivy could feel his passion. For the first time, she had the sense that she was seeing the real Arnold. Plus, she had seen invoices on the computer that listed some armored car services. "You sound as if you really like it."

He wrapped his hand around his iced-tea glass and inclined his head. "I do. I like matching wits with these guys. Every criminal always believes they are smarter than the system. I like disabusing them of that notion by outthinking them. For a while, I had considered going into police work, but I have more independence as a private investigator."

Marla sat up straight. "That's exciting. Do you pose as an employee? How do you do it?"

Arnold smiled. "It depends on what the company wants. But yeah, I've gone undercover as an armored car driver. I was able to gather information on two other drivers planning a heist. We had the cops there when they tried to pull off the job."

"You're not afraid? I mean what if these guys find out what you're doing? Can't they Google your name or something and find out you're a private investigator?"

"I'm careful, I don't use my real name, and I change my appearance. Just like Clark Kent and Superman, people just see what I want them to see. As a last resort, I have a gun and I know how to use it."

Chills ran down Ivy's spine. Trip had died of a gunshot wound. "A gun?"

Mallory glared at her. "He knows what he's doing. That's why he's helping me."

Marla said, "I'll help too." She turned to look at Ivy. "I love my job at the radio station, so I want to help."

Ivy nodded, "I know, thanks, Marla."

Arnold kept the conversation going with, "What's your background, Marla? How did you get into radio?"

"I wanted to sing but never really broke in. I hung around the fringes and learned a lot. I ended up working in several recording studios and radio stations over the years—"

A cell phone ring cut off the rest of what Marla had been going to say. Ivy got up, walked to her purse, and pulled out her cell. After she looked at the screen, she answered the phone. "Hi, Leah. Can I call you back later?" When she had privacy to tell her boss what they'd learned so far.

"Ivy, turn on the TV. It's your dad."

Chapter 11

"My dad?" Ivy repeated to her boss on the phone as she hurried to her mom's TV, picked up the remote, and turned it on. She heard the others coming into the living room, but she stared at the screen. "What channel?"

"*Crime Probe.*"

Damn. Ivy turned it to the channel that featured *Crime Probe.* The camera showed her dad sitting on one side of a large desk. He was cleaned up, wearing a jacket and tie. His too-long hair had been neatly cut, and makeup covered most of the broken veins on his face. He faced a serious-looking lawyer-turned-pseudo-crime-reporter, Daphne Finch.

"Mr. Beaman, have you talked to your daughter since the news broke about the murder in the radio station where she works?"

Her dad shook his head. "I've tried to reach her, of course, but she's not taking my calls."

"Are you close to your daughter?"

He looked up to the camera. "When she needs money. Otherwise, you know how kids are." He shrugged with some of the old charm that had attracted her mother.

Ivy tasted the sandwich in the back of her throat. How could he do this? What was he doing? He'd never given her money. Ivy gave him money.

"They must be paying him, that rat-bastard," her mom said from behind her left shoulder.

Daphne said, "This isn't the first time Ivy York has been in trouble, is it?"

Her dad spread his hands flat on the desk, one hand on either side of the coffee mug. "She was cleared of those charges. My Ivy is very clever."

Oh God, he made her sound like she had stolen the money and gotten away with it!

Daphne pounced. "Are you saying she outsmarted the police three years ago when the three million dollars was stolen from her clients' accounts?"

"I'm not saying that at all. Just that she's really smart. You watch, she'll turn this whole murder and theft to her advantage. She'll probably get job offers and all kinds of money and endorsements. She'll use this as a springboard from that dinky radio station to the big time. You watch."

Daphne's serious journalist voice turned giddy. "Rumor has it that she's working with the Urban Legend. Do you know anything about that?"

Her dad frowned. "What's the Urban Legend?"

"He's a famous treasure hunter known for seducing women."

"Oh, well, there was a man at her house. Could have been him. She wasn't wearing much, so I guess she was dressed for him."

She was going to throw up. A man was dead! Her mom was in trouble. And her dad was calculating how much money he could soak her for while destroying her reputation. The tragedy was that people would believe this stuff. Remembering her boss on the phone, she said, "Leah, I'm so sorry. I don't know what to do."

"We use it, that's what we do. We turn this thing around, come out swinging. Ivy, you do what you always do—tell the truth. You are working with the Urban Legend."

Between the radio show she'd heard earlier and her dad's

comments, she sounded like a slut and hypocrite. "But my dad made it sound like—"

Her boss cut her off. "So what? All you have to do is make it clear that you're using Luke, not that he's using you. He's just scratching an itch for you while finding the statues. You are being smart and not falling prey to the economic sex hex. He's not getting access to your bank accounts or anything else."

She remembered all the women who had appeared on tabloid media looking for their ten minutes of fame by claiming to have slept with Luke. She wouldn't do it. Damn the ratings and her reputation. "No, I won't do that. I refuse to discuss my sex life in any case."

"You don't have much of a choice," her boss said calmly. "Our advertisers are making ugly noises. The body was found in the radio station, and now KCEX, you, and your show are getting huge publicity. People are going to draw some nasty conclusions."

Pain clamped in a vicious band around her head. "It was a murder! People can't think we'd kill someone for publicity."

"Ivy, this is your chance to prove who you are. How you handle bad things says a lot about your character. So what if you work with, and sleep with, the Urban Legend? People will be interested and tune in to see how you, the Ice Princess, handle the ultimate bad boy. You can teach your listeners how to do it."

Was that who she was? A woman who had become that cold, that calculating? She didn't know. "We'll talk about it tomorrow." She hung up.

Ivy worked downstairs in her home office. She double-checked every thread of Trip Vaugn's financials that she could find. It was easier to think about numbers than what her father had done. It cut deeper than she would have thought possible. She shoved it away and focused on the numbers. The eight-thousand-dollar cash deposit.

The radio station was a central part of the puzzle. How did the killer get in? Had it been the original buyer? Maybe Trip had upped the price and the buyer decided he'd paid enough? So he or she killed Trip?

Was someone at the radio station connected? There were, on any given day, dozens of people in and out of the station. The different on-air personalities, sound engineers, interns, janitorial service, various repair people, her mom . . . where did she start?

She couldn't just break into everyone's bank accounts, assuming she had their information. She needed to narrow down the suspect list, then decide what to do.

She closed down Trip's screen and opened Beth Lawrence's file on the computer. It hadn't been hard to track down the account that Beth's husband had set up for himself. It was at a different bank, but the moron used the same username and password. It took a little doing, but she managed to find the bank, get into the account, and learn the grim truth. Out of the fifty thousand Beth's mom had left them, only seventeen thousand remained. They needed to act fast to save that amount. She wrote the report and planned to suggest that Beth get a lawyer on Monday and freeze that account.

At least she accomplished something tonight. She got up and arched her back. Her mom had been asleep for a couple hours. Ivy went upstairs and turned right to go down to her room.

She paused by the bedroom Luke had slept in the previous night. The one they'd made love in. In the quiet night, she wondered what it was about Luke that pulled at her? She headed down to her room and crawled beneath the cool sheets and thick comforter. She closed her eyes and fell asleep.

"Ivy, damn, you still sleep like the dead."

She jerked awake, her heart pounding. Blinking, she tried to get her eyes to focus in the gloom. She felt the weight on the side of her bed before she saw him. She opened her mouth to scream.

He slapped his hand over her mouth. "Shh, it's just me."

She bit his hand.

"Ouch, damn it!"

Ivy tried to roll the other way to get off the bed, but she was yanked back by her hair. Sharp pain made her yelp and she dropped to her back. Real fear sizzled along her spine and pressed on her bladder. The bathroom nightlight gave enough illumination for her to see Dirk Campbell. Even after three years, he still looked like a high-school football star. But his green eyes were colder than she remembered. "Dirk?" She'd never been afraid of him, but maybe she should have been.

He leaned down with a grin. "Miss me, babe?"

"What are you doing back in the States? The police—"

"I want the statues, Ivy."

"Huh?" Her brain was still trying to process that Dirk was in her bedroom at one A.M. in the morning.

His hand tightened on her hair. "The jade statues, where'd you stash them?"

"I don't have them! Did you hire Trip to steal them?" Her thoughts whirled and tumbled. She didn't remember Dirk being an art lover. But he did love money. Maybe he'd planned to turn the statues around and sell them at a profit?

His green eyes studied her. "Once I'd have believed that. God, you were dumb. But I've listened to your radio show and you've turned into a cold-hearted, money-hungry bitch. Let's see if you're still dumb. One more time, where are they?"

"I don't have them!" She started to sit up, the fear draining out as the preposterousness of the situation dawned on her.

He moved fast, letting go of her hair, then slapping her hard enough to slam her over onto her side. The pain bloomed hot and sickening, making her eyes tear up. Rage roared in her head. She kept rolling, willing the nausea back, and got to her feet on the floor.

"You prick!" her mom's voice bellowed.

Ivy managed to look up just as her mom leaped onto Dirk's back, pounding him with her fists.

Ivy reacted with sheer instinct. Diving back across the bed, she yanked open the drawer of her nightstand and grabbed the can of pepper spray.

Dirk threw her mom to the floor with a thud. Her mom shrieked and flailed around.

Taking the opportunity, Ivy aimed and shot the pepper spray into Dirk's eyes.

"Goddamned bitch!" He covered his eyes, shoved her mom with his elbow, and stumbled out of the room.

Her mom started to follow, but Ivy grabbed her. "No!" She yanked her mom into the room, slammed the door, locked it, and called 911.

Luke grabbed the phone on the second ring. He sat up and threw his legs over the side of the bed to shove away the dregs of sleep. Glancing at the clock, he saw it was two A.M. "Sterling."

"Thought you'd want to know. Had a 911 call from Ivy York's house tonight. An intruder. The guy was gone when we got there."

What the fuck? Luke shoved to his feet and started moving. "Owe you one, Mark." Slamming down the phone, he yanked on his pants, a shirt, and shoes. He grabbed his wallet, a light jacket, and his gun, then took off.

The lights were blazing at Ivy's house. Luke ran up the stairs and pounded on the door. "Ivy, it's Luke. Let me in!"

She pulled open the door and frowned. "What are you doing here?"

"I've made a couple friends on the police force in town. One of them called me." It's his standard operating procedure. Buy the cops some drinks, cooperate, and never screw 'em over. He had a solid rep and it paid off at times like this. He walked in, shut the door, and took a look at Ivy. She had on a robe, her hair was sleep mussed, and a bruise was forming on her left cheekbone. "What happened?"

She said, "Luke, it's late and—"

"Dirk Campbell broke in and hit her! That's what happened, Sterling. Where the hell were you when he was smacking Ivy, huh?" Mallory stomped from the kitchen and shoved a bag of frozen peas at Ivy. "Put it on your face." Then she turned back to Luke. "Well? What do you have to say for yourself? Thought you were protecting Ivy! If this is the way you protect my daughter, you purely suck at it!" She stormed back into the kitchen.

Luke blinked. He hadn't been dressed down like that since he'd been in basic training.

"She's in a bad mood," Ivy said dryly.

He turned back to Ivy and his gut went cold. He took a step closer. "How bad did he hurt you?"

"Just a slap. That's it. He threw my mom to the floor. As soon as her temper dies down, she's going to be hurting worse than me. I told her she needs to take a hot bath and see if she needs a doctor."

"I don't need a doctor! I need a gun. A big ugly gun to kill that ugly son of a bitch." She handed Ivy a glass of wine. "No lip from you, go sit on the couch and drink it."

Luke was really starting to like Mallory York. She might have her quirks and faults, but right now, there was no doubt she loved her daughter. He took Ivy's arm and led her to the couch.

Mallory followed them. "Do you have a gun, Sterling? With you now?"

Luke turned back to look at Ivy's mom. "Yes." He reached behind him and pulled out his Glock. "I've shot and killed. I don't miss."

Her mom nodded. "You stay with her. I mean it, none of this separate bedroom shit. I want you glued to her side. You hear me?"

She was yelling loud enough for the neighbors to hear, but in her brown eyes Luke saw tears of real fear. "Yes, ma'am. I hear you."

A knock on the door stopped him from saying anything else. He got his gun back out, and said, "Both of you stay here." He strode to the door and looked out the peephole. It took him a second to place the face he saw in the porch light. He turned to Ivy. "It's Isaac."

Ivy kept her gaze on Luke. "Let him in."

Mallory yelled, "Ivy Rose York, what did you do?"

Luke opened the door. Isaac barely glanced at him and his gun. He stalked past Luke and kept going until he was nose-to-nose with Mallory. "She called me because she said you wouldn't go to the emergency room. You're going now."

Luke shut the door, locked it, and hurried over to Ivy. This was a hell of a lot more interesting than TV.

Mallory shouted back, "I'm not leaving Ivy and you don't boss me around! I decide if I'm going to the emergency room, and I've decided I'm not! Go home and leave us alone!"

Isaac's face and nearly bald head reddened. "I'm not leaving. Not this time. You're in danger, and so is Ivy."

"Got Ivy covered," Luke said helpfully.

Ivy elbowed him.

Isaac glanced over at Luke. "Good. You stick with her, and I'll watch over Mallory."

"No, you won't!" Mallory turned on her heel and started for the door. "You're leaving."

Isaac caught her arm. "Not a chance, hellcat. Unless I'm taking you to the emergency room, I'm not budging."

Luke frowned and looked at Ivy. "He's grabbing your mom."

Ivy met his gaze. "He won't hurt her. But she could be injured. I . . ."

He nodded. "Got it. He'll force her to do what you can't."

"He won't hurt her," Ivy said again.

Isaac pulled Mallory into his body, and said, "I'll make a

deal with you. Let me take a look at your hip where you hit the ground. If it looks okay, I won't try to make you go to the emergency room tonight."

Mal's shoulders relaxed just a little bit. "I'll look," she said defiantly, but Isaac was already guiding her into the hallway, then either the bathroom or bedroom. Luke didn't care which; he'd seen what he needed to know, Isaac's careful, protective body language.

"She landed on her hip," Ivy said. "I saw him throw her down." She shuddered.

"Your mom must have run into your room when she heard something."

Ivy looked up at him with her deep blue eyes. "With no plan, no weapon, not even stopping to call 911. She'd have gone after Dirk if I hadn't stopped her."

Luke guessed that most moms were like that. Fiercely protective of their kids, even their grown-up kids. "I'm going to check out and secure the house. Tomorrow I'm getting an alarm system installed." He pushed himself up to his feet.

Ivy said, "I think Dirk got in through a window in my office downstairs."

"Go to bed, Ivy. I'll be there when I'm finished. And tell your mom and Isaac to sleep upstairs tonight." It would be easier to protect them if they stayed close by and on the same floor of the house.

Luke spent the next half hour checking every opening in the house, cutting some strips of wood to double-lock accessible windows. He briefly talked to Isaac. He and Mallory had more words, but Mallory was losing every argument. The last he saw of them, they were both going into the upstairs guest room.

Luke went into Ivy's room and had to smile. She'd lit a couple candles and had the TV on low. With any other woman, he might think seduction. With Ivy, he knew she was just comforting herself with hominess and trying to banish the memory of Dirk from her room. Probably chasing out his scent.

She looked small and lovely in her huge bed, surrounded by fluffy pillows and the thick, snowy white comforter tucked neatly under her arms. She held the bag of peas to her face after another lecture from her mom. He walked over to the bed and sat down. "Let me see, Ivy." He took the bag of peas from her. "It's not too bad."

She rolled her eyes, then winced. "It was just a slap. You and my mom are making too big a deal of it."

"The hell we are. And by the way, baby cakes, your mom has a nasty temper."

She cracked a small smile. "Thank you for staying the night. I'll get an alarm system in tomorrow and we'll be fine. Move, so I can go put these peas in the kitchen."

"Stay there. I'll take them." He grabbed the peas, dumped them in the kitchen, then went back into the room. He blew out the candles, then stripped down to his boxers. "Do you want to keep the TV on?"

"No." She picked up the remote and turned it off.

Luke slid into the bed. It was soft and comfortable. As soon as he inhaled, he smelled Ivy. The warm scent of her. The thought of Dirk scaring and smacking her ripped through him. He reached out and slid his arms around her, pulling her into his body. He just wanted her to feel safe. He had to touch her to know she was safe. "You're safe."

"I know."

He could feel her relaxing and drifting off to sleep. He closed his eyes and willed himself to sleep.

Luke tried not to step on them, but he looked down at his boots. They were covered in blood. He kept stepping on his dead and bloody friends. Only this time it was worse . . . Ivy was one of them. "No!"

"Luke, wake up."

He woke up to see Ivy on her knees and leaning over him. *It was a dream, just a dream.* He reached out and took a handful of her hair, it felt warm and silky. She was safe and alive. "I woke you?"

"Nightmare?" she asked softly.

Framed by the thin glow of the nightlight she kept in her bathroom, her eyes shimmered with concern. Mixed with the feel of her silky hair wrapped around his palm and her soft hand on his chest, it made him feel vulnerable. Almost like he had something to lose. It was the fucking nightmare, seeing her dead and mutilated. The nightmares were what kept him a loner—he didn't get attached to people who vanished from his life, sometimes brutally. His life was about chasing down legends, art, and jewelry, the stuff that lasted. Not people with their fragile lives and even more fragile commitments.

All he was after was the statues.

He let go of her hair and made his voice harsh. "Go back to sleep. I'll spend the rest of the night on the floor."

A line marred the smooth space between her eyes. "Don't be stupid." She stretched out next to him and burrowed into his side. "Do you want sex? Will it help you sleep?" She ran her hand over his chest.

Holy Christ. His dick jerked enthusiastically while his belly warmed and coiled with raw, aching need. His mouth dried, and blood pounded through his body. He wanted her, needed her. That thought scared the shit out of him. Terrified him. He grabbed her wrist, flipped her onto her back, and covered her with his body. Looking down at her, he growled out, "Don't try to fix me."

Her breathing grew shallow and a faint heat washed across her cheekbones. "I'm ready to get naked."

She threw his own words back at him. "That so?" He was so fired up, so blasted hard, his body primed and ready for release. He knew he shouldn't do this, knew he was using her. Knew it.

Didn't care.

Couldn't stop.

His heart pounded in time with his dick. Only the faint

bruise on her cheek kept him from devouring her mouth. Instead, he reached down and shoved up her top.

In the faint light, he saw the pale mounds of her breasts with mouth-wateringly dark nipples, and nothing would stop him. He slid down and lapped at the underside of her breast, feeling the shiver wrack her; then he sucked her long nipple in the heat of his mouth. He used his thumb and finger to gently squeeze the other nipple.

Her fingers dug into his shoulders, her body lifting beneath his.

He dragged his hand from her tit, down her belly and beneath her shorts and panties. Spreading her folds, he found her hot and slick, and Jesus, the feel of her on his fingers intensified his craving—a primitive, bone-deep demand that he sink his cock into her, into the sweet oblivion that was Ivy. He took his hand from her long enough to get to his feet, skim off his boxers, grab his last condom, and shove it on.

He looked at her on the bed. Her hair was messed up, her little tank shoved up to her neck, her shorts yanked partway down. And then she moved, shoving her shorts all the way down and off. He saw her from her breasts, down her belly, the pale curls of her hair and her long legs. Dragging his gaze up to her face, he clenched his fists to hold himself in place. "This what you want?"

She looked away. "Yes."

"Just sex." He pushed harder.

She looked back at him. "I want you."

Damn it. He should run like hell, but instead he put his knee on the bed and slid his hand between her thighs, stroking her clit and down her folds. He refused to let himself close his eyes and inhale her the way he wanted to; instead, he watched her face. Watched the shivers of pleasure that tightened her nipples and made her eyes half close. "This is what you want, Ivy." He slid one finger into her and took it back out. Then in again. "You want the pleasure. You want to come. I can give you that."

She stared at him, a helpless look sliding over her face. "Luke . . ."

"No, damn it." He stroked her clit with his thumb. She was getting hotter, wetter; her walls were tightening. He added a second finger inside of her. "You want to come, Ivy. Say it."

She closed her eyes. "Please."

He hadn't ever hated himself as much as he did in that moment. When he'd made her admit to a half truth to get a little wash of please. A little release. Something he should have given her without conditions. But he was too fucked up and he knew it. Instead, he leaned over her and sucked her nipple while he stroked her deeply with his fingers and his thumb circling her clit.

She held on to his shoulders, panting, and then her voice broke into soft cries as she came.

The noises she made drove him over the edge to madness, it was an excruciating ache to be inside her. He pulled himself up her body, spread her thighs, and pushed himself in.

Bliss. She was bliss. Her small hands ran over his shoulders and held him close. Luke buried his face in berry-scented hair and thrust. High. Deep. Going where only he could go inside of Ivy. She began to pitch her hips, and icy-hot pleasure ripped through him. He forgot everything but her, her body taking him, and her cries against his shoulder as she came again. The feel of her orgasm milked him until white-hot pleasure raced down his spine and exploded as he shoved himself deep inside of her. He pulsed endlessly, pouring out everything he had inside of Ivy.

She tried to gentle him by stroking her hand down his back in a comforting rhythm.

With his lust spent, what returned was a yawning ugliness inside of him. Luke pulled out of her, slid off her body, and went into the bathroom to get rid of the condom.

When he came back in, Ivy had pulled on her shorts and straightened the covers. She looked like a princess.

He wanted her again. He wanted to make slow, easy love

to her, tell her that she'd never have to beg him for an orgasm. Prove to her he wasn't a complete bastard.

But he was.

So he walked to his side of the bed, snatched the pillow off, and sank to his knees to slap the pillow down on the carpet. He would leave her the hell alone.

"Luke?"

Her voice floated over the bed and ripped open the hunger for her. Then he remembered her as she had appeared in his nightmare—bloody and dead—and the hunger turned to pain. "I'm sleeping on the floor." He put his head on the pillow and willed his body to calm down and relax. After that orgasm, he should be comatose, but instead, he was edgy.

He heard her breathing. Forced breathing. The kind everyone does when they try to pretend they are okay. In-out, in-out, pause, shudder, deep careful breath, let it out, in-out, *shit*. "Do you need ice or Advil for your face?" Maybe her face hurt. He knew he was being cruel, but it was better this way. He'd warned her, told her he was good for sex and nothing else. Somehow she slipped something else in. She was trying to comfort him with sex that was more than sex.

Finally, she answered in a soft voice. "It's okay. I took some before we went to bed. You can sleep up here, I'll stay on my side."

Her careful words made him grit his teeth. "I don't want to wake you with another nightmare. I'm fine on the floor."

He heard rustling, then Ivy was leaning over, covering him with her thick comforter.

Jesus. How was a man supposed to keep his priorities in line when a woman did shit like that? "It's not you."

She laughed. "That's a break-up line, Sterling. 'It's not you, it's me. I need space.' You can't break up with me because we're not dating. We just had sex. No big deal." She patted his shoulder, then retreated to the bed.

The second her hand left his shoulder, he felt the loss. "I don't usually date women twice." He wanted her to understand.

"Got it."

But he hadn't really dated her, had he? No, he hadn't taken her to dinner, made her laugh and complimented her until they'd both wanted sex. He'd used her. *Twice.* And he wanted to use her again. Sex was real, feelings were not. He closed his eyes, determined to shut it all out.

"Have you ever been in love, Luke?"

He snapped his eyes open. "No."

"Then we're more alike than you think. Love makes you weak, vulnerable. Stupid. Love is a choice, but people act like it's a compulsion. An illness they can't fight. Who wants to be out of control like that?"

She was talking about her mom. "You loved Dirk," he pointed out.

"Exactly. And because I decided to love him, I didn't see what I should have."

It was weird talking to her from the floor. He couldn't see her, it was nearly dark, and it didn't seem as odd of a conversation as it probably was. Curious, he said, "Have you ever loved anyone else?"

She didn't say anything for a bit. The only sound was their breathing. Then she answered, "Once, back in high school."

"What happened with the boy in high school?"

"Turned out he didn't like brainy girls after all. He was using me to get to my mother. My mom was the hot mom. Always the hot mom. I used to be so embarrassed . . ." she trailed off into silence.

He winced for her. Luke had seen pictures of Ivy in high school. She looked like a cheerleader now, but then she'd looked gawky and brainy. But her own mother? "Your mom didn't . . ."

"No, my mom tried to warn me, but I didn't listen. Later, he told his friends he was banging my mom and I was too stupid to know. It got all around the school."

He felt for her. God, no wonder she didn't trust her own judgment. "Ivy, are you sure your mom—"

She snorted, the sound carrying her amusement. "My mom showed up at his football practice and told him—in front of his jock friends—that she doesn't date little boys so knock off the lies because they just proved he was a little boy not a man. Oh, and if she ever heard him say one thing against her daughter, she'd tell everyone that he'd tried but couldn't get it up."

Lying on his back, he stacked his hands under his head. Her quilt was soft compared with the hardness of the floor beneath him. "Damn, you're mom's a scary woman. But she obviously loves you."

"I know that. I've always known that. No matter how awkward or bad things got, I knew my mom loved me."

His gut hollowed out. The emptiness inside of him echoed. He didn't know what that felt like, but he was damned glad that Ivy had it.

"What about you, Luke? Ever been in love?"

She hadn't bought his denial the first time. How was it that Ivy always saw the real him? He opened his mouth to launch a sarcastic reply, but instead he said, "Once. In high school just like you. Her name was Kelly and she was another foster kid. I was a hellion and in trouble all the time, but for her, I'd have done anything, even become clean-cut and respectable. She might have changed my life." He hadn't thought of her in years. He never wanted to think of her. But it seemed okay in the mostly dark room, with him on the floor and Ivy in the bed where he couldn't touch her or see her.

"What happened?"

The memories surprised him. He hadn't really *felt* in so long, then suddenly he was back in high school and Kelly was gone. He'd loved her, adored her, wanted to be a better man for her. She had been a reason to fight and struggle and to just plain try, damn it. She'd been his reason for breathing; then she just disappeared from his life. He didn't want to talk about it anymore, except the words slipped out, "One day she was just gone. Vanished. I went berserk, threatened her foster parents if they didn't tell me where she was. They told me she'd been moved to a new foster home in the middle of the night to get her away from me. That I was a dangerous influence, a bad seed, etc. I went to my case worker and pleaded with her to help me find Kelly. Eventually, she convinced me that Kelly was better off away from me."

Ivy said nothing.

Luke wondered if she had fallen asleep. Or if she didn't know what to say because really, what the hell was he doing telling her this shit? It changed nothing.

"She didn't fight for you."

His throat hurt with the effort of holding back the old anger. The rage. The knowledge that he simply hadn't been worth fighting for. Or even a goddamned phone call. Since the clusterfuck of not getting his friends out of harm's way, he had pretty much stopped feeling. Until now.

Until Ivy.

"Go to sleep, Princess."

"Why do you call me that?"

Because to him, that's what she was. A princess. He'd never have her, not really. A woman like Ivy was the real thing. Honest, loyal—look at her loyalty to her mom. Luke admired the hell out of that. She fought for her mom tooth and nail, going so far as to beg him for help when she hated everything Luke stood for.

That was what Luke's deepest desire had always been. If those statues truly had power, they had unearthed his raw, aching, painful need for real love from a woman who would fight for him. The need that he had successfully suppressed. The risk was too great, too horrible. His nightmare had shown him that he couldn't survive loving and losing. Hell, he didn't even know how to love, or be in a family. Or in a relationship. He just didn't know. His life was about puzzles and sex.

Ivy was the princess he'd never have. To answer her, he said, "Because you're a princess in your sound booth where you can cast out your judgments about others but don't have to take any real risks yourself."

Chapter 12

"Today on *Stranger Than Fiction*, Ivy York, talk show host of the popular radio show, the *Economic Sex Hex,* is joining us."

"Hello, Whitney, thank you for having me," Ivy replied, struggling to keep her voice calm and confident as she sat in the sound booth at KCEX radio station on Sunday morning. Leah worked the control board, capturing Ivy's interview that she was doing with another radio station to run pieces on Ivy's show tomorrow.

Whitney recapped the events of the Jade Goddesses being stolen, Trip's murder, rumors of the Urban Legend, and any other scandalous piece of gossip possible. Then she asked, "Isn't this whole situation something right out of your sex hex warnings? I mean, how could a woman reputed to be as smart as Professor Regina Parker allow a bad boy like Trip Vaugn to get her statues?"

Ivy slid into her professional skin. "Yes and no. My theories are just that, theories. They are meant to warn women, and some men really, to take care of their economic health. But in real life, we're dealing with real people. Professor Regina Parker is a smart, savvy woman, indeed. But she's also human. Trip made himself useful to her, and somehow just became part of her life without setting off alarm bells. It happens all the time."

"So you don't blame the professor?"

"No, what's the point in blame? It happened, and now we try to fix it. What's really sad is that Trip Vaugn had to pay with his life. The police, of course, are doing everything they can to find the murderer."

"Including looking at your mom as a possible suspect."

"I can't comment directly on that, but I will say the police are doing their job, and everyone is cooperating. We all want the same thing, the killer caught and the statues returned to the professor where they belong." Ivy was careful with her answers relating to the theft and murder, as instructed by KCEX lawyers.

"This is where it gets really sticky for you personally. Your father went on TV and made insinuations that you have gotten away with stealing in the past."

Her stomach clenched and her palms grew warm and damp, but training kept her voice smooth. "I was exonerated of that theft. The police know exactly who stole that money, and they will get him if he dares to set foot back in the States." She took a breath, letting that threat float out to Dirk and hoped he choked on it. Then she went on, "And I think it's important to point out that I hadn't even seen my father in well over a decade until I started getting some attention with my radio show. My father and I are not, nor have we ever been, close."

"Did the lack of a father in your life help form some of your opinions that some men never grow up and just go from boys to bad boys who use women?"

Hearing questions phrased like that made her blink in surprise. "There are good and bad men, and shades in between, just as there are good and bad women. What I strive to do on my show is to give women the tools to protect themselves. The tools work for men as well."

"But you do focus on bad boys. Particularly the Urban Legend. You've criticized him repeatedly on your show, and now your name is being linked with his. Talk about stranger than fiction!"

Ivy's mouth went dry. She glanced at Leah, and then her

heart sped up. Luke had shown up a few minutes ago; he stood in the control room with his arms crossed, dividing his glare between her and Leah. Realizing she had dead air, she jumped into an answer. "I can't control how my name is linked with the Urban Legend. All I can say is that it's true that he's looking for the statues, and I hope he finds them." She grabbed her water bottle and took a sip. It was tempting to blurt out the truth: He's a better lover than the rumors, and a better man than she'd given him credit for. But the sting of being rejected after sex helped keep her mouth shut. What was Luke doing here?

"Are you in a relationship with the Urban Legend?" Whitney's voice was tinged with conspiracy. "All the women out there are dying to know if he's as good as everyone says!"

She set the water bottle down, trapped in Luke's stare. "No, we're not in a relationship. We both want the statues and murderer found. That's all." *Well, except that he's turned me into a sex addict. I throw myself at him and beg him for sex. But he probably gets that a lot.* She saw Luke's jaw clench tighter and wondered at it.

Disappointment colored Whitney's next words. "Oh. But would you really admit it if you were? I mean, people are calling you a hypocrite."

Recalling Luke's words about her last night, she looked away from him. "Right now, I'm more concerned with finding the killer and the statues than my career or what people think of me."

Whitney ended the interview. Off the air, she thanked Ivy and said, "I did an interview with Professor Parker a couple months ago. She wouldn't talk about the Urban Legend either. Can't blame a girl for trying."

"Regina and Luke are just friends," Ivy said absently.

"I really tried just to spice up her tale about those statues. I mean, who wants to hear old legends? Now the flesh-and-blood, extremely hot Urban Legend, that's what gets people listening. I told her that she should get him to talk about the statues on the air." Whitney laughed, then said, "Gotta go. Thanks again."

Ivy sighed and considered hiding out in the sound booth until Luke went away. But she couldn't do that, other people needed the booth. Besides, she was tired of being a coward. She took off her headset, got up, and walked out.

Luke demanded, "What the hell were you thinking leaving without waking me up?"

"I have a job to do," she said in a quiet voice, hoping to bring down the tension in the room.

Leah leaned back in her chair, picked up her coffee, and enjoyed the show.

Luke took a step toward Ivy. "Dirk is skulking around somewhere and he wants those statues. He's risking his freedom by coming back to this country to get them. He obviously thinks you have them. That bruise is nothing compared to what he might do to you if he gets a hold of you again. Especially after your veiled threat in there!"

Why was he yelling at her? "Isaac walked me out to my car, and Leah met me in the parking lot. We have extra security here, Luke. I'm being careful, so quit yelling at me! I'd think you'd be happy I wasn't there when you woke up!" She wanted to smack herself for that last comment.

His gray eyes narrowed. Then he turned away from her to demand from Leah, "What was so important that you are willing to risk Ivy's life?"

Leah's eyebrows shot up into her curly hair. "Damage control. Ivy's show is important."

"Ah."

Ivy didn't like his tone. "Ah what?"

Luke stared her down. "You'd risk your life for that damned show."

Why exactly was he so mad? "I'm not risking my life, I'm doing my job. It was a phone interview with another radio station, and we'll use some of it on my show as well. I also taped a quick interview with Roland Meyers, my old boss that fired me. He absolutely stated that I was cleared of any involvement with stealing that money."

Luke narrowed his gaze. "Why would he do that? You're the one who allowed Dirk access to the accounts."

She tried simple logic. "Because I let him know that Dirk was back in the country. I also called the detective on the case to let him know. Mr. Meyers appreciated that I'm trying to help."

Long seconds ticked off before he said, "Bullshit. What are you not telling me, Ivy? How the hell did you pull together an interview with Meyers and the radio show in such a short time?"

She should have known he wouldn't fall for it. "Okay, fine, it was Pierce Jordan's idea. He called me this morning. He saw the interview with my dad and had an idea how to handle it. Then he talked to Mr. Meyers and got him to agree to do the taped piece with me. And his client is the host for *Stranger Than Fiction;* so he was able to pull some strings. I guess he got Regina on the show a month or two ago."

Luke's entire body puffed up, sort of like a ticked-off bullfrog. "Pierce Jordan isn't a man who gives away favors without a price."

Getting tired of this conversation, she said, "That's not your problem."

Luke's gray eyes turned mirror hard. "Fine. You want to climb your way to fame, I'm not going to stand in your way. All I want is the statues."

She hated the truth of that last statement. She hated standing so close to him, close enough to smell the rich scent of him, and that she was nothing more than a convenient orgasm to him. He made that clear last night when he'd chosen to sleep on the floor rather than next to her. He cared about the statues, not her. Dirk was another clue, and Luke meant to be close by her because that's where the clues were showing up. She refused to let him see how much it bothered her, refused to let him know how she'd fallen into the sex hex just like the women who called in to her show. "I'm going to go over all the employee records and see if I can find some trail. Maybe someone listed Trip Vaugn somewhere on their employee records. I'll be fine here, you can go do whatever."

He ground his jaw and a nerve jumped in his temple. "Don't go anywhere else without telling me. I'll be at your house installing a security system."

Oh no. She wasn't depending on him, on anyone. Ivy had rules for a reason. "No need. I'll take care of it."

His face flushed. "Your lawyer friend doesn't know shit about electronics, baby cakes. That's my expertise. I'll install the damned system." He turned and left.

That's what did it, what kept her from being able to believe that Luke was the cold, emotionless man he wanted her to think he was. He cared enough to make sure there was an alarm installed and done correctly. It made her grind her teeth that he just wouldn't fit into the categories of men that she understood—either bad boy or nice guy. And worse, she knew no one had ever fought for Luke, showed him that he was worth it.

Sex hex, damn it. She was falling so deep and hard she should do a reality TV show on herself. TALK SHOW HOST SUCCUMBS TO SEX HEX WHEN SHE FALLS FOR DAMAGED AND DANGEROUS BAD BOY. WATCH EACH EPISODE AS SHE DESPERATELY TRIES TO FIX BAD BOY WHILE COLLECTING NIFTY ORGASM.

Leah interrupted her thoughts. "He's really hot."

Ivy turned to her boss. "Oh, shut up."

She grinned. "Well, he is. Did you see his butt in those jeans? Those arms? That chest? Is he any good in bed?"

Yes. Not that she cared. She was going to stop caring right this Goddamned-freaking-second. But Luke was a generous lover. Until him, she hadn't realized what she'd been missing. She'd sat behind her microphone and preached vibrators and good money sense. But she really hadn't understood that a woman could become addicted to a man. To the touch of his hand . . .

"That good, huh?" Leah's voice was smug.

God, Ivy *had* to get control of herself. "I'll be in my office." She walked into the hall, turned right, and went into her little sanctuary. Her safe place where everything was supposed to make sense.

Yet, she still felt edgy. Her skin tingled, her throat was tight, and her stomach was knotted. She couldn't concentrate—her brain seemed to keep tuning in to the Luke Channel. Luke sleeping, Luke making love to her, Luke talking to her, Luke laughing . . . Enough. She was in control of her own actions. She went to her filing cabinet, pulled out a stack of employee files, and started work. She refused to think about Luke.

Three hours later, her eyes burned, her back ached, and her stomach was on strike from coffee.

"I brought you a burrito."

Ivy's heart slammed up into her throat. "Luke! God. You scared the bejeebers out of me!"

He arched an eyebrow. "Bejeebers?"

She shrugged. "My mom. When I was little and got scared, she used to call it the bejeebers."

He smiled, set the bag down on the desk, and started pulling out food.

The smell made her stomach growl. "Thanks for the food. You didn't have to do this."

He set a burrito and iced tea in front of her. "I needed to check on you and figured I'd better bring food to get back on your good side."

"Good plan." She dug into her burrito. She hoped it was the food that lightened her mood and not Luke. "Did you get the system installed?"

"No sweat. I'll show you how to use it later. I've already shown your mom and Isaac."

She'd seen Isaac this morning while her mom slept. He'd looked tired and harassed. She hadn't known what else to do but to call him to watch over her mom. No one else could possibly understand how scared she was of losing her mom.

"You did the right thing."

"What?" She looked up from the burrito.

"Isaac. He and your mom have been bickering all day, but I'm dead sure he'd protect your mom with his life. Stop second-guessing yourself."

He knew what she was thinking. How did he do that? But she supposed it was his job as a private investigator. After all, she'd begged him to help save her mom. She'd told him she would do anything to protect her mom. Changing the subject, she got onto more comfortable ground. "So you're an electronics whiz?"

"I'm good with electronics."

"Where'd you learn it?"

"Military."

Sarcastically, she said, "Wait, not so fast, I can't keep up with all this information you're tossing out."

A grin spread over his face. "It's not that interesting. I can fly most any plane or helicopter and I'm good at electronics. Pretty good at explosives. Deadly with a gun. I also play a mean game of hoops."

She took that in. "Why'd you stop flying when you left the military?"

He stopped eating, his gaze settling heavily on her. "I'm grounded."

"Oh." She didn't quite know what that meant, but she could see it was a sore subject. "About the security system. How much do I owe you?"

He just kept staring. Finally, he said, "The shrinks grounded me. After that, I left the military."

He was giving her pieces of himself. Trust. It was like a fragile bird in her palm. She wanted to hold it carefully and guard it with all she had. "Why were you grounded? The nightmares?"

"Post-Traumatic Stress Disorder is what the head-shrinkers said. Flashbacks of landing my helicopter on top of . . ." He looked down at the food and seemed to change his mind. "Never mind. The point is that Arnie's right about me being screwed up. Just not the way he wants you to believe."

Her stomach dropped to her thighs. She reached across her desk, taking his hand.

He looked up at her. "There you go again. You're going to get hurt." He said the words softly.

Maybe, but no power could stop her from touching him. Trying to ease him. She hated the loneliness that rode Luke hard. Somehow he believed that he deserved to be alone. "I'm just being a friend. No strings attached."

Luke took his hand out from under hers. "Hand me half of the files you have left to look at."

She let it go. There were only a few files left. She handed him two and opened the next one herself. It was Marla Rimmer. Her eyes were tired, the words were blurring. She had to force her eyes to focus. Her last address was . . . "Sherman Oaks. Well, that's a coincidence. That's where Pierce Jordan has his office."

Luke jerked his gaze up from the file. "I don't believe in coincidences."

"And she worked at a recording studio. I checked her reference there, everything seemed fine." She frowned. Did it really mean anything?

Luke set his files on the desk. "What did she do at the recording studio?"

"Sound engineer." Ivy liked Marla in a colleague way. But now things were starting to bother her. "She was so freaked at Trip's death. I mean, she wouldn't do her job, Leah sent her home."

"That bothers you?"

"She seems so I've-seen-it-all. Nothing throws her on the air." Ivy shifted her gaze from the file to Luke. "But like you said, murder is different."

"When did Marla start?"

"Six weeks ago." Ivy's mind kept turning. "It's just kind of odd that she lived in the same town as Pierce Jordan and worked at a recording studio. He's an entertainment lawyer . . ." She didn't know where she was going.

"His girlfriend, Simone Waters, was a singer. I didn't get much on her without a birth date or social. I was going to follow up on that Monday . . ."

Ivy felt a shiver of excitement hiss inside her. "Yesterday, Marla said, 'I wanted to sing, but never really broke in. I hung around the fringes and learned a lot. I ended up working in several recording studios and radio stations over the years.' What if her stage name was Simone Waters? What if she was Pierce's girlfriend?" Okay, it was a leap. A big one. Luke would laugh at her.

Instead, he said reasonably, "Go online. Get a picture of Simone Waters." Then he got up and came around the desk to watch.

Ivy Googled the name, and finally, she came up with a head shot.

Luke leaned down so that his breath touched her face. "Well, what do you know. That's quite a hunch, Ivy. It looks like Marla does have a connection to Jordan. Can you get into her bank accounts? See if there's an eight-thousand-dollar withdrawal somewhere? Let's get facts."

Ivy studied her paperwork. "Marla has her paycheck automatically deposited. Maybe. I have the bank, the checking account number, her birth date, and her social security number. But I need to figure out her username and password." She flipped pages in the file, trying to get to know Marla. "Username is most likely her name. People usually keep it simple." She turned to her computer.

Luke sat down on the desk, watching over her shoulder. "We need to figure out the connection between Pierce Jordan and Marla."

Ivy called up the bank's Web site; then she put "Marla Rimmer" in the username space, then tried "Rimmer31" for the password—Marla's last name plus her age.

That failed.

She dropped her hands, studying the screen. "I don't know enough to do this." She turned her chair to look at Luke.

"We have to think. Let's say Marla hired Trip. Is she in it with Pierce? Or did she learn of the statues through Pierce and decide she wanted them?" Ivy turned back to the screen. What was she missing? "Could Marla really be a killer? Could the statues drive her to kill? Did the statues bring out something in Marla, some deep desire, then Trip got in the way? Or was it just money?"

"Anyone can kill if they have enough motivation," Luke said softly.

"So we need to know what motivated Marla. She seems so confident and competent." Ivy liked her calm, straightforward manner. "She obviously knew her way around a sound board and a radio station, and she had a connection to . . . oh, I have an idea." She pulled up Google and typed in "Marla Rimmer and Pierce Jordan." Several items popped up. Social functions where the two of them were photographed. Ivy started pulling up the files. "It seems like Marla, as Simone Waters, was singing in clubs and trying to find her break. But then a few months ago, she just stopped. What happened?" She looked over her shoulder.

"She got too old," Luke said. "But how does that connect her to the statues?"

Ivy thought about it. "The economic sex hex."

"What?"

She kept thinking out loud. "Okay, she had it all right? She's dating a successful lawyer, she's ready to break out, and then it all falls apart. Women have to be young and sexy to make it in entertainment. And they usually don't make as much as their male counterparts, but that's not the point."

Luke smirked. "And yet, you did get it in there."

Ignoring that, she said, "She can't do anything about the career, right? But what about her boyfriend? Did Pierce drop her because she's old news? Did Marla really love him? Is she being *stupid* over a man? So determined to get him back that . . ."

He finished her sentence, "She'd steal the statues she knows he wants." Luke stood up, pacing around behind her desk. "Maybe even believing that if she got those statues, she'd get Pierce."

Ivy swung her chair around, switched the screen back to Marla's bank, and typed in the username of "Marla Rimmer." For password, she used, "Mjordan31." And she was in. "Holy cow! It worked!" Damn, she was good!

Luke leaned over her to watch the screen.

"Let's see what her account activity has been." She clicked through to get to recent savings account activity."

Luke whistled softly. "Damn, Ivy. There it is. Eight-thousand-dollar withdrawal a couple weeks ago."

A shiver raced over her skin. "It really is Marla. She's a thief. She hired Trip. But did she kill him?"

"I'm going to talk to her."

Ivy looked up to his face. "We need to tell the police, Luke."

He looked right back. "We're going to. But I want those statues. They are Regina's life's work. If Marla knows where they are, I am going to find them. But if someone else stole them out from under her, she may know who."

She got it. Luke wanted to talk to Marla before the police made her unreachable. "Okay, let's go."

The apartment building had about 200 units off Foothill Boulevard in Claremont. They found Marla's unit and knocked. There was no answer.

"What now?" Ivy asked. She was so out of her element and still stunned that she had hired a woman who was using the radio station to pass stolen merchandise, and maybe murder. "Do you think she's skipped? Left town?"

Luke reached into his pocket and pulled out a tool of some kind. "Let's take a look." He glanced around, then dropped to one knee and slid a thin doohickey into the lock.

Horrified, Ivy said, "You can't break in!"

He kept his gaze on what he was doing, but he smirked. "Sugar, you just broke in to a bank account. I wouldn't be throwing stones." He turned the doorknob, stood, and stepped in. "Hello? Marla?"

Ivy heard the empty echo of the apartment. "She's not here. We have to leave."

Luke grabbed her arm, tugged her into the apartment, and shut the door. "You can stand here and struggle with your precious integrity, but I'm going to look for any leads or clues." He turned away and walked through the apartment.

"But we broke in to Marla's house!"

Luke strode across the copper-colored living room carpet to the desk pushed up against a wall. "She paid Trip to steal the statues from Regina. Which is worse?" Holding a stack of papers, he turned and looked at her. "Or have you forgotten that your mom was implicated in this mess? Pick a side, Ivy. You don't get to play for both teams."

He turned his back on her, his shoulder and neck muscles tight and bulging beneath his T-shirt. She was being stupid, she knew it. But the fear constantly brewed and simmered in the very pit of her belly. The fear that her life would blow up in her face again if she didn't keep tight control of it.

Newsflash, she thought, it had blown up. And Luke was trying to help her fix it. So why was she giving him a hard time?

Because she was scared. Always scared. No matter how confident and professional she may look to others, inside, Ivy was always scared. Never sure that she could trust her own judgment. Forcing herself to ignore the fear, she said, "Tell me what to do."

Without looking at her, he said, "Trust me." He dropped into the chair and booted up Marla's computer.

Taking a deep breath, she looked around the living room. It had a couch, TV, and stereo system with shelves. Music, Marla loved music. She had wanted to be a singer. It all just sort of tumbled through Ivy's mind. The kitchen was to the left. She could see the white refrigerator over the bar. On the right of Luke were two doors. He had already looked in there, obviously to make sure Marla wasn't asleep in the bedroom or in the bathroom. Finally, she walked over to Luke. "What are you doing?"

"Seeing what she's been surfing. People research every-thing on the Internet." His voice was cool, efficient. "Regina's Web site on the Jade Goddesses, including the legend page. Wedding planners. Blogs. PMS relief. Armored car companies. *Variety* magazine, *Entertainment Weekly.* There's also you and your mom. She's been doing searches on you. Nothing on Trip Vaugn. But I'm there as the Urban Legend and so is Sterling Investigations."

Standing at his shoulder, she looked at the drop-down screen that showed Marla's last visited Internet sites. She was stuck on the fact that Marla researched her and her mom. Okay, it made sense that Marla would research her before she was hired on, but now? And why search out her mom? What was Marla doing? "We are sure she hired Trip, then something went wrong. I don't think she has the statues or she'd be gone . . ." Ivy stopped talking, abruptly heading through the opened door into Marla's bedroom.

"What?" Luke called after her.

"Maybe she ran. Maybe she got the statues back somehow and left." The room had a double bed in the middle and an old dresser parked next to a single-door closet. Ivy went to the chest of drawers and pulled open the one on top.

Underwear.

Very few women leave without their underwear unless they are in danger. She checked the other drawers—more clothes.

The closet had clothes, shoes, purses, and belts.

She went into the bathroom through the sliding door from the bedroom. It also had an entrance from the living room, and Luke stood there watching her. She checked the medicine cabinet. Toothbrush, birth control, and a couple prescriptions. Going through the drawer and cabinet, she found makeup, cleaning products, hair dryer, hot rollers. She stood up. "Marla didn't pack up and leave. I don't think she has the statues; she's still looking for them."

"Okay, that tells us she plans to come back to the apartment. She drove somewhere in her car since it isn't in her parking space. I'm going back to check out her desk."

Ivy followed him out. "So what was she looking for in searching us out?"

"The statues, I think." Luke settled into the desk chair. He opened drawers and rummaged through them. Peeking into bill envelopes, looking in cases for glasses, folders, looking everywhere. "Ah," he said, pulling out a folder. He opened it. "Here's a statement for cashing out a fifteen-thousand-dollar 401K. Just recently. She paid the penalties." Frowning, he looked up at Ivy. "Where's the money? Is that part of the eight thousand that was withdrawn from her account?"

"I'm betting she had it in cash to pay off the statues. Or it could be in another bank." She tried to think.

Luke set the folder down, reached into the middle drawer, and pulled out a desk calendar. The type that lay open, each page a single day. It was still on yesterday's date. Scrawled on there was a phone number. "Recognize it?" Luke asked while pulling his cell phone out. He put the number in and hit Send.

"No." She couldn't figure it out.

"No answer, generic voice mail." Luke hung up. He flipped back and stopped on Thursday. There was a notation: "T.V., midnight KCEX."

"T.V., that has to be for Trip Vaugn. He was murdered Thursday night or early Friday morning. Marla must have been going to buy the statues from Trip at KCEX at midnight since the station is off the air during the dark hours. So what happened? How did Trip end up dead and Marla without the statues?"

"Trip met with someone else," Luke said, drumming his fingers on his thigh while staring at the calendar. Then he turned it to Friday. In dark shaky ink, it read, "Find them!" It was underlined over and over.

"You're right. So Trip must have met with another buyer before Marla. Then Marla showed up—"

"And Trip was dead. But she saw enough to think she could find the killer who stole the statues. Blackmail." Luke shook his head. "Very stupid. Whoever it is already killed once." He grabbed a sheet of printer paper and copied down everything. "And if it's her boyfriend, Pierce—"

Ivy finished it, "She might try to blackmail him to marry her." Why would someone want to be married that badly? To a person who didn't want them?

Luke looked up, startled. "Well, women have been blackmailing men into marriage since the beginning of time. But they usually do it with pregnancy."

She made a face at him. "Get serious."

He folded up the paper and stuck it in his pants pocket. "I'm serious. As I was saying, if Pierce used Marla to get him the statues, then somehow swooped in and got them himself, killing Trip—"

"Marla's in danger."

"Grave danger."

"I thought you checked his alibi, that he was in New York when Trip was killed."

"I did, I checked out the airline tickets he told me about. It doesn't mean he didn't take another flight back to the West Coast, killed Trip, snatched the statues, then hurried back to the East Coast." Luke flipped through the calendar, backward and forward.

Everything else was just appointments and reminders, nothing helpful.

"We'd better go. I'm going to see if my Web group has any information on Marla and do a full background check. I think we need to take a drive up to Sherman Oaks and drop in on Pierce Jordan at home. See if Marla is there. Talk to him. Pressure him."

"We have to tell the police—" Ivy's cell phone rang before she could finish her thought. She pulled it out. "It's my mom, I'd better answer."

Chapter 13

York Interior Designs looked like a tornado had blown through. It was a small office off Indian Hills Boulevard that Mallory had decorated herself. Very Victorian, and decorated with dollhouses that she had built. Little replicas of dream homes exquisitely decorated.

They were set on specially made tables and positioned to be the first thing customers saw when they entered.

Now they were destroyed. Crushed.

Mallory slid to her knees amid the splintered woods, broken china, ripped fabric . . . It was all too much. She didn't care about the rest of the office. She lifted a miniature girl's bed set that Ivy had painted white with pink flowers, and Mallory had draped with pink netting. A little girl's fantasy.

Ruined.

"We have to call the police," Isaac said behind her in a voice frosted with fury.

She got up and walked through the office toward the back room, noting that her handpicked pieces, desk, conference table, chairs, and tea service were all destroyed. Drawers had been dumped, pictures pulled down off the walls . . . "They were looking for something."

"The statues. Jesus Christ, Mallory!" Isaac exploded.

She kept walking across the luxurious carpet and didn't look at him. She felt nothing but grief for the dollhouses.

Nothing else. She would not feel a damned thing about Isaac and his blasted accusations. Because she knew they were coming. "You're my lawyer, nothing more. Start acting like it. Call the police and do lawyer stuff." She disappeared into the back room.

Isaac followed her, got in her face, and stared down at her. "Was he worth it? That's all I want to know. Was the sex worth all this?"

She hated him almost as much as she hated herself. "Yes." She pushed by him and went past the counter that held a sink and coffeepot with a half fridge underneath and stopped to look around. The back room she used to display drapery, wall treatments, and various other decorations, as well as storage.

It was ravaged like the rest of her office.

"The police will be here shortly."

"Fine." She pulled out her cell phone and called Ivy, just like she always did when she was in trouble. One day she'd call and her daughter just wouldn't answer anymore.

Just like her parents.

God.

Ivy answered her phone with, "Mom? Where are you?"

Her throat tightened, but she fought it. "My office. It's been broken into. Someone destroyed it, everything." It was all she could say. Squeezing her eyes shut, she struggled for control.

"Oh, Mom, the dollhouses?"

It took a deep breath to say it. "Yes."

"I'll be right there. Mom, call the police. Uh, is Isaac with you?"

Funneling her grief and fear into anger at Isaac was easier than dealing with the loss. "Yes, he's already asked me if the sex was worth it." Damn. It didn't work. She brought her hand up to press on her eyes, to hold back the tears. If she didn't have Ivy . . .

"He said that?" Ivy sounded stunned. Why was she stunned?

Everyone knew Mallory York was a slut for boy toys. Everyone knew it. Mal had known it ever since her dad had told her she was a slut. Why should Isaac be any different? "I have to go." She hung up.

Everyone was tense, including Luke. He was climbing out of his skin. Pierce didn't answer his phone, or return Ivy's calls. They couldn't find any clues to where Marla was. The phone number from her calendar was untraceable, probably a prepaid cell.

Where was Pierce? With Marla someplace? Did they both pull off the heist? Who broke into Mallory's business? It had to be someone looking for the statues? Marla? Dirk? Pierce? Arnie? Ivy's dad?

Who was doing what? Where were the statues?

The police and detective on the case had left. Mallory was trying to salvage the dollhouses, which made him even more nuts. They were dollhouses, for crying out loud. Not multimillion-dollar statues! Ivy was checking Mallory's bank accounts to make sure that the thief hadn't gotten access. Isaac called the insurance company, took pictures of everything, and made notes for documentation.

Luke looked around one more time. "We're going home. You all are going to lock yourselves in Ivy's house, and I'm going hunting." God, he couldn't believe how stupid he'd been. He kept going to Ivy's house instead of out looking for the statues.

Ivy looked up from the computer. "You're leaving?"

It was a struggle not to flinch at the harsh tone of her voice. "I'm doing my job, Princess. Going after every lead. I need to see if I can find Jordan and/or Marla."

Ivy shut down the computer. "I'll go—"

"I don't think so, Princess. This isn't accounting with tidy little numbers. I'm going into dark places looking for dark people. You stay home and do your thing online. See if you can find anything. Go back to Trip, Marla . . . everyone."

She blanched, her blue eyes filling with hurt. But she simply said, "Fine. Let's go."

Luke got them settled at the house and left for Sherman Oaks around six P.M. He dragged back to Ivy's house around midnight, completely frustrated. Jordan's office had been closed up tight, but he'd expected that. He'd done a background on Jordan, so he'd gone to the house, his favorite restaurants and hangouts, badgered Regina for more information by phone, prowled any place that was open Sunday night. Nothing.

He'd found the place where Marla used to live. No sign of Pierce, Marla, or either of their cars.

He'd gone back to Claremont and checked Marla's apartment. Not there. Nor was Pierce or either of their cars.

Luke unlocked the door to Ivy's house and disarmed the security system, then reversed the process. The house was quiet. Ivy had left the stove light on in the kitchen for him.

Shit. Small gestures and they touched him. He opened the fridge and saw a plate of food with a Post-it note that said "Luke" in Ivy's tilting scrawl.

Hell.

He stared at the plastic-covered plate and dragged in a deep breath. Lust and need wound tightly in his gut and groin. He wanted Ivy, wanted all of her. She loved the way he made her come—hell, he was good at sex. Lust he could handle.

It was the need for her that scared him shitless. The desire to be the object of the incredible loyalty and affection that she lavished on people she loved. The way she loved was so real and genuine. Piss her off? She told you. Get hurt? She was there. Work late? She left dinner in the fridge.

He shut the fridge. He was good for sex, nothing more.

It was slipping into something more.

He was going to sleep on the couch.

Ivy woke up. Again. Rolling over, she looked at the green numbers of her alarm clock. It was 2:37 A.M. She hadn't slept much. First, she'd waited until she'd heard Luke come in.

Then waited to see if he'd come to bed with her.

She dozed off and on, but now she finally gave it up. Her mouth was bone-dry and her eyes felt gritty. Getting up, she pulled her robe on over the panties she'd worn instead of her usual tank and boxers, and headed out the door of her bedroom. She walked softly down the hall.

The porch light spilled in through the front window to show her Luke sprawled on the couch. He was too big, his feet hung over the edge. His face was pulled tight, and his hand twitched on his bare chest. The afghan he used as a cover had fallen to the floor.

He looked hard and safe sprawled on her couch. Her fingers curled with the need to touch him. He'd come back. She'd wondered if he'd come back to the house or go to his apartment. After all, they were safe enough with the security system and Isaac in the house.

He was there to protect her, and her mom. Ivy knew it right down to her core. The man who hadn't had any family of his own since he had been six was working damn hard to protect hers.

Her chest grew hot and thick.

Luke insisted he was only good for sex.

She thought of his words last night—that she was a princess in a sound booth who couldn't handle real life. In other words, she was a coward hiding behind a microphone instead of living. Isn't that what her mom had told her? And maybe she was.

God, she was tired of being afraid. Maybe it was time to accept that she was going to get hurt. Life had a way of doing that no matter how hard she tried to protect herself. Look at Dirk. She'd believed he was a safe investment broker. Then he'd turned out to be a bad-boy thief. Finally, she had thought she was safely rid of him. Yet, he'd showed up in her room in the middle of the night.

There was no such thing as safe. No such thing as protecting yourself with rules for living.

She forced herself to swallow the emotion building in her chest and traveling up her throat. She turned away from Luke and headed into the kitchen for a bottle of water.

She heard Luke shift and cry out in a tortured whisper, "Holy God."

Another nightmare. Nothing could keep her from him. She rushed back, this time going around the couch and dropping to her knees by him.

"Blood, too much blood." He rolled toward the back of the couch, seemingly trying to escape something.

Ivy put her hand on his bare shoulder, struck by the sheer heat coming off of him. "Luke, wake up. It's just a dream."

His body tensed; then he shifted to his back and looked at her.

In the amber porch light coming through the front window she saw the white lines of tension around his mouth and the grooves of fatigue around his eyes.

He said in a thick voice, "You're still alive."

She wasn't sure what to make of that. "Yes."

He rolled up to a sitting position and ran his hands through his hair.

She stood up. "Want some water?" She hurried around the couch into the kitchen. The light over the stove was on, making the big flowers on the border of wallpaper look like strange shadows. The wood floor was cool on her bare feet. The light-weight robe moved softly around her calves. She hadn't even belted the robe. She yanked open the fridge, pulled out two bottles, shut the door, and turned around.

Luke stood in the doorway of the kitchen. All six feet plus of sleepy-eyed, muscular, almost-naked-but-for-the-boxers male leaned against the doorjamb.

She'd never been a woman to experience lust before, but now—whoa. Lust bloomed hot and wicked in her belly and breasts, and it spread like a forest fire. Her robe stuck to her skin, irritating her, making her want to rip it off.

She dropped her gaze down his length, down the smattering of hair over his chest, down his belly until she caught sight of a huge erection tenting his boxers. Oh God. What did she say now? What did she do?

"Water?"

She jerked her gaze up to his face. His eyes. With the light over the stove, she could make out the blue warming the gray color. "Uh, sure." She tossed him one of the bottles, afraid to get too close.

He caught it and nodded his thanks.

Ivy opened her bottle of water and sipped it. It didn't do a darned thing to cool her down.

"You're staring."

Heat crawled up her chest and into her face. She was staring at the green boxers straining to hold in his erection. Forcing her gaze up, she said, "It's a nice view." Oh, clever. But she didn't know how to do this, how to deal with her own overwhelming desire to touch him and to feel his arms around her. She actually wanted to bury her face in his chest and inhale the rich, tangy scent of his skin. She shifted her weight to her other foot. "Umm, you can go sleep in my bed. I'll watch TV out here." If he moved out of the doorway, then she could escape to the living room. Because she was feeling really desperate. Out of control. This time she was staring at his chest and arms, remembering how it felt to be held there.

Safe.

God, she needed more than water. Turning around, she pulled the fridge open again and searched for the bottle of wine. She grabbed it, slammed the door, walked to the cupboard to pull down a glass, and dumped in some wine. She drank half a glass without breathing.

Laying one hand flat on the cool counter, she stared at the sink and willed herself to get control. What was happening to her? What made her need Luke? It wasn't just lust, was it?

Luke moved behind her, grasped the lapels of her robe and pulled it open, easing it back over her shoulders. Then he stopped when the tops of her shoulders and breasts were exposed. "What am I good for, Ivy? Be a good girl and tell me, and I'll fuck you until the only thing you can think or feel is pleasure, until you are so exhausted you will fall asleep."

She shivered, sexy chills running down her spine while denial stabbed at her brain. The confusion didn't help. She reached out and lifted her glass of wine, draining it. She slapped her glass down. "No, I won't."

Luke dropped the edges of her robe and stepped back.

Ivy twisted around to see his taut back. "Turn around, you coward!" She knew the alcohol was fueling her chaotic emotions, knew she was on the edge of someplace she'd never been.

Someplace she'd always been afraid of.

But she couldn't stop, couldn't put on the brakes before she crashed into a wall.

Luke stopped, his shoulders bunching up. He turned.

She yanked her robe off and dropped it to the ground. "You're a man, not a walking vibrator. I want a man. I want you." She wasn't yelling, she was whispering as loud as her tight throat would allow. But right now, she didn't care if her mom came running. Or Isaac. Maybe they all needed to know that Ivy was done being a coward. That she was done being afraid to try, afraid of getting hurt. She hadn't been living, she'd just been existing. Luke changed her. He made her want to live, to feel, even if it meant pain later.

His gray eyes widened, flaring raw, hungry heat as he ran his gaze over her. Down her puckered nipples, her belly, her scrap of lacy white panties, and her legs.

She was trembling with too many feelings, too many needs. A wet streak of a tear trickled down her face and she brushed it off. No crying. No turning back. If he was going to turn her down, then he'd do it to her face, by God.

She saw Luke's dick twitch hard, his thigh muscles bunched, and even his stomach muscles tightened. He said, "Ivy . . ."

She didn't want to hear it. "You once accused me, right

here in my kitchen, of being afraid to go after what I want." She went right up to him until her bare toes touched his, and she could feel the head of his dick press against her belly through his boxers. Tilting her head up, she said, "I'm going after what I want." She put her hands on his chest, slid them down and felt his stomach contract and his dick jump. Catching the edges of his boxers, she shoved them down. And before he could react, she slid to her knees, curled her hand around the base of his dick, and caressed the head with her tongue.

"Shit. Okay. Shit." His breath rushed out.

Ivy slid him deep in her mouth. She loved the feel of him riding her tongue and growing bigger, harder. Giving him pleasure made her bolder, and she cupped his balls, using her thumb to stroke the sensitive skin in between.

Luke caught her beneath her arms and hauled her to her feet, then into his arms and crushed his lips over hers. He opened his mouth and plunged his tongue in deep. His large hand settled on the small of her back and pulled her into the heat of his body. She melted into the hard muscles and hot skin. Her heart rate shot up. Blood pounded in her ears and pooled between her legs, swelling the wet folds of her sex. Making her desperate for Luke's touch. Her breasts were oversensitive and yet she arched into him, seeking any relief. Seeking more, with Luke it would always be more. She'd never get enough of him. She wanted his huge body wrapped around hers. Inside of her . . .

He ran both hands down her back, under the panties, and curled his fingers over her butt. Then he lifted her. Pulling his head back to see her, he said, "Legs around me."

It flashed through her head that he was damned strong, powerful. He settled her so that the seam of her sex rubbed the length of his cock with only her thin panties between them. The instinctive need to get closer had her hook her ankles behind his back. Then she discovered the intense pleasure of rubbing herself against him.

Luke rumbled a noise deep in his chest, then licked her ear, and said, "More, Jesus, Ivy. Your pussy feels like silk, hot . . ."

She shivered, feeling sensual and protected and wild all at the same time. Everything felt more intense, and her body throbbed, ached, needed. "My panties," she tried to explain. "It's not, uh, me."

"It's you." His words were throttled low and gruff. "Do it, keep doing it until you come."

"But you—"

He thrust against her, his hard length rubbing her clit. At the same time he took her mouth again.

The feel of his tongue stroking hers rivaled with the sensations of him rubbing her with his dick. She tightened her legs, her thighs clenching, and she moved. Hard. Against him. Faster. Until she couldn't breathe, couldn't see, she could only feel. Luke was everywhere—holding her, kissing her, shoving his cock against her. She exploded, and Luke tightened his arms around her.

He tore his mouth from hers. "Oh, yeah, I can feel you soaking your panties and my cock." He sucked in a breath, his eyes hot and pleading. "Please tell me you have condoms?"

"My bedroom."

Chapter 14

He knew he was out of control, but nothing could stop him. Not with Ivy's sweet little body in his arms, her pussy torturing his cock through the panties. Nothing would stop him. He'd kill anyone who got between him and Ivy.

Sex. He meant between him and sex with Ivy.

Shutting the door with his foot, he said, "Where're the condoms?" He needed them now.

"Top drawer of the dresser, right here."

She gestured to the dresser at his left elbow. Luke eased her down to the top of the low dresser. "This drawer?"

She nodded.

He pulled it open, found the unopened box, and stared. Unopened. Not used. It meant something but he was so damned horny he couldn't . . .

"Are they the wrong ones?"

Luke grabbed the box and ripped it open. Then he dug out a packet and tore that open. "No, perfect." He rolled the condom on.

She scooted to get off the dresser, but Luke stepped between her legs, holding her there. He looked into her face. "Legs around me."

She lifted her legs, but said, "My panties."

He looked down between them. With her legs wrapped around his waist, she was tilted and exposed. The thin white silk clung to her. He could see her swollen clit and lips, smell the fragrant musk. He had to be inside her. Had to. Now. He used his thumb to move the panties aside, feeling her shiver as he stroked her sensitive skin. "No time." Then he stepped forward and pressed inside of her. Her wet heat sucked him in.

She tightened her legs around him and grabbed his shoulders. Lifted her hips, pulling him in deeper.

Sweat burned his upper lip, his back. His balls tightened and the pressure against his lower back made him shove hard, burying his cock all the way in her. "Can't stop." He tried to plant his feet. Tried to tighten his muscles to get control.

Ivy reached up and put her hands on his face. "Do it, Luke. Hard. The way you need to do it. Until you come."

A wave of white-hot lust broke loose. The only thing more powerful than the lust, the sharp painful drive to fuck her, was the primal instinct to protect her. He leaned in enough to get his arms around her before he lost control. Thrusting hard and deep into her. Her breathing turned ragged; she dug her fingers into his arms, dug her heels into his ass. Her thighs clenched around him and still he drove into her. Going deep until their skin was slick with sweat. Her head fell back, her mouth opened, and he knew she was going to come. That drove him to pull her tighter against him so he'd feel every pulse and shiver of her orgasm. Then pleasure burst and raced through him in wave after wave of spasms.

Luke could feel her heart hammering against his chest where he held her. Her head was titled down so he just saw the blond hair falling around her. Saw the curve of her shoulder, her long back and her sweet butt resting on the dresser. He felt his dick twitch. Holding her was the closest thing he'd ever get to the real thing.

No way in hell was he going to let Ivy get hurt. Or her mother whom she loved so much. He didn't know shit about families, but he could protect Ivy's for her. Leave her with at least a memory of him that was more than just an orgasm.

She made him want to be more than just an orgasm.

* * *

The stirrings of real panic left him in a cold, gut-cramping, sweat. Where were they? He could only see big splotches of wet red on the ground as he brought the bird into land . . .

"Luke? It's a dream, come here."

He opened his eyes to see Ivy on the bed facing him, with her hands trying to pull him into her arms. He'd been sliding into his nightmare. But Ivy was alive, safe and warm in bed with him. He reached up, moved her hands off of his shoulder, and hauled her up to his chest. She smelled like berry shampoo, warm skin, and sex. Just feeling her curled up against him eased his muscles. He threw one leg over her hip to keep her where he needed her, then closed his eyes. And slept with her in his arms.

The phone woke them up Monday morning. Ivy grabbed it and glanced at the clock. Just after seven A.M. "Hello."

"Ivy, you have to help me."

She sat up. "Dad?" Damn it she couldn't deal with him before coffee. "Why would I help you? You told the world I got away with embezzling."

Luke sat up next to her, watchful but quiet. He appeared rested so he must have slept well.

Her dad said, "No! She twisted my words! You know how sneaky those TV people are, editing and splicing and tricking people!"

It was always someone else's fault. "Dad, I have to get to work."

"You don't understand, I'm in trouble! He'll kill me!"

What the hell? She swung her legs over the side of the bed and stood up. "Who will kill you?"

She heard Luke get up and come around the bed to stand next to her. She tilted the phone so they could both listen.

"Dirk! He threatened to kill me if I don't get the statues, those Jade Goddesses!"

"Dirk?" Her mind clicked along, trying to make sense of it all. "You don't even know Dirk. I hadn't seen you in years when I dated him."

"But he knew me! He found me and threatened me! You have to give me those statues!" His voice climbed to a piercing whine.

Ivy looked at Luke. He stood so close, she could feel the heat off his body. His very naked body. She forced herself to focus. "Is Dirk there now?"

"No, he said he'll come back tonight."

She didn't think her dad was in real danger. "He's bluffing, Dad. Just stay somewhere else tonight and you'll be fine." Okay, yeah, Dirk had slapped her and tossed her mom to the ground, but she didn't think he'd kill her dad. Her shoulders and jaw tensed. What was going on? Who was doing all this? They knew Marla hired Trip to steal the statues, so how did Dirk get involved?

"I should stay there. It's supposed to be my house anyway. I should move in there."

She gritted her teeth and squeezed the handset of the phone.

Luke shook his head and put his hand over the mouthpiece. "He's scamming you."

She whispered back, "He never met Dirk."

"Dirk was in the news after the embezzlement. He'd know about you and him."

True. Shifting the phone to move his hand off the mouthpiece, she said, "What did Dirk look like?"

"Green eyes, black hair, uh, he said to tell you that he always hated those dollhouses. Whatever that means."

Her skin went cold. She looked at Luke. His gray eyes were grim. She knew that meant the dollhouses in her mom's office. Dirk must have broken in there, looking for the statues and destroying everything he could. Probably in a fit of rage. What was making him so angry? Was he in trouble? Would he really kill her dad? She came to a decision. "Okay, tell you what, I'll reserve you a room for a couple days in a hotel." This time she didn't look at Luke. She didn't need his approval or disapproval.

"That's cold, Ivy. My sister was ill and you tricked her into giving you that house! She—"

Yeah, yeah, heard it all before and still didn't care. "Ten seconds to decide, then I'm hanging up."

"I'll take it."

"The Doubletree on Foothill. You can check in this afternoon. And, Dad, stay away from the media, or I'll toss your ass out of the hotel." She hung up, sat on the bed, and said, "What is Dirk up to? Why is he risking his freedom for those statues?"

Luke crossed his arms over his chest and said, "He's determined and pissed. When he didn't get what he wanted from you, he broke into your mom's office. He probably figured the police had searched her house, so the office made sense. And he was seriously pissed about not finding them judging by the destruction he left behind. Then he searched out your father, who you said Dirk never met, and decided to threaten him to get you to cough up the statues."

"I don't have them!" She fought down the frustration with a deep breath. "But my dad thinks I might, so he probably told Dirk anything he wanted to hear just to save himself. If Dirk hit me," she felt an ache in her cheek from the memory, "I'm sure he was more than willing to smack around my dad." She clenched her fists. "I'm not going to let him hurt my family!"

"I'll take care of it."

Startled by the deep threat in his voice, Ivy looked up. Luke's gray eyes were flat and hard, his jaw bulged, his shoulders and chest flexed. She could trace the lines of his muscles and veins he was so tense. Anger? Frustration at not finding the statues? Looking lower, she saw that he was half hard. She tried not to flush, but heat rushed through her. Desire, which was stupid when they had other things to worry about. But when she dropped her gaze again to his penis, he got harder. "Uh," forcing her gaze up, she said, "you'll take care of what?"

His gaze bore into her. "Beating the shit out of Dirk Campbell for smacking you. Scaring you. Hurting your mom, and now terrorizing your dad. Then I might turn him over to the police." His crossed his arms over his chest. "Or not."

She stared at him open-mouthed. "But . . . uh, you can't . . ."

"Can and will."

"But the law—"

"Don't care."

"Luke!" She didn't understand! "You're not being reasonable. You can't just beat someone up because . . . because . . ."

He arched an eyebrow. "Because they hit you?" he asked silkily. "Any man would do the same, Princess. Any man. So save your breath. But we need to figure out why he's here and why now? He came late to the game of chasing the statues, but he wants them bad."

She dropped her gaze again. He was hard. Ready. Sexy. Hot. Luke was nothing like Dirk—he'd always needed a lot of attention to get hard and stay hard.

Luke's voice rumbled into her thoughts. "Keep looking at my cock and I won't be able to think."

Oh. Oh my God. That's it! "I might know a reason why Dirk's so determined to get the statues. They are the Goddesses of Fertility and Virility, right?"

He eyed her. "Yes."

"I think Dirk might be interested in the virility part."

He dropped his arms and moved to sit next to her. "He had sexual problems? Couldn't get hard? Stay hard?"

The bed dipped down, tilting her toward him. The urge to lean into him was strong, but she resisted. "Not, uh, not like you do."

"Sex by the numbers," he muttered as if swearing. Then he said, "That prick tried to blame you, didn't he?"

She looked over at him. "It was subtle. And I didn't like sex very much. I mean it was just . . ." She shrugged.

"You've had sex since then? You had to realize it wasn't you."

"Couple times, and yeah, I knew Dirk was blaming me when he had a problem. But sex was still blah, so I didn't really care. Basically, a lot of fuss and heavy breathing and it hardly seemed worth the effort." She looked up at him and smiled. "Now I get it."

Luke stared at her.

She started to feel like a weirdly fascinating bug crawling by. "Anyway, maybe he's trying to get the statues to increase his virility or sexual function. Knowing Dirk, he'd do anything to prove his manhood. Men like him would think all their manhood is in their penis."

He reached out and touched her face. "If he didn't get rock hard and ready being with you, then he's out of his mind if he thinks a couple statues will give him a hard-on." He took her hand and put it on his dick. "Don't ever settle, Ivy. This is what a man who wants you feels like." She held his rigid penis in the curve of her palm, while Luke's warm hand wrapped around hers. "But it's more than this"—he squeezed his hand gently around hers cradling him—"it's wanting to make you feel good. Watching you come excites me like nothing else. That's the kind of sex you deserve. You can find a man who will make you feel safe and still give you this."

She shivered, and tears rushed her throat. She had to fight it back. Luke made her feel safe, as well as confident and sexy. He didn't see himself that way, didn't understand that he was a man worth so much more than just sex. Using her thumb, she stroked the head of his penis. "Show me again. Or better yet, let me show you."

He groaned and tugged her hand away. Then he scooped her up into his arms and kissed her.

Warmth flooded her and she sank into the kiss, into his arms. She tasted his mouth and it wasn't enough. Pulling back, she tried to straddle his hips for more control.

"Condom."

She looked down at his rigid jaw and blazing eyes. "Right. I'll get it."

He stood, set her on her feet, and went for the condoms. When he returned, he put his arms around her from behind. He kissed her neck and caressed her breasts and rolled her nipples. She reached behind to stroke him. He drew a slow line down her belly and said into her ear, "Lie down and let me take the panties off of you."

She started to turn.

"On your stomach."

Ivy didn't think, she just did it. She sprawled across the messy bed and let herself relax and just feel. The moments she had with him would be gone, but she would remember.

The bed dipped with his weight. She discovered it was sensual and exciting, to have him behind her, not quite knowing what he was doing.

He leaned over her, used his fingers to brush her hair aside, and kissed her nape. "Close your eyes."

She let her eyes slide shut as she felt his mouth trail sensations down her spine. A kiss, a lick . . . she shivered. Her arms were over her head and she squeezed her fists.

Luke's hands followed his mouth. He pressed a kiss just above her panties. Then he was easing them down.

Oh. God. The worries and fears of late were shoved out of her mind, replaced by deep lust and longing. She wanted his hands on her, his mouth, and his body covering her. She wanted all of him. Filling her up. "Luke, I can't wait." She tried to turn over.

He put both hands on her hips, holding her there. "What do you want, princess? Tell me." His mouth touched her backside, trailing a hot blaze downward.

She squeezed her thighs together. Trying to ease the violent ache that fired between her legs. "I want you inside me!"

"Open your legs."

Biting off her argument, she eased her legs apart.

His hands pulled her hips up until she was on her knees. And then, "Damn, you are wet."

He was at the base of the bed, looking at her. She grabbed handfuls of the bedsheet, more excited than she'd ever been. "Luke," she begged. What would he do?

He didn't keep her waiting. First, a finger stroked her, then his tongue. Her whole body shuddered. She writhed and made noises in her throat. She was pretty sure she begged him. Nothing mattered but the feel of Luke against her. Everything in her coiled into agonizing tightness.

Then it stopped. "Feel good?"

She nearly cried, "Yes!" She heard the condom package tear open.

He was back, easing inside of her. More of him. And more. She heard him draw a ragged breath as he eased out. Slowly.

"You're torturing me!" She wiggled her butt.

"Damn right. You're going to come hard." He slid back in. Slowly.

"Too slow." Frustrated tears squeezed out. She didn't care. She shoved back against him.

He tightened his fingers into her hips. "No cheating, baby girl. You're going to kneel there and take it, aren't you?" He slid a hand up her hip and along her spine.

Ivy was done playing. She waited until he was deep inside of her; then she squeezed her thighs tightly together, contracting every muscle she had from her thighs to her womb.

"Oh hell," Luke snarled. Then he pulled out and filled her up. Hard. Deep. Pulled out again, then demanded, "Can you take it?"

"Yes. More." She wanted it all. She wanted him as desperate for release as she was. He drove back in and Ivy stopped thinking or hearing. Only feeling Luke. She rose higher, and when the crash came, Luke curled an arm around her waist, wrapping her in his body as she rode the spasms. She was still shuddering when he pumped into her and released, his breath harsh behind her.

He pulled out of her, rolled her to her back, and covered her body with his. Looking down into her eyes, he said, "That was damned sneaky, Princess."

She smiled up at him. "Are you complaining?"

He leaned down, kissing her. "Complimenting, not complaining."

Luke handed Regina a cup of coffee. She was a little pale, her eyes tired. "Regina, what did you find on Dirk Campbell?"

"Two e-mails. The first one he inquired if I would sell the statues. The second one he tried to convince me to sell and asked for my phone number."

"Did you give it to him?"

"No. Do you think it's him?"

Luke shook his head. "He doesn't have the statues, but he wants them bad enough to be a dangerous complication. I need to know everything I can about him."

At his left elbow, Ivy hung up her cell phone and started booting up her laptop. "Leah's going to play the interviews and a partial tape from a show. But Marla didn't show up for work. She's still missing."

Luke nodded; they had to check, but he'd been sure Marla wouldn't show up for work today. There was no way he wanted Ivy out of his sight, he was relieved that she'd agreed to skip work.

Regina shook her head and looked down into her cup. "I should have guarded the statues more carefully. More people are going to die if we don't get them back soon." She looked up at Luke, ignoring everyone else at the table. "Every time the statues are stolen, people die. They keep dying until they are returned. And this is really selfish, but I can't hold off canceling the tour much longer."

He and Regina both understood the power of antiques

that outlive generations of people, and the power of legends. "I think we're getting close. We just need to find Marla Rimmer and Pierce Jordan."

Regina said, "I tried to contact Pierce this morning. He didn't answer his cell phone or the e-mail I sent. All his office would tell me is that he had a client emergency and is out of contact." She pulled her mouth tight, then added, "I can't believe he might be involved. Maybe the statues are influencing me, blinding me to what I don't want to see."

"Ah," Mallory spoke up. "You want Pierce but he doesn't want you."

"Mom!" Ivy glared at her over the laptop.

"It's okay, she's right," Regina said. "I accepted that Pierce was only interested in friendship. He goes after younger, hotter types. Not middle-aged college professors."

For the first time, Isaac spoke up, "Then he's stupid. A woman his own age would be infinitely more interesting. Just the same as a man your own age is more interesting than a silly boy toy."

Mallory snapped her head around to Isaac sitting at the other end of the table. "You're a sanctimonious prig."

He crossed his arms. "And you're a scared little girl. I'm losing my patience. I'm beginning to think you need a good spanking."

Luke rubbed his forehead. "Stop it." He did not want to think of Isaac spanking Ivy's mom. Although feeling Ivy's ass under his palm was appealing, he wouldn't hurt her, just a little sex play . . . shit. He needed to get his priorities in order. Focus. On the case, not Ivy. Christ. Sex with her had scrambled his brains.

"Ivy!" her mom shrieked. "Did you hear that? Did you hear what he said to me? And you think I should date him?"

Luke turned to watch Ivy stare down her mom. "Isaac loves you. He's not your father. He would never raise a hand to you." She turned her head left and glared. "Because if he did, I'd kill him. Now, if you two don't mind, shut up. You're both making me queasy."

Luke wanted to sweep her off her chair and into his lap. She loved her mom, but she also knew her mom for who she was. And still loved her.

What was that like? To be loved anyway? Even when you didn't measure up? Damn it, he was drifting again. He turned back to Regina.

But Regina was staring at Mallory. "You're under the influence of the statues, but you're fighting it. Oh my God, it's incredible. All three of you are under the influence. Isaac is not. His passion has been on the surface for a long time. But you three"—her gaze swept Mallory, Ivy, and Luke—"you're all vibrating with passion. And you were only exposed to them for a short time. It's perfect!"

Lust was more like it, but Luke let that pass. Regina lived for the statues, so she'd naturally look for people who were affected by them. "Back to Jordan. He's smart and slick enough that he could have been pulling strings all along. We can't discount him."

Ivy frowned, dragging her gaze away from the computer screen to ask, "If Pierce got Marla to hire Trip to steal the statues, then why kill Trip? She could have just paid him off and the two of them walked away with the statues."

Luke answered with, "Unless Marla tried to blackmail Pierce to marry her. So he took matters into his own hands. Killed Trip and got the statues."

"Then where's Marla?" Ivy said. When no one said anything, she winced as she realized the answer. "You think he'd kill her too? I can't believe it."

"There's another scenario," Isaac suggested. "Perhaps Marla hired Trip, was double-crossed, and then went to Pierce for help. Wouldn't Pierce Jordan be the likely person a thief would contact to sell the statues to? How bad did Jordan want those statues?"

"Bad," Luke and Regina both answered.

Ivy let out a frustrated sigh. "It's so complicated."

He hated how much this was troubling Ivy, scaring her and making her worry about her mom. "Because we don't have all the pieces to the puzzle. We have to keep looking and pushing until we get them."

Ivy nodded and went back to working on her laptop.

He looked at Mallory. "When Marla and my cousin were at your house, what did they do?"

"They just helped me clean. Washing silverware tossed on the floors, putting cushions back on the couches, books in the bookcase, cleaning off the surfaces, vacuuming."

Luke pushed harder. "Did they stay with you or roam the house?"

"Everyone did different chores. They were just helping! Marla's always been friendly, and Arnold's been helping me all along, free of charge."

Isaac snorted.

Ivy jumped in. "Luke? Why are you asking about Arnold? You don't think he could be involved, do you? We didn't find anything in his office that pointed to him."

He shrugged. "I think he's just trying to find the statues before me, but I'm not eliminating anyone. Most likely, he was covering his bases in case you and your mom had something to do with the statues being stolen. He used the excuse of helping your mom in order to search her house and look for clues to where you two might have hidden the statues. Just like Marla probably did."

Mallory said, "But he said he'd help me, and that you were dangerous. That we had to protect Ivy . . ."

Luke refused to answer that.

Isaac turned on Mallory. "Ivy's never been safer than she is with Luke. And just where is Arnold-the-Knight-in-Shining-Armor now? Gone like all the rest of your trophy boys."

Mallory shot to her feet. "I hate you. I hate the way you're so sure you know it all. So sure I'm a screwup. So sure no man would be interested in me." Tears welled up in her eyes. "At least boy toys don't try to boss me around and tell me I'm a loser."

Luke was getting a pounding headache.

Isaac uncoiled and stood. "I have never called you a loser."

Silence rolled down the table.

Mallory sniffed, lifted her head, and squared her shoulders. "Yeah, you do. Ivy's wrong, you are exactly like my father. You would have tried to take Ivy away from me too." She stormed past Isaac and stomped down the stairs.

Ivy moved the laptop, shoved her chair back, and got to her feet, but Luke grabbed hold of her hand.

Isaac turned a sickly shade of white. He turned to Ivy. "What does she mean?"

"Her dad smacked her around and tossed her out when he found out she was pregnant. A few years later, he took her to court and tried to get custody of me. My mom fought him and won."

"Jesus, he tried to take you away from her? Why? Why would anyone do that?"

Luke held her hand tightly. He felt the tremor.

"Because he didn't think she was capable of being a mother. A good mother, at any rate. Said she was too flighty and a slut to boot."

The sickly color gave way to a deep flush. Isaac flexed his jaw several times and sucked in a breath. "A slut. He called his daughter a slut."

Softly, Ivy said, "Ever wonder why she flaunts the men in front of you?"

"Waiting for me to call her a slut. And leave her. Or take away something she loves, like you."

Ivy shook her head on the last one. "She knows better than that, Isaac. I love you; but if it came to a choice, I'd choose my mother. She knows that."

He sank down in his chair.

Ivy's back practically arched. "You're giving up? Now?"

Luke could feel the anger shafting through her.

Her voice grew harder. "You've pushed her and pushed her until she told you the truth. And now you're going to bail on her?"

Luke hated the pain in her. He let go of her hand and put his arm around her shoulder, trying to give her . . . something. He didn't even know what. Just . . . something.

Isaac blinked, took his glasses off and cleaned them on his shirt.

Luke feared for the man's life.

Then he put them back on, fixed his gaze on Ivy, and said, "I don't ever give up on people I love. I'm waiting for you all to clear out. Your mom's days of running scared are over."

"Amazing," Regina said.

Everyone turned to look at her.

"You all can't keep focused on anything but each other."

Luke narrowed his eyes. "The hell I can't. I'm on this, Regina."

Chapter 15

While Luke walked Regina out, Ivy kept searching on the Internet. She'd gone over Trip's bank accounts again. All she could find was the eight-thousand-dollar cash deposit.

Nothing else.

She checked her mom's accounts just to make sure that Dirk hadn't decided to help himself to her money. But they looked fine.

She didn't have enough information to get into Pierce Jordan's accounts, but she was reasonably sure he wouldn't leave a trail anyway.

She'd even dipped back into Arnold Sterling's accounts, the ones she could get access to, but nothing of interest was there. Everything looked normal.

Isaac put a fresh cup of coffee in front of her, then set his hand on her shoulder. "I love her, Ivy."

She laid her hand over his. "I know." She looked up into the intense brown eyes that she'd come to love almost as a father. But it wasn't her choice, it was her mom's decision. "You can't keep doing this to yourself, Isaac. My mom needs men's attention. She just . . . does."

He squeezed her shoulder gently. "She needs to trust me. I can't let her go. She makes me feel alive just being with her. She makes me want to fight for her."

Maybe Isaac was as dysfunctional as her mom. And who was she to throw stones? She kept pulling down her panties for Luke, a man who swore he was only good for sex. She craved him like a drug. Without thinking, she said, "They are addicting, aren't they?"

His gaze gentled. "Oh, honey, you're in love with him."

Thank God Luke was walking Regina to her car and couldn't hear. "I thought I had a choice in this, that I could choose a man like you to love."

Isaac's smile was slow and sweet. "Thank you, but you don't need a man like me. You and me together? We'd have a tidy relationship and no spark. No passion. No one to make us feel, you know? We need them as much as they need us. You just have to decide if you have the courage to go after him." He leaned down and kissed her head. "Either way, I'll always be here for you."

How did a girl get so damn lucky? "I feel the same for you."

"I know. And I know you are worrying about helping your mom clean up her office today and deal with the insurance. I'm going to ask you to stay with Luke—and I mean do not leave Luke's side—and leave your mom to me."

She stared up at him, her thoughts skidding around. Her mom was starting to come apart from the stress. Ready to crash and burn as Ivy had seen countless times over the years. Her best memories of her mom while growing up were those nights she'd wake up to hear her mom furiously working, sewing, stripping wallpaper, painting, building shelves, assembling a dollhouse, and Ivy would get out of bed and shuffle out in her nightgown. Each and every time, when the latest man was gone, Mallory would turn to her daughter. They'd work for hours and talk and just be a mom and daughter.

It had always been Ivy who took care of her mom when the crash and burn happened.

And just how sad was that? Was she going to sabotage a chance for her mom and Isaac to work something out between them, something that she knew right down to her soul was special and real, because she couldn't let go of the need to rescue her mom? Be the caretaker?

Isaac waited patiently. He was so much like her, thinking things out in a methodical way.

"Just swear you'll take care of her. I know you will, but swear to me anyway." If he was insulted, too bad.

"I swear, Ivy. I will take care of her. And I swear, if she needs you, I will find you."

She nodded, grateful in a way she couldn't yet name.

Taking his hand from her, Isaac looked at her computer screen. "Any luck?"

"Not yet. There's no way I can get into Pierce's accounts. I just checked Marla's yesterday. We have to find the two of them."

"Try Marla again. Maybe she's charged something."

The possibility skittered down her back. "Right! She could have charged a meal or a pedicure or . . ." she trailed off and accessed the account. They desperately needed a break, a clue; hell, she'd take a soggy breadcrumb at this point.

Ivy typed in the username and password just as Luke came back in.

The screen popped up. She skimmed the details of the accounts and stopped.

"Look! There! The SuperHaven Motel! See it, Marla charged a room at the SuperHaven Motel Saturday night. It probably didn't post until just this morning." Luke came up on her right, but she turned to Isaac. "You're brilliant and sneaky."

"That's what lawyers do," he said with a grin.

"Do you know where that is?" Luke asked, leaning on the other side of her to look at the screen.

His scent reached deep inside of her, but Ivy stayed focused. "By the Ontario airport. Do you think Pierce is with her?"

Luke turned his gaze on her. "One way to find out. Let's go, Princess."

"Hold on, I have to go tell my mom." Before Luke could answer, she left the two men and hurried down the stairs. She paused to see the material her mom had chosen for the drapes laid over on the floor of the spacious entertainment room. Her mom's sewing machine was set up against the wall. She must have been working on it last night after Ivy went to bed.

She hurried down the short hall, stopping at the bedroom on her left before the door that led to the garage. Her mom stood in front of the mirror over the dresser, wearing a short denim skirt that revealed lots of smooth leg, a tight, low-cut sweater, and high-heeled sandals. Suspicion fisted heavily in Ivy's gut. "Mom, what are you doing?" Or more to the point, where was she going and who was she trying to seduce?

Her mom brushed out her long dark hair. "I have things to take care of this morning. My office is destroyed. Someone has to clean it up."

Not good. "Isaac will help you, or I will when I get back. Please, Mom, stay here. Don't go anywhere."

Smacking the brush down on the dresser, she glared at Ivy. "I'm not a child, Ivy. I'm a grown woman with a business to run. I have to get my office cleaned up and do some work."

The awful suspicion grew. "What have you done?" It had to do with a man. Dressed like that, it had to be a man.

Lifting her chin, Mallory said, "I'm doing what I have to."

Ivy looked around the room, spotted her mom's purse and lunged for it.

"Ivy Rose York! What do you think you're doing!"

Ivy pulled her mom's cell phone out, pushed the buttons to show the last calls, and stared at the number. The fist in her gut tightened. "You called Arnold Sterling? Have you lost your mind?"

"Don't you start lecturing me, Missy. Who do you think picked up your robe and the *Urban Legend's* boxers off the kitchen floor this morning?"

"That's different!" Ivy couldn't believe this. Her mom was

spiraling out of control just when things seemed to be getting the most dangerous.

"Different my ass," her mom yelled back. "For all your high and mighty talkin' you've fallen for the biggest bad boy out there. And he's going to hurt you, and then you'll go back to hiding in your safe little life. Passing judgment on people who are stupid enough to call you on your precious show. Well, no thank you. I don't want that. I never wanted that. Because safe doesn't exist, Ivy. It's not real. It's just another kind of cage, a cruel cage! So I'm going to go out and be free, free to screw any man I want to."

The words hit their mark and froze her in a blast of pain so cold and brutal she could only stand there and take it. Endure it. Her mom thought the same thing everyone else did. That she was an emotional coward. How did the gulf between her and her mom get so big? So . . .

"That's enough, Mallory."

Ivy tore her gaze from her mom's tight and tortured face to see Isaac in the doorway.

"Ivy, Luke is waiting for you. Go on."

She was on the other side of the bed, with her mom in between them. "I . . ." She what? Didn't want to go? Wanted to go? Finally, she dropped the phone in her mom's purse and took a step. Then another.

Her mom loved her. Ivy knew that. Always had known that.

She took another step.

"Ivy, don't leave me here—"

The next step brought her even with her mom. Turning to face her, she hugged her tightly. No words could ever destroy their relationship. Instead, she said, "I'll be back. Call me if you need me. I love you, Mom." Then she let go and hurried out.

When she got to Isaac, she looked up at him. "You swore."

"And I meant it. Go on."

* * *

Mallory heard Ivy and Luke leave. She was stuck here with Isaac, but that didn't mean she had to talk to him. Listen to him tell her what a terrible mother she was.

In the entertainment room, she dropped to her knees and ran her fingers over the fabric she'd found for the drapes, visualizing how they would look in Ivy's living room. When Ivy saw it, she'd forgive her for the ugly things she'd said.

Ivy always forgave her.

She refused to think about Isaac. For two days, he'd been all over her ass, bossing her around, demanding that he stay in the same room with her.

But he didn't touch her.

Didn't try to make love to her. They'd made love a couple times over the past year. Okay, twice, when she'd been weak. Isaac might be kind of boring to look at, sort of like a comfy afghan, but he made her skin heat when he touched her. But when the sex was done, he was still Isaac and she was still Mallory, the slut. Never good enough. Stupid. But she wasn't stupid, she couldn't be stupid with a daughter like Ivy. She was creative.

That's what Ivy always said.

Thinking of Ivy made her stomach clamp tight, and worry marched up her spine to pound in her head. There was no one she loved as much as her daughter. In one way, she was thankful that Luke was around to protect her baby girl. But she knew Ivy was falling in love with Luke. And Luke was just like Mallory—commitment-phobic. Mallory had felt the chemistry between Luke and Ivy from the first day. Luke would protect Ivy from Dirk, but what about the heartbreak of falling for Luke?

"You've been sitting there for five minutes staring at that material, with scissors in your hand and a ferocious look on your face."

Her shoulders tightened up further at Isaac's voice. "I thought you left." She knew he hadn't, but it was all she could think of to say.

"Left you alone?"

She heard the anger. "Don't get your panties in a wad. I don't need you to protect me." She didn't need him. She didn't need anyone. Not like that.

He walked over the fabric and toward her.

"Get off! Don't walk on this! It's for the living room!" Horrible, awful, bile-tasting rage poured through her. Climbing to her feet, she glared at Isaac. "You've ruined it! These were perfect for Ivy, and now you've ruined it." She cried too damn easy. "I looked everywhere to get her the perfect—"

Isaac didn't stop until he was in her face. "She'll still love you, Mallory. She'll always love you."

She shook her head. "You don't understand!"

He put his hand under her chin. "I do. You think all you have to offer your daughter is your incredible talent as a decorator."

She jerked away from him. "You have to leave me alone. Just leave me alone. I won't let you cage me." Just the thought made it hard for her to breathe. Her parents had tried to cage her. Private schools, and—she didn't want to think about it. She hurried down the hall toward the downstairs bedroom. If she got there, she could lock him out and breathe. Just breathe. Her short denim skirt twitched as she walked faster and faster. Hanging a left, she went into the room and tried to close the door.

Isaac blocked the door, his brown eyes furious. "Cage you?" He backed her into the room. "How the hell can anyone cage you!" He slammed the door. Hard. "What do you think I'm going to do, Mal? Slap an apron on you and turn you into a Stepford wife? What don't you get about me? That I like your creative mind? Your sexy body? Your total focus when you get into a project, so total that you'll work through the night and forget to eat?"

She couldn't get a breath. It scared her, terrified her that he could understand so much about her. "You nag me when I don't eat!"

"Damn right I do. Now think hard, when I nag you about not eating, do I drag you into the kitchen and command you to cook?"

No. He'd either gone into her kitchen and found her something to eat—he made lovely omelets and crepes—or he ordered in. He would bring the food to her, handing her a plate and telling her to eat. "No, but you'd tire of that."

"Damn it, Mal, you are the most irritating woman I've ever met! I like taking care of you!"

"Like a child? Is that it? I'm your charity case?" That hurt, it all hurt. She was so tired of it hurting. "Guess you weren't up to a pity fuck the last couple nights. Your charity doesn't go that far." The words were out her mouth before she realized it.

The silence hung there, with only the sound of a car driving by and the antique clock ticking on the nightstand. And the echo of her words. Pathetic and crude.

He turned around and walked away.

Good, that was what she wanted. She knew he would leave her. Be disgusted with her. It was fine. Perfect. Just great. She was so damned happy that tears of joy choked her up.

She heard the lock turn in the door.

Her throat tightened until it was torture to drag in a breath at all.

Isaac turned. Watched her with eyes that missed nothing. Isaac never missed anything. It's what made him such a good lawyer. He saw everything.

Including her.

He started unbuttoning his sweater vest.

Nervously, she asked, "What are you doing?"

The sweater vest landed on the chair in the corner, and he went to work on the shirt.

Naturally, he had an undershirt on.

His chest was broad and tight with muscles. His belly was white with a rounded gut from the wine and beer he enjoyed.

He sat on the bed and pulled off his shoes. His dark socks.

He had big feet with long toes. Such stupid thoughts! Nerves danced all over her skin. Made her stomach tingle. Her back tight. "What are you doing? Have you lost your mind?"

He stood up from the bed and undid the belt on his pants, then the fastening and the zipper. He dropped his pants. His thighs had muscle to match his chest. Stepping out of his pants, he tossed them to the rest of the pile. Stood in his boxers. "When I'm done with you, you will never accuse me of pity-fucking you again. You want to call it fucking, you go right ahead. Screwing, absolutely. Making love? Bet your ass." He shoved down the silk boxers and stepped out.

His dick was hard. Big and pulsing. Dark red with thick blue veins. Isaac might be a man in his fifties, but he was perfect.

"For the record, I didn't make a move on you for the last two nights because (A) you have a bruise on your hip from that miscreant Dirk; and (B) I didn't give you a choice about sleeping in your bed, but you sure as hell had a choice about sex."

She opened her mouth.

He cut her off. "Don't even bother telling me you don't want it. You just told me that I hurt your feelings by not making love to you. I'm going to correct that oversight. And I'll know soon enough if you really want me, won't I? For sure, I can't lie about wanting you." He lowered his hand to brush over his dick, making it bounce with excitement. "You can see how bad I want you."

Off balance, she'd never seen this side of Isaac before. Not this confident determination, this almost uncanny reading of her. Somehow the power in their relationship had flipped from her to him, and she couldn't quite grasp how that had happened. Only that it was leaving her weak-kneed and needy. It was too much. She knew from experience that Isaac wasn't like a young man—eager, horny, and unwittingly selfish. He wouldn't let her be disconnected from the sex. She struggled to regain the power and push him away. "You're embarrassing yourself. Put your clothes on."

"You'd have more effect with that speech if you didn't keep looking at my cock." He walked over to her, easy with his nudity. With his arousal.

It wasn't working! Half panicking, she shifted tactics. "Fine. I want it. Let's just do it." She went at him, thinking she could strip off her underwear, take him inside, and make him come. Fast. Hard. Leave her wanting and she'd remember the lesson.

He caught her wrist and yanked her into his arms. He wrapped her in his arm, holding her against him, and whispered, "I'm not one of your boy toys, Mal. I know exactly how clever you are. I never underestimate you."

She shivered, feeling a sob climb up her throat. No one had ever known her this well.

He sank his hand into her hair, tugged her head back, and kissed her. A deep kiss from a man who knew how to get the job done. How to make her feel feminine and safe and excited. Then he slid off her sweater, unhooked her bra, drew down her skirt and her panties. Mallory kicked off her shoes and let him push her back on the bed.

Isaac's gaze skated down her body in hot approval, followed by his tongue. He spent time at every spot, her collarbone, her breasts, her nipples, until she was digging her fingers into his shoulders. The soft undersides of her breasts, her ribs, her belly.

Then he stopped.

She saw his hard expression when he looked at the bruise on the outside of her hip. He gently touched it, then pressed his lips against it.

Mallory closed her eyes, tears burning. He did take care of her. And it terrified her. Excited her. Made it easy for her to spread her legs and let him put his mouth on her center. Where he didn't leave until she was flushed and hot with orgasms. Then he covered her body with his and looked down at her. His mouth was wet from her; his eyes were bright with lust and deep with tenderness.

Resting on his elbows, he cradled her face. "This is real, Mal." He slid his cock deep inside of her. "When you stop fighting and give because you want to. Because you know you're safe with me."

He thrust into her, high and deep. And he didn't stop until she was surrounded by him, just him. Felt him pressing against her hips, her belly, her breasts, his mouth slanting over hers, his tongue sliding up against hers, his hands holding her face. She couldn't fight, all she could do was feel. He made love to her with the same patient intensity he did everything else.

She shattered beneath him, her entire body quivering.

Isaac broke the kiss, rose up on his arms, and threw his head back so that she saw every muscle clench as he drove into her one last time and came.

Mallory couldn't understand how he wrung so much more out of her than any other man. It wasn't the orgasm or excitement, it was that when he touched her, she felt cherished and safe. Worthy. Valuable. For more than just Pilates-toned thighs and enhanced breasts. How in God's name could she trust that?

Ivy tried not to worry about her mom as Luke circled around the motel building, getting the lay of the land. The rear of the hotel faced the back of a restaurant and the freeway.

Luke said, "It doesn't look like anyone can slip out the back of the rooms."

"Do you think Marla used blackmail and got the statues back? Then she is going to meet Pierce here and try to blackmail him into marrying her for the statues?"

He shrugged. "I've seen crazier shit in my life. Marla might also believe the statues have the power to make Pierce love her."

Ivy jerked her head up. "Do they? Have that kind of power?"

"Regina says no. She says their power is in unearthing what is already there, not like a love potion." He turned the car into the SuperHaven Motel.

The layout was typical of cheap lodging by airports. It was two stories, set up in an L around a parking lot. It looked like it hadn't been painted in a dozen years; the color scheme was faded green with dirt-colored doors. The wrought-iron railing on the top story had dripped a rust-colored sludge onto the sidewalk below when it was damp or rainy.

"There's Marla's Jetta. Do you see Pierce's black Escalade anywhere?"

Ivy saw the light green Jetta parked at the very end of the parking lot. It was nose-first, pointing at a room. She looked around for the big SUV but didn't see it. "No, just Marla's car."

He slid his car into the empty spot by Marla's Jetta.

The room had the blackout drapes drawn tightly closed over the window, so she wouldn't be able to see inside. How did they know if it was Marla's room?

Luke said, "Call the motel and ask the desk clerk to put you through to Marla Rimmer's room. Hang up when she answers." Then he got out of the car and walked up to the room.

Understanding that he was going to listen to see if the phone rang inside the room, she took out her cell and dialed. "Marla Rimmer's room, please." The call was put through. She got out of the car and walked up next to Luke.

The phone inside the room started to ring. And ring. Marla didn't answer. No one answered. It was the correct room, so where was Marla?

Putting her phone away, Ivy asked, "Do you think she's with Pierce?"

His face was blank. "Might be." He raised his hand and knocked hard on the door.

Nothing. No answer, no movement inside.

"I don't think she's in there."

Luke turned his full attention on her. "Let's go to the motel office and talk to the manager."

Her stomach tightened into a big knot and she shivered, but she nodded and started walking across the parking lot. Inside the office, it smelled like old socks, fresh coffee, and Lysol. The old man behind the pock-marked Formica counter looked up from his newspaper as they walked in. "Need a room?"

Ivy quickly scanned the office, noticing a couple folding chairs dotted the small area and a TV mounted in the corner played ESPN. There was a table with a couple boxes of store-bought donuts and a coffeemaker.

Luke answered, "One of the women staying in a room here works for this lady, Miss York. She didn't show up for work today and we're concerned. We'd like you to check her room or let us do it."

The man squinted toward her. "York? Ivy York? From that radio show? Is that you?"

She took a breath and said, "Yes, it's me. Right now I'm really concerned about Marla Rimmer. It's not like her not to show up for work. She's not answering her cell phone. Can you check her room and make sure she's all right?"

"Oh." He typed into the computer and read the screen. "What room did you say she is in?"

"Room number one hundred and seventeen." Ivy assumed he was double-checking.

He looked over at her. "Well, since I recognize you, I can't see the harm. I'm Walter, by the way." He unlocked a drawer and took out a key card. Then he went around the counter, and as they walked outside, he said, "I listen to your show every day."

Ivy kept up light chatter all the way across the parking lot just to control her nerves. She didn't like lying. She didn't like any of this. She hated being out of control. But if they could find Marla, they'd find answers.

The three of them stopped at the room.

Her stomach flip-flopped.

Walter knocked on the door, waited about thirty seconds, inserted the key card, and then opened the door.

She heard the increased hum of the air conditioner. Then Walter said in a strangled voice, "Oh no. Damn."

"Call the police, Walter," Luke instructed; then he slipped by the frozen old man.

Ivy stood on the sidewalk and shivered. She didn't want to go in there. Didn't want to see. She just didn't want anyone else dead.

Walter leaned against the wall outside of the room, his face pasty white. "We get suicides every once in a while."

She tried to focus on him. "Do you have a cell phone with you?"

"No."

She pulled her phone out, dialed 911 and handed it to him.

He took the phone and talked to the 911 operator.

Ivy took a breath and forced herself to step into the room. The buzz of the air conditioner sounded overly loud, and the air made gooseflesh stand up on her arms. She saw Marla immediately.

Slapping her hand over her mouth, she cried out, "Oh God." Marla lay faceup on the bed, her legs hanging off, and the top part of her head missing. It looked like she'd been standing, then the force of the gunshot threw her back onto the bed. Dried blood soaked the paisley bedspread into a gruesome thing.

Black dots swam in her vision. She jerked her gaze away to see Luke going through Marla's purse. She focused on him, on the way he did the job no matter what.

Sensing her appraisal, he looked up, his gray eyes hard. "Go outside."

She heard the anger in his voice. He wasn't angry at her, but that Marla was dead. It made her feel better. Luke cared that people were murdered. She hugged herself, her icy fingers biting into her own arms. In the distance, she heard the wail of sirens. "Should I do something?"

He said, "Her cell phone is gone. I didn't see it in her car either. Whoever did it took her cell phone but left her purse."

She couldn't stop herself and looked at Marla. Hot dizziness assaulted her and bile burned up her throat. The howl of the approaching sirens grew louder, and voices outside gathered. Ivy fought to think, think about Marla's apartment. "Where's the money? From cashing out her 401K?"

"Nothing in here," Luke said.

Dragging her gaze from Marla, she looked at the carpet and concentrated on breathing to control the nausea. The carpet was olive green and thin . . . What was that? "Luke, here's something." She pointed to a quarter-sized chunk of pink plastic.

Luke hurried over and dropped to his haunches. "I'm guessing her cell phone. She must have dropped it and it broke."

Ivy filled in the rest. "The killer picked it up. For the text messages? Phone numbers?" She dragged her gaze from the pink plastic to Luke. "Or a picture on her cell phone? Did Marla see who killed Trip?" It was all so crazy.

Just then they heard the sirens swell and tires squealed into the parking lot. The sound cut off and voices rose. Luke moved quickly, grabbing Ivy's arm and leading her toward the door to deal with the police.

Chapter 16

Mallory kept busy, it was the only way she could cope. Between the horrible news about Marla, and Isaac . . . And her guilt.

She had to keep moving. Since Isaac wouldn't let her out of his sight, he'd come with her to clean up the office. Having him around just put her more on edge.

She was sifting through the remains of the dollhouses, but there was nothing to be saved. They were destroyed. Her heart ached at the countless hours she and Ivy had worked together on them.

It had started when Ivy had only been three. She wanted to know what Mallory did at work. Mallory had bought a dollhouse, furniture, and made little drapes and assorted accessories to show Ivy. Her baby girl had been intrigued. Then when Mal had extra wood and supplies from projects, they started building their own dollhouses.

It was one of the few things they both liked. Agreed on. They didn't read the same books, watch the same shows, or date the same kind of men.

But the dollhouses were just things. Keeping Ivy safe was what really mattered.

She was jerked out of her thoughts when Isaac came back into her office and asked, "How much more to go to the trash?"

They'd cleaned up most of the office after meeting with the insurance guy. Wiping her hand on the jeans she'd changed into, she said, "I guess we might as well throw all the dollhouse stuff away." Why had she slept with Isaac? Again! She knew it was stupid, a mistake. He seemed to think he had a claim on her now.

And if Isaac knew how different sex was with him than any other man, he'd gloat. Puff up with that massive male ego. He'd find a way to use sex to control her. He'd try to make her into something she wasn't. Into something she'd never be.

"Mal, you're tired. Let's go back to Ivy's. Get something to eat."

She turned on him. "Eat? Marla is dead! Murdered. How can I eat? What if it had been Ivy? What if he gets Ivy? Who is doing this?" Her hands started to sweat. Fear gripped her belly. This was her fault. She was the one who brought Trip into . . . *Oh God*. She shoved her palms against her eyes. It was her fault.

Isaac grabbed her shoulders. "Mallory! What's wrong?"

She couldn't tell him. Not him. Tears burned her nose, her throat. "Let go of me!" She twisted away, putting distance between them. It didn't matter, she had to remind herself of that. What she'd done, it didn't have anything to do with the statues or the murders. It was just Mallory being a slut. Nothing new there. "I want to go back to Ivy's." She would work on the drapes for Ivy. And the chair rail molding. Helping Ivy make that old rambling Victorian into a home made Mal feel needed by her daughter. Valuable.

He squeezed her shoulders. "Mal, damn it, when are you going to trust me and stop running?"

She looked at Isaac. He would call her a slut and a bad mother. She'd never tell him. Never. "I don't want you. When are you going to understand that? I've told you over and over! Just take me back to Ivy's and get the hell away from me!"

*   *   *

Luke hung up the phone. "Regina hasn't heard from Pierce. She's really starting to panic. Her tour is in a few weeks." He gripped the steering wheel of the car. They'd lost hours dealing with the police. Ivy had now found two dead bodies, and that was enough to make any cop uneasy.

He was uneasy. It was too close to Ivy. He looked over at her. Even pale and tense, she was beautiful. It took his breath away to look at her.

She turned her gaze on him. "The police have a better chance of finding Pierce than we do."

He nodded and turned back to watch the road. He knew that, damn it.

"I think we should go to my father's place and see if Dirk shows up. He said he was coming back tonight. If we find Dirk, he might have some answers."

She was smart and cunning. But no way was he—

She cut him off before he could finish the thought, "Don't even try to suggest dropping me off at my house. I won't tell you where my dad lives unless I go with you."

He glanced over at her. "You drive a hard bargain."

"Damn right. It's time I faced Dirk."

He actually understood that. He didn't like it, but he understood it. Not having a choice, he said, "Okay."

"My dad lives in a mobile home he got in the settlement from his ex-wife. Off Foothill in Pomona."

"Do you have a key?"

She met his gaze, "No, will that be a problem?"

That was interesting, she seemed to be bending her rules. "Taking a walk on the dark side, Princess?"

Her blue eyes never wavered. "With you, yes. I trust you, Luke. Two people are dead, we have to find answers."

He shut up and shifted his gaze to the road. Ivy trusted him. His methods. But eventually he'd do something to change her mind. It always happened. Luke knew the score. He'd lived it over and over. New house, new family, and it was all nice until he did something wrong. Then he was thrown out. Like garbage. He'd only belonged in one place—Special Ops, until he became too broken for even them. After he had gotten his two best friends killed because he couldn't fix the helicopter fast enough.

He didn't want to do that with Ivy. Not with her. He couldn't bear to see her begin to hate him. Detest him. He'd rather walk away clean.

He headed to Pomona and followed Ivy's directions until they pulled into a mobile home park that ranged from nice double-wides to rust buckets. Greg Beaman had a peeling-paint double-wide with a thick blue tarp covering a portion of the roof. The unit was surrounded by weeds and rocks. Luke didn't stop, he just glided by the place slowly.

"What are you doing?"

"Parking somewhere else. We don't want to tip off Dirk that we're waiting for him." He went down to the guest spaces that were out of sight from her dad's mobile home. After parking, he opened the glove box and took out a canister of pepper spray. He handed it to her. "You know how to use this. Don't hesitate."

She nodded. "He didn't show a gun or anything at my house that night."

Luke put his hand on her thigh. "But you didn't take any chances either. You grabbed your mom to keep her from following Dirk. Smart, Ivy. Damned smart, and it also tells me that you believe Dirk can be dangerous."

She put her hand to her cheek. "He never hit me before. Ever."

Oh yeah, he really wanted the bastard to show up. Breaking that knife-wielding weasel Ed's arm was nothing compared to what he'd do to Dirk. "I won't let him touch you. I swear."

She set her jaw and narrowed her eyes. "I'm not afraid, I'm pissed." Then she swiveled around and got out of the car.

Luke caught up to her, and said, "I'm going in first to make sure it's safe. Got that?" He led them up warped steps to the front door.

She nodded and stayed quiet. Luke nudged her up to a wall beside the door; then he dropped down to study the lock. It was so simple he could open it with a bobby pin. Her dad wasn't much on security. He slid the long tool in, felt the catch, and turned the knob. Rising to his feet, he put the tool in his pocket and took his gun from the small of his back.

He looked at Ivy.

She stared back at him and nodded.

Knowing she'd stay there, he went inside and wrinkled his nose. The thick smell of old grease and beer made it hard to breathe. He quickly walked over gold shag carpeting, dodging clothes, towels, newspapers, and fast-food wrappers. The kitchen had brown linoleum and a trash can overfilled with beer cans.

He left the kitchen and headed down the short hallway. He checked the bathroom, second bedroom, and stopped in the master bedroom. "Shit." The place was a pig pen, sheets and blanket tangled on the bed, clothes everywhere, but it was the smashed window and torn screen that infuriated him.

"Dirk's already been here," Ivy said behind him.

He turned around, glad that she at least had the pepper spray uncapped and ready in her hand. The one thing he knew with Ivy, she wasn't stupid. He could count on her to use her huge brain when in danger. "I'd say so. Your dad didn't answer the door, so Dirk found another way in. He left the same way when he realized your dad wasn't here."

She looked around. "How come he didn't trash this place?"

"Not worth the effort. He wants your dad to get to you."

She doubled back to the living room and stopped, staring at the couch, coffee table, and TV. Newspapers, food debris, and beer cans covered the coffee table and couch.

"Looking for something?" he asked her.

She picked up a section of the newspaper. "He's circled properties that are for sale. Houses like mine."

Luke felt his gut kick. "You know what he is, Ivy."

"Yes." She dropped that newspaper and picked up another.

An article about the theft of the statues. Another about Ivy's "connection" with the thefts, and a rehash of the money Dirk had stolen. "He believes I stole that money. Probably with Dirk."

"Let's go." He reached for her arm.

She slipped away, picking up another newspaper that had an article about Ivy's radio show and her as a rising star. She dropped it and kept searching. "That's weird, it's not here."

Baffled, Luke asked, "What are you looking for?"

She stood up. "The blueprints to my house. I came over once, stupidly believing Greg wanted to have a relationship with me. But of course he wanted the house. He has the original blueprints. The house has been in his family since it was built. When his parents died, they left the house to his sister, my Aunt Betty, and the family business to my dad. He ran the business into the ground."

Luke watched her wading through all the debris. "Do you think the blueprints are important?"

"To him." She stood up and shook her head. "I don't know. It's stupid, let's go." She skirted around him and went to the door.

Luke followed her, turning the flimsy lock and pulling the door closed behind him.

"I'll get his window fixed tomorrow," Ivy said as she got in the car.

He'd never figure her out. "Why would you do that? Let him pay for his own window." Her father lured her to his house, playing on her emotions of wanting a dad, then tried to get her to sign over her house. She didn't owe him anything. When she didn't answer, he looked over at her. "Ivy?"

She said, "You could make Arnold miserable every day. Hire a battery of auditors and hound him. You could take your half of the money, but you don't. Why?"

He merged onto the freeway. "Not the same thing. It amuses me to dangle the threat over him, to keep him wondering when I'll show up, what I'll do."

"You're full of shit, Sterling."

He set his teeth. "The hell I am." The old anger rushed through him. He kept his gaze fixed on the road, one hand on the wheel and the other curled in a fist on his thigh. "I'm waiting for the day that bastard has it all. A woman he loves, a life that depends on that business; then I will destroy him. Take it all away. Insist on all my back pay and bring in auditors to get it." His chest hurt with the need to strike back.

Ivy touched his arm, her fingers cool against his hot skin. "You're lying. You won't do it because you loved your aunt. She screwed up, she let you go into the system. But she somehow figured it out, didn't she?"

He was done with this conversation. "Ancient history."

"What really happened that day when your grandma died?"

Luke didn't want to talk about it. "I'm sure Arnold told you."

"He told me you stabbed him with a kitchen knife. Was it an accident? Grief?"

Luke turned to Ivy and met her gaze. "You believed him? Don't feel bad, Princess, so did his parents. His mom cried, his dad threw me across the room and dislocated my shoulder." He jerked his gaze away from her horror-stricken face. From the memories. From it all. Just get her home and go do his job.

Get away from her. Away from all the things she made him feel.

"Luke! How could they . . . what happened? Tell me, I'll believe you."

She wouldn't. No one did. Not even the social workers or the shrinks. "Really, Princess? Do you believe a ten-year-old boy stabbed himself so he didn't have to share his parents with his six-year-old cousin?"

"I . . . he stabbed himself?"

Disbelief. Oh yeah, he knew it well. "He was always afraid his mom would love me more than him, as he believed our grandmother did. So he made damn sure she never got the chance."

"How did your aunt find out? She found out, right?"

Luke took a deep breath. "When I got out of the service, my aunt gave me a job in Sterling Investigations, her company. Arnie was furious; he got drunk and came after me with a knife. She saw the whole thing, and she heard Arnold screaming at me that he should have finished the job the first time."

"Did you hurt him?"

Luke snorted. "He was drunk. Too easy. I took the knife and left." Just got the hell away from the scene. Because he could never do the family shit right. Ever. He always fucked it up somehow. Every chance he'd had, he'd blown.

"I'll replace my dad's window because Dirk broke it trying to use my dad to get to me. I owe my dad that much, as much as I'd do for any human being, but I don't owe him anything else. That's how I live with myself and sleep at night."

He pulled into the driveway of her house. "I use sex to sleep at night."

Ivy walked into the house to the sound of her mom downstairs working on the drapes and Isaac upstairs pacing like a caged animal. "I should spank her. I swear I'll do it!"

Ivy dropped her purse and rubbed her temples. "Your talk didn't go well?"

He stopped pacing. "It went perfect. So damned perfect until she started thinking again. If I kept her in bed, this wouldn't happen!"

Luke hurried into the kitchen and made a lot of noise. Ivy rolled her eyes and said, "I don't want to picture you and my mom having sex. In my house. Try to have some boundaries." She didn't dare close her eyes. She'd either see poor Marla or she'd see her mom . . .

Isaac dropped down onto the couch. "I'm worried. Mal is hiding something, and nothing I've done will get her to talk. She's scared. And since you called to tell us about Marla, she's almost in a panic."

Ivy knew what her mom was like when she felt cornered. "I'll talk to her." She started toward the staircase when her cell phone rang.

She walked to her purse and pulled it out. She recognized the number. Putting the phone to her ear, she said, "Arnold?"

Luke roared out of the kitchen, his gray eyes intent on her.

In her ear, Arnold said, "Ivy, I've been tied up. Kat Vaugn's house was broken into last night. She got away, but she's been terrified. I have her with me."

"Kat's with you? Did she see the intruder?"

"No, heard him, grabbed her purse, and went out the back. My card was in her purse. She called the police, then called me. Her house was torn apart. The cops used sirens, so when they arrived the intruder was gone."

She sank down onto the arm of the couch. "Someone looking for the statues."

"Yes, I heard about Marla too. Ivy, Luke won't talk to me. Won't take my calls. I've tried to talk to Regina Parker, but she's refused. But none of this sounds right to me, and after talking to Kat . . ."

Luke sat next to her. She tilted the phone so he could hear. "What doesn't sound right?"

"How did Trip Vaugn pull this off? He's a small-time con artist, not a master thief. And Regina Parker is a professor, and she has those statues booked for a tour. How did she let someone like Trip steal them?"

Ivy tilted her gaze to Luke. Before either of them had an answer, there was another call beeping on her cell. "Arnold, hang on." She switched the phone to the other call. "Hello?"

"Ivy York? This is Ann Mitchell, producer of *Celebrity Now* TV show. We'd like very much to interview you about the sex hex and the Urban Legend. Tonight."

Leah gave them her phone number? She was trying to catch up.

"This is the first time any woman has turned the tables on the Urban Legend. It'll be a hot story. And I don't need to remind you, it'll help raise the profile of you and your radio show."

Luke had stiffened next to her, but nothing showed on his face. "I'm not—"

A little more forcefully, she said, "Actually, Ms. York, your boss said you would do the show."

Had she? "My boss was wrong." She switched back to Arnold and tried to calm down. "Arnold, I need to take care of something. I'll call you back."

He sighed as if being brushed off. "Okay."

With the memory of Marla hovering in her mind, she added, "Arnold, keep Kat safe with you. Please."

"I am." He hung up.

She picked up the remote and turned on the TV. She flipped to different stations that had soft news. Marla's murder featured prominently, as it should. But the statues were getting a huge amount of attention, and so was Ivy and Luke.

One station even had a grainy picture of her and Luke standing outside the on-air booth, staring at each other, their bodies leaning in toward one another. The shot screamed "lovers." Ivy recognized it from when Luke had come into the station when Ivy was doing the interview with the radio show *Stranger Than Fiction*.

Only one other person had been there. *Leah*. She had to have snapped the photo with her cell phone. "Leah's been the one leaking information to the media."

Luke put his hand on her shoulder.

Isaac said, "Ratings."

She tried to grasp it. Her mind tumbled, almost like falling down a flight of stairs, bouncing on bits of information along the way. Finally, her tumbling thoughts landed on the host of *Stranger Than Fiction* telling Ivy she'd interviewed Regina and suggested that Regina needed the Urban Legend to bring real attention to the statues. Ratings and attention—that's something the Urban Legend would do, ratings for KCEX and attention for the statues. Ivy pulled herself together and focused. "I checked all the employees, but I never checked Leah." Grabbing her laptop, she went to the table and booted it up. Leah had her personal bank accounts at the same bank she used for the radio show.

Ivy's phone rang again. She looked at the display of her cell, and answered with, "Leah."

"Ivy, you have to do *Celebrity Now.*"

She squeezed the phone until her fingers hurt, still wanting to believe that Leah hadn't done the unthinkable. She said, "Marla's dead, Leah. I'm not up to publicity."

"Exactly, Marla's dead. We have to do everything we can to help find who killed her. The more attention we bring to this, the better. I'm trying to help you here. Your dad caused a lot of damage with his TV appearance."

Guilt. Nice touch. "I'm sorry, Leah, I just can't."

Leah let the silence stretch out, then finally conceded by saying, "I'll do a call-in interview in your place. Ivy, you'd better pull yourself together." She hung up.

Ivy clicked on to the bank Web site and didn't let herself think about anything but the numbers. She typed in Leah Allen for username, then for password . . . it was too easy. When would people learn to change their passwords? As smart as Leah was, she hated trying to remember passwords. So she used the same one everywhere. For password, Ivy typed, "KCEX820."

And she was in.

She started paging through the accounts. She scanned the transactions until she came to a withdrawal.

Four thousand dollars.

Her pulse picked up, her heart raced, and she could hear her blood pounding in her ear. Three weeks ago, Leah withdrew four thousand dollars. Right after Regina's party where Trip was the bartender but before the statues were stolen.

Had Leah gone to Regina's party?

Luke moved up to her side. "What do you have?"

She looked up at Luke. "A withdrawal for four thousand

dollars. Half the amount of the money we found in Trip's account." She forced her mind to stay on track, follow to the logical conclusion. "What if we were wrong? What if Trip didn't steal the statues because Marla hired him to? What if he stole them because Leah and someone else hired him to?"

"Who?"

She knew he didn't want to hear this. "Who is really profiting from all the attention on the statues? And Arnold had a point—how did Trip Vaugn manage to steal them from a woman as smart and passionate about the statues as Regina?"

Anger washed over his face. "Regina? I checked her out. It's the first thing I do on any kind of insurance case. And you're forgetting, she has this whole tour set up and has been aggressively promoting the tour. It's the most important thing in the world to her. She needs the statues; she wouldn't risk losing them."

"What if she didn't think it was a real risk? What if her passion got the better of her common sense?" Ivy went to the Web site for the radio station that had the *Stranger Than Fiction* show. She pulled up the interviews and clicked on an excerpt of the interview with Professor Regina Parker. "Listen," she told Luke.

> *"Is it true you know the Urban Legend? Is he as hot as everyone says?"*
>
> "I thought we were going to talk about the Jade Goddesses of Fertility and Virility. The statues are at least five centuries old and have a fascinating legend of sex, love, and murder. Once you see them, you'll feel their power."
>
> *"Sex, love, and murder, wow. That sounds like something that would attract the Urban Legend's attention. Has he seen the statues?"*
>
> (Audible sigh) "No, he's been too busy treasure hunting and honing his reputation as a sex legend.

Now, can we talk about the statues? I will be taking the statues on tour—"

"How do you know he's honing his reputation as a sex legend? Have you had . . . uh . . . personal experience?"

(Bigger sigh) "No, back to the statues, they were carved by a powerful sorcerer to set up meetings with the woman he loved but could never have. They used the statues to pass messages of where and when to meet to conduct a passionate affair."

"Oh my. How romantic."

"Indeed. As best we can tell, the Jade Goddesses of Fertility and Virility came from the Aztecs. They had a highly structured society based on religion, magic, and science. A society that prevented two star-crossed lovers from being together. The powerful sorcerer would not be denied, however, and he carved the statues out of two pieces of jade, including the traditional oblong space for a jade heart. But when he crafted the hearts to fill the oblong space, he made them hollow. The two lovers communicated by leaving messages inside the hearts to set up clandestine meetings."

"They wrote notes to each other?"

"They didn't have the same written language we have today. We believe they left markers of some kind inside the hearts that indicated a place and time—perhaps gems, locks of hair, who knows? It's quite romantic to consider—until, of course, the tragedy struck."

"Tragedy? What happened? Were the lovers caught?"

"Infinitely worse. Someone stole the hearts of the goddesses, and the legend goes that the two lovers died instantly."

"That's horrible. But how could such a thing happen?"

"Because the man who carved the statues was a sorcerer, and the two hearts were crafted with the blood of their love. It's said the statues have been looking for their deepest desire ever since then. Even today, the power of the statues lives on. They bring out people's deepest desire, deepest lust."

"What does that mean exactly? If someone like the Urban Legend came in contact with these statues, he'd get even more sex? That wouldn't really be anything extraordinary, would it?"

(Pause) "It would depend on what the Urban Legend's deepest desire is. What he really lusts for."

"Hmm, you might want to guard those statues carefully, Professor. A lot of women may want to steal them to seduce the Urban Legend." (Shuffling, clearing of throat) "Or maybe some woman out there thinks she can use the statues to catch the Urban Legend permanently. Now that would be extraordinary."

(Academic sniff) "The statues aren't a match-making service; they are an exceptional and exquisite piece of history with a fascinating and provocative legend."

Ivy clicked off and looked at Luke. "Regina couldn't get the media to focus on her statues the way she wanted them to, so she found a way to create excitement. And give the world a demonstration of the statues' power. Remember when she was here? Talking about how we couldn't concentrate because we were under the influence of the statues? She's using us . . ." She had to swallow down her anger, betrayal, grief. "Two people are dead!"

Luke walked away.

Ivy jumped up and ran after him. She grabbed his arm. "Where are you going?"

Luke looked down at her, his gray eyes cold. His entire body was tense. She could feel him leashing his anger. "I'm going to find out the truth."

Think. Luke didn't like being used any more than she had. If they were right, both Regina and Leah had picked Luke because the media made his life, his work, into an endless series of sexcapades. *I'm good for sex, nothing else,* he'd told her. "I'm going with you. Let's try the radio station first. I'm betting Leah will do the call-in interview from there. And she might just have her cohort in crime with her."

Luke pulled into the parking lot of the radio station, still furious that he'd missed the obvious. His dick had taken over his brain, and he had missed the fact that Trip should never have been able to get those statues. It made sense when he thought Ivy had been directing Trip because she was smart enough to do it. But once he realized Ivy hadn't been the one directing Trip, he should have known. One look at Ivy York, and he'd become an idiot. His cousin, his limp-dick cousin, figured it out before he did. To Ivy, he said, "Leah's and Regina's cars are here."

Ivy nodded and got out.

Grabbing her arm, he followed her in, waiting while she quietly unlocked the front door; then they slipped into the reception area.

They heard voices. The radio station was off the air for the evening, but they were in the control room outside the sound booth. They'd left the door open. Ivy put her finger to her lips.

Luke nodded.

"We're in a grip of trouble, serious trouble."

Luke recognized Regina's voice.

Leah's voice answered, "No one will know. Trip's dead; there's no way anyone can prove we had anything to do with it. As long as we find the statues, everything will work out. *Celebrity Now* is another great opportunity to promote the statues, Regina. Don't panic and screw this up."

Ivy turned and looked at him.

Luke felt her betrayal. The same as his own. They had been used.

Regina said, "I don't understand what went wrong! None of this makes any sense. Trip was supposed to get Mallory to stash them in the station and disappear. I can't believe he tried to sell them. Luke told me Marla was trying to buy them. This is a nightmare."

"No, it's not." Leah's voice was sharp but calm. "Don't you see? This clears us. Everyone will believe Marla hired Trip. They can't blame us."

"But I have to get those statues! The Jade Goddesses are my life's work!"

Leah dropped her voice to a reassuring tone. "We will. Those statues are more famous than ever now. They are all over the media, everyone is fascinated, they will turn up. Your tour will be more successful than you ever imagined. You know Luke and Ivy will find them. They have to, we made sure of it by implicating Mallory."

Ivy snapped her back straight and hissed.

Luke put his arm around her shoulders, pulling her into his body. Rubbing her upper arm, he listened.

"Are you sure? What about Ivy? She refused to do that interview tonight."

"You let me handle Ivy. I'm making her famous. She's ambitious and she cares more about dollar signs than anything else. When I sell the station, her show will be syndicated. She'll thank me." Leah's voice paused, then she added, "Hell, she should thank me for the sex too. I never met a woman who needed a good fuck more than her."

Rage like he'd never felt boiled up inside of Luke. If Leah were a man, Luke would slam his fist through her mouth for that remark. No one talked about Ivy that way. She was sweet, giving, and real, all the things he could wish for in a woman and a lover. He realized he'd taken a step toward the offices when Ivy's hand landed on his arm. He looked back.

She shook her head and tugged on his arm.

He struggled with himself, needing to be the one to stand up and defend her. But she was right, too much was at stake for him to lose it now. They quietly went out, got into the car, and headed back to Ivy's house.

His gut churned as he drove. Too much adrenaline coursed through him. He had to focus on the case. Think about the puzzle. Not Ivy, not her entire life being destroyed. He'd already screwed up because of his . . . lust . . . for Ivy. She was quiet, too quiet. He looked over at her. She had her head back on the headrest, her eyes closed. "You okay?"

"I couldn't face Leah tonight. I have to face myself first. And deal with the fact that she doesn't care that Marla is dead. Marla was a friend. I know she tried to do something wrong, but I understand it. I understand wanting so desperately to be loved. She didn't deserve to be murdered for that."

Luke clenched his fingers around the steering wheel, hating her pain. Her grief.

"I keep seeing her like that, her head half gone, and now she'll never have that love she craved. And Leah didn't care." She shivered, wrapping her arms around herself.

He didn't know what to do for her. How to help her. This was the shit he didn't get, never would. Pulling to a stop in front of the house, he parked and said, "Look, we'll find the statues. You'll get your life back."

She turned to look at him. "Leah can shove my job up her ass. I don't want it. I want love. Family. The real thing. I want to matter to the people I care about. I won't be just a commodity to someone. Not ever again."

Chapter 17

Ivy didn't talk to Isaac or her mom. She didn't talk to Luke. Her shame at who she allowed herself to become was so deep, she didn't know how to deal with it. She stripped out of her clothes and got in the shower, trying to wash away her guilt, shame, and grief.

Marla would never get her chance at real love.

Her head ached. Tears rolled down her face and mixed with the shower. What did it matter? No one would see her. But maybe somehow Marla would know that Ivy was sorry. If Ivy had taken more time to be friends with Marla, maybe she could have stopped her.

Had Pierce killed her? Killed the woman who loved him that desperately? Or Dirk? Or someone they hadn't even thought of yet?

The bathroom door slid open. "Get out," Ivy said. It had to be her mom or Luke. She was betting on her mom.

The curtain slid back.

Not her mom.

Luke stood there wearing nothing but a pair of jeans riding low on his hips. Huge, powerful, his gray eyes fierce on her. His shoulders filled up the opening to her shower, his chest rippled with tension, and his stomach was tight. A large bulge pressed against the front of his low-riding jeans. "Come here, Ivy."

She closed her eyes, the pull of Luke so powerful she was even more ashamed. What had she just said in the car? That she wouldn't be a commodity. That's all she was to Luke—a way to get the statues. And sex. "Don't. Just go away. I want you too much, I crave a man who thinks of me as a . . . coward and . . ." A sob choked her. Why did she tell him? He'd only use it against her. She understood her mom. In this moment, she got it. Be the one to screw and run. It hurt so much less. She backed up a step against the cold wall.

The water went off.

Snapping open her eyes, she said, "Get out. Leave me alone!"

He stepped into the tub, crowded her until he slapped his hands against the walls of the enclosure and trapped her. "Your tears make me bleed inside, and I don't know what the fuck I am supposed to do about that. I want to kill that bitch Leah. I will pulverize that prick Dirk when I find him. And I will not leave you the fuck alone."

Stunned stupid, her mouth dropped open.

He reached back, grabbed a towel, and dragged it over her body. Ivy sucked in her breath when the terry cloth rubbed her nipples; then Luke moved it down her belly, between her legs. She shivered. She looked down at him. He was crouched before her, his big shoulders at her hips, looking at her. He seemed to shake himself like a big wolf, and drew the towel down her legs. Standing up, he threw the towel to the floor and lifted her in his arms.

"Luke?" She put her arms around his neck. What did he want from her?

He sat on the end of the bed and cradled her on his lap. His arms held her to him, skin to skin, uncaring that her wet hair dripped all over him. Ivy felt like she couldn't get close enough to him, and yet, the feel of his skin against hers was more erotic, and more tender, than anything she'd ever felt. Finally, Luke said, "When I got out of the helicopter and saw the remains of my two friends, my mind snapped. I gathered them up in a blanket and flew them back. I don't remember doing that, but they tell me I did."

"Oh God, Luke." Lifting her head, she looked into his eyes. Saw the lines of sheer agony around them, and in the gray depths, she saw his smoky grief and guilt.

He met her gaze. "I'm telling you this so you understand something. You are a woman who deserves someone who can love you. I can't be that man. I've tried in the past and failed. I was never enough, not for my aunt and uncle, not for any of the foster parents, not for Kelly, and I wasn't enough for the two men I loved like brothers. I brought them home in pieces, Ivy. I can't care about you that way. I can't."

Her chest hurt. She was already in love with him. But he wouldn't believe her. He'd never had anyone fight for him. He'd never had anyone forgive him. Love him. Show him what real love and family meant. She tightened her arms around his neck, unwilling to let him go.

He reached up a thumb and gently wiped her tears. "I swear to you, I won't be too late to save you. Or your mom. I won't let either of you get hurt. Can you just believe in that?"

"Yes." She didn't hesitate.

Relief eased the tense lines around his eyes, and the color of his eyes deepened into a molten gray-blue. "I have to touch you."

The words were throttled low, desperate. She could feel them rumble in his chest, feel his need. His gaze left her eyes and trailed down her body. Her skin heated, her womb softened, and she felt herself melting into his arms, letting him look.

He brought his hand up and traced her mouth with his thumb. "You're going to let me, Ivy. I'm going to touch you everywhere." He pressed his thumb into her mouth.

She sucked him in, tasting Luke. She couldn't tell him she loved him. But she could give him what he wanted. Freely. No strings, no guilt, no recriminations. Total trust in him.

Sliding his thumb out, he drew his hand down her neck, over her chest, to cradle one breast. He stroked the distended tip with his wet thumb.

The sensation shot from her breast straight to her womb. Her clit ached, and she let her thighs fall open, silently begging him.

He shifted his gaze down her belly to her thighs, then back to her face. "So beautiful. And mine. For now, mine. All of you."

A deep tremor went through her. She could feel his cock straining against his pants beneath her. But something else was going on, something more than sex. Something so personal and intimate, it shoved out the entire world and it was only them. Luke and her, and their need to feed each other's desires. "Yes," she whispered. And she wrapped her hand around his arm, pulling his hand down her belly. "Touch me."

His face flushed, his breathing roughened. "God, yes." Taking over, he slid his fingers into her pubic hair, separating her folds and finding her clit. His arm around her tightened, pulling her into his chest. "You're so hot, wet. Jesus . . ." he broke off, pressing his fingers into her.

"Luke," she curled her fist against his chest. Her hips rose, seeking him.

"God, I just want to feel you on me. Feel your slick, hot little body sucking me in." He lifted her with one arm and unbuttoned his pants. Shoved them aside.

Ivy looked down, saw his cock spring free. Big, thick, straining. She looked into his eyes.

"I won't come. I swear. Just want to feel . . ." Getting both hands around her waist, he lifted her so that her knees rested on either side of his hips. "Never mind." Leaning around her, he reached over to the bedside table and grabbed the box of condoms.

Ivy trusted him. Luke knew her, knew she was very careful not to accidentally get pregnant as her mom had. Knew she didn't sleep around. Knew she didn't take risks. And he stopped himself from asking her to take a risk for him. But for him, she'd take any risk to bring him into her body with no barriers, no lies, no pretense. Only their honesty in the moment, their connection. She reached down, taking hold of him, and lowered herself on him. Took him in. Felt him pressed through her folds and inside her. She took him an inch at a time. He kept one hand on her back to steady her, his gaze hard on her face. When she had him fully inside her, when he touched her womb, he wrapped his big hand around the back of her head, pulled her forward, and kissed her. He tongued her mouth while his body shuddered with the effort of holding back from thrusting into her. Then he lifted his mouth from hers. "I just had to touch you, feel all of you. Feel every part of you. For a moment I had my very own princess."

Her eyes filled, but she blinked the tears back. She lifted off of him, took the condom and rolled it on. And took him back inside of her where he belonged, and rode him until he wrapped his arms around her, held her tight, and they both exploded.

A part of her heart cracked, but it belonged to Luke now, and she'd never regret that.

The phone woke her out of a deep sleep. Ivy lifted her head and looked at the clock. Three minutes after eleven P.M.

"It stopped ringing," Luke said in her ear. He hauled her back against his chest, pulled the covers up around her shoulders, and added, "Go back to sleep."

As soon as he said the words, someone knocked on the bedroom door. "Ivy, phone for you. It's Greg. I'd hang up on him, but he says he'll keep calling until he talks to you."

"Let go," she told Luke.

He lifted his arm off her and slid his heavy thigh off her hip. Ivy threw back the covers and got out of bed. She grabbed her robe and put it on.

"Answer it here," Luke said.

She looked at him in the nightlight from the bathroom. He

was huge, taking up most of her bed. Her heart did that weird flutter. "Go back to sleep. I'll take it in the kitchen." She wanted him to sleep. Turning around, she walked to the door and slipped out into the hallway.

Ivy frowned. "Mom, you look tired. Why aren't you sleeping?" She obviously had been in the kitchen when the phone rang.

Mallory glared at her. "Everywhere I try to sleep, that dumb ox tries to get into bed with me. If I go downstairs and get into bed, he shows up. If I go upstairs and sleep in that bed, he shows up. He says I can't outrun him."

Rolling her eyes, she said, "You two are sick, you know that?"

Her mom shook her head. "No, just him. He's like . . . stupid or something."

Ivy looked into her mom's brown eyes and saw real fear. "Whatever it is, you can just tell him. He knows you're keeping something from him."

She lifted her chin and folded her arms beneath her breasts. "I don't have to tell him anything."

"No, you don't. But you could, Mom." She turned and went down the hallway and into the kitchen. Her mom had put the phone on hold. She picked it up. "What do you want, Dad?"

"I have a deal for you."

Her mom came into the kitchen. Then Luke came in, wearing a pair of jeans and sexy bedroom eyes. God. "What deal?"

"I heard that girl was murdered today. For the statues? Everyone is looking for the statues. I know where they are."

She snapped up straight, her robe slapping gently against her calves. "You what?" *What the hell?* "Are you drunk?"

"I've known for a while. If you want them, I'll tell you where they are . . . when you sign over the house to me. It's supposed to be my house. Then we both get what we want."

"I'm not giving you my house!" Outrage boiled hot and thick, making her head pound.

"What?" Luke roared the word out.

Ivy looked at her mom and Luke. "My dad says he knows where the statues are. He'll tell me if I sign over my house."

Isaac appeared in the doorway too. He wore a pair of navy blue sweatpants and his hair stood out like a chia pet. But his plain brown eyes were alert.

Her dad said, "You will, Ivy. Because if you don't agree to my plan, I'm going to call the police and tell them where the statues are. Then you and your mother will go to prison."

A chill dripped down her spine. She clutched the phone so hard her fingers hurt. "Where are they?"

"In the house. They've been there all along. You'll never find them. Only I know where they are."

"How? How do you know?" She was so furious she knew if her dad had been standing in her house right then, she'd have attacked him.

"Trip and I knocked back a few beers. Shared some secrets. I always knew those hidden compartments in the house would come in handy. I found them when I was a kid. I know where he hid those statues. Ten A.M. tomorrow. You give me the house or I'll make sure you and your mom get what you deserve."

She opened her mouth but nothing came out.

"Put him on hold." Luke's voice was flat. Emotionless.

Ivy did, then told them all exactly what he said. "But how would Trip hide the statues in my house? He's never been in my house." She rubbed her forehead with her fingertips, trying to make sense of it.

Isaac said, "That doesn't matter right now. What matters is finding the statues."

Luke put his hand on Ivy's shoulder. "I'll go over and deal with your dad. I'll make him tell me."

Ivy pulled herself together. "No, Luke. I don't want you beating up my dad."

"Ivy . . ."

"No." She shook her head.

"Ivy, don't do it. Don't give in to his blackmail." Her mom said, huge tears pooling in her tired eyes. "We'll give him my house. Okay? Please, make him take my house. Not yours. I don't care, just—"

"Mom!" She stepped toward her, reaching out to calm her down.

Isaac turned Mallory to face him. With both hands on her shoulders, he said, "Is this what's been eating at you?"

She nodded her head. "It's my fault. Isaac, I don't care what you think of me, you have to help Ivy. Don't let Greg do this to her. Trick him and give him my house."

Ivy felt the old dread take hold. "Mom, what are you talking about?"

She twisted her head to look at Ivy, most likely to avoid Issac, and said, "I brought him here. Trip. I wanted to show him . . . I don't know! But he saw your house. And he could have easily gotten my key to hide the statues later."

Ivy saw Luke wince. She ignored him. "Mom, do you know where the statues might be hidden?"

She shook her head, tears tracking down her face. "No, but these old homes often have secret little holes. We'll never find them, but if Greg tells the police exactly where to look—"

Ivy nodded. "Fine, we'll give him what he wants. Isaac, can you draw up a fake document that looks real enough to fool Greg?" She saw that he hadn't let go of her mom.

"Yes. I'll have it by morning. Tell the bastard to meet me at my office. Ivy, I'll take care of this."

She nodded, picked up the phone, and told Greg to meet her lawyer at his office at ten A.M. Then she hung up.

The silence hung there until Mallory finally turned and looked at Isaac. In a whisper, she said, "Go ahead, call me a slut. I don't care."

He dropped his hands. "Not now, Mal. You three start looking while I go draw up the papers. Ivy, I'm going to use your office."

* * *

Mallory had sent Ivy and Luke to bed at one-thirty A.M. Everyone was exhausted. But she wouldn't stop, wouldn't give up. Not that it would matter, Isaac would get Ivy out of this.

She had taken everything out of the cupboards in the kitchen, looking for a fake back wall. Nothing. She'd tried every closet—closets and cupboards were popular for fake walls or floors. Giving up in the kitchen, she went into the dining room and the built-in hutch that they had stripped down to bare wood.

Her neck ached, her eyes burned, and her stomach was queasy. Opening the doors, she traced the back wall of the hutch that had carved scrolls, maybe it was fake backing? She tried to concentrate on her task, not Isaac. Somehow she cared what he thought. How had it happened?

He hadn't even wanted to talk to her. She wished he'd called her a slut. Said something. Told her he hated her, couldn't stand to be near her. Anything but just walked away. Or if he'd walked out on all of them, but no, he was hero enough to save Ivy's house. Isaac loved Ivy like a daughter.

She gave up on the hutch and sank down on the hard dining room chair. And faced the truth. It was her, Mallory, that Isaac was disgusted by.

A sob worked up her throat. She drew her legs up on the chair, bit her lip, rested her forehead on her knees, and just tried to breathe. Don't make noise. Don't let anyone know. Isaac must have finished up the papers and gone to bed downstairs. She forced her feet down to the floor and stood. She'd go in the room, close the door, and get through the night.

Then she'd get through tomorrow.

Then all she had to do was get through the rest of her days.

She was so damned tired. Tired of running. Tired of proving the world right, that she was a slut. Tired of being afraid.

Tired of being alone.

She cared so much about Isaac that it terrified her.

But really? What did it matter now? He had no illusions, did he? So what if he called her a slut? She'd been called worse and her heart kept beating.

Maybe it was best to just face him. Get it over with. Let him say whatever he wanted to her. He deserved that much, he deserved more. Isaac wouldn't walk out on Ivy for something Mallory did. Why hadn't she seen it before? Seen the real man instead of just her fear?

If she had told him first, been honest when he asked her what was wrong, would he have forgiven her? Forgiven that she endangered her daughter by bringing a boy toy to Ivy's house? Mallory would never know. But she could do one thing right. She could tell Isaac . . . something. Make him believe she loved Ivy and that she hadn't meant to endanger her.

Ivy knew that. At least Mallory had that much—her daughter knew she loved her.

But Isaac, he deserved words from her. Apology. He'd arrived when Ivy called him, he'd been there for both of them. Mal was the one who destroyed everything, even their friendship.

She'd never really known she could be friends with a man.

She walked forward, turned right, and went down the steps. She clutched the wood banister rubbed smooth by years of use. She could hear the gentle slap of her bare feet. She could taste her fear, but she could also feel her resolve.

The light was on in Ivy's office.

She took a breath, went around the corner, and walked in.

Isaac sat behind Ivy's desk, a short-sleeve shirt thrown on but not buttoned, his head bent as he read over documents he must have printed. Slowly, he lifted his head and looked at her.

"I'm sorry." It was all she could think to say. Then words started rushing out. "I want you to know that I appreciate everything you're doing for Ivy. I know you're doing it for her, not me, but I appreciate it anyway." She reached out and clutched the back of a fabric-covered chair. "I wanted to tell you, but I was so afraid. I brought Trip to Ivy's house when I was dropping off wallpaper. He claimed to be interested, and I showed him the house because Ivy is the one thing in my life I'm proud of."

She stopped talking. Swallowed. Forced herself to look at him. His glasses sat on his intelligent face. His eyes were brutally honest. She'd never imagined a man like him loving her. Being her friend. At least she could hold on to that. Yes, she killed his love, his friendship, but for a period of time, he had genuinely loved her. "Okay, I'll leave. I just wanted you to know . . ." She turned away.

"Wanted me to know what, Mal? That you appreciate me helping Ivy?"

She turned back to him. Frowned. "Yes, and me. All that you've done for me." She was trying, but she knew she wasn't doing a good job.

He put the papers down on the desk, took off his glasses, and leaned back in the chair. "That's all you got?"

She tried again. "And that I'm sorry."

"Baby, I know you're sorry. That's not what I asked."

She started to shake. Real fear set into her blood and rushed everywhere. "What do you want from me?"

He gaze was steady, level, and demanding. "I want you to tell me what you really want me to know."

She wanted to look away, but his gaze was magnetic. She'd told him she was sorry, that she . . . her mind slid back to this morning. To Isaac making love to her. Not sex. She'd had sex with lots of men. Just sex, a little pleasure and no heart. With Isaac, it was making love. And she knew then why he could reach her as no one else ever had.

She was in love with him.

And if she told him, would he use it as punishment? Tell her he doesn't love a slut? But Mallory was tired, tired of running. Her mouth went bone-dry. She felt cold from the inside out. "I'm scared."

His face softened, while his eyes grew more intense. "I know. You'll just have to decide if I'm worth the risk."

She got this far. Came down the stairs. Told him stuff. She was standing here in the office. What could he do? Throw her out of her daughter's house? No. Tell her it was too late? Okay, he could. But wouldn't it be better to know? She shifted, putting one bare foot over the other, wrapping her arms around herself, trying to find enough warmth and courage. Finally, she forced her jaws to open. She said the words "I love you." Then she just stood there and waited for it.

Isaac shoved his chair back from the desk and opened his arms. "Come here, Mal."

She hurried toward him, terrified he'd change his mind. Isaac reached up, pulled her down onto his lap, and held her against him. "I love you, Mal. God, stop shaking. I'm not going to hurt you."

"But I hurt you."

"Only because you didn't trust me enough to tell me." He rubbed her back.

She leaned her head back and looked into his eyes. "How can you love me? I screwed other men!" She didn't understand.

"You screwed them because you were afraid. Of me and what you and I have. Love. I let you run because I figured you would tire out. And you have tired of running, haven't you?"

Hot tears brimmed in her eyes. Her throat thickened. "Yes." It was a whisper.

He touched her face. "When you give me your word, I believe in it. When you tell me it's me and no other man, I believe you. You've never lied to me, Mal. You told me you wouldn't date just me. You told me all of it. The only person you've ever lied to is yourself."

She shivered and leaned into him, melting against his body. His arms wrapped around her. "You know, don't you?" she said into his chest.

His voice thickened with knowledge and pride. "That you only come for me? Yes. Because you cry every time. Like I've given you a precious gift."

"I don't want anyone else. Just you." It didn't take any real courage to tell him anymore. "I love you."

He kissed her head. "Tell me again when I'm inside you."

Sanders and Ray sat in the back of the helicopter. Luke knew it was wrong. They were whole. And alive. Razzing the shit out of him. Calling him "Urban Legend" and laughing their asses off.

He looked back at them. "Stop it, you're dead!"

They stopped laughing. "We know that. Dead doesn't make us stupid."

Furious, he yelled at them, "Stupid is what got you dead. All you had to do was stay alive until I got there! I would have gotten you out!" God, why hadn't they stayed alive?

They looked at each other, then him. "But, Luke, you did get us out. You brought us home."

Luke opened his eyes in the cool, dark early morning. For the first time in years, he could remember them as they'd been alive. Not dead. It sent a shaft of raw, burning pain through him. He missed them. He actually felt real grief.

He never had. All he'd felt was the mind-crushing guilt.

But now, now he could see their faces when they laughed, the times the three of them got shit-faced drunk and did dumbass things. All the memories rolled through his mind like a movie.

On his back, he turned his head to see Ivy had scooted to the side of the bed, far away from him. He frowned, thinking of what he'd told her. The thing he tried so damned hard not to think about. He didn't want to remember gathering up the torn pieces of his friends. And Ivy, God, she had cried, saying more with her tears than all the words shrinks had thrown at him. Because her tears were real; her tears understood you don't fix this, you just find a way to live with it. Rolling to his side, he reached out and pulled her into his arm. She tucked herself into him, and he could feel her breath on his chest.

Better.

"Okay?" she asked in that silky voice of hers.

He kissed the top of her head. "Sleep, Princess." He just needed to touch her, feel her warm and alive in his arms.

He closed his eyes, letting himself sink into sleep.

Chapter 18

"I should go with Isaac," Ivy said. "Greg might be suspicious if I'm not there." They stood in the living room with the morning light spilling in the front window. Isaac was wearing a button-down shirt and tie, and holding his briefcase in preparation to meet her dad at ten A.M.

Luke shook his head. "No, we need to stay in the house, and I'm not letting you go anywhere without me. And I'm not letting Dirk or Pierce, or your dad if he's playing us, get in here and snatch the statues if we're gone."

Isaac walked up to her. "He's right. Relax, Ivy, I can deal with Greg. I will call you when I get the information. And don't forget, I'm going to videotape this for the police."

"But what if he has a gun?"

"I have a gun too."

That didn't make her feel any better. She was cat-jumpy, worried. "You shouldn't have a gun."

Isaac smiled. "I won't need the gun to deal with your dad. He believes we're going to give him the house and he needs me for that. He's a lot of things, but he's not a killer. I've checked his background."

Ivy wasn't surprised. Isaac was a defense lawyer and he was good. She took a deep breath. "It's just a house, Isaac. If your life is in danger, give him what he wants."

Her mom sucked in her breath from where she stood next to Ivy. "That won't happen."

She turned to her mom. "I know, but Isaac is more important to me than a house. Than any material thing."

Her mom smiled. "To me too."

She had no idea what happened between her mom and Isaac last night. Her mom still looked tired, but some of the strain was gone. "I know." She reached out and took her mom's hand. Just held it.

Isaac shifted to the left so that he faced Mal. He leaned down and kissed her. Then he left.

Luke shut the door and armed the alarm. He had on jeans, tennis shoes, a T-shirt, and his gun. His gray eyes were alert, watchful. He said little. Ivy could feel his tension. It was part of what made her so jumpy.

Plus the knowledge that it was nearly over. And Luke would leave. He'd been honest with her. Given her what he could. She turned and went into the kitchen, poured herself a cup of coffee, and stared out the back window. She loved Luke. Did he love her? She didn't know. But she was going to fight to find out. She was in the game of life, of love, and she was going to risk the pain to find out if she and Luke had a future together.

"What's wrong, Ivy?" Her mom walked in and poured her own coffee, then went to the fridge for cream.

"Just thinking, Mom. I'm going to quit my job." She didn't want to talk about Luke, not yet. Not until she was ready.

"You can get a job at a bigger station." Her mom leaned against the counter.

She nodded thoughtfully, but said, "No, I don't want it."

"What do you want?"

She looked at her mom. "I want to be an accountant, but I don't think it's going to happen. My reputation is destroyed. No one hires accountants who can't be trusted."

"Then go out on your own. Do forensic accounting. Isaac

said lawyers use them. And you can have private clients like the divorce cases you work. Stop being afraid, Ivy. Trust yourself."

She leaned her hip against the counter and thought about it. "I could, couldn't I?"

Mallory smiled. "Honey, if I can have my own business, you can. God knows you're the one who kept my business going since you were about nine."

The phone rang and Ivy froze. Her mom's smile dimmed. "It's too soon, right?"

"Answer it," Luke said from the doorway of the kitchen.

Grabbing the phone, she said, "Hello?"

"Where are you? I thought you were coming in today?"

"Leah," Ivy said to let her mom and Luke know. "No, I'm not coming in." What should she tell her?

A pause, then, "You have a job to do, Ivy. If you don't do your radio show, it'll look like you're hiding."

The anger surged up in a huge wave. "Nah, after all the leaks you've let out, my listeners will just think I'm busy using Luke for sex." She hung up.

Both her mom and Luke stared at her.

"What?" She glared right back at them.

Her mom started laughing.

Ivy rolled her eyes and turned to Luke.

His gray eyes danced. "Hey! I'm the victim here. I'm being used for sex."

"Shut up."

The phone rang again.

Ivy narrowed her eyes, turned, and yanked it off the hook. "I'm not doing the show today!"

"Hello to you, too, Ivy."

"Oh, uh . . ." The unexpected voice surprised her. Then her heart kicked against her ribs. "Pierce? Is that you?"

Luke shouldered up to her so he could listen too.

"Yes, I've spent much of the night at the police station and morgue. The police have cleared me. I was with a client, driving her up to a rehab in Arizona and trying to stay off the press's radar."

She looked at Luke's eyes. The twinkle was gone, they were flat and cold. "How do I know that's true?"

"Call the police and ask them. Anyway, I'm returning your calls. Did you need something? I'm still catching up with the news, but it looks like you're a hot commodity now."

She winced at the word. "I don't care."

"I was afraid of that."

Luke moved away, pulling out his cell phone and dialing a number. Ivy said to Pierce, "What do you mean?"

"It's cliché, but I could make you a star. But all along I knew you weren't interested. Too bad."

"Yeah, well, first I have to deal with my current contract."

"You want to break it?"

"Probably. Maybe. But before I decide about that I have to deal with . . . some things." Her thoughts shifted. "She really loved you."

Silence, thick and heavy. Then Pierce said, "I know. I didn't love her like that. But I cared. She didn't deserve this. Everything just fell apart for her at once. Her career, then I dumped her." He went quiet, then added, "Marla wasn't a bad person. She just got a little bit lost."

It made her feel better that he did care. That he defended Marla. "I know." She saw Luke make a cutting motion to her. "Listen, Pierce, I have to go. We'll talk later."

"Okay. If you need help getting out of your contract, come to me. I'll help you."

She believed him. "Thanks. Bye." She hung up.

"I checked with the police. Pierce is telling the truth."

Relief and fear mixed. "Dirk?"

Luke said, "We're not taking anything for granted."

"So we wait for Isaac to call. If we have the statues, we get them out of the house and set up a meeting with the police and insurance company. The video from Isaac will help convince the police we didn't know the statues—"

The phone rang. Again. Ivy startled in a jerk.

Luke reached out, putting his hand on her nape. "Easy. Want me to get it?"

"No." She forced a confident expression, then reached for the phone.

Luke slid his arm around her.

"Hello?"

"Hey, babe."

Oh God. "Dirk."

Luke's arm around her shoulder hardened to steel.

She asked Dirk, "What are you doing?" What did he want? Why was he calling her?

"Thought maybe we could hang today. You know, chat about old times? By the way, your dad is a screamer. Did you know that?"

She sagged. Luke yanked her up against him, caught her gaze and stared. Hard. Ivy pulled herself together. "What have you done?"

"I want those statues, Ivy. I will kill your dad and the lawyer if I don't get them."

A tremor rocked her and erupted into a scream, "What have you done!"

"Busy morning. Broke your dad's hand. He cried and screamed, then told me everything I wanted to know. That lawyer was some piece of work."

"Was!" *Oh God. Not Isaac.* She looked at her mom standing frozen by the counter. "Did you hurt Isaac?" It came out a desperate whisper.

The cup slid from her mom's hand, and she cried out, "No!"

Luke had his head bent to Ivy's as they both listened. He shifted to look at her mom and held out his free arm to her.

Mallory ran to him, and Luke pulled her against him, leaned away from the phone, and whispered to her, "Hold on, Mal. We have to find out." Then he pressed her mom's face into his chest.

Ivy knew in that moment she would do anything in the world for Luke. Including let him go. Anything. He took care of her mom in the midst of a crisis. He understood her mom, and that made Ivy love him a million times more.

"I'll tell you what I will do to him, and to your dad. I will kill them." The next words sounded farther away, "Tell them, asshole."

"He broke my hand!" her dad's voice sobbed. "In the newel posts! Get the statues. Give him whatever he wants!"

"Hear that, babe?"

A coldness spread inside Ivy. Her dad was a broken, pathetic man. For Dirk to hurt him was sick. *Think*, she told herself. Okay, they knew, hopefully if her dad was telling the truth, where the statues were. She asked, "Yes, now let me hear Isaac. I'm not giving you anything until I know he's alive."

"Nope, he's in the trunk trussed up like a hog."

God, please let him be alive! She focused on what might help them figure things out. If Issac was in the trunk, they must be driving. Where? She put her hand over the phone and looked up at Luke.

His gray eyes met hers. He whispered, "Get the terms."

Terms? She fought hard to think past her fear. He meant the terms to trade the statues for Isaac and Greg. Taking a shaky breath, she looked at Luke's big hand pressing her mom into the shelter of his chest. "You want to trade the statues for my dad and Isaac. Tell me where and when."

"Too bad you weren't this smart when we were together."

Isaac in the trunk. Her dad in the car and in pain. It tormented her. She had to fix this. Had to. "Dirk, don't waste my time. We both want something the other has. Let's make the trade and get on with our lives."

Luke ran his hand up and down her arm in a gentle show

of support. He was spreading his strength between her and her mom.

"Just you, Ivy. No tricks. I know that scam you tried to pull on your dad. Fake documents. You try anything like that, I'll kill them both, and then I will kill you."

"Right. Got it. Threat noted. Very scared. Where and when?" She should be more scared, but damn it, she was getting mad.

"Perhaps you don't believe me. Shall I kill your dad now? Do you want to hear him begging?"

Her dad screamed, an unspeakable sound.

"No! Okay, I'm sorry! Don't!" She gagged on the sheer horror.

Her mom sobbed against Luke.

"I'm not fucking around."

"I know." She could barely talk. "Just tell me what to do."

"Bring the statues to your dad's house. Alone. Just you, Ivy, and bring your cell phone. No police."

He'd kill her. Not a doubt in her mind. What did she do? Let Isaac and her dad be slaughtered? Tears poured down her face. "You'll let them go?"

"When I have the statues."

"And me?"

"We'll just have to see, won't we? You have an hour; then I shut your dad up for good. A half hour after that, the lawyer dies." He hung up.

Luke took the phone from her hand, and said, "Issac appears to be alive, Mal. Now we have to get them out."

Ivy's panic spilled out. "Call the police! He'll be at my dad's, the police can—"

Luke let go of her mom and took Ivy by the shoulders. "If we do that, the police will bring them out in body bags."

She couldn't breathe. She felt her mom's pleading eyes on her, but she didn't know how to fix this. She didn't know. It was her fault, being so damned smug. Thinking herself so smart and dragging Isaac into this mess. "I have to go. You have to stay here and protect my mom."

His features hardened into stone.

Terror tightened the muscles in her neck and cramped her stomach. They knew where the statues were now. Luke could just take them and leave. "Luke, please! You swore you wouldn't let my mom get hurt! I have to give him the statues. I have to!"

"Ivy, no! You can't . . . Oh God, he'll kill you!" Her mom's brown eyes were huge pools of pain.

"Enough," Luke said. "We tried this your way, Ivy. It didn't work. Now we're doing it my way."

His harsh voice helped her focus. "Which is?"

"I'm going to remove the threat by killing him."

Ivy felt the house tilt. "But—"

He leaned down, putting his face in hers. "You don't have to like it, you don't have to approve, but you will damn well do what I tell you. I will make sure you, your mom, Isaac, and your dad live. Then you can spend the rest of your life hating what I am." He let go of her and turned away. He pulled his phone out and dialed.

Ivy shivered.

Luke turned back. "Go get the statues."

"Come on, Ivy." her mom grabbed her hand and pulled her away and down the stairs to the newel posts at the bottom floor. Together, they worked until the top of each of the newel posts was pried off. And inside, wrapped in black cloth, were the statues.

Ivy's hands shook. She pulled out her statue and carefully unwrapped it. "My God." They were exquisite. Eight inches high, carved from a pure clear jade, beautiful and ethereal except for the rectangular hole that stood out like a gaping wound. The space for the hearts, the hearts that had been stolen centuries ago. Unable to help herself, she brought her finger up to touch the stone. The jade was warm, like skin.

She pulled her hand back and met her mom's eyes.

Mallory's gaze held the same depth of both admiration and horror. People had died for the statues, murdered for them. And now the statues held the lives of Isaac and Greg. And probably Ivy's too.

Finally, her mom said, "You can't take these to him."

She looked down again at the statues resting in the black cloth. "I have to. It's our only chance of getting Issac and dad out alive." She lifted her gaze. "Luke will get me out, Mom. Believe that. Both Isaac and I will come home to you."

Her mom whispered, "You believe it?"

"Yes." She did believe it. Luke always brought people home.

They had very little time. Luke told Ivy, "Open your shirt." They were in her bedroom and he was going through his box of assorted tools.

She unbuttoned her shirt without a word.

He turned with the wireless mike and stopped short. She stood there with her blouse hanging open, her breasts encased in a delicate pink bra, her eyes steady and full of a combination of trust and determination.

Luke moved to her, close enough to catch her berry scent mixed with pure Ivy. He forced himself to focus on the job. Getting them all out alive.

Not in pieces.

Don't think about it, he told himself. *The job, the mission, think about that.* Gently, he inserted the mike into the cup of her bra, refusing to feel the warm softness of her skin.

Ivy shivered.

He looked into her huge eyes. "I'll hear you. You won't be alone. You're going to keep Dirk occupied at the front door; I'm coming in the back window. If I can't get in that way, I'll get in another. I swear."

She nodded.

Luke pulled Ivy's blouse closed, slipping the buttons through the holes. Then he moved her hair back and put the earpiece in. After placing her hair over it, he cupped her face. "You'll hear me talking to you. Don't answer me, Ivy. Don't react like someone is talking to you. But if I say, 'Ivy, down,' you hug the ground. Whatever command I give you, follow it exactly."

She took a deep breath and nodded.

He knew damn well Ivy wasn't being passive. Her brain was working, he could feel it. She was taking in information and assimilating it. His princess was not a hothead, or a blowhard. She was incredibly smart. Her skill wasn't going to be in fighting, and she didn't try to pretend it was. He loved that about her.

He loved her.

Goddammit, not now. He couldn't think about it now. Just do the job.

He went back to his box of toys, brought out a pen and held it up. "Pepper spray. See the clicker that depresses the ballpoint writing tip?"

She nodded.

"It's really a trigger that will depress a shot of pepper spray." He slid it into the left side of her jeans in the front. "If you get in a tight situation, you pull it out, shoot him, and run like hell. Try to give me some warning first so I can cover you."

Again, she just nodded, and dropped her gaze to where he'd tucked the pen into her jeans. Then she looked up. "I'm ready."

He didn't want her to do this, but he'd never get close enough in the allotted time without her. If that asshole Dirk had waited until nightfall, Luke could have hugged the shadows and gotten in. He might still be able to do it in the daylight. . . .

"He'll kill them before you get in. This is a better plan."

Curious, he asked, "You trust me that much?"

"Yes."

Her simple answer touched him in a place he'd thought was long dead. Closed off. Ivy made him want to live again. To be a better man that deserved her, that could have her. "What happened to that woman who had rules to tell the bad guys from the good?"

She put her hand on his chest. "I don't need rules to tell me who you are, Luke. I know you."

His chest tightened. He wanted to be her hero, but Luke knew that life rarely worked out that way. He was just a man, a damaged and dangerous man. She'd see today just how dangerous he could be. He had no words, so he put his hands on her face and drew her mouth to his. Kissed her deeply. Unable to help himself, he wrapped an arm around her and pulled her close to fulfill the primal need to shelter and protect her with his body. His instincts surged into crystal clarity: Anything that threatened her, died.

His cell phone rang. Luke broke the kiss and answered, "What do you have, Arnie?" It pissed him off that he had highly skilled buddies all over the world, but no one close enough to help them in the slim time frame. He had to rely on his pissant cousin. The good news was that Arnie knew security and could shoot. The bad news was that he was Arnie.

"I can't get much closer. I see an old tan Sentra in the carport of the mobile home. No other cars close by. I think I can see wires across the windows and doors, except the front door on the opposite side of the carport. The area around the mobile home looks quiet."

The car was Ivy's dad's, so Dirk must have used that car. He'd gotten her dad first; then they went and got Isaac. He didn't like this—it was too organized, indicating a tightly controlled operation. Luke started focusing on the obstacles. "What do the wires look like to you?"

"Quick job, electric shock."

Prep work, so Dirk did have a plan. "I can cut through

that, I doubt he's had time to set up a second-layer system. What else?"

"Drapes are closed, can't get a look inside."

"We're leaving now. I want you as close on the front door side as you can get." He hung up.

Luke turned to Ivy, "Let's do it."

Chapter 19

Ivy tried to swallow but her mouth was bone-dry. Adrenaline made her hands shake. She drove up to her dad's mobile home.

Her dad's car was in the carport on the kitchen side of the house. They figured Dirk had used her dad's car. How he got two grown men into the mobile home without rousing suspicion was anyone's guess.

Luke was on the other side of the fence at the back of her dad's property. Hidden from view. As soon as Ivy knocked on the living room side of the house, and hopefully distracted Dirk, Luke would go over the fence and get into the house.

It was safe. Nothing bad would happen.

Luke's voice was gentle in her ear, "Ivy, any time you're ready. I'm here."

It calmed her. Luke calmed her. He made her feel capable, and for the first time in her life, he made her feel like she had a partner. To distract herself while parking the car across the street from the mobile home, she said, "Sterling, you'd better live up to your legendary reputation." She picked up the statues her mom had carefully packed into a canvas bag.

His teasing voice said, "I'm supposed to be a sex legend, have I failed you yet?"

Warmth settled in her stomach. Dropping her voice to a

soft purr, she said, "I'm not a very good judge, not enough experience."

He rumbled in her ear, "You're perfect, so damned perfect."

She closed her eyes, sucked in a breath, and forced herself to keep it light and easy. "Is this how you conduct all your missions?" A beat of her heart passed.

Then he answered, "Just the important ones."

She was ready. Time to do what they came to do. "Getting out of the car and going to the door now."

"See you on the other side."

She wasn't sure what that meant, but she knew Luke was nearby. That gave her more courage. She walked up to the living room side of the mobile home. It was weird as hell to be carrying over five million dollars worth of statues in a tote bag up to her dad's house. Statues that people had killed for. Up on the porch, she went to the door and knocked.

Her cell phone rang, nearly startling her into dropping the statues. She dragged the phone out of the holder on her pants. It was Dirk. "What?"

"Come inside."

She didn't want to go in there. To buy time, and to keep Luke informed, she asked, "I don't think going inside is a good idea."

In her ear, Luke said, "Good. Just keep him talking."

Dirk said, "Don't screw with me. Get in here. Now."

Cold with fear, she tried to think. "Uh, my hands are full with the statues and the phone. I don't want to drop them. Can you open the door for me?" The drapes on the window were tightly closed, so she added, "If you look outside, you can see that I'm alone. I'm following your instructions."

In her ear, "Good, keep it up."

A muffled groan/scream sounded from inside the mobile home, followed by sobbing. Then Dirk said, "One more minute until the one-hour time limit is up. Then I kill your dad."

"No! Dirk, listen to me!" she screamed into the phone while staring at the door, her heart slamming against her chest.

Luke's low voice rumbled, "Steady, sweetheart. I'm almost in."

Oh God. They were going to be too late. "Dirk?" She got as close to the door as she could.

A muffled voice cried, "Please, Ivy! Oh God, please, help me!" Her dad's voice begged through the phone. "Come in. He'll kill me! It's your fault. You did this! Don't let him— no!"

"All right! Okay, Dirk, I'm coming in!" She shut the phone and shoved it into the holder on her pants.

"No! Christ, Ivy, no!" Luke whispered frantically.

"I have to," she whispered, then reached out and turned the doorknob, easing the door open. It was darker inside after being out in the sunshine, making it hard for her to see anything but shadows.

"Step in."

"No." Luke's whisper was frantic.

Ivy took a breath. "I'll hand you the statues. Send out my dad and Isaac."

"If you don't get the fuck in here, I'll shoot him now. Count of three."

"For the love of God, Ivy!" her dad yelled.

Following his voice, she saw her dad duct-taped to a kitchen chair. His eyes were red, his face swollen from crying, and his hand . . . She looked away from the swollen mess. Behind him stood Dirk with a gun to her dad's temple. A few feet away, Isaac was taped to another chair. His skin was pale green, his eyes barely open, and he seemed not to be able to focus because his gaze kept jerking to her right. A piece of duct tape over his mouth kept him quiet. Blood appeared to be caked on the back of his head. Gunshot, or had he been hit with something? Where was Luke? She didn't know what to do.

"One," Dirk said.

She couldn't watch Dirk kill them. She had to keep everyone alive until Luke got inside. Even as part of her brain screamed at her not to, Ivy took a step in the house.

"Farther," Dirk said.

Luke's low hiss, "I'm in. Don't do it!"

She shook with icy fear. Dirk had the gun to her dad's head, and he could see the hallway Luke would have to come out of. Ivy had to get in and make him turn away from the hallway. "Okay, Dirk." She took another step, clutching the canvas bag. "I'm doing exactly as you . . . argh!" Someone grabbed her by the hair, yanked her head back, and stopped her.

Who was behind her? Frozen by the death grip on her hair, tears burning in her eyes, she said, "What's going on?"

Dirk ignored Isaac and Greg and walked toward her. "It seems like you might have some unfinished business with Ed here. You really do know how to piss a guy off."

Ed leaned close to her ear and snarled, "I wanted those statues, you dumb bitch."

Ice dripped down her spine. Ed, he was the man who attacked her in her office, the one Luke saved her from. What had Ed said that day? *Payback. You cost me a hell of a lot of money, bitch, and I'm gonna get my payback. Where are they?* He'd been there for the statues. But she hadn't known anything about the statues then! That's why it hadn't made any sense. She stared at Dirk. "You're giving Ed the statues?" Could Luke hear her? There was only silence in her ear.

Ed said, "Trip was such a dumb shit; he bragged to me about his big auction for the statues. I was trying to get the statues out of the radio station before he moved them. Figured you'd know where they were. I planned to make a little money. Do you know how much you've cost me? I'm going to get my revenge!" He yanked hard on her hair.

Dirk grabbed the canvas bag from Ivy before she could react. Stepping back, he laughed at her. "I bailed Ed out

Monday morning with the money that I took from Marla. That bimbo thought I had the statues and tried blackmailing me with a cell phone picture of me leaving the radio station after killing Trip."

"How did Marla find you?"

Anger washed over his features. "I took Trip's cell phone, the one he'd used for the auction. My one miscalculation was that Trip died before he told me exactly where the statues were. All I got out of him was York, so I knew one of you had them. But I took his phone just in case, and Marla left a message on it. I called her back."

"We didn't know we had them!" Now they knew where Marla's 401K money went, and that she had taken a picture of the killer—Dirk. She had to be desperate to try and blackmail him.

"But your dad did. He told me he could get you to cough them up, but then he was going to double-cross me. Can't trust a hustler." He sighed as if he were really disappointed.

She had to keep him talking so Luke could make his move. "But you trust Ed? He was trying to steal the statues before Trip sold them!"

"It's business, I paid him." His expression turned to a sneer. "And you're his bonus."

Ed yanked her head back far enough to smell his thick, greasy breath. "You have a lot to make up for, my broken arm, my marriage . . . I'm going to make you pay."

She was in real trouble. The full impact slammed into her, making her sweaty and sick. She could feel the hardness of the cast on Ed's other arm behind her. She had no idea if he had a weapon or not. But she knew Luke wasn't going to be able to save her, Greg, and Isaac. Ignoring Ed, she tried to appeal to the man whom she'd once loved. "Dirk, don't let him do this. Please. Take the statues, take my car, but don't let him—"

Dirk moved to a table where he set the bag down. Keeping his gun in one hand, he used the other hand to take out a statue and unwrap it. He lifted his gaze to her. "You think I care?" He laughed. "You were nothing more than a meal ticket to me. I'd like to stay around and watch, but you know, places to go . . ." He finished unwrapping a statue and held it up. "Worth millions, huh?"   •

She stared at the beautiful Jade Goddess and her anger kicked in. Hard. She was not going to curl up and let someone else fight her battle. She moved her hand to the edge of the pen in the pocket of her pants.

Where was Luke? He wasn't talking, so she assumed he was inside. Waiting to make his move? Assessing the situation? The biggest threat seemed to be Dirk. Ed was holding her by the hair, which left only his broken arm free.

She had to do something to get Dirk off balance, to give Luke an opening. "But you don't want the statues for the money. You want them so you can be a real man. The kind of man who can actually pleasure a woman." She eased the pen out of her pocket.

"Ivy." Just that word in her ear. Just enough to let her know Luke was nearby.

Dirk snapped the gun back up and leveled it at her face. Leaving the statues on the table, he took a step toward her. His cold green eyes rested on her. "I had planned to help Ed tie you up, then leave. Now I think I'll stay and watch. You never liked sex much." He walked up until he was in her face, until his green eyes froze on her face. "You're really going to hate it now."

She had to get out of this! She opened her mouth—

Dirk reached up and snatched the earpiece from her. "What's this?" Rage fired his gaze. *"What the fuck is this?"* He brought his hand up and backhanded her hard enough to rip her hair from Ed's hold and throw her to the ground. Ivy landed on her left side.

Moving up on her, Dirk bellowed, "What is it?"

Think! "For my cell phone!" She rolled to her hands and knees, praying nothing was broken, and that she could get up. Every instinct she had screamed at her to get on her feet so she could run. Bone-deep terror sizzled through her. She had to keep them all alive. She started to rise from her hands and knees.

"You lying bitch!" Dirk shoved his foot into her side, throwing her over and cracking the side of her face into the coffee table leg. Bright lights exploded in her head. The pain bloomed hot, spreading furiously. The left side of her face felt like it had been slammed into a sizzling-hot frying pan. Nausea greased her gut. Fighting to breathe, to stay alive, Ivy forced her eyes open. Dirk dropped to a knee, the gun aimed at her face. "Who else is here?"

His voice had calmed down. He thought he had her cowed, thought he still had control. Ivy squeezed her left hand.

It was still there.

"Just this," she said, and brought the pepper spray pen up and shot it directly into his vile green eyes. At the same time, she shoved the gun away from her face.

All hell broke loose.

Dirk recoiled and screamed.

Luke's voice bellowed.

Ed tried to get to her, but Arnie burst into the mobile home and took him to the ground.

The noise was deafening. Her mind spun. Ivy had to help, had to make sure Isaac and her dad stayed alive. She tried to roll to her side and force herself to get up.

"Ivy"—Arnold knelt down next to her, "stop moving. You're hurt." He put his arm around her back and eased her to a sitting position.

She took her first look around. Her dad and Isaac were still tied to the chairs in the dining room, but they were alive. Ed was out cold on the living room floor. Dirk was face down, his arms were behind his back, and Luke was on his knee looping a plastic thing around his wrists. Dirk's face was turned toward Ivy. His nose was crunched and his lip was torn open and bleeding.

"Thought Luke was going to kill him," Arnold said. "But he didn't. He stopped. I think I would have killed him."

Luke stood up and strode to her. She didn't know how it all happened so fast. She'd never even seen him rush into the room. Her body was starting to want to pay attention to the pain, but she ignored it. "I didn't know." She wanted to tell him she didn't know about Ed. Or something.

"Don't talk." He looked at Arnold. "Go see to Isaac and her dad." Luke dropped to his haunches beside her. He pulled off his shirt, rolled it, and held it against her face. Then he looked into her eyes. "I told you not to go in the house."

He was crouched beside her, his chest naked, glistening with sweat, the strength and power of him so obvious. She heard sirens. "Arnold called the cops?"

"Yes, he wore an earpiece to hear what was going on." He leaned closer. "Let me look at the cut, Ivy." He leaned over her, taking the shirt away to peer at her face. "Christ," the word was torn from him. He put the shirt back against her face.

She looked at his eyes. "It's okay."

He met her gaze, full of regret and pain. "You're going to need stitches. Have a scar. You'll never be able to look at yourself without remembering that I let you get hurt."

"No." She didn't care how much it hurt to talk, he had to know. "What I'll remember is that you kept your promise and got us all out alive."

Ivy woke up alone. She looked at the clock, it was after one A.M. Luke had done so much—dealing with the police, getting her mom to the hospital, checking on Isaac and her dad, and sitting with her while the doctor stitched her face. Her wound wasn't that bad; it'd only taken a few stitches and she'd have minimal scarring, mostly by her left ear. They were keeping Isaac overnight for a mild concussion.

Getting out of bed, she went looking for Luke.

He jerked his head up from the TV when she walked into

the living room. Then he surged to his feet and came toward her. "What's wrong? Do you need a pain pill?"

She had no room for lies, or games. "I need you. If you don't want to come to bed, I'll just sit here with you."

He put his arm around her. "You need to be in bed."

"No." She refused to let him get rid of her. "It hurts to lie down, throbs by the stitches. I'll sit up with you. Did you have a nightmare?"

Luke shifted direction and guided her to the couch. He sat down on the left end of the couch and pulled her down on top of him, gently pressing the right side of her face to his chest. Then he picked up the afghan and covered her. "Close your eyes and see if you can sleep. I'll keep you upright so it won't hurt so much."

Ivy felt the sting of tears at his gentleness. He cared. This man who she had told the world was the ultimate bad boy was, in truth, the ultimate man. But that didn't mean he could trust her, or her feelings. She knew that now. Understood that he had to do what he did. "You're going to leave."

He rubbed her back. "I have to finish the job. The insurance will file a complaint to have Regina and Leah arrested for insurance fraud. And the statues, that's going to be complicated."

"You've already talked to Regina?"

"Yes." He kept gently rubbing her back. "She knows I'm helping the insurance company file charges. Her chance at the show is over. She'll never get anyone to insure the statues while they are in her possession. She's going to consider putting them in a museum. Where they are safe. Where they won't be able to get out of control again."

"I'm surprised she'd do that. She loves those statues more than anything else."

"I think the horror of the murders, and that we narrowly avoided three or four more murders, made her take a hard look at herself."

Ivy knew he meant the murders of her, Isaac, Greg, and

probably Ed. No one really thought Dirk had been going to let any of them go. Ed was just purely stupid. Dirk needed him to help control the situation; then Dirk would have killed him. The good news was that Dirk faced charges for two murders and he faced the embezzlement charges from three years ago. The horror of what Dirk had done affected many of them, including Regina. "I'm sorry, Luke," Ivy said. "Regina was a friend."

"We all got caught up in the power of the statues. Including your boss Leah."

"I'll deal with Leah. What's odd is that the cold part of her, that ruthless need to succeed, was always there, and I even admired it. But I thought there was more to her. I thought she cared about people, about her employees. She didn't care that Marla was murdered."

His hand stilled on her back. "She used you."

"I don't care anymore. I just don't. I'm going to ask Pierce to break my contract." She put her hand on his bare chest next to her face. He was warm and made her feel safe. Okay. She felt like she could handle things with Luke by her side. Luke had shown her who she didn't want to be—the woman who judged others while sitting safely behind a microphone. She wanted to live, to take the risks for the bigger rewards. Like love. Ivy lifted her head to look up to his face. "You think it's the statues, don't you?"

Luke shifted his gaze down to her. There was no pretense in his gray eyes. "I don't know. How can you forgive me? I thought you were the thief in the beginning. Then your mom. And most unforgivable, I kept getting distracted and screwed up." He took hold of the long braid down her back, and said, "I knew Dirk was dangerous, but I never considered Ed. I dismissed him when I found out he was in jail the night Trip was murdered. You'll carry the scar of my screwup the rest of your life."

The torment in his gray eyes hurt more than her face, or her sore side. Nothing hurt like Luke's pain, his inability to believe simple truths. "The statues aren't here now, Luke. It's just you and me." She could feel his arousal, one that he'd been steadfastly ignoring.

"Lingering effect," he said softly. "It's not real, what you think you feel for me. It's never real."

He was giving her so much of his truth, it shocked her. The Urban Legend, a man renowned for selfishly screwing women for pleasure and information, held nothing back from her.

Some people might believe that Luke used her for sex and to get the statues. That she had been nothing more than a commodity.

The old Ivy would have believed that. But not now. This Ivy believed in Luke. She reached up to his face, settling her palm over his flexing jaw. "It's real. I love you, Luke. And I will fight for you."

"Ivy, I can't—"

She put her face down on his chest and heard the painful thumps of his heart. "I know. You told me." The night she'd known her heart no longer belonged just to her. But she'd given it to him freely. With no strings. She wasn't going to demand something back from him. She closed her eyes, tired to the bone. She didn't want to sleep, didn't want any last moments with Luke to slip away from her. But with Luke's arms around her, his body warm and safe, she felt herself slipping away.

The last thing she heard was Luke's thick voice saying, "Don't stop believing in me, Princess. I'm coming back to find out if what we have is real."

Chapter 20

A week later

Luke dropped the file on Arnie's desk. "Done." They had worked together to tie up all the loose ends, including getting the statues to the museum Regina had chosen. The two of them ran the security to get the statues moved. Now Luke was going after the most precious treasure ever.

Ivy.

Never had he wanted anything or anyone more. He just hoped that her love for him was the real thing, and not an illusion caused by the statues. He was going to find out. And he was going to do it right, treating her as she deserved. He had plans. . . .

Arnie sat back in his chair. "I hear Regina has all kinds of offers for movies, etc., on her story." He folded his hands and looked at Luke. "I've had serious offers on the Urban Legend's story."

Luke shifted his thoughts from Ivy and sat in the chair facing his cousin. "And?"

Arnold leaned his head back to look at the ceiling. "God, I hated you. From the time you were three and moved into Grandma's house, I hated you."

Ah. Was that what had been in it for Arnie all this time? Was that why he butted into Luke's case? For a week they had worked together and not once had the past come up. He wanted to hate his cousin, but the power behind the feeling was gone. Arnie had done the right thing by protecting Kat Vaugn, and he'd backed Luke up to get Ivy out of Dirk's clutches. It was time to end this, for both of them to move on past the old bitter hate. "You've wasted your time and energy if you did all this to get leverage to make me give you my interest in Sterling Investigations. I'm signing it over to you. It's yours."

Arnold flushed and demanded, "Do you ever get tired of being a fucking saint?"

Luke folded his arms and glared at Arnie. "A simple *thank you* would have been enough."

"Thank you?" He leaned forward and slapped both hands on his desk. "I'm sick of your noble shit. You won't take the money owed you from the business. You treat me like an annoying pain in the ass instead of a man. And you have never, not once, called me on what I did to you. I should thank you for your fucking noble act!"

Where the hell was this coming from? "Noble? Your dad dislocated my shoulder when I tried to defend myself. Then the social workers insisted I admit to the truth. And later, your mom didn't want to know. That wasn't noble, you stupid son of a bitch. It was self-preservation."

Arnold sank back in his chair and shook his head. "When I attacked you with the knife, I thought for sure you'd react. What the hell is wrong with you?"

Luke felt a punch of shock. "Jesus Christ, you wanted to fight?"

He nodded. "Hell yes. I wanted it over. I wanted you to take your shots and put it behind us."

Luke stared at his cousin and remembered that day. Arnie had been drunk, and he'd come at Luke with a knife. But the bastard knew who Luke was, and he knew Luke could hurt or kill him. He was giving Luke his shot. His payback. And what had Luke done? Taken the knife and walked away. No wonder Arnie was brewing batch after batch of bitter hatred. For the first time, it all just didn't matter anymore. "You were ten. A stupid kid. I don't blame you." He'd stabbed himself, not Luke. All these years later, Luke had to wonder, what kind of desperation made a kid do that?

Arnie got up, walked over to his media center, and looked back at Luke. "I made a promise that I'd get you to listen to Ivy's show today. Pierce broke her contract, and Ivy insisted she was doing one last show. As far as the business goes, I want you in, as a full, working partner. But it's your call." He turned on the radio and started to walk out of the office.

Luke stared at his cousin's back. "I never told you thank you. For saving Ivy. For watching both our backs. Thank you."

Arnold turned, his blue eyes serious. "That goes without saying. I can see you care for her. Just as I know you cared about my mom."

He pulled the door closed behind him, leaving Luke alone with Ivy's voice. As soon as he heard that silky velvet of her voice, the need for her slammed him, pinning him in his chair as her words washed over him.

"Someone told me recently that I've been a coward. That I wasn't really living my life, but sitting on the sidelines and judging. He was right. And so I am leaving the *Economic Sex Hex* to live my life. But before I go, there's something I have to say. I was wrong about the Urban Legend. I judged the man without ever having met him. Everyone wants to know if the Urban Legend is as good as his reputation."

Luke's heart started to beat fast and furious. What was she doing? All kinds of thoughts blasted through him.

Ivy went on, "I don't know. Because I met the man, not the legend. The man I met is strong, loyal, passionate, smart, and tough. He makes hard choices and he lives with them. He fought to save my family . . ."

Her voice thickened, making Luke rub at a hollow ache in his chest.

"The man I met cares about justice, and about people. He

keeps his promises. He gave me courage to be myself, to take emotional risks. As you can all probably tell, I don't have these words prepared. I'm just telling you the truth.

"I'm telling *him* the truth.

"Luke . . ."

Swear to God, his heart couldn't take it. He couldn't sit still, but he was afraid to so much as breathe in case he missed her next words. He put his elbows on his knees, folded his hands, and bowed his head. Waiting.

Her rich voice flowed out of the radio, "I've never met a man more worth fighting for. I love you."

"I want you to know, for what it's worth, I'm sorry." Leah stood in the doorway of Ivy's office. She looked ten years older, and ten pounds thinner.

Ivy put her college graduation picture, the one with her mom, in the box. She was gathering up her last things. "Sorry that the big conglomerate isn't going to buy your station? Or for what you did?"

"For what I did. For what both Regina and I did. I don't know how it all got so crazy." She walked in and sat down. "It seemed harmless at first. Just hide the statues, bring in the Urban Legend, and make a big splash for KCEX and Regina's tour with the statues."

Harmless? "You knew it was wrong."

"I know. And I'll be paying for it."

Isaac had told her it was unlikely Regina or Leah would get any jail time. They'd probably get a form of restitution and probation. Was that enough? They hadn't killed Trip or Marla themselves, but they had set the events in motion.

"The thing I'm sorriest for is losing you for a friend, Ivy. We were friends. I don't know . . . I just got caught up. I'm turning forty, my biological clock is running out, I don't have time for romantic relationships, and my radio station is small-time. I just wanted to make my mark." She rolled her head to stretch her neck. "If it's true about those statues, that they bring out our deepest desires, then I didn't like what I learned about myself."

That she understood, she hadn't liked what she'd seen herself becoming. But her deepest desire? It wasn't success, the statues showed her that. It was Luke. A man who never let Ivy lie to herself, who was strong on integrity, who cared about people, going so far as to hold her mom when she was terrified during the phone call with Dirk. And he'd held her. Ivy had slept in Luke's arms that last night. She forced her mind back to now. She finished packing her stuff and looked at Leah. "Two people were murdered."

Leah's eyes slid away. "I liked Marla. I know you won't understand this, but once people started dying, the lies I told myself got bigger."

She picked up her box and her purse. "I do believe you. But I'm done with radio. I'm going back to what I love doing, accounting." Ivy was going to lease a small office in Isaac's building and do what she loved—investigative accounting. Bob Harris would be her first case, the man who needed to know how far in debt his wife had gotten them. Isaac had other referrals and it would work out. She was good at accounting, numbers made sense. It was time to go live her life, whatever that would bring.

Leah stood up and followed her down the hall. "The media is out front. Your last show stirred them back up. They love the story of you falling in love with the Urban Legend. That was some sign-off show you did."

Ivy stopped in front of the on-air studio and looked in. A new sound engineer was at the control board. She looked into the booth and felt nothing. Looking back to Leah, she said, "You could have fought breaking my contract." Pierce said she pretty much rolled over to all Ivy's demands.

A ghost of her old smile touched her face. "Consider it a gift in memory of our friendship."

Ivy nodded, accepting that. Then she turned and walked

through the reception area and out the door into the bright sunlight.

Throngs of reporters started yelling questions at her.

"Did the statues make you fall in love?"

"Is the Urban Legend as hot as the rumors?"

"Did he seduce you and dump you like all the other women?"

She ignored them, keeping her focus on her car, only stopping when she almost ran into a man. She struggled to keep her balance and hold on to the box.

It was lifted from her arms.

Ivy looked up and felt the world tilt. "Luke! What are you doing here?" He wore jeans, a black T-shirt, intense gray eyes, and a grin so sexy it should be labeled dangerous.

"It's the Urban Legend!" Reporters jammed in around them, shouting questions.

The case of the Jade Goddesses had made him even more famous, more in demand. He could have any case he wanted, go after any legend.

Sleep with any woman.

It hit her then just how stupid and naive she'd been. Luke had been around the world. She'd grown up in Claremont. He was an adventurer, a treasure hunter. She was an accountant.

She needed to go home. Her throat filled, her eyes burned, but she would keep her dignity. She reached for the box, trying to slide it from his grip. "I'll get out of your way."

A reporter shoved between them, forcing Ivy to step back as questions were pelted at Luke.

The loudest question was, "What's your next case?"

Luke's deep baritone rang out, "I'm going after the only treasure I've ever wanted for myself."

She realized then that he had another case. Forget the damned box. It was just stuff. She turned to walk to her car now that all the focus was on Luke.

"What is it?" The reporters were whipping into a frenzy. The Urban Legend had never granted an interview before.

"A treasure more valuable than any jewel or precious metal or stone."

Ivy kept her head down, dug her keys out, and frantically beeped her car door open. She noted that Luke's voice was moving, meaning he was moving. So were the reporters, no doubt trotting alongside him, begging for details.

Luke answered their questions. "A woman that I love."

She stopped with her hand on the door of her RAV4. She turned around.

Luke stood there, his gray eyes had veins of blue in them. She didn't know where the stupid box was, his arms were empty. Quietly, he said, "If she'll have me. Will you have me, Princess?" He held his arms open.

Ivy ran into them. He closed his arms around her, being careful of her face. Leaning down, he said, "I've missed you. Everything about you. Come with me?"

She nodded against his chest.

He led her to the car, pushed her into the passenger seat, and took her keys to drive.

Inside the car, Ivy was a bundle of nerves. "What about your car?"

"Don't care. We'll get it later." He looked over at her. "I want to do this right. The way you deserve. Will you trust me for just a little longer?"

Confused, she said, "I don't—"

He reached out and touched her thigh. "Please."

"Okay."

A little while later, Ivy was strapped into the passenger seat of a small airplane. Luke was at the controls running through his preflight check.

He looked over at her. "Ready?"

"I don't know."

Luke pulled off his headset, unfastened his seat belt, knelt by her seat, and took her hand. "You're afraid to fly with me?"

"No!" She trusted him with her life. "I'm just . . . Why are you doing this? Borrowing a friend's airplane? You don't like to fly—"

He squeezed her fingers. "Ever since I told you about Sanders and Ray, my ghosts are gone. I remember most of bringing them home now, Ivy. And I remember them alive. This is the second time I've borrowed my friend's plane. The first time was when I flew to where Sanders and Ray are buried. They are home where they belong, and I have a life to live. A life with you. You are the home I never had, Ivy."

Tears welled up in her eyes. "Oh, Luke . . ." She felt too much for this man. Facing his ghosts took a courage few people had. She remembered him asking her to believe in him when he thought she'd been asleep. She did believe in him, she always would.

Clasping both her hands, he added, "I want to take you to Carmel. It's beautiful there, although not as beautiful as you. I want to take you to dinner, walk on the beach, and spend time with you. We'll talk about our future and how many kids we want together. Then I'm going to take you to our room and make love to you. And when I'm deep inside of you, I'm going to tell you over and over how much I love you." He brought her hands to his mouth.

He gave her so much of himself, every part. Kids—she knew what a huge step that was for Luke who had grown up in foster homes. But he trusted her and loved her. "I love you, Luke."

He leaned up and kissed her mouth, careful not to jar the left side of her face that was still healing.

Ivy didn't know how it had happened, how the safe accountant and dangerous bad boy had fallen into a powerful love. But they had, and she embraced the gift. "I'm ready. I want to fly with you."

Don't miss Sylvia Day's latest,
A PASSION FOR HIM,
available now from Brava . . .

"**Y**ou should not be out here alone," he said, rubbing her ribbons between his thumb and index finger. He could not feel them through his gloves, which made the action sensual, as if the lure of fondling something that belonged to her was irresistible.

"I am accustomed to solitude."

"Do you enjoy it?"

"It is familiar."

"That is not an answer."

Amelia looked at him, noting the many details one can see only in extreme proximity to another. Montoya had long, thick lashes surrounding almond-shaped eyes. They were beautiful. Exotic. Knowing. Accented by shadows that came from within as well as from without.

"What was she like?" she asked softly. "The woman you thought I was."

The barest hint of a smile betrayed the possibility of dimples. "I asked you a question first."

She heaved a dramatic sigh just to see more of that teasing curve of his lips. He never let his smile go completely free. She wondered why, and she wondered how she might see it. "Very well, Count Montoya. In answer to your query: Yes, I enjoy being alone."

"Many people find being alone intolerable."

"They have no imagination. I, on the other hand, have too much imagination."

"Oh?" He canted his body toward her. The pose caused his doe skin breeches to stretch taut across the powerful muscles of his thighs. With the gray satin spread out, she could see every nuance and plane, every hard length of sinew. "What do you imagine?"

Swallowing hard, Amelia found she could not look away from the view. It was a lascivious glance she was giving him, her interest completely carnal.

"Umm . . ." She tore her gaze upward, dazed by the direction of her own thoughts. "Stories. Faery tales and such."

With the half-mask hiding his features she couldn't be certain, but she thought he might have arched a brow at her. "Do you write them down?"

"Occasionally."

"What do you do with them?"

"You have asked far too many questions without answering my one."

Montoya's dark eyes glittered with amusement. "Are we keeping score?"

"You were," she pointed out. "I am simply following the rules you set."

There. A dimple. She saw it.

"She was audacious," he murmured, "like you."

Amelia blushed and looked away, smitten with that tiny groove in his cheek. "Did you like that about her?"

"I loved that about her."

The intimate pitch to his voice made her shiver.

He stood and held his hand out to her. "You are cold, Miss Benbridge. You should go inside."

She looked up at him. "Will you go inside with me?"

The count shook his head.

Extending her arm, she set her fingers within his palm and allowed him to assist her to her feet. His hand was large and warm, his grasp strong and sure. She was reluctant to release him and was pleased when he seemed to feel similarly. They stood there for a long moment, touching, the only sound being their gentle inhalations and subsequent exhales . . .

. . . until the gentle, haunting strains of the minuet drifted out on the night zephyr.

Montoya's grip tightened and his breathing faltered. She knew his thoughts traveled along the same path as hers. Lifting her mask to her face, Amelia lowered into a deep curtsy.

"One dance," she urged softly, when he did not move. "Dance with me as if I were the woman you miss."

"No." There was a heartbeat's hesitation, and then he bowed over her hand. "I would rather dance with *you*."

Touched, her throat tightened, cutting off any reply she might have made. She could only rise and begin the steps, approaching him and then retreating. Spinning slowly and then circling him. The crunching of the gravel beneath her feet overpowered the music, but Amelia heard it in her mind and hummed the notes. He joined her, his deep voice creating a rich accompaniment, the combination of sound enchanting her.

The clouds drifted, allowing a brilliant shaft of moonlight to illuminate their small space. It turned the hedges silver and his mask into a brilliant pearl. The black satin ribbon that restrained his queue blended with the inky locks, the gloss and color so similar they were nearly one and the same. Her skirts brushed against his flowing cape, his cologne mingled with her perfume, together they were lost in a single moment. Amelia was arrested there, ensnared, and wished—briefly— never to be freed.

Then the unmistakable warble of a birdcall rent the cocoon.

A warning from St. John's men.

Amelia stumbled, and Montoya caught her close. Her arm lowered to her side, taking her mask with it. His breath, warm and scented of brandy, drifted across her lips. The difference in their statures put her breasts at level with his upper abdomen. He would have to bend to kiss her, and she found herself wishing he would, wanting to experience the feel of those beautifully sculpted lips pressed against her own.

"Lord Ware is looking for you," he whispered, without taking his eyes from her.

She nodded, but made no effort to free herself. Her gaze stayed locked to his. Watching. Waiting.

Just when she was certain he wouldn't, he accepted her silent invitation and brushed his mouth across hers. Their lips clung together and he groaned. The mask fell from her nerveless fingers to clatter atop the gravel.

"Good-bye, Amelia."

He steadied her, then fled in a billowing flare of black, leaping over a low hedge and blending into the shadows. He headed not toward the rear of the manse but to the front, and was gone in an instant. Dazed by his sudden departure, Amelia turned her head slowly toward the garden. She found Ware approaching with rapid strides, followed by several other gentlemen.

"What are you doing over here?" he asked gruffly, scanning her surroundings with an agitated glance. "I was going mad looking for you."

"I am sorry." She was unable to say more than that. Her thoughts were with Montoya, a man who had clearly recognized the whistle of warning.

He had been real for a moment, but no longer. Like the phantom she'd fancied him to be, he was elusive.

And entirely suspect.

You'll definitely want to try
REMAIN SILENT,
the new title by Jamie Denton,
in stores now from Brava . . .

66 It's stupid, I know, but I don't think I want to hire a private investigator," she said quietly. "I don't want to find out that another person I trusted wasn't what he appeared to be."

"What do you mean?" he asked, wondering who had betrayed her. He supposed any number of the adults in her life could've been responsible, from the social workers who'd placed her in one home after another, to the various people she'd been sent to live with following her mother's death. Or maybe some guy had hurt her, although he had his doubts on that score since she rarely allowed anyone that close to her. "You do realize looking into Linton's past could mean the difference between a death sentence and freedom."

"I know that," she said. "I do. But I'd hate to find out I was wrong about him. Besides, it's just . . . it just seems so far-fetched. Like what? Jonathan was leading a double life that I didn't know about?"

"It's entirely possible." He loosened his hold on her and slid his hands up her arms to her shoulders.

"What if I don't want to entertain the possibility?"

The hurt in her eyes made him curious, but also resurrected the protectiveness he'd always felt toward her. An emotion he knew from experience could lead him right into a world of trouble neither of them needed.

That knowledge didn't stop his hands from drifting upward to cup her satiny soft cheeks in his work-roughened palms. "Look, Laurel. My job is to keep you alive. I'll do whatever it takes to ensure that happens."

The barest hint of a sad little smile curved her lips. "You know that as much as I protested, I don't know if I could get through this mess without you."

He smiled. "Sure you could," he told her. "You're a strong woman, Laurel. Don't forget that."

Something flickered in her eyes, but this time he recognized the emotion. Desire. That other emotion in her gaze he'd mistakenly thought could be fear, hadn't been fear at all.

Man, was he ever in trouble.

"I am glad you're here, Damon," she said softly.

God help him, he had to kiss her. "Me, too," he said.

Tension radiated between them. Before he could debate the wisdom of his actions, he lowered his head and kissed her.

Telling himself kissing Laurel was nothing more than a measure of comfort for a friend in need because she was facing such a difficult situation was a bald-faced lie. The instant his lips pressed against hers, the sweet taste of her mouth fired his libido and blindsided him.

He didn't believe she'd actually meant to slide her body along his, or return the kiss in a way that defied the boundaries of friendship or that of a client and her attorney. There was no way in hell either of them had imagined for a minute the air around them would crackle with an energy that could only be described as sexual in nature, but when her lips moved beneath his in an erotic dance of seduction, his testosterone shot through the roof.

Heat stirred in his belly and burned hot in his groin as her tongue demanded entrance. She tasted sweet. And hot. So hot. Like mind-blowing, sweat-drenched bodies, and tangled-sheets sex. The kind they used to have.

God help him, he wanted nothing more.

He should stop the insanity, but he couldn't. He wanted Laurel.

Instead, he moved his hands, sliding them around her rib cage to chase down her back, settling on the curve of her bottom, pulling her closer.

He brought his hands up, gliding along her side, and stopped on her rib cage again. With his thumb, he traced the underside of her breast. She trembled in his arms.

She slid her hands from around his waist to wreathe her arms around his neck, the movement creating more friction as their bodies moved together. Through the thin fabric of her top, the pebble hardness of her nipples brushed against his chest.

His cock throbbed. He knew he should stop. Stop before they went too far. He also knew he'd wake up in the morning with more than regret, too, if he didn't end this craziness—now. He'd wake up in bed with a beautiful, sensuous woman. A naked woman.

For the space of a heartbeat, he figured spending the rest of the night making love to Laurel would be worth every regret thrown at him. The temptation of having her in his bed again was too much for him to ignore.

He waited for common sense to prevail.

It didn't.

Thank God.

And here's a sneak peek at Lucy Monroe's
DEAL WITH THIS,
coming next month from Brava . . .

The best part of the tour by far was Jillian Sinclair.

The worst part was the effect she had on him.

He found himself standing closer to her so he could get more of her elusive scent. She didn't wear perfume. The springtime freshness was too subtle for that. Probably her shampoo, but even knowing the fragrance was something so mundane did not diminish its addictive appeal. of course, the fact that the unmistakable feminine musk underlying it was all Jillian did not help.

Alan wanted to nuzzle right into her neck, and various other enticing places, and just inhale. Okay, and then maybe taste and touch . . . shit . . . he wanted this woman.

"Alan?"

"Huh?"

Jillian was looking at him questioningly. "I asked if you wanted to see more of the technical behind-the-scenes stuff."

"Yeah, that would be great."

Jillian knew more about the technical workings of the sets and the show's production than he would have expected. He took copious notes on everything she said. "I feel like I'm taking Film 101."

She laughed. "Bored?"

"Not at all. Just surprised you know so much."

"I never went to college, you know? I took some classes on

acting though, but for the most part? Boring. Having someone else tell me how to do what I love best just didn't work
for me. I found I liked knowing how everything worked
more. So, I took classes on set design, editing, prop design . . .
you name it, I've probably taken at least one class on it."

"So, you really are a jack of all trades."

"Well all trades related to the film industry."

"Do you have dreams of directing one day?"

"Yes. And eventually, producing. I'm supposed to direct
two episodes next season. It's part of my contract."

"That's great."

"Yeah, I'm pretty excited." She led him out of the prop
room. "If this show goes for enough seasons, it will be my
last full-time acting gig."

"Moving to film?" he asked and promptly tripped on one
of those big black cables.

He fell toward Jillian, her hands automatically coming out
to steady him and his grabbing onto her. They ended up with
her leaning on the wall, him leaning against her with one of
his hands on her hip and the other her shoulder.

It was the perfect position for kissing and his body perked
up, hormones screaming at him to take the plunge.

Reason prevailed and he managed to apologize rather than
lock lips.

"No problem. Are you okay?" she asked, both of her
hands planted firmly against his chest.

She wasn't pushing him away and he wasn't quite up to
the task of stepping back. Yet.

"Yes. I forgot to watch for the cords."

"It's one of the first things you learn."

"It would have to be."

"Yeah . . ." She swallowed and licked her sweet bow lips.
Damn.

"Maybe you should hold my hand and guide me," he said
in a low voice that he usually reserved for the bedroom.
Double damn.

"If it will make you feel safer." Her voice was huskier than normal too and her pupils had almost swallowed the emerald green of her irises.

Triple damnation. She was turned on.

He willed himself to step back.

Nothing happened.

She stared up at him, silent but for the short little breaths she took.

His head began to lower while his libido cheered and his brain shouted at him to go to the men's room and soak his head under a cold faucet.

Her mouth opened slightly, ready for his to descend.

"Miss Sinclair?" It was Ralph, the security guard. "I just got off the phone with the Prop Master. He wanted to request you not tour his room."

Alan found his lagging self-control and sprang backward.

Jillian sidestepped and moved toward the security guard. "I don't know what he thought we would do."

"Probably break something. He's pretty protective of his stock."

Jillian made a little growling noise. It was cute. "Yes, I know. He's quite the *artiste*," she muttered aside to Alan. "We just won't tell him we already toured the room, yes?"

"Whatever you say."

"If he asks, I'll tell the truth," she said on a sigh.

"Let me know if he asks."

Her brows drew together. "Why?"

"So, I can keep our stories straight."

She groaned. "I hate subterfuge."

"I know."

That made her eyes widen, almost with fear. Like the idea of him knowing her worried her. The woman was a 3D Chinese puzzle and he planned to have all the pieces put together before this case was over.

"Thanks, Ralph."

"No problem, Miss Sinclair."

She turned back to Alan, her smile almost too bright. "So, what were we talking about?"

"I had asked if you planned to do movies once this series has run its course."

"Maybe . . . I'd like to do a movie or two, but mostly? I want to work behind the camera and I'm hoping I can make that happen in a full-time way."

"What's stopping you?"

"From directing? Experience. Mostly. From producing, which is my real love . . . the green stuff. It takes a lot of seed money to build a name as a producer, not to mention some killer scripts."

"Another reason to rent rooms out in your house."

She laughed. "That's mostly to cover living expenses. My friend Amanda has almost all of my acting income in an aggressive investment plan. She's helping me realize my dreams."

"She sounds like a good friend to have."

"We've always been there for each other."

"I've got a brother like that. He's my best friend."

"That's great. That you're close to your brother like that. It's the way family should be."

"Do you have any siblings?"

"Yes. A younger brother. I haven't seen him in a while."

"Why?"

"It's hard to get home. He's talking about coming to visit. He might even transfer to the University of Vancouver next year. Our parents aren't too happy, but I'd love it if he lived closer."

"I hear that. My brother and I do a lot of IM-ing, e-mails, phone calls . . . it helps. But sometimes, we just have to get together face-to-face. Even if we didn't want to, Sir would insist on it."

"Who's Sir?"

"My grandfather. He raised us since our parents died when we were teens."

"And you call him *sir*?"

"He's got his quirks, but he did a good job with us."

"I'm sure he did."

"What about you? You're originally from Southern California, right? I bet you call your parents by their first names."

Jillian laughed, but the sound was edged with something not in the least humorous. "No way. We had a very traditional home. At least once my mom married my stepdad. I had to call him Dad even though my own father is still living."

"That must have been hard."

"It was, but not because of any feelings of disloyalty I felt toward Scorpio. The truth is, he never played much of a parental role."

"Scorpio, the painter?"

"Yes."

Well, he knew where Jillian got her red hair from. But she didn't seem to have much else in common with her famous father. Scorpio was legendary for his affairs with young, gorgeous women and throwing parties that rivaled the decadent depravity of ancient Roman orgies.

"I guess you were lucky to have a stepdad then."

"You'd think so, wouldn't you?"

"You don't." He was getting tastes of Jillian's secrets and they only made him thirstier for more.

"One thing I learned growing up is that appearances can be and are often deceptive." She sighed. "Not that I think living with Scorpio would have been better. Sometimes, life doesn't give you any good choices. But you know? I realized after moving out that it could have been a lot worse too."

Despite his temporary insanity that prompted his request she hold his hand, Alan kept his distance for the rest of the tour. If Ralph hadn't shown up, Alan would have kissed Jillian senseless. He couldn't believe his own behavior. No matter how strongly she impacted his libido, he was not some rookie agent to be derailed by a pretty face. Or even a beautiful face. And intriguing personality. And charming personality. And the same sense of humor as his own.

Practically growling with frustration at himself, Alan forced out question after question about how things worked and who did what on the set and in the studio.

True to what she'd told him earlier, Jillian had enough knowledge to give him elucidating responses to every single query.